WANT SOME
GET SOME

6/19

WANT SOME GET SOME

PAM WARD

KENSINGTON PUBLISHING CORP.
http://www.kensingtonbooks.com

DAFINA BOOKS are published by

Kensington Publishing Corp.
850 Third Avenue
New York, NY 10022

Copyright © 2007 by Pam Ward

All Kensington titles, imprints and distributed lines are available at special quantity discounts for bulk purchases for sales promotion, premiums, fund-raising, educational or institutional use.

Special book excerpts or customized printings can be created to fit specific needs. For details, write or phone the office of the Kensington Special Sales Manager: Kensington Publishing Corp., 850 Third Avenue, New York, NY 10022. Attn. Special Sales Department. Phone: 1-800-221-2647.

Dafina Books and the Dafina logo Reg. U.S. Pat. & TM Off.

ISBN-13: 978-0-7582-1775-2
ISBN-10: 0-7582-1775-7

First Kensington Trade Paperback Printing: March 2007
10 9 8 7 6 5 4 3 2 1

Printed in the United States of America

To my supersonic daughters
Mari and Hana

Acknowledgments

Much gratitude to: My wonderful, sassy mother, Bonnie Moore, who drove us around in a VW bus and taught me the meaning of *family;* my unstoppable father, the architect, James Moore, who zoomed his 911 with zest (rest in peace, Daddy); my blood sisters, Linda and Lisa, whose cars died or blew up on freeways and who helped and hoorayed me in countless ways; my brother, Jimmy, whose ride always stays clean, thanks for all the raw material and always being there; my cousin Rachel who typed this from chicken scratch, we won't say how many cars she had; to all the rest of my family, especially my sweet Grandpa George who gave up driving at 90 but still has steam in his eyes.

To Michelle Clinton and Bob Flanagan of Beyond Baroque Literary Arts Foundation; to Leonard Miropol's proofreading eyes; to Eso Won Books, the World Stage and Beyond: Wendy, Wanda, Vee, Nancy, Michael, FrancEye, Peter, El, AK, Merilene, Kamau, Watts Profits, Rafael Alvarado, SA Griffin and to Eric Priestley who peeped me some game; to Terry Wolverton and Heather Haley of the Woman's Building and to Guava Breasts: Michele Serros and Nancy Agabian; to Arvli who encouraged all my artistic endeavors, to Rob Cohen of Caffeine; to my home-girls, Alane O'Rielly, Claudia Bracho, Jeannie Berrard and Francine Lescook; to my new son, Ryan, to Michi and Ron Sweeney and the entire Abrahams family.

To my amazingly tenacious agent, Stephanie Lee, who believed in me from day one; to Selena James at Kensington and to my editor Stacey Barney who put gasoline to this dream. And lastly, to my beautiful and brilliant daughters, Mari and Hana, wear your seatbelts and roar and to *mi amor*, Guy Abrahams, an Olympian who held my hand the whole way and showed me the road to true bliss.

Want some get some,
bad enough take some!

A schoolyard threat sung before a fight.

1

Flo and Charles

Some folks will do anything to get what they want. Sell their mama in a heartbeat and not miss one note. Oh, they'll smile; grin so big they show all their back molars. But don't turn your back. Shoot, you better not blink. 'Cause there's those who'll yank a bone from a starving dog's jaw, or climb a tree just to peek at the stuff in your yard.

It was May, and L.A. was a bronze deep-fried hot. In 1997 was the worst ever heat wave on record. With all the windows gaped wide there was still no damn breeze. With his head in the freezer, Charles could not cool off. He looked at Flo's scowling face and groaned. All he wanted right now was to get out the apartment. In his mind's eye, he could already see Trudy on stage. It was the tragic way she swayed, singing with eyelids half closed, looking half sleep or strung out on dope. She was stacked. Had a break-your-neck-just-to-look kind of body. Men who'd already grabbed their car keys and stood up to pay sat back down in their seats and ordered more whiskey when Trudy came out on stage. When she sang, all the men would lean up in their seats, 'cause her hug-me-tight dresses showed off plenty of meat and sent waitresses back for more shots. Just watching her made Charles feel like he committed a crime but he took what he could like a crook.

And now he was in deep. There was no turning back. Charles stared at the intricate veins in his hand. It was dangerous but Trudy said they would go fifty-fifty. Wiping the sweat from his brow, Charles bit his own fist. He wanted it so bad that he could taste it.

Looking back, it all started with that smashed liquor bottle. Charles was coming home late, well past twelve on some nights, and Flo couldn't take it much more. She had a locksmith come over and change the locks on the doors, then she waited for Charles's car. Oh, he pounded like mad trying to get in that night. He ran to the front, then around to the back, yelling "open the door" over and over again, insanity soaking his eyes.

They lived in a backyard duplex, and the man upstairs groaned. Moving his arm under his pillow, he reached for his gun. He wanted to shoot through the floor.

During the racket, the neighbors began clicking on their lights. Some of them drifted outside in their robes trying to see what the heck was going on.

Flo didn't budge. She sat in the living room amused.

"Serves him right," she said smugly. "He can just sleep outside. That's what he gets trying to creep in this late."

But something inside Charles snapped while he pounded that door. Like a dropped glass, or the sharp blasting sound of a gun, or a bat someone swung in a car. He grabbed a giant ceramic pot, aimed it at the back door, and tossed it right through the paned glass. Charles stuck his hand in, twisted the lock, and walked through the busted pot and chunks of dirt on the floor.

Flo ran to the kitchen to survey the damage. "Are you crazy? Look at all this mess!"

"Why the fuck did you lock me out?" Charles edged toward her face. He wasn't tall but he was broad-shouldered and wide. He looked like a hotel front door.

"Because," Flo told him. "I'm sick of this, Charles! You're always coming home late. Always out at the club. What the hell is really going on?" Her anger only masked a sad, bitter wound. A hurt so deep that her bottom lip started quivering hard until she had to bite her lip with her teeth.

"You don't know shit!" Charles yanked the liquor cabinet open. He rarely drank more than an occasional beer. But during these last two fast weeks, he'd been drinking a lot. He couldn't eat. He couldn't sleep. He was butchering his job. But how could he tell Flo that? Grabbing a Jack Daniels bottle, he took a big, sloppy swig. "Stay the fuck out of my business, okay?"

"You better not be cheating." Flo's narrowed brows scolded. "If I find out, you'll live to regret it."

Charles held the throat of the fat liquor bottle. He watched Flo out of the rim of his eyes. He was seething from being locked out, and she was threatening him now! This was too much for Charles to bear. So after wielding the bottle around for one lunatic minute, he flung it against the wall, smashing it to bits, just inches away from Flo's head.

Vicious shards scattered all over the room. Glass bashed into the porcelain sink and the booze left a huge ugly stain on the wall.

Charles grabbed his keys and rushed out the door.

"Come back!" Flo screamed, her voice like a mallet. "You better clean this up. I'm not playing with you, Charles!" She chased Charles through the weeds and down the long, busted-up driveway. She chased him all the way out to the grassless front lawn. She chased him right into the middle of the trash-ridden street, her whole face a wreck with hot rage.

But Charles walked fast. He refused to look back. He hurried down the walk and jumped back in his car.

"Go ahead and go, you postal-working punk. But if you leave, I may not be here when you get back!" Flo smacked her own ass, letting her hands trace along her hips. "I know you want this, huh? You begged for it last night!" She smacked her ass again, stretching both arms toward the sky, then she licked one of her fingers and touched her behind, making a fried bacon sound with her tongue.

Charles didn't look back. He switched on the ignition. He revved it so long some of the neighbors held their ears. And when he shoved it in reverse and backed the thing out, his tires left dark marks in the driveway.

"You want me!" Flo screamed, but only his taillights noticed. Charles was already gone.

Flo and Charles played the same routine a hundred times before. Flo pretended she didn't care. She tried to act nonchalant. But she loved Charles as much as a junkie loves his drugs. Craved him like a drunk does that last sip of scotch and even in her rage, standing in that cold concrete street, she'd suck a golf ball out a water hose to keep him.

But deep down something had begun to eat at her lately. Each day she felt something was slipping away. Oh, she laughed with her friends, pretended everything was okay. "Charles is just singing that same tune again. He'll be back," she'd say, making her voice seem upbeat, but those worry lines came just the same. Flo was thirty-four and a good twelve years older than Charles. Not many folks knew. You couldn't tell by looking. But Flo felt the age gap growing wider each day. Though she joked on the phone, she was really afraid, scared that Charles would make a play for a woman his own age.

Squeezing the steering wheel, Charles raced through the streets like a demon. He could still see Flo's smiling face in his mind. It was that cold laugh of Flo's that Charles hated most. It said he would never be anything in her eyes. It said she saw him in all of his smallness. It was that laugh he wanted to smash when he snatched that glass bottle. It was that laugh he wanted to leave, to drown out completely as his tires ate the road back to Dee's.

But wait now, we're leaping ahead of the story. There's a whole lot of mess that went down before this.

2

Dee's Parlor

"Hit me again, damn it!" Tony smacked down ten dollars. "They say money'll bring out the worst in some folks." Pearl smiled over the arch of her worn yellow cards. "Some'll kill just to get the last five from the jar."

"No one gives a hot fuck 'bout five bucks in a jar." Tony smacked his hand hard on the table again. "You gonna play cards or sit there and yap?"

Pearl ignored his remarks and munched on some pretzels. "Where's Miss Dee, huh? I ain't seen her in months. You got her hidden in some room or did you bury her in the yard?"

Tony ignored her and downed the remainder of his beer.

"I see what you're doing and I'm telling you it's ugly."

"Ain't this about a bitch. Have you looked in a mirror lately?" Tony slapped his friend Stan so hard on the back that Stan's drink sloshed all over his hand.

"You come up in the world, Tony," Pearl told him, unfazed. "Wasn't that long ago you were living hand-to-mouth on the street running a sneak game outta some fool's garage."

Tony stared at his cards and ran a hand around his stomach. He was a whale of a man, leaning on the mean side of fifty with a black, gummy smile, a bad smoker's hack, and a deep love for Johnnie Walker Black Label scotch. Tony was a pasty man who thought being fat was an asset. His conked hair was feverishly brushed to one side and held with a thick coat of Murray's grease.

He ate rich food and resented having to ever work hard. If he did work, he spent more time eyeing the shapely legs going by, examining women's calves and trying to sniff at their breasts as they bent down to look through his stacks.

See, before working at Dee's Parlor, Tony sold these cheap posters. Used to lean them against the front of Dee's wall every day. The kind of bad art you see at gas station corners. Awful blurred drawings of Malcolm and King. Sadly drawn kids holding balloons in a tub in frames so damn cheap they put nicks in your hand.

"Seems like yesterday Tucker brought you into this place. It was '91, wasn't it. You wasn't but fifty and some change. In six years you're running the whole got damn club." Pearl shook her head slow, staring around the club sadly. "Hiring you was the worst thing he did before he passed."

"Tucker liked me. He hired me for my great gift for gab." Tony smacked Stan again and Stan's drink sloshed over his arm. "Hell, he told me my people skills dramatically increased the bar's tab."

"Humph." Pearl ignored him. She studied her cards.

Tony smiled, wiping the table until it gleamed. He threw the dirty rag across his broad shoulder. He poured his good friend Stan another stiff drink. Stan came to Dee's and stayed drunk every day.

"Tucker was glad he picked me. He considered me an asset." Tony nudged Stan, and Stan smiled at his glass. Agreeing with Tony meant he could drink free.

"You an ass, all right," Pearl said. "I will give you that."

Tony leaned like he wanted to take a good swing at Pearl.

"Oh, I really wish you would," Pearl said without flinching. Eventually Tony slowly sat back.

Pearl looked around the club. It had changed so much lately.

Dee's Parlor was a low-lit supper club that sat on the south side of neglect. It was on the hit-and-run corner of Washington and Tenth Avenue. Used to be an aquarium shop owned by a Chinese family, in the sixties. But after the Watts riots broke almost thirty years ago, the Chinese folks packed and left, moving to the west side to be with the whites. Washington Boulevard wasn't Watts, but it didn't matter back then. It was too close to all that black skin.

"Hit me again!" Tony barked, scratching the table with his cards.

"When Mr. Tucker bought the place it had been boarded up for years. He cleaned it, bought some used stools, tables, and chairs. Miss Dee cooked them big vats of well-seasoned food. Dee's Parlor used to be the best known black-owned restaurant in town." Pearl smiled and fanned her chest with her cards.

"What about Leo's on Crenshaw or Phillips in Leimert Park?" Tony lit a cigarette and blew the thick smoke.

"Or Johnny's Pastrami," Stan said, wiping his lip.

"And everybody knows Woody's keeps 'em lined up over on Slauson. You can smell their smoked beef from the curb." Tony rubbed his gut and smacked his lips as if he could already taste it.

"Those are small take-out shacks where folks get food in brown sacks. There's not many sit-down places to go any more. Green's shut its doors, and Memory Lane closed down. The Parisian Room is only a memory now. Shoot, Dee's Parlor is the last of the few standing."

"Why you telling me?" Tony asked. "Shoot, I was there too. You gonna play Tonk or you gonna get your photo book out? No one gives a hot fuck 'bout none of that stuff now."

But Pearl didn't care what Tony said and kept on talking. Stan didn't care either. He didn't want to talk. All he wanted was another free beer.

"Restaurant used to be a nice place you could take your lady after a date. You could catch a show or get a quick nightcap. An alligator bite went for one forty-five. A pucker shot set you back only a buck and a quarter. 'Member when well drinks were barely two dollars a glass? Shoot, a whole pitcher of draft was just one ninety-five." Pearl smiled, fanning her cards in her face. "Things were real nice back in the day."

"Back in the day's all you talk about now. Who cares what stuff used to cost way back then? Them days is gone. All I care about is how much to charge folks right now." Tony studied his cards. He scratched the side of his head and looked concerned. Stan pretended to look concerned too.

"I remember the singers. Shoot, we had the best talents! Esther Phillips sang here twice; we had Little Milton and Millie Jackson. O. C. Smith sang here so much the place was practically his home. Dee's rocked from Tuesday to four a.m. Sunday. Used to hear laughing and champagne bottles popping all the time. Oh, we had us a grand time back then." Pearl stopped and looked around; a sweet smile was on her face, but it changed looking at the rundown tables and chairs. The ugly black bars on the windows and doors made the once-bright place musty and dark. "We used to have *good* people. Didn't need them damn bars. Now all you hear is crashing bottles of beer and rowdy, loud, shit-talking men shooting craps."

"Shoot. We got people!" Tony stared at her hard. "Plenty of folks be lining up to come to Dee's now!"

"Different kinds of people." Pearl glanced at Stan.

"All people's the same. They all got the same wants."

"How the hell do you know what all people want?"

"I know what men want, and it's always the same." Tony held his cards with a confident air. He had a nine, a jack, and an ace. "They want money, and a good place to get a cheap drink, and some nice leg to see while they're there."

Stan nodded at Tony. Tony smiled back.

"Humph," Pearl muttered. She stared at her cards. She thought Tony was as dumb as a sack of manure. "If I had a dollar for every cockamamie thing I heard in here, I swear I'd be a damn millionaire." She stared hard at Tony over the rim of her glasses.

Tony got annoyed waiting for Pearl and sat up in his chair. "You gonna play or just sit and talk shit?"

"I dreamed about Miss Dee." Pearl smiled at her cards.

Tony squirmed in his seat. He tapped out a new Winston. He did not like this subject at all.

"She told me she doesn't feel safe anymore." Pearl held his eyes until Tony twisted in his seat.

He took a deep drag, blowing the smoke nice and slow. "Girl, please, nobody cares about your stupid-ass dreams." He didn't want to show she intimidated him one bit, so he stared straight back at her face. "Why don't you just mind your own business and play?"

But Pearl was no fool. She knew what he was doing. In these last months, Tony acted like Dee's Parlor was his. He put bars on the windows. He bought a wrought-iron door. He had the door hung with the hinges screwed on the right so the cops would have a time busting in. He started gambling and all kinds of betting on sports. He hired a strong-armed ex-boxer named Percy to stand watch and a felon who worked part-time named Ray Ray.

"I ain't dumb. You got them bars so no one barges in here—the same kind you put all over Miss Dee's house right before you carted her away. I remember. I saw Miss Dee change. She slipped down to nothing in no time at all. She's a pitiful size six if she's a day. You never feed her. She barely got out the bed. She stopped coming to the club after Mr. Tucker passed. I bet you got her holed up somewhere with the shades all pulled down. I still remember the last thing she said. She said, no matter how sunny each L.A. day blazed, to her everything turned gray. Like the whole world got old. Like some white clothes that got washed with a batch of black socks."

"I don't give a fuck 'bout no got damn black socks. Miss Dee was getting too old for this place. You got to have a man to run a hard place like this."

"This place wasn't hard until Miss Dee met you."

"She likes me." Tony grinned, "Whatchu want me to say. She had a twinkle in her eye whenever I came by." Tony held in the smoke. He let it float through his teeth. His smile was as wide as the Hollywood sign. "Don't hate the player, hate the game."

"You been eyeballin' Miss Dee like a fly does a steak. Hovering around her shoulders like a moth-eaten stole, waiting to swoop down and make your next move."

Tony drank a huge gulp and vulgarly belched. Stan took another swig too.

* * *

Truth was, the best part of Miss Dee's day was when Tony stopped by. Over the past year, she saw him at least once a day. She was never good at keeping the books at the club. She couldn't make heads or tails from the papers he shoved under her face. She'd sign them all fast to get them out of the way so she could ask Tony if he wanted some cake or a piece of See's candy, anything to make Tony stay.

And Tony kept coming. He liked telling Miss Dee lies. All of them were about someone dying. "You know, Miss Jenkins passed today. They found her dead in the tub." Tony would relish it with graphic details about flies. He liked watching the fear lodge inside Miss Dee's eyes.

All the stories about him always ended the same. He always had some financial problem. Some, "I'm so broke" woe. His car was on the blink or he had a leak in his apartment or his bum knee was messing with him again. Then he'd wait while Miss Dee wrote him a check. He made a mistake once and told the truth about Trudy. Miss Dee was so upset she wrote Trudy a big check. But Tony endorsed Trudy's check to himself. He wasn't about to let some young fool cut in on his pie. Especially that fast little tramp.

From then on, whenever Miss Dee asked Tony about Trudy, he just made up stories. "Why, she's fine, Miss Dee. Trudy's doin' real fine lately." Tony picked up a dark, nutty piece of See's candy and plopped the whole thing on his tongue. "Why, that girl is a regular college gal now. She's up at U-C-L-A, yessirreebob." Tony licked his bottom lip, sucking off the soft chocolate. "Naw, Miss Dee," Tony assured her. "You ain't gotta worry about her. That gal's got big plans on her mind."

It was fun for him. Old folks were such cupcakes. Most of 'em never knew what the hell was going on half the time. Tony layered the frosting thick, said whatever he wanted, said whatever popped into his lopsided head.

Later that night, Tony went back over to Miss Dee's around seven. It was Monday, and the club was closed, so he had lots of time. He went in the living room and clicked the Lakers game on.

He was just about to fall asleep when the wooden porch squeaked. Tony sat quiet in his chair.

Trudy stopped by Miss Dee's to give her a nice plate for dinner. It was winter, but the heavy plate kept her hands warm. A bluish glow leaked from underneath the shade. A frayed blanket covered a knee. Trudy leaned closer and squinted both eyes.

"Miss Dee?" Trudy whispered, straining to see. "Miss Dee, is that you?"

When she placed her palm over the cold metal knob, someone pulled the front door from her hand.

Tony's pale, balding head glowed under the moon. His heavy frame blocked Trudy's way.

"Oh . . . Tony . . ." Trudy stammered. "I didn't know you were here. I stopped to give Miss Dee some food." Trudy smiled, trying her best not to show she was startled. Her hand shook while holding the plate.

"Oh, you did? This damn late? You know old folks eat early. You shoulda called first. Miss Dee's gone to sleep." Tony's fat fist stayed gripped to the knob. He started to ease the door closed.

"Tony . . . wait!" Trudy said, putting one big leg between the door and the jamb. "I haven't seen Miss Dee in such a long time. I just want to check on her a second."

"Sorry, baby," Tony said, leaning against Trudy's leg. "Ain't nobody checking for shit." Tony smiled and sucked on his fat bottom lip. He rubbed both hands slow over the warm, brimming gut. He let his leg graze across her thigh.

Trudy moved her leg and glared Tony in the eye. "Look, all I want to do is go give her this plate." Trudy took another step. Her left foot was shaking. She could feel the hot warmth of his breath.

But Tony wasn't listening. The low porch light gleamed. The light rolled all over Trudy's firm, curvy body.

"Mercy alive," Tony said. "I'd sure love to taste some of yo' mashed potatoes and gravy." Tony ran his tongue around his top and bottom lip. "Look at you, girl. You done growed up! You got ripe in all the right places." He took a long drag, tossed the butt toward the sidewalk, then reached out and boldly squeezed Trudy's breast. He did it like it was the most natural thing on Earth. Like she was a fresh loaf of bread at the store.

Trudy lurched away and dropped the plate she was holding. It smashed the porch like a shot bird. Trudy was so shocked she stood numb and said nothing. Shame flooded her face and her anger made her rear back to slap him.

But Tony reached up and caught Trudy's hand in midair. "I wouldn't do that if I were you. I might hit you back." Tony held her arm but Trudy violently snatched it back.

Tony leaned back and smiled, admiring her frame. "Boy, I wish I had some of that hot fire on my stage."

Trudy stepped back but still held his gaze. "I'd never work for you, and don't touch me again, you freak!" Trudy glared at him like he was scum.

"Ewwwww wee! Girl, you just like your mama. Lotta hot fire running through both y'all's veins."

Trudy ignored him and angrily walked down the street.

Tony smiled from the door, licking his fingers and thumb. "That's one fine piece of tenderized meat."

Tony decided he'd have to play it safe from now on. He had been just about to leave once the Lakers game went off. Trudy's late visit had surprised him. He couldn't have folks sneaking around Miss Dee now, poppin' in whenever they wanted. So Tony got a slim cot and dragged it right in the room. He set it right next to Miss Dee's own bed and slept there each night just in case.

Folks say it was just to make sure Miss Dee left her Parlor to him. Others say Miss Dee never left Tony squat. Said he took that bar like he took everything else in life. Lord knows, some folks sure come out of the woodwork when folks get up in years. Showing up during the final months like they'd been coming around for years. Usually it's the ones who didn't so much as spit when the dying could still breathe. Visiting at the last minute, putting on a good face, hoping the half dead would leave them something in their will. But it sure was a shame the way Tony did Miss Dee.

See, Miss Dee and Mr. Tucker never had any children. She was glad to have a strong man like Tony around. She couldn't understand why a nice man like Tony wasn't attached.

"Why haven't you been married?" Miss Dee asked him once.

Quietly, Miss Dee was pleased Tony didn't have a woman. She was glad he didn't have to run home at all. She missed a man's gentle affection.

"Oh, I tried, but they don't make 'em like you anymore." Tony leaned real close with his crocodile smile. Shoot, Miss Dee couldn't see what a crowbar he was, that no woman in her right mind would have him.

"Well, you can't be from around here. I suspect Mississippi. You act like my people in Natchez. There aren't many people as kindhearted as you," Miss Dee said. She felt bad that her girl-friends had abandoned her so completely. She didn't know Tony was keeping them away.

Tony didn't care nothing about Miss Dee at all. All he wanted was her club and that big house she was sitting on now. Shoot, the area was already starting to change. The '92 riots were at least three years back and all the boarded-up businesses were being fixed or reclaimed. The mansions were starting to get fresh coats of paint. Tony was getting itchy. He always wanted more. He wasn't happy with small-change money. He wanted Miss Dee's house. He wanted her club. He wanted money and property and power and new things. He was sick of seeing all those late no-tices and bills. Tony never owned nothing. Not a car, not a home, not even a bike, and at fifty-six he was dealing with three women who all thought he was their man.

Tony had waited a long time for an opportunity like this. He'd seen Mr. Tucker fading away more and more each day, whittling down like a worn piece of wood. Like a mint in the middle of your tongue. Fact was, Tony was the one who saw him fall in that cellar. He waited a full twenty minutes before he called anybody. He checked around to see if anyone heard the thud of his body and watched while Mr. Tucker held his hand to his chest, heaving against the cold concrete floor. By the time the paramedics got there it was already over. Ol' man Tucker was gone.

Mr. Tucker was the last thing in Tony's way, and Miss Dee would be a piece of cake to do in. Tony would smile nice and real friendly while handing her legal papers to sign.

"Just sign this last one," Tony asked Miss Dee, "and I won't be bothering you no more." He handed her a pen and Miss Dee scribbled her name, and Tony quickly slipped the papers into his briefcase. Lord, it got so Tony could taste owning that club. Every time the boys would rattle the dice, his teeth would chatter with a greedy need to have it all. Have it all now! He just couldn't wait for Miss Dee to kick off. But she just lingered on so. He moved into her place but he couldn't stand it in there. The rank stench of her rotting body and wet filmy cough made him want to jump out his own skin.

So Tony started creeping in her bedroom at night, whispering into Miss Dee's ear.

"Die, Miss Dee," he'd say harsh and low. "Hurry up, Miss Dee. Go on and let go. Die, die," he told her each night.

Miss Dee woke feeling like someone was trying to grab her from the floorboards, like a black fog seeped inside her lungs.

Well, one night it damn near worked. When Tony came to check Miss Dee, she was laying stiff from stroke. She barely had a pulse and her whole left side was frozen. Her hands clutched the blanket and her chalk face was drawn. Her eyes looked like forty-watt bulbs.

Pearl called everyone she could and they gathered at Miss Dee's house. Everyone knew it was bad, but nobody could believe the hideous sores on her backside when the ambulance came and wheeled her out. Mercy alive! Giant bed sores the size of huge saucers, raw weeping wounds all blood red and rotten. Her paper skin ripped when they lifted her up and her howl was so long and so deep and so bad that folks had to suck in their breath.

Everybody looked at Tony a real long time, but he just smiled and shifted back and forth on his feet.

"Shoot, Miss Dee never did get up," Tony said low. He downed a quick drink from his silver flask and belched. He took a deep drag from his Winston and coughed. Slowly they all looked away.

So that's how Tony got the club. Got everything in fact, the bank book, the house, the black drop-top Caddy, all that liquor they kept locked up in storage. And even though he put his name up in orange giant lights blinking TONY, everybody still called it Dee's Parlor.

Miss Dee's friends were so mad they wouldn't even walk on that side. The old men would mumble, shake their heads at the club, and some of them would rear back and spit. But Tony didn't care what those old-timers thought. Most of his new clientele were working-class folks. They were postal workers, plumbers, jackleg mechanics, sales clerks, and staffers from Kaiser Hospital off Venice. Folks who worked hard but liked having a really good time and wanted an easy place to talk shit and drink.

Pearl eyed Tony hard over the edge of her cards and then laid down an ace and a king. "I know what you're doing. Don't think I don't. I can smell when a dog's pissed on the floor."

Tony threw his losing cards down, ignoring Pearl's glaring face. "Come on, Stan. Let's get the gambling room ready upstairs."

"You know doggone well Miss Dee don't go for no gambling. I got a good mind to tell her about it myself." But Pearl knew this was futile. She didn't know where Miss Dee was. Pearl was a big woman and wasn't afraid to speak her mind. "I've been working for the Tuckers too long to let it go downhill. Nothing but hooligans and ragamuffins coming in here now. I ought to call the police and have them search this place now."

Tony stacked up the cards. He never liked losing. "Listen," Tony said, blowing his smoke in her face, "I'ma say this one time so you won't forget." Tony took a deep drag, holding it down in his gut. "Stay the fuck out of my business. I'm warning you, hear? I don't pay your big ass to think."

"Miss Dee pays me," Pearl triumphantly said.

"Oh, really? Since when? Who signs yo' check? All you need

to worry about is whether there's enough hot sauce on them wings. If you don't like it, then you can just get to steppin'. I got five other fat cooks just lickin' they chops, ready to step in and take yo' damn place."

Pearl stood up to leave but Tony blocked her way. He inhaled his Winston and held in the smoke. "Look at you standing there acting all high and mighty. I've seen ya skimmin', thinking no one's around. Seen you take cuts of meat and vegetables too, not to mention them wine bottles you been cartin' off lately in that bottomless pit satchel you call a purse." He stood there and waited but Pearl remained quiet. "Now get yo' ass outta my face."

Pearl stepped way back and let Tony pass. What he'd said was true. She'd been skimming a bit. Nothing big. Nothing anyone would notice. Besides, she had three little grandkids to feed and her salary at the club didn't cut it. And how in hell could she tell Miss Dee about Tony, when her own arm had been in the cookie jar too. Slowly, Pearl went back to the kitchen, but not without mumbling, "I'm watching yo' ass. You ain't slick, sucker. I'm telling you Pearl's eyes is watching." She opened the freezer and slammed it back shut. She lifted a plant and peeked between a pile of plates. Her fifty-year-old eyes were always hunting for some kind of clue.

Tony smiled at the crowd growing inside Dee's doors. He didn't care what Pearl thought. He was holding all the cards. The club's atmosphere changed once he hired that girl. Her X-rated body had them coming there in droves and she sang like her whole life depended on each note. Shoot, even the old-timers who used to spit on Dee's steps were sneaking back over after their wives went to sleep to snatch a quick drink and watch Trudy sing.

3

Trudy with the Booty

"Look, man, here she comes."

Two men sat huddled near a liquor store wall. Their folding chairs scraped against the brick as they stared. At three o'clock, in the sticky-clothes heat of '97, the men were already three or four beers deep.

Without letting his eyes leave the hot scene across the street, the older man placed his icy-cold beer on the ground. His age-spotted hand gripped the hook of his cane. With a dead, eaten-out face he looked two snaps from death. Only his eyes were alive.

"Hey, gal!" the old man growled, wiping beer from his chin. "Lemme taste some of yo' dumplins."

The younger man sported a big auburn perm. "You gonna need some Vi-ag-ra, old man." He laughed in his weather-beaten face.

Trudy's thick, big-boned body strutted along the sidewalk on Bronson. It was a mean strip of squat apartments where bottle-caps and domestic brawls were as regular as junk mail. Where crackheads hung out at liquor-store corners, where whole packs of pit bulls ran wild. Trudy was one hellified bitch herself. Had to be on that block. It didn't pay to be soft. She walked bold and threw out a "don't fuck with me" look so folks would leave her alone. Trudy wasn't real attractive but she did well with what she had. And if big tits and hips were grocery mart items, then homegirl owned a whole store. She was a cinnamon woman with plenty of beef on her bones and a head full of slick, well-kept braids. By the time she was nine, she had a woman's full body. At fifteen, she was splitting the seams of her skirts. At eighteen, she spilled easily from a 42D. And now at twenty, her wet melted Popsicle smile could bring most men down to their knees.

Trudy kept walking fast. She glanced across the street. The tall auburn-haired man was Lil Steve.

"Why you walking so fast, baby? Hold up a minute." Rubbing his thighs, which were open as wide as unhinged pliers, he watched her like a hungry kid eyeing the stove. A neat stack of videotapes rested between his feet. He sold them for fifteen bucks each.

Trudy's razor eyes stayed straight. She kept stepping fast. She ignored the turkey-carving look in their eyes and kept her own glued to Dee's neon sign. When she passed the older man, he licked his wet chops and spat, "Girl, you a bitch and a half."

Suddenly, a car came screeching wildly down the street. It leaped over the curb and blocked Trudy's path. Its hood skidded inches away from her knees. Trudy lost her balance and fell hard against the wall. One of her fingernails ripped at the quick and bled.

"Hey, Trudy with the booty! I've been looking for you, girl!"

The Cutlass Supreme rattled as the man leaned from the car. "I want you to be in my movie!"

Obscenely, the man grabbed and held his own crotch. "I got something to put in your next scene." The man laughed, slapping his hand across his knee. His wide-spaced teeth looked like a loose picket fence.

Trudy steeled her body. She circled around the car.

"Ah, girl! Don't even try to be mad. You the one witcho ass all on Front Street."

"Hey Lil Steve," the man screamed. "Gimme another Trudy tape. I made the mistake of lending mine to Shawn and his ass left it out in the sun."

All the men watched Trudy as she strolled down the block.

"Mercy!" the Cutlass Supreme man said. "You're putting a hurting on us, girl."

As Trudy got closer, a woman sneered and crossed to the other side, covering her son's eyes with her hand.

Hiding her pain under sunglasses and casting an armored car strut, Trudy wedged her way toward Dee's Parlor door. And then suddenly she stopped and stared at Lil Steve hard. A smirk crept across her thick maroon lips. It was the kind of smile you gave your boss when he caught you sneaking off early or gave a sales clerk when you tried to return something you already wore.

Lil Steve wanted to follow her to the club but he was banned from Dee's Parlor. His lids followed the roll of her hips toward the entrance.

See, three summers ago no one knew Trudy's name. It was the second summer after the '92 riots. People were starting to feel strong. Some of those burnt buildings were back. People were throwing huge bashes all over town with the last bit of riot liquor left.

Trudy couldn't wait. She was going to a Crenshaw High party! She was nervous about going but someone special would be there. She usually went to the movies during her mother's late dates. Trudy would sit in the dark watching the same show for hours, eating bon bons and Red Vines and warm popcorn in tubs. She sat, mimicking every single character's line, until her mother finally picked her back up.

But that night she wanted to go to a party. Ray Ray was meeting her there and Trudy begged her mother to take her. She took a long bath, spraying her neck with vanilla and piling her hair high on her head.

Joan watched her get ready without saying a word and then flatly told Trudy no. "Besides," her mother said, "I don't like that bucket-of-blood area, so wash off your face and go to bed."

Trudy was devastated. She'd been planning to go to that party for weeks. It was the last one before high school was over. "Please!" Trudy begged. But Joan shut her door and Trudy wept alone on her bed.

But by ten, almost all of Joan's vodka was gone and she needed to go to the store. They drove in dark silence from Seventh to Degnan. When they hit Fiftieth, she made a left turn. Her mother studied Trudy's lace dress and her piled-up hair. She looked beautiful but Joan only glared at her daughter, swearing at her for wearing all that "war paint."

Trudy's leg barely cleared the car as her mother took off. "Catch a ride back," her mother yelled at her daughter. "I'm too tired to get you tonight."

Trudy stayed by the DJ so she didn't seem alone. Her friend Vernita was supposed to come but she wasn't there yet. Suddenly she saw him, outside with a whole bunch of guys. Ray Ray was standing in a sea of white T-shirts and creased khakis. He held court; the other guys circled his broad frame. He had a deep voice and a beautiful naughty-boy smile. Ray Ray was the reason she'd come to the party. And he stopped talking as soon as he saw her.

"Hey, girl, when'd you get here?" He brilliantly smiled. He gently took her hand and led her to the balcony outside. Trudy couldn't help staring at his black flawless skin and that grin he aimed only at her. And that's when she saw him. This thin, janky-looking guy. He shot her mean, dirty looks the whole time but Ray Ray didn't notice and Trudy ignored him. All she could think of was how close Ray Ray stood. He felt good. She could smell him. She inhaled his clean male skin. When he touched her it felt like her whole insides glowed like the cool bluish ray of blacklights. When he slowly brought her close, her mouth grazed his lips. She could feel the hot need steaming under his skin. And then suddenly it was over. The blacklight glow was gone. In a flash, everything took a harsh turn for the worse. Lil Steve came up and whispered something in his ear and Ray Ray ignored her the rest of the party. In fact, she couldn't get a ride and had to take the bus home. When she got there her mother was sipping a pink drink. "Don't worry, girl, men are just vehicles, honey. Just grab hold of one with a full tank of gas and ride that damn bitch 'til it kicks."

See, Ray Ray ended up going to jail that night and Lil Steve kept sniffing, kept coming around her house. It took a long time and a lot of rides to where she worked at the mall. It took flowers and showing up every day at her door, but Lil Steve was determined. He always played to win, and after a while he broke Trudy down.

"Don't wait for Ray Ray," Lil Steve whispered in her ear. "With his record, that nigga's gettin' fifteen, at least."

Trudy tried to avoid him but he was there all the time. He was always walking her home or asking her out, begging her just like a dope fiend. One day she agreed to go see a movie. "Please," Lil Steve said. "I only want to see this with you. Look," he said, showing Trudy the stubs, "I already bought both the tickets."

But when it came time to go he made her wait in the alley. She watched Lil Steve mack the girl working the counter. The girl smiled big and let him come in for free. Lil Steve opened the back door and let Trudy creep in. They did that every single time they went to a show. But Trudy didn't mind. It was fun sharing Cokes and watching all those flicks. Trudy, who used to sit alone in those red velvet chairs, now sat in the dark with a warm arm around her shoulders. She liked how he put the popcorn right in her mouth. No, Trudy didn't mind it at all.

After the movies he took her on shoplifting sprees. Trudy would watch Lil Steve talk while his hands smuggled items. He got alarm clocks and watches and dozens of cameras, which he sold out the back of his car. He showed Trudy the fat rubber bands attached to his pajamas, which he wore underneath his loose pants. He had elaborate ways to steal all kinds of stuff, between your legs, down the back of your shirt, jewelry stuck deep in your hair. He would go in and instantly scope the whole room, ceiling cameras, stuff that didn't have sensors on, all those dumb undercovers.

Trudy was fascinated with this life. She became a quick study. She realized her wide, shapely body was an asset. Her cleavage became a deep and reliable pocket. She started to take small things too.

But Lil Steve had his eyes on a different kind of prize. He licked Trudy's neck sitting next to her in the dark. "I want you bad, girl. You know you're my heart. When you gonna gimme a taste of them yams?"

Trudy laughed and threw popcorn at Lil Steve's head. But he gently kissed her cheek and let his elbow graze her breast.

See, Lil Steve was a pro. He knew how to take it slow. When they got home he kissed her fingers and played with her hoop earrings. His palm barely touched her bare knee.

"I know people, baby. I could make you a star. You look a helluva lot better than them chicks on the screen." He playfully stroked Trudy's braids.

At the time, it didn't seem like much. No one else had asked for it. So she gave it like somebody who gives a nice present. She lotioned it, dressed it up in beautiful fabric, dabbed a floral scent behind her neck and the back of her calves and then draped it across her clean bed. She thought it would be like all those girls in the movies as she waited for the wonderful thing to begin. But Lil Steve ripped through her body as if she were paper. He crumpled it, shoving the wrapping aside, and the sweet gift she'd saved was like knocking over a bottle that juzzled all over the floor.

The next thing she knew, it was done and wiped up. Tossed out like yesterday's trash. It was over so fast without any emotion. Lil Steve didn't say or do any of those things in the movies. But it was too late to play the scene over again. She was stuck with the ending, whether she liked it or not. So she kept giving him some, thinking this time would be different. Trudy even felt glad when he pulled out his camera. She was flattered. In her dream world she was becoming a star. She was pleased when he aimed the video recorder toward her skin. She thought Lil Steve felt exactly the same. That he wanted to remember these candybar moments. That he wanted to save her sprawled out on these sheets with the moon streaming straight through the wide Venetian blinds, branding her with animal stripes. She watched Lil Steve's thumb gently press the Play button. She saw the camera's red light bleeding against his front teeth. And as the slimy film rolled around the video camera's mouth, Trudy's own lips curled up and grinned.

But Lil Steve's eyes were focused on something else now. He saw Trudy's nude body as a window, a door, a new way for him to make money. He was a tall, fine, light-skinned, goateed, Iceberg Slim type who used women as easily as napkins.

"Everybody knows money and clothes make the man," Lil Steve said, smiling at himself in the rearview mirror as he drove. "A real woman knows how to keep her man happy." Lil Steve took a 'do rag from his glove compartment and patted his auburn perm down.

But Trudy found out that keeping a man happy meant buying him stuff and lending him money and letting him have sex when he asked. She wanted to drop him and asked her mother for advice. "What? Are you crazy? Fine men like him don't come every day. You're lucky he looked at you twice."

She worked at Macy's in the mall and saved nine hundred dollars. But in three months, Lil Steve borrowed five hundred of it. In six months, her money was gone.

"Just spot me fifty," he said, kissing her cheek. "I swear I'll pay it back to you by Friday." Lil Steve always had some quick money-making scheme. "I'll double your cash, baby, you watch."

But Friday came and went and he still borrowed more. When Trudy stopped lending, Lil Steve got mad. He figured if she wouldn't lend it he'd just have to pimp her. He convinced her to do it. "I want to remember you forever." He told Trudy to lie down naked and made a movie of her in bed, and then he hawked the video shot all over town. That's how she got the name "Trudy with the booty." Everybody in the neighborhood called her that behind her back. Lil Steve said her ass had such a wide natural ledge, he could put a shotglass on it, a small bowl of pretzels, and still play a quick hand of Tonk.

It killed her to find out he was selling her nude film. Something died deep inside that she never got back. See, Trudy's life changed once that video came out. It was little things at first. Women eyeing her sideways. Or gripping their men's arms whenever she passed. She couldn't leave the house without men whistling loud or yelling lewd comments or blocking her path whenever she walked down the street. People threw things at her. They laughed when she talked. Women tossed her change when she came to the store.

"I ain't touching nothing from you," a store clerk told her once. "You're that filthy, lowdown slut from the movie."

Trudy couldn't believe Lil Steve had stabbed her in the back. Her body boiled into a pot of simmering hot greens when she confronted him outside Dee's Parlor.

"Baby, you know you got back," Lil Steve said, playing it off. "Ain't a damn thing wrong with showing off yo' stuff." Lil Steve smiled in the car mirror, continuing to comb his thin mustache. "Didn't I say you'd be famous?"

"How could you do me like that?" Trudy screamed. She was standing in the street, at the driver's side of the car. "And when are you going to pay back my money?"

"Now wait, girl, stop tripping," Lil Steve said, hanging from his car window. "Nobody never said nothing about no loan. You gave all that money to me." Lil Steve never blinked when he looked in her eyes. His face was as cold as a shovel.

Just then, a girl came out of Dee's Parlor. She was dressed in cool cream from her head to her toes. Her beige leather shoes matched her small, expensive purse. She smoothed down her dress and gently knocked on the passenger's door.

"Baby," she said in a high, whiny voice, "when are you coming back in?"

Lil Steve unlatched the passenger's side and the cream woman slinked in. She moved her small frame next to Lil Steve's thighs and his arm circled over her shoulders.

Trudy glared at Lil Steve and at the cream woman, who grinned while applying pink lipstick.

The money was one thing, the nude movie another, but seeing Lil Steve sitting with this cream-colored thing was an icepick rammed straight in her chest.

"How could you dog me like that, Lil Steve?" Trudy's whole face was ruined. Her makeup was smeared. Tears drained from her mascaraed eyes.

"Dog you!" Lil Steve laughed in Trudy's strained face. The cream girl looked back and laughed at her too. "Shoot, you the one hounding me. Following me around all the time. When's the last time I called your big ass?"

Trudy thought back and realized it was true. She'd been calling him. Been tracking him down. He was always on his way. Always telling her, "I'm coming, I'm running a little late." Trudy would wait by the giant picture window for hours. Waiting and watching the dented cars go by. Listening for his rumbling engine.

But those cold, hardcore facts just made Trudy mad. She watched Lil Steve and the smug cream-puff woman. To this day, Trudy still didn't know why she did it. She didn't want Lil Steve. He made her sick. But she had to do something to stop feeling so bad. So Trudy grabbed the latch and yanked the cream girl right out. She got in herself and slammed the passenger's door hard. "I'm not moving," she fumed. "You can't make me go! I'm staying 'til we get this thing straight."

Trudy sat in the passenger's seat like a rock while hot tears leaked down to her lap.

Lil Steve couldn't stand watching her sit there and weep. It made him feel sad. It made him get angry. The cream girl was screaming and wiping her foot. "Look what your ghettofied bitch did to my shoe!"

Lil Steve leaned across Trudy and swung open her door. "Get out," he said flatly, with no emotion at all. He said it low like he worked in a morgue.

But Trudy was fuming. She wouldn't budge one bit. She sat on the seat like a whole mountain range. She thought of all those nasty men hassling her lately. Leering and calling her lewd vulgar names. "Fuck you," she said. "I'm not goin' nowhere. Your skinny ass can't make me leave!" She slammed her door shut and clenched her back teeth. She'd be damned if she moved one inch.

Folks were coming out of Dee's doors and circling the car, eager to watch a big show.

Lil Steve remained calm. He rose from the car slowly. Smoothing his auburn hair down, he strolled over to her side and then yanked her door handle like he was uncapping a beer. Flinging his thin arms around Trudy's thick heavy waist, Lil Steve tried to snatch Trudy out.

But Trudy was big-boned and wouldn't come easy.

"Get out!" he said loudly. He was very angry now. "You're embarrassing yourself. I don't want you no more! Can't you see I got someone else?" He pried each hand loose from the steering wheel she held and jerked her frame out from the seat.

Trudy could see the people from Dee's Parlor lining the curb three folks deep. They watched holding shot glasses and small bags of chips. There was nothing more fun than seeing other folks squabble. Tony sucked his big bottom lip and stared. The other menfolk grinned, squeezing their tall sweaty bottles. The cream girl wickedly screamed with joy, twisting her hair in her fist. Shirley, the waitress, could hardly get enough. She pushed her vicious smile toward the front and wildly popped her gum. When a hand reached to help, Shirley held their arm back.

"Don't go getting into other folks' mess," Shirley said.

It was awful to watch. Some folks turned their heads. Trudy struggled back fiercely but you could see she was lost. Suddenly there was a horrible clothes-ripping sound and the crowd tightened up at the curb.

"Stop!" Trudy shouted. She was kicking and screaming. Her red face was scratched. Her makeup was smeared. But Lil Steve had her. Had her thick juicy waist. He slammed her down hard. Tossed her there on the lawn. Laying her flat like a big sack of weeds. Trudy struggled against him. The short grass itched her back. Her dress was hiked up to her waist.

He could have fucked her right there, Lil Steve thought to himself. Shoot, he wanted to. He could feel himself getting hard. It was fun feeling her firm body squirm against his. It excited him touching all that strong, sexy flesh. Her wet agonized face made him just want to kiss her, to wipe off her tears, make her pain go away. But vanity made Lil Steve pull away. All he had left in the world was his pride. He'd die first before becoming weak. Besides, all these people were watching him now. So Lil Steve left her and never looked back. He walked inside Dee's with the cream-colored girl and ordered a tall whiskey sour.

Trudy slowly rose up, brushing the dirt from her dress. Her

hair was a mess and one shoe had come off. Half a breast peeked out from her bra.

"Slut," someone mumbled.

"That's what the bitch gets."

"She's the video chick, huh?"

"Yeah, that's that heifer."

"Serves her right, being so damn fast and nasty."

The folks from Dee's Parlor started throwing out comments. The men were unconsciously stroking themselves, while the women sucked hard against their tongues.

But Trudy stayed on the ground and stared everyone down. She let out a howling melodious scream. The hate in her face made them all look away, and one by one they went back into Dee's.

Tony lingered by the door. He inched toward the curb. He leaned down and offered her his fat outstretched hand. Reluctantly, Trudy let Tony lift her back up. He cracked open a pack of Big Red cinnamon gum as Trudy adjusted her dress.

"You held that audience, gal." Tony inhaled his Winston. His eyebrows rose up as he slowly exhaled. "That yell was at least seven octaves." Tony put a warm stick of gum into Trudy's sweaty palm. "I'll give you a shot on the stage if you want."

"Yeah, right!" Trudy bitterly said, brushing dirt off her behind.

"Naw, girl, you have talent!" Tony eyed her backside. "You can sing at my club anytime you want."

Two years ago, Trudy had turned him down flat. But this time, when he flipped her a matchbook, she gingerly took it.

Tony waddled toward Dee's doors and then stopped and glanced back. His eyes rolled across Trudy's curvaceous body. "You been blessed, girl. I wouldn't waste it. Besides"—Tony lit a match in his palm and sucked the flame toward the tip of his Winston—"stage sits about three and a half feet off the ground. You can glare 'em down real good from there."

Trudy didn't shed one teardrop when she got to her house. She walked up in time to see her mother at the window, slowly closing both the drapes.

When Trudy walked through the door she could smell cooking meat. She looked at her mother with pain in her eyes. But Joan kept on ironing and spraying starch on her cotton dress. She was wearing see-through pumps and a pink satin slip. Her latte skin glowed with the friction of pressing.

Joan noticed Trudy but avoided her eyes. She didn't have time. Hall was on his way over. She kept spraying and pulling the dress with one arm. Joan kept the place spotless. The house stayed impeccably clean. Joan believed a clean house reflected who you were. She worked hard to be perfect herself. Though it was an old craftsman home, everything in the place sparkled. The polished wood made it look rich.

Joan held down the iron. She checked the watch on her wrist. Trudy followed her arm as it pressed the taut fabric. Her mother scowled while applying more pressure.

Joan finished the dress and pulled it off the board and wove a hanger in through the neck.

Trudy wiped her eye. A tear ran across her hand. She unwrapped the soft piece of gum.

"I don't know why you're eating that. I told you to watch your weight. You're just one plate from being obese."

This was not true, but Joan, who was built like a stick, thought that anyone beyond the trim side of a nine was just plain ol' fat, without question.

Joan walked to the mirror and started fussing with her hair. It was an enormous red wig, which she teased, hard and scratched and sprayed so much Aqua Net over the thing until the whole room filled with a dense mist. She reapplied her lipstick and doused herself with cologne. The house was a kaleidoscope of fumes.

Joan was a good-looking woman who stood over five-seven. And at forty-eight she still looked great for her age but she was the last one to know it. No, the only thing Joan saw when she looked in the mirror was crow's feet and moles and the faint hints of gray and fine lines that grew deeper each year. Though she layered on the makeup, she could not stop the clock. She was furious every time she looked in the mirror and always cursed before walking away.

"Hall's on his way, so don't mess anything up!" Joan slammed down a vase and filled it up with fake flowers. She sprayed the mahogany table with Pledge. Trudy was out of high school and Joan was annoyed with her now. She was pissed Trudy still lived in the house.

Joan feverishly rubbed the wood back and forth until it glowed. She stopped suddenly and looked dead in Trudy's eyes. "What is it? Why are you standing there staring? What the hell do you want from me, huh?"

Trudy started to say something but Joan glanced at her watch.

"Look, I need you to get me some ice from the store and pick up my stuff from the cleaners, okay?" Joan created errands to get Trudy out of the house. She gave her an endless list of things she wanted to have done and if she couldn't get rid of her that way, she dropped Trudy at the show, anything to get her out of the room. But no matter where she sent her, no matter the task, Trudy would always come back. She couldn't stand the way Hall started to look at her daughter. She saw his eyes. The way they traced her young frame. It made Joan sick to no end.

But Trudy couldn't go out now. Not after what just happened. She went in her room and closed the door.

"What did I tell you?" Joan asked, following her in. "Hall's on his way here. I told you I need some ice and I don't need you sashaying around here."

Trudy frowned, holding her pillow to her chest. Warm tears rimmed the edge of her lids.

Joan got in her face. She spoke to her slow. "I need ice," she said low. Trudy felt her hot breath. "Get up and go get it now, like I said!"

When she still didn't move, Joan popped her leg with the rag.

Trudy quickly got up. She rubbed her stung thigh. But something snapped before she reached the front door to leave. See, Trudy was eighteen and not a kid anymore. After what happened at Dee's, Trudy didn't care what happened next. And that word she held down for so many years, well, it crashed like a mug on a porcelain floor. It jumped from her throat and raced from her tongue way before she could snatch the word back.

"Bitch," Trudy said.

Yes, there the word was. It was as bold as a cherry in a clear crystal glass.

Joan dropped the rag and stared hard at her daughter. A smile passed over her red, pursed-tight lips. It was almost as if she'd been waiting for this moment. Trudy gave her a reason, an excuse to release her fury. Trudy became a place for Joan to stash all her rage.

Trudy tried to back away but Joan snatched her wrist. Joan wheeled back and whacked Trudy's face with the back of her hand. Trudy's whole head swung back and she fell against the wall. So hard in fact, Joan's own hand stung from the blow.

Joan walked from the room and fumbled through the kitchen drawer. She came back with a long wooden spoon. Joan smacked Trudy hard across her legs and her arms. She gripped the spoon's handle like it was a weapon. She covered Trudy's body with tiny welts. Trudy yelped as the wood ate her skin.

"You want some more of this, huh? Calling me out my name! You dumb, stupid, big-butt slut!"

Trudy tried to lurch away. She tried to avoid Joan's raised fist.

"I saw you in the street with your legs in the sky." Joan covered Trudy's thighs with a dozen quick smacks.

"I'm not having my man think I live with a tramp!"

Trudy tried to ward off the blows but Joan didn't stop. It felt like a million bees stinging her skin.

Joan struck her with the spoon until it snapped right in half. Joan was outdone. She had lost all control. Her anger wasn't just for Trudy but she didn't care. All she could feel was a tidal wave of rage. An anger that grew harder to manage each day. She struggled between wanting to hold Trudy tight and tossing her against the back wall. It was Hall she was furious with but she'd never admit it. It was Hall she thought of when her hands circled Trudy's throat. She only let go to answer the phone.

"Oh, hello!" Joan said quickly. "No, baby, I'm not breathless, I just came in from taking out the trash. Uh-huh. Oh, yes, you can come over late. I've got a nice roast on and a boysenberry . . . Oh, you ate. That's okay. No, I'll still be up after one." Joan kept her voice upbeat but Trudy could see the change. Hall was going to be late again.

Joan walked to the closet and grabbed a rotted-out suitcase. She threw it toward Trudy and it slammed against the bed. "Get out!" was all she said.

The next thing Trudy knew, she was out on the street. She stayed at a friend's place for a couple of days, then got a dumpy one-room unit off Western.

Trudy got clothes conscious after being kicked out by her mother. And as the video began to circulate more and more, her exterior was what mattered to her now. What she wore became important. It was her focal point now. She wanted to prove she was better than the girl in the nude movie. Trudy became hell-bent on reinventing her image. Stealing was merely a means to an end. It became a game. It felt more like a sport. Each store was a quest. A victory. A challenge. It satisfied her unquenchable desire to feel special and a hot, burning quest for revenge.

In two months, her closet was jammed full of clothes. Trudy never left the house unless everything matched. She'd snatch something out of every store she ever walked into. It could be a small pair of gloves or a full-length wool coat. She stole so much and so long, it was part of her now. It was way beyond habit. It was like a disease. Clothes became her drug. She was totally addicted. Stealing satisfied an insatiable craving she had. She would glide both her hands across rack after rack. She loved touching fabric. She loved rubbing new textures. There were hundreds of colors in a variety of weights. Silk and the glorious smoothness of satin or the animal feel of cashmere.

Clothes allowed her to be completely new every day. Clothes lifted her up, above all those mean wagging tongues. Clothes became a shield from the dull poverty of her life. It made her life finally feel alive and exciting. And that wild panic she got from getting away clean almost felt better than sex.

Trudy loved stealing from the male shop owners best. The

power she felt was intoxicating and intense. When she went in she felt like a strong sexual magnet. In the dressing room she would always leave the door slightly ajar. They saw her wiggling out of her skirt. Saw it fall to the floor. They watched her dangle a leopard print shoe from the end of her toe. The show she put on got those men so distracted. They were so busy watching her thick luscious hips or her jiggling cleavage that they never once looked at her hands. Trudy stole in the open. Right out in front. That's where the thrill was. That wild, crazy panic. Where her heart beat so loud her eardrums were bursting. The lunatic moment before her feet hit the door. When her blood raced and her breath sounded like a chased dog. When each foot turned to stone and the world moved in slow motion. She would try to walk natural, force herself not to run. It was maddening to breathe while her whole body screamed. Like car alarms were going off in her brain. It was hard trying to appear calm, passing stock clerks, or managers and those damn undercovers, keeping her eyes locked on the cool freedom outside, during the eternal long stroll to the door.

So in three summers Trudy's life had dramatically changed. She was no longer a lace-dressed girl, eager to go to a party. She got kicked out and took Tony's offer and started working evenings at Dee's. In no time, she was living in the fast lane herself. She met scammers and sharks and slick-talking women who came to Dee's Parlor every day.

"Hey!" Lil Steve screamed but Trudy ignored him. He wiped the sweat off from this boiling-hot day.

The men whistled loud. They made awful sucking sounds. But Trudy walked tall. She kept her head high. She climbed the two steps to Dee's wearing a plum silky sheath and four-inch-high brown snakeskin slides. Before Trudy cleared the door she smiled sweetly at Lil Steve and then disappeared behind the door.

"Shouldn'ta let that thing go," the old man told him.

I know, Lil Steve said to himself.

*   *   *

Trudy walked down the hall to the dressing room door and sat by the giant chipped mirror. She hid her purse underneath a big pile of clothes and changed into a long, glittering gown. Trudy sat still and stared. She sighed to herself. She glanced at the big pile of shimmering clothes. No matter how many new outfits she put on or tore off. No matter how many new looks she paraded around town. No matter how much she wanted to feel like she sparkled, inside she felt deader than lead.

There was only one time Trudy felt truly alive. One crystal moment when she shimmered within. That was just before Sonny leaned and gave her the nod. When the house lights went dim and she glowed in the strobe light. Singing on stage filled her up with a new kind of blood. It erased all the traces of her bottlecap life. She imagined herself a bright, giant star. She could rule the whole room with her drumming hipbones. She could hypnotize them with each wiggly dip. She saw their eyes melt like ice cubes while watching her body. She could stop folks from talking. Hold them hostage with each note. Her throat, wet glossed lips and big hips were weapons. She drowned out the occasional cackles of women because their men sat there spellbound, straining to hear, glued to each sultry move. And even though most of those eyes never rose above her neckline, even though some got drunk and spilled booze on her dress, even though some of them pinched her or snatched at her body. They were reaching for her. It was her they were after. Not the gambling or liquor or the buffalo wings. All those hot thrusting hands were stretched out for her. The feeling from being on stage stayed after the house lights switched off. Long after the sounds of their glorious clapping. She became dizzy to please. She lost all inhibitions. She was determined to sharpen all their dull, worn-out lust. Like a drunk she swayed recklessly over the stage. She shook her big juicy breasts in front of their faces. With one foot near the edge it felt like she might fall. She flung out both arms, bent her neck back and roared. Because this moment, this one time she felt like she shined. Like a diamond, she felt totally see-through and free. Tony thought he was lucky getting this young chick to sing cheap. But the hot power she got from being on stage, she'd have sung in Dee's Parlor for free.

But something gnawed at her awful, like an old cat with fleas. Each day the stealing got progressively worse. Each time she took something she wanted something more. That victorious feeling would never last long. She wanted something else. Her thirst for revenge was a constant burn. She tried to stop lots of times. She knew it was wrong. But her hunger kept growing, kept itching her skin. Sometimes she'd wish she would get caught to make it stop. Sometimes she wished someone would just snatch back her hand. That someone would notice all those bags she dragged home, but nobody ever did.

4

Vernita's

It was a mean, nasty hot in '97 during summer. A new tube of lipstick could ruin the bottom of your purse. If you wore your hair down you wanted to go have it whacked just to get that hot stuff off your back.

Flo sat in the chair as warm water filled her ears.

It felt good to finally get her hair done again. It was one of the few pleasures she had. It was a place she could go and feel right at home. Having her whole head a mess gave her a sense of abandon. The close way you sat while someone worked on your locks. The quiet dignity you kept while your hair stood on end. It was intimate. It made you all feel connected. Giving you a kitchen-chair nearness, like mother to daughter. The genuine laughter, the low, hushing tones. The comb gliding slick or fighting through knots. The "wait now," "girl, hush" or "if I'm lyin', I'm flyin'" that rocketed across the hot room. But underneath the brush and the warm, calming water, over the robe at your throat and calm hands at your neck, there were pitchforks and ovens that could sear off your skin. Hot metal combs that could mar both your ears. Chemicals that bore through the first layer of your scalp and could singe the hair right out your nostrils. The beauty shop, the pit stop to glamour and pain. A place somewhere between holy hell and home.

Vernita's shop sat near the corner of Adams and Tenth, on a little side street called Mont Clair. Mont Clair was a warped piece of urban decay. Auto shops sat squat next to sewing machine stores or markets selling old milk or dusty piñatas and big stacks of Mexican bread. The painted brick buildings were tilting from earthquakes and the stucco walls were ugly from cracks. Film crews used that small stretch of street a whole lot because it was such a wrecked piece of neglect. But even in that miserable condition, if something wasn't nailed down, you can bet it'd be taken. Snatched before you had a chance to turn around fast, and before you figured what happened, before a cop answered the call, it'd be sold out of someone's beat-up van. People bought steel gates, pulled them across each shop entrance with padlocks hanging from chains like lots of loose teeth. But it didn't stop the stealing, only slowed the flow some. Because in the street there was always a steady flow of eyes, waiting for you to drop or misplace your keys, wondering if you left one of your car doors unlocked or your window rolled down, hoping for some kind of opening.

"You didn't hear?" Vernita whispered into Flo's lobe. Vernita put the last roller on a heavyset lady who was now sitting under a loud, blaring dryer.

"Girl, you late. The shit happened months ago." Vernita pulled the comb through Flo's thick black hair.

"I'd believe anything about that hussy," an older lady muttered. All you saw of the woman was her swollen neck and thick legs. Her head was slung down in a rinse bowl.

"Serves her right," Shirley said, scratching her scalp with long nails. Shirley was the cocktail girl at Dee's Parlor. She was always in everybody's business. "Didn't I say she'd get what she deserves?"

"I remember like it was yesterday the night she showed at my place. Her whole face was covered in welts," Vernita said.

"You inviting trouble having that tramp at yo' house," Shirley warned. "I'da got her a map and a bus pass."

"That was awhile ago. She got her own place now." Vernita frowned. She wanted to say something back to Shirley, but she was a good paying client. So she held the curling iron a little too close to her neck.

"Watch it!" Shirley snapped as she turned around.

Vernita left Shirley and started working on Flo again.

"Poor thing, you shoulda seen her. All black and blue." Vernita pulled the comb sadly. Flo's thick hair lay flat. "Joan must have smacked her ass fifty-two times." Vernita pulled the comb again but left it too long. It sizzled when it got to Flo's ends. "Trudy couldn't even show up to work the next day. Said she got up to go but hid in the yard. Didn't want everybody to see those large, ugly welts. Gruesome skin oozing with juice."

"I bet her mama had enough. She had to throw Trudy out. Anybody can see how skanky she is. She's your friend, Vernita, so you know better than anyone else. Joan probably couldn't take all her bullshit no more." Shirley rubbed the red lipstick off her crooked front teeth. The sun showed her pitted complexion.

"Well, I heard Trudy called her mother a bitch. Now see," Shirley said, "ya'll know she was wrong."

The washbowl woman made a loud smacking sound with her tongue. "If my daughter said that she'd be lucky to still be breathing."

"But ain't that the pot calling the kettle black," Shirley told the washbowl woman. "Both of 'em bitches, if you ask me."

With wet hair leaking over her smock, the older woman said, "I know that's right."

"Isn't Joan still shacking with some poor woman's husband?" Flo asked.

"Stole him like someone does your clothes off the line."

"And got the nerve to still put her big foot in church."

"Um um um," the older woman said, ending the exchange and laying back down in the bowl.

Vernita pressed the hot comb near Flo's neck and she flinched.

"That's no reason to beat her or toss her into the street. Trudy told me she ain't talked to her mother in months," Vernita told them. When she brought the hot comb to Flo's head once again, Flo covered her ear with her hand.

"Some women can't stand having their men near other women," Flo said low. She thought about Charles. The hair fumes upset her stomach. She wished Vernita would stop gabbing and finish.

The older woman leaned up from the washbowl again. "That Trudy ain't got nothing but hot sin in her body." The woman wore so much mascara on each of her eyes, they looked like they were lined with black flies. "My Waymond don't want to do nothing no more but creep out at night to that damned hoodlum club to hear that skanky gal sing."

"It's the same with my Joe," another woman sighed. "I caught him drooling at her in the front row one night."

"Y'all call that singing?" Shirley laughed loudly. Extending her hand, she examined her nails. "I don't care if she's Joan's daughter or not. I bet Joan got tired of Trudy sticking her ass in Hall's face. Trudy was a threat living inside Joan's house."

"Amen," the older woman said, wiping dead hair from her shoulder.

Suddenly, Trudy's Aunt Pearl rushed through the door. "Morning, everybody," Pearl said, glancing around. She was a short, husky woman with brown, flawless skin, with a smile like she just hit the Lotto. She was one of those old-time singers who'd spent time in Detroit. Told you anything you wanted to know about Motown. "Hotown," she called it. Said everybody in there was fucking. At fifty, she could sing rings around Trudy and the other girls in Dee's Parlor, and her D-cups looked damn good in sequins. Pearl showed the new girls like Trudy the ropes and made sure they weren't dealing no dirt. Nosirree, Dee's Parlor might be sliding a bit, but Pearl made damn sure it wasn't no brothel. She was a bonafide lady but not too sidity. A saucy woman who had her own stable of men who hung near her dressing room door.

"Hurry up, Vernita! I need me a touch-up. My stuff ain't layin' right no more." Pearl tossed a stuffed 99-cent-store bag on the floor. She stuck one hand in her purse and started rummaging inside. It was a great big black bag filled to the brim with Lord knows what. Her arm fumbled around until she found what she wanted. She popped a large gumball inside her jaw.

"Well, I think it's that dirty ol' man of hers," Vernita said. "She told me how Hall was nothing but hands. Trying to reach for her braids or the hem of her skirt. My uncle eyed me sideways like that from day one. Watching me, pretending to read."

"Fill me in. Who y'all talking about?" Pearl loved good gossip as much as the next. Her eyes flickered around the packed room.

"Now, Miss Pearl, you know I mean no disrespect. But Trudy and her mama, they both the same," Shirley said. "Snatch yo' man if you ain't got him chained."

Pearl looked around the room, realizing she'd walked into a storm. She eyed Shirley like she wanted to stab her right there. Trudy's mother, Joan, was her sister.

"The apple don't fall far from the tree," Shirley sneered, ripping a hangnail off with her teeth. There was nothing she liked better than stirring the pot. She showed plenty of chipped tooth when she grinned.

"Tree, my black ass. Look, y'all don't know squat. That child's hurt. Any fool could see that." Pearl shifted farther up in her seat.

"Poor thing's been living hand-to-mouth ever since Lil Steve started this mess," Vernita said.

"Hand-to-mouth, my foot. That heifer dresses better than me," Shirley said. "And what do you mean 'child'? The girl's twenty now. Lil Steve didn't do nothing but document the shit. That video proves what kind of woman she is."

"I saw her wearing a gold Chanel suit with these ice-pick-high sandals."

"I saw that suit too. That shit wasn't cheap. I know she's not shopping at Ross."

"Must be selling her stuff on the side," someone said.

No one knew Trudy got her clothing from stealing.

Pearl shot the woman a cold eye. "She ain't selling squat."

"Maybe she's giving it away," someone else laughed.

Shirley loved the way the conversation was going. She thought it was time to toss in a lie. "I've seen her outside of Dee's with a lot of different guys sitting in dark cars for hours."

Everyone in the room started talking at once.

"See?"

"What'd I tell you?"

"Girl, you were right!"

"Anybody seen the video?"

"Uh-uh."

"Not me."

"I heard Joan found the nude tape wedged inside Mr. Hall's Bible."

"Ol' nasty freak."

"Pork chop–eating prick."

"Joan should've put a spoon to his ass," Vernita added.

Pearl stared out the window a real long time. She wished Trudy could come stay with her but Pearl lived in an apartment house for seniors and they had strict rules on who could come in. "All I know is the menfolk have been bothering Trudy bad."

"Drooling like she's something warm from the oven," Vernita added. "That video did her in. That's all I hear people talking about now, and Lord knows working for Tony don't help."

Flo was trying to sort some things in her mind. "Exactly how long has Trudy been working at Dee's now?" Charles had been there at least three times that week.

"Girl, where you been?" Vernita asked. "Trudy's been working there for months."

"I helped her get started," Pearl said. "She needed the money."

"And y'all should see how she's singing up in there." Shirley glanced quickly at Pearl. "You know I ain't lying." Shirley stood up and started dancing real raunchy, sashaying and grinding her hips. "Got all them men in there looking at her sideways. Pearl, I know you seen her. She got all them men sprung."

Pearl shot her a look, and Shirley smiled and sat down.

"And look at you," Pearl said to Shirley. "Jeans all bunched at the crotch, looking like kitty in the meat box watching that tight fabric fight."

Vernita laid the comb down and let it heat back up. She didn't like them talking about Trudy and tried to change the subject. "That fight's coming up. Anybody taking bets?"

"Bets. Ain't that about a bitch. Black folks sho' know how to waste some good money," Pearl said. "Gamblin' is just throwin' it away."

"Gone and speak the truth." The older woman liked this subject. "Buying quick picks and playing the Daily Three every day instead of letting it build up at the bank."

"Bank! Hell, I don't even have an account," Shirley said proudly. "They'll never get their hands on my money."

"What money?" Pearl asked dryly. "You're always borrowing from me."

"I deposit mine each week. I don't play with mine, honey, and I got something if someone wants to act funny." The old woman patted what looked like a gun in her purse, then she smugly sat back in her chair.

Pearl stared at Shirley. "Some'll walk over a dollar to pick up a dime."

Vernita saw a customer coming. She went to the window to wave, but the woman raced into the shop down the street.

"And some rob you before you ever see 'em coming," Vernita said flatly.

Pearl let the gumball roll against her tongue. "And leave you to bleed in the street."

"That's what Trudy did me," Shirley snapped back fast. "That bitch stole the best man I ever had." The nail file she held gritted across her rough tips.

"Your man? You wouldn't know a man if his teeth bit your rump. Only man I seen you with left you sitting at the curb with a window cracked down, breathing on the glass like a dumb smashed-faced dog." Pearl grabbed a bra strap and hiked up both breasts. "If you gonna tell it, then get the shit right!"

"Trudy's just getting what she finally deserves," Shirley said.

"Nobody deserves the hand she got dealt." Pearl's eyes got as tight as two steak knives.

"Lil Steve started this mess," Pearl told the room again.

"Choosing the wrong man can lead you astray," the older woman said.

"Well, all I know is"—Vernita finished Flo's hair and spun her toward the giant mirror on the wall—"Trudy's a hundred percent Scorpio. Homegirl don't play. It might be today, it might be next week. You fuck her over, she don't forget. One day she'll pay yo' ass back."

Flo didn't say she was a Scorpio too. She didn't know Trudy well, but Flo did know one thing. Men beamed whenever

Trudy's young frame came around. She had caught Charles eyeing her at the gas station one night. Trudy looked like the kind of woman who could have any man she wanted. At thirty-four, Flo had been around the block a few times. She watched young women like Trudy out the side of her eye.

Shirley popped her gum and grinned at the room. "Well, I'm sorry. But I don't feel sorry for that girl. Trudy's gonna get it one day, wanna bet?" Shirley pointed the nail file tip at the door. "Game recognizes game. She ain't fooling me. I work with her. I've been watching her lately. I got a good feeling she's got something cooking up her sleeve, and believe me, it ain't on the same side as right."

"You ain't been on the right side in years." Pearl gave her a harsh, deadly stare.

"Hey, Flo," Vernita yelled, quickly changing the subject. "You still breastfeeding that fine younger man?"

Flo's eyes darted around the shop. She hated discussing age. But she gave a fake laugh and began fanning her face. "That man is making me crazy."

"Don't downplay it, Miss Flo, you know Charles is fine." Vernita was glad Flo had her a nice younger man. "He's quarterback wide and got a flat six-pack stomach."

"And gives skull like a pro, once I showed his ass how." Flo whispered that last part. She didn't want that on blast.

Vernita smiled, letting her hand rub across her round head. She was a very light-skinned woman with razor-short hair. Her green eyes gleamed in the sun. "I know exactly what you mean," Vernita whispered back.

"Hold up!" Pearl said, happy to finally change the subject. She scooted all the way up in her chair. Vernita had half of Pearl's hair perfectly curled on one side, and the other was sticking straight out. At fifty, she easily looked ten years younger and her body was as strong as a vault. "Y'all can keep them chicks; give me a rooster. Give me an older skilled man working over my back and, Lord, girl, I turn right into butter." Pearl practically rolled from the beauty shop chair. "Somebody better come mop me up."

Flo faintly smiled and fanned herself in her seat.

"Miss Pearl, you ol' hussy," Shirley said, smiling.

"Ain't no freak like an ol' freak," Vernita said, approving. She liked Miss Pearl. She always spoke frank. Real women like her were rare.

"If a man goes down south, pleases my Mississippi, I'd pop his big gun for free." Pearl smacked her own thigh.

Shirley and Flo laughed; even the washbowl woman chuckled.

"And I'd freak his ass in fifty-two ways if he knew what to do when he got there," Vernita said, snapping her fingers, waving her arm in one large arc.

"But y'all better use a jimmy. Mama don't play," Pearl said, wiping the front of her smock. "I'm done with them urine cups and trips to the clinic. Y'all keep that stuff if you want."

Flo dabbed the warm sweat welling out from her temples. She picked up a magazine and threw it back down. She did not want to talk about sex.

"Y'all laughing now but wait 'till you got a screaming brat on your back. Tell me about what feels good then!" Pearl looked at Shirley in the beauty shop mirror.

Shirley had five babies from four different guys. She sure wasn't the sharpest knife in the drawer.

"Tell him, 'no glove, no love.' Have that jimmy hat ready. Cuz I done known plenty of men in my life, but I don't know any women—once a man gets it—had any luck getting him to take it back out," she said, laughing.

"Amen," the older woman echoed.

Suddenly, the room got front church pew quiet. Flo nudged Vernita real quick in the arm as Joan strolled in the shop door.

There was only one woman who could turn a loud, rowdy shop into a Catholic church service. That was Trudy's holier-than-thou mother, Joan.

Joan was the kind of woman who rarely smiled. When she did, it was with a half-curled-up lip that quivered like she couldn't quite hold it. She never laughed big or showed any teeth. And if she did it was only at someone else's expense. She was younger than Pearl but her face was more lined. She was the kind of light-skinned woman who felt better than most women. She spoke low, carefully enunciating each word, and walked stiff like a pool stick ran straight up the back of her dress. Although she wore a red wig, she came for the same press and curl, for the same tidy bun she'd been wearing over twenty-two years.

Flo watched Joan pick a nonexistent piece of lint from her over-starched collar. At five-seven and in heels, she easily towered over them. Acting all high and mighty with her light eyes and pasty loose skin. Joan was always talking about the good hair and keen features that ran in her family, like anybody gave a hot damn. Shoot, her hair couldn't be that good, Flo thought to herself, if she was getting it done like everyone else.

"Hello, everyone. Hi, Pearl," she coolly said. Joan took a napkin from her purse and wiped the chair before sitting down. Carefully applying some lotion to her manicured hands, she said, "Vernita, I need a full set today."

Vernita left Pearl's head to hand Joan a magazine. She got the foot pan, rinsed it in hot soapy water and plugged it in next to Joan's legs.

"That bitch makes me sick," Vernita whispered to Flo.

Flo ducked her head in a magazine and sat quietly.

"Joan ain't nothing but a white-looking snob," Shirley whispered to Flo so Pearl couldn't hear. "Whole damn family ain't nothing but crooks. Everybody knows she stole Mr. Hall from his sick wife's back door. And he charges too damn much at his store."

"You know," Vernita whispered back, bending down, "the real reason she threw Trudy out was because she was jealous. Didn't want no daughter looking better than her." Vernita dropped her comb and let that sink in.

Everybody in the neighborhood talked about Trudy and Joan. Joan did this or Trudy did that. The fine clothes Trudy wore, the Mercedes Joan drove. And even though the Benz was old and smashed on one side and their house was down the street from the rowdy Dee's Parlor, it still was the best-looking one on the block.

Joan was holding a video case in her hand. "Look at this!" Joan waved the tape all around. "Can you believe they're still selling this crap out on the street? My God, could my life get worse?"

They all stood around Joan's thin, narrow hips.

"Is that the video?"

"How'd you get a copy?"

"She ruined my life," Joan told anyone who'd listen.

"Oh, I don't think . . ." Pearl tried to stifle her sister. Joan could be so damn dramatic.

Everyone gathered tightly around the TV to see. They'd all heard about Trudy's nude movie but none of them had seen it up close.

"Girl, don't show them that!" Pearl tried to turn the set off.

"Pearl, I'm talking. Please don't interrupt. Mama taught you better than that." Joan pushed the tape inside the VCR. "Now, I'm not some dumb turnip dropped from the truck. There is absolutely no way to make a picture this close, a video this clear, without you having to know. Look at it! Sitting right there in the air. All that black nakedness hanging for the whole world to see."

Everyone stared close. Even Vernita peered in. The movie showed a young woman rolling around naked in bed.

"She posed for it. Look at her dry humping that bed!" Joan got so close, the set touched her nose. "Look at those overgrown breasts and that awful behind rising." Joan snatched out the tape and carefully sat down. "I tell you it's just plain dis-gusting!"

To Joan, a behind standing high was plain vile. She didn't understand why black women stuck their butts out like that. They should hide it, or drape it with long flowing fabric. Or walk like her own mother had taught her to do—with her hips jutting forward and her behind tucked back in.

"And her hair? Just as nappy as can be!" Joan sucked her teeth and shook her head back and forth, like Trudy's natural hair was a sin. "It's a shame the poor girl looks like her father. She didn't get anything from me."

Pearl stared amazed at her younger sister but decided to hold her tongue.

The other women didn't know what to say. Joan made them

feel small. She was so knowledgeable, so dignified; she looked so damn rich. She didn't have a pot to piss in or a window to throw it out but you'd never know it by the elaborate way she dressed. She stared at the other women, flipping her long red wig hair. See, this was the nineties. The sixties were long gone. All that black pride had turned into perms, fades and weaves. Extensions were the only rage now.

Joan yanked the tape from the black cassette holder.

"She's my daughter, so I can say whatever I want." Joan pinched her nose and clenched her china-cabinet dentures.

"She's a slut. She's a big lying bitch. Turned out to be just like her father. Didn't get any of my family's genes." Joan flipped her fake hair and looked at her sister, daring Pearl to comment. She picked up an *Essence* magazine and eyed the dark-skinned woman on the front cover. "Nobody that dark should wear white."

Flo stared at herself in the mirror a long time. Her body wasn't that different from Trudy's. They were about the same size, had the same drenched-maple skin; Joan easily could have been talking about her. Flo rushed from the shop and raced down the street. All the hair-burning fumes were making her sick. She was glad to get out of there today.

5

Vernita and Trudy

Trudy waited in her car until the last person left Vernita's shop. She watched Vernita click the lights, twist the deadbolt and pull back the grate until it latched.

"Vernita!" Trudy whispered once she got near her window.

Vernita jumped and her purse slammed against a shop door.

"Damn, girl, you scared me. What are you doing here? I know none your braids have fallen a loose 'cause I tightened you up good myself." Vernita leaned in and examined Trudy's brown scalp.

"Get in," Trudy said. "I need to talk to you a minute."

Trudy opened the passenger's side and Vernita glided right in. She handed her a heavy paper bag.

"What's this?" Vernita asked, peering inside. "Ah, girl, you sho' know what a working girl likes." Vernita pulled a pink wine cooler out from the bag. Twisting off the top, she took a deep, thirsty swig.

"Damn, girl, it's hot. I been doing heads all day." Vernita placed the cold bottle against her forehead.

"So did you talk to Lil Steve? Did he take the bait?"

"Girl, please," Vernita said. "Mommie knows how to talk to a man. That boy took the bait and ran with it, chile. He and Ray Ray been whispering all day."

A girl with a cute, sassy bob pulled up across the street. When Vernita saw the girl, her expression completely changed. And even as she downed two more large gulps, her eyes never left the car's dash.

"That's that Keesha girl I was telling you about." Vernita watched Keesha get out of her brand-new black Nissan. "Trained her myself. Taught her all my hair tricks. Now the bitch up and got her own shop."

Keesha's shop was half a block from Vernita's. Vernita's business had slumped as soon as it opened. Even her regulars were starting to peek in on Keesha, and all the new business went there without fail.

"She got lots of exotic plants and them red chairs I wanted and wood cabinets that go from the ceiling to the floor." When Vernita downed the rest of her cooler, Trudy handed her another one from the bag.

"She's been stealing my customers. Takin' 'em all, one by one. Last month I had to go into my stash to make rent, and this month is fifty times worse."

"Nobody does hair as good as you, girl." Trudy tried to cheer her friend up. She saw the pain in her eyes.

"I swear no one out here is loyal no more. I really helped that girl. Taught her everything I knew, and this is my fucking thanks."

They watched Keesha lock the gleaming black car.

"I oughtta key her new shit now." Vernita opened Trudy's door.

"Don't be stupid, Vernita!" Trudy held her friend's arm. "You know that won't solve nothing. Don't stoop down to her level. Besides, I think I can help." Trudy looked straight in her eyes.

"How?" Vernita asked, staring back.

Trudy took a wine cooler from the bag and drank half.

"'Member what we did working the hash line in high school?"

"Hell yeah, I remember. How could I forget? Both our arms hung heavy at the end of the day from all that money we stuck up our sleeves."

"'Member that ol' white lady that worked with us too? She loved your ass. You couldn't do no wrong."

Vernita smiled and added more gloss to her lips. "She was

sweet. Just a little ol' grandmommie type. I stole steady next to her every day."

"She was sweet 'cause her lily ass thought you was white."

"She did not!"

"Yes she did. All of 'em thought that. 'Cause when everyone got caught and they asked us all those questions, they interviewed everyone except you."

"'Cause I was good. Color had nothing to do with it."

"Good my black ass," Trudy shot back. "Them white folks thought you was one of them is what it was."

"Well, I can't help what stupid white folks think."

"And you never said different. You sat there all quiet."

"Well, what was I supposed to do, huh? Scream in their face, 'Hey, y'all forgot one. Come over here. I want you to question me too?' Shoot, just 'cause their lily-white asses were dumb didn't mean I had to be."

Trudy always noticed how people treated Vernita. Her skin tone made folks treat her less harsh. Like they were glad to have her around. Vernita's hair was real long and feathered back then. Trudy never understood why she'd cut it off.

"All I want you to do is what you did then."

"What?" Vernita asked with her piercing light eyes.

"I just want you to play white."

Vernita's eyebrows rose up. She lowered the bottle to her lap. "A white girl. What, you're asking me to pass? You want me to play an ofay?"

Trudy knew that Vernita felt this was a personal insult. Although she was as light as most white folks come, she never considered herself anything but black.

"Why I gotta play white for your *big* plan to work?"

"'Cause a white girl in a bank does not look suspicious. White girls got privileges us dark sisters don't. They can walk anyplace and no one ever thinks twice. People don't follow them in stores like they're gonna take something. White girls got it easy. No one suspects them. They're like American Express. They just glide through the system and nobody ever thinks twice." Trudy pulled a blond wig and a beautiful white linen suit from out the back seat. "Just put this on. No one will ever know you're there. All I want you to do is be a decoy."

"I thought all you wanted was to get Lil Steve. Pay his ass back for dogging you so bad. Now you want me to be a damn white decoy too."

"I do, but I been thinking about it, Vernita. We can dog him and get paid ourselves."

"'We'? I ain't down for robbing no banks. Y'all can be a fool by yourself."

"I'm not asking you to rob the damn bank, Vernita. You said yourself you wanted to redo your shop. Come on, girl, I need your help."

"So me helping means I have to act like I'm white."

Trudy smiled at her friend. "Well, I sure can't do it." Trudy stroked her dark skin and fingered her long braids.

"Get some Porcelana, hell. Rub that fade cream shit on," Vernita said sarcastically.

"Yeah, that's right." Trudy downed a swig herself. "I'll turn white when pigs fly."

"Well, hell, look at Michael. Homeboy had his shit dyed."

"And I'll look like I'm going to a Halloween party. Look, you did it in high school. How is this any different?" Trudy stared down the litter-strewn street.

"I wasn't doing *it* in high school! I can't help what fools think. And I damn sure wasn't robbin' no banks. We just took a few bucks from the hash line, my God!" Vernita stared at her friend. Trudy had changed a lot lately. "You got cocky ever since you started working at Dee's. Them drunks and small-time thieves got you thinking like them."

"Just help me, Vernita. I gotta leave this place. I'm staying in that backyard unit near Vermont. It took me five weeks to get the place clean."

Vernita had seen Trudy's place. All the walls were rotten. The pipes leaked and someone had burned a hole in the floor. Lots of hard-looking people lived next door. She looked at Trudy's strained face. "Girl, don't be dumb. Just call her and tell your mother you want to come home. I'm sure y'all can work this thing out."

Trudy stared at all the trash leading to the liquor store door. A man stopped near their car and leaned toward her window. He licked his lips slow before speaking.

"Hey, movie girl," he said, grabbing between his legs. "I think I got what you need. Let me get a whiffa yo' stuff!"

"Step the fuck off," Trudy yelled sharply, "or you're gonna need to get some new teeth."

"Bitches!" The man spat, walking away fast.

"I can't stand it here anymore. It's getting worse and worse. I can't go anywhere without someone saying something or grabbing me or throwing things at me. And the women are as horrible as the men."

"Ignore them. Or do what you just did, tell 'em to step the fuck off."

"I do, but it's hard." Trudy's eyes filled with tears. "They're vicious, Vernita, the comments are much worse. That movie Lil Steve did really ruined my life. If I could take five minutes back, I swear, it would be that. I can't stand to walk down the street anymore. I got to do this job so I can get the hell out."

Vernita stared at her friend. She really wanted to help Trudy. She knew everything she said was true. She'd heard those cruel comments firsthand. But hitting a bank was no god damn joke.

"This ain't high school. This is a fuckin' bank you're talking. Cameras be everywhere. Even in the bathrooms. This ain't like taking nickels and quarters from school," she said.

"Look, I've already thought this thing through. We don't have to touch any of the money. Lil Steve does the work for us. He handles the drama. All you do is play decoy and leave."

Keesha must have forgotten something, because she ran from her beauty shop and out to her Nissan again. Her silver rims sparkled in the streetlight.

Vernita looked seriously back at her friend. "All you want me to do is walk in. That's all?"

"I'm telling you that's it. No sweat, I promise."

"I don't want to get caught." Vernita stared dead into her eyes.

"Being caught is not even an option, Vernita. See, we're not the ones who'll be doing the crime. That punk who fucked up my life, that's his god damn job. Not getting caught is Lil Steve's problem. You and me are going to be fine."

6

Ray and Lil Steve

"Wake up, you homeless muthafucker!" Tony screamed loud. He was banging on Lil Steve's fender. It was nine o'clock at night and the streetlights were on. A slight mist had fallen on the lawn.

Lil Steve was sound asleep in the backseat of his car. The pounding sound made him bump his head against the door. He saw Tony's sour face pressed against the window. He knew what Tony wanted, but Lil Steve remained calm. As his head throbbed, he reached over and put his Ray-Bans back on. Then he slowly rolled the window halfway down.

"If you give me two weeks, I'll pay it all back with interest."

Tony smiled at Lil Steve. He took a pack of cigarettes from his pocket. "If ifs were fifths, we'd all be drunk. Now pay up and don't give me no lip." He wasn't about to be intimidated by this dumb stupid punk whose dick just got big last week.

Lil Steve pulled up his pants leg and peeled down his sock, taking a C-note out from his ankle.

Tony stared at the bill like it was nothing. "You 'bout four yards short." Tony lit his match, sucking his lips hard against his Winston.

"I'ma have it by Friday," Lil Steve told him coldly.

"You better have, Junior." Tony's gummy grin was broad. He dropped his lit match on the front seat of the car. It made a tiny burn mark on the oily green vinyl. "If you don't, you gonna need to get a new home." Tony grabbed the money and walked to Johnny's Pastrami. He ordered three pastramis, two fries and a Coke before laboriously getting back in his Caddy. Lil Steve leaned forward, watching him close out of his clean sideview mirrors. He rolled down the window, grabbed the parking ticket from under the wiper, balled it up and tossed it out toward the gutter.

"Yeah, get yo' fat ass back in yo' ride." Lil Steve took another hundred from under the car mat and jammed it inside his sock. He got out of his car and wiped the chrome of his Impala. He folded the rag and put it back in the trunk. The car might be old and nicked on one fender, but Lil Steve kept his ride clean.

Lil Steve sprayed Armor All on the burn mark and flicked the match out. "Muthafucka," he said under his breath.

In the criminal world there were all kinds of types. Gangsters, straight thugs who would murder your mama and not shed one drop. Ballers who pulled up in white, gleaming Bimmers to hand out their small rocks to sell. Players and pimps who liked dealing women and hid in a shroud of giant permed hair with fat gold chains waxing their necks. Hustlers were the ones you got free cable from. Sold those black bootleg boxes at a hundred a pop. Or maybe they worked for the phone company once or some video shop and walked home with a bag full of tools or a catalog of CDs and movies. They did insurance fraud, real estate and credit card scams. They might carry guns, but they weren't your murdering type. Just had heat if some shit broke off raw.

See, Lil Steve was one of these. A confidence man. The kind you got to do the talking. He'd only been to juvie on a credit card scam. He walked and talked fast. Always thought he was smarter. His young-looking face lived on a stack of fake ID's. He prided himself on never getting caught. Never went to the pen once. You could tell by the crazy way he talked.

"Chili dog, chili dog!" Lil Steve screamed to Ray Ray. He walked the short blocks to Dee's Parlor.

Ray Ray was standing outside against the wall. He had just been hired as a bouncer.

"What's hap'nin, man?" Ray Ray smiled back.

Big Percy grinned too, giving Lil Steve a pound.

"Walk with me a minute," Lil Steve whispered to Ray Ray. He threw a quick glance at Big Percy's back. "Nosy brother always trying to co-sign."

Ray Ray's black leather jacket blew in the night breeze. Lil Steve stopped when they got out of earshot.

"Every word I tol' you is the got damn truth, man. This dude is like clockwork. Every Friday at three o'clock he strolls in the bank with his double-breasted suit and puts in twenty-five grand. Blam! Just like that." Lil Steve popped his fingers into Ray Ray's burnt face. He took out a Kool and lit up the end. The match glowed against his baby-smooth skin. "But at the end of the month he takes the whole hundred out." Lil Steve pulled the tab on a Colt 45. He kept the can inside the brown paper bag.

"All we got to do is follow the dude and jack his ass on the ride home. Simple as that. Easy money, homie. That's fifty G's apiece in our pockets." Lil Steve took a swig from the bag. He passed it to Ray Ray to sip.

Ray Ray waved the can away. He leaned against the wall. He stayed icy cool, but everyone knew he was crazy. He'd already done time for battery and assault and the word was still out on the boy in a coma. If the parents unplugged him and the little kid died, they could still charge Ray Ray with murder. That's the kind of dude Ray Ray was. Straight thug. Strong-arm man. Half Panamanian, ex-heroin addict, and you'd better watch out when his temper flared up 'cause there was no telling what he might do with a knife.

Ray Ray's narrowed eyes sliced into Lil Steve's face. Homeboy always came up with these crazy-ass schemes. Nigga talked more shit than anybody he knew, but they'd been best friends since fourth grade.

"Who told you about the suit, dog?" Ray Ray asked casually.

"Vernita hooked me up. Her girl Trudy works there." Lil Steve took another swig from the can and looked down. He never looked Ray Ray in the eye when Trudy's name came up. "Homechick still got the best ass on the block!"

"Shouldn't have let that one go," Ray Ray said matter of factly.

Ray Ray had learned early to keep his emotions in check. No one knew how he really felt about Trudy. Like a cellblock, he looked colder than concrete.

"Man, I know," Lil Steve said, wiping his mouth. "I done had plenty but Trudy was the best. That girl had a whole lot of heart."

They both stopped and watched a woman walk down the street. She balanced a fat grocery bag on her hip. Her thin skirt swirled around her large calves.

"A bitch'll flip the switch once she knows yo' ass is sprung," Ray Ray said, flicking his ash. "No point going out like some punk." He said that last part more to himself. Jail had given Ray Ray a long time to think. "So, y'all still hang?" Ray Ray asked casually.

Lil Steve looked at the trash cans lining the street. "I had to cut her loose, dog. My shit was all fucked up. That's when I owed Tony that money."

Ray Ray remembered. Word was, he still owed him some.

"Man, how'd you get her to make that nude movie?" Ray Ray knew lots of women who did lots of freaky shit, but never in front of a camera.

"Had forty copies made the same day," Lil Steve bragged.

Ray Ray had one too but he never did watch it.

"Nigga, how you even think of some crazy shit like that?" Ray Ray put half a smoked joint in his mouth.

"Common sense, loc. Marketing is all. I told her I was gonna make that big ass a star. I said Hollywood's not ready for the body she got. Man, her shit looked way better than them babies in *Playboy*. I couldn't believe how easy they sold. All the barber shops wanted 'em, auto mechanics, men hanging at the car wash were asking for some and them dudes sitting up high at the track. I even rocked 'em at a few of my friends' bachelor parties." Lil Steve stopped to laugh at his own crazy antics. "Never had a problem having cash after that."

"You was flowin' for a hot minute, player." Ray Ray nodded. He blew his smoke out real slow.

"I sho' didn't expect her to find out, though, dog."

"I'm surprised she's even speaking to yo' ol' janky ass." Ray

Ray took another long drag. "How you know this bank shit ain't her getting you back?"

"'Cause she's sprung. That's a damn woman for yo' ass. You dog 'em real bad and they still call you back. Trudy ran the thing down to Vernita the other day. Told me somebody could make some quick money off that white boy. Said they better move soon before the deal dries up. Said the tan-suit man's been talking about leaving that bank. I'm telling you, fool! We could make a killing putting that cash on the fight." Lil Steve wiped his mouth with his sleeve. "So, whatchu say, homie? You in or you ain't?" Lil Steve leaned closer into Ray Ray's marred face.

"I'm thinking about it, man."

Ray Ray was fresh from the pen and didn't want to go back. He looked down at the long silvery scar on his arm from the last time.

"Study long, study wrong," Lil Steve shot back. "Look, this Friday is the day. That gives us just enough time to place our bet and bust Tony's fat ass for good. You know he be treating you wrong at the club. Messing around with your scrilla and shit. Talking about hold your check till next week. You know that ain't right. Got all kinda money coming in every day and he talkin' 'bout hold your damn check."

Lil Steve took the forty out of the bag. He downed the rest of the can, wiping the corner of his mouth, and let it roll down to the curb.

Ray Ray stared Lil Steve straight in the eye.

"Straight up, man, is this shit legit or what? You ain't in it just to bust that big ass again, is ya? How I know you the one who ain't sprung?"

"Me sprung? Nigga, please. You must be sick. You know every woman I hit turns into an addict. She just wants my black juicy dick."

Ray Ray studied Lil Steve's smooth face. He knew Trudy wanted something. But he didn't know what. "So how's this shit s'posed to work?"

"Damn man, I done tol' you twice! Dude comes in and takes

out the cash. Been taking it out every fuckin' month. All we got to do is gank his ass and go. No guns, no drama, no bullshit, all right? Man, I'm trying to tell you it's cool."

Ray Ray knew it had to be cool. He had just come back from doing eighteen months in Norco. If this went bad he could face eight years upstate. Ray Ray picked up a bottle and threw it out in the street. It crashed next to an old Dodge.

"I need to get my hands on some ends, fast," Ray Ray said. "Tony don't pay on time at the club, and things getting worse around the house." Ray Ray worked at Dee's Parlor as a bouncer. It was the only job he could get as a felon.

"Your moms don't sew at that factory no more?" Lil Steve asked.

Ray Ray fingered the cross at his throat. He re-lit a Newport and sucked the dank smoke, blowing it out long and slow.

"When I was locked up she worked late at the shop. Used to have to leave my little niece Kelly alone. So this social worker comes nosing around, asking questions and shit. Kelly lied. Told the lady Mama went to the store. You can't tell those welfare folks you got a gig, no matter how below minimum wage it is."

"Dig it," Lil Steve said, cleaning his shades.

"So the lady say, 'You here all alone by yo' self?' Man, you seen them Section Eight wenches with they wide, bulging eyes, tapping they clipboards and shit."

"Running up in here like some roaches," Lil Steve said.

"So the bitch hauls Kelly off to a foster care ward. Said Mama's unfit. Some endangerment law. Man, my moms ain't been the same since."

Ray Ray threw a rock at a parked beat-up car. It ricocheted off of the curb.

"I was locked down and couldn't do a muthafuckin' thing. All she does, dog, is just sit in her chair in a big apron, staring. Looking out at the busted-up pavement outside, blinking at nothing but the hot sun."

"Damn, man," Lil Steve said. That's not what he heard. He heard Ray Ray's mama was smoked out on Sherm.

"When I finally got out, I tried to watch her myself. Bought food, cleaned up the place some. Tried my best to cheer her back up. But, man, it's no use. I can't leave her alone. Almost torched the place once when she fell asleep with the stove on." Ray Ray rubbed the large burn on the side of his face. "I gotta pull all the knobs off the oven when I go." Ray Ray popped open his Newports and pulled out one more smoke.

"Look at this." Ray Ray pulled up his sleeve, revealing large, pumped-up arms. The kind you only see on wrestling shows, or on men who just got out the pen. Ray Ray lit his cigarette and held in the smoke.

"Man, I tried to go legit, but every interview's the same. Muthafuckas always asking, 'What skills do you have? Where have you worked?' I want to leap across the desk and slap the smirk from they mugs. Punks always asking questions. What can you do, what have you done? White boys don't want you to *learn* no new shit. They got all the fuckin' power. Own every got damn thing and do the hiring too. My parole officer told me to go work for Roadway. I don't want to sit in no funky-ass truck. Riding all damn day in a jail cell cab. Getting hemorrhoids and shit, breathing cheap gas and fumes, just to bring home minimum wage."

"That's right," Lil Steve added. "That's what I'm talkin' 'bout, dog!"

"Chump change once they gank you for taxes. Look, man," Ray Ray said, showing the inside of his arm. "I've been selling my own blood to get me some cash."

Lil Steve studied the bruises of Ray Ray's thick arm.

"They stab a long needle deep down in my veins. Make me lay down and give me cups of grape juice to drink while I watch my blood fall in a jar. I get $15 a pop each time I strap down. When I ain't manning the front door at Dee's Parlor, dog, I'm feeding Mama on plasma donations alone."

Lil Steve didn't know if homeboy sold blood or not. But he did know Ray Ray used to like him some heroin. "Listen, G, if we do this, you gotta be straight. You can't be fuckin' with no needles and shit." Lil Steve didn't want to do no heist with no addict.

"Well yo' ass can't be up on that cheap liquid crack." Ray Ray looked at Lil Steve's empty malt liquor can. But he smiled at him too. The deal sounded smooth. A little too smooth. But he had to admit, Lil Steve was one of the best hustlers he knew. Ain't been caught on no serious shit yet.

Lil Steve squinted his eyes at him hard. "So what you say, nigga? Is you down or what?"

"Yeah, man, I'm down. Handle yo' business. Meet me at the club and let's work this shit out. But listen, cuz, don't fool around and fuck this shit up. I ain't playing with yo' crazy ass. Call ol' girl and pick her brain about this mess."

"You ain't got to tell me. See, I'm Teflon, baby! Nothing sticks to me." Lil Steve flashed Ray Ray a big gold-tooth smile. "Wooowee," he said, wild. "We gonna jack his ass and be counting fifties on the freeway, baby!" He gave Ray Ray a pound and did a little backyard boogie dance.

Ray Ray flashed him back a mild smile. "You's one crazy fool." He took one final drag and dropped the butt to the ground, smashing it out with his toe.

7

Joan and Pearl

Pearl poured her sister Joan a shot glass of tequila. Two frosty margaritas sat next to each short glass. They liked to sneak a quick shot before the club opened up. The metal fan rattled trying to beat back the sun. The weatherman said they were in store for a scorcher. It was supposed to hit a hundred and one.

Joan sat there stiff with her gold cigarette lighter. Her long legs were crossed, her nails immaculate. She wore a tight pencil skirt and a white low-cut Danskin. Though her wig was pinned up off the back of her neck, her scalp heated up like a skillet. She kept studying the room like she smelled something bad and kept wiping her lap with a napkin. She would only visit her sister in the day while the club was all closed. She thought the women at Dee's were beneath her and cheap. Joan would never be caught dead in Dee's Parlor at night.

Pearl pulled open a drawer and peered deep inside. She brought out a giant stack of old mail. One by one she held each piece to the sun.

"What in God's name are you looking for, Pearl?" Joan asked.

"Tony's not slick. Something's here, I can feel it. He shipped Miss Dee off to some home who knows where and I swear I will look till I find it. 'Member what Mama used to say to us all the time? If you keep looking, nine times out of ten, you bound to stumble on something." Pearl's glasses slipped farther down her nose.

Joan looked at her sister like she was a fool. "Nine times out of ten you'll find something you don't want. Admit it, you like snooping in others folks' junk. You're like an old dog gumming away at some shoes."

Joan sipped her drink. She twirled her gold lighter. She noticed the chipped plates and wobbly-looking chairs. "How can you work here? This place is a dump."

"'Cause, if I stay, I may find something out about Miss Dee and I'ma keep looking until it's all said and done."

Joan shook her head in disgust and popped open her compact. She urgently started plucking hairs from her chin. "Growing old ain't no joke. Tony sure dogged Miss Dee bad."

"Acting all slick just to get in that will," Pearl said. "'Member what Sally Jenkins did to poor ol' Mr. Wade?"

"Dumb man shouldn't have trusted her with all his life savings! That bitch woulda pinched a penny from a dirty hog's ass."

"That's the same thing Tony did to Miss Dee. The last time I saw her I asked her point-blank, I said, 'Excuse me for prying and I mean no disrespect, but that man ain't worth spit and I know folks, Miss Dee. Been working here too long to let it go down like this. Every time I see that fool he got his hand out and you keep greasin' it like some damn Vaseline.' You know what she told me?"

"What?"

"Told me Tony was nice." Pearl sneered.

"Nice! Did you tell her that man's half iguana?" Joan opened her compact again and dabbed on more lipstick. "The man's skin's so thick I bet he can't even bleed."

Pearl adjusted the pull of her giant bra strap; it snapped against the skin on her shoulder. "I remember telling Miss Dee, you know what I told her?"

"What?"

"I said, 'Miss Dee, he's stealing.'"

"You told Miss Dee that?"

"Sure did," Pearl said. "But she didn't do shit." Pearl downed her shot and wiped off her lip. "She told me she knows. 'Been knowing,' she said. Said the little bit he takes she don't miss."

"Little bit!" Joan screamed. "Shit, the man has it all!"

"She told me Tony was the only one that comes by to see her. Said he perked up her day. Girl, you should have seen her smile. It gave me a window to the girl she once was."

"Tony drove all her good friends away. Always hanging at her door like some old hungry vulture. No one wanted to see Miss Dee with his big ass around."

"The ones bold enough to come, he wouldn't let get upstairs. He just takes their plates of food and don't even say thanks, lets the screen door smack back in their faces." Pearl studied Joan's face. She watched her and waited.

"Trudy tried to see her once," Pearl continued softly. "Told me Tony got out of line."

"And you believed her. Girl, you know how she lies. She must have led Tony on."

"Led him on! Tony don't need any leading."

"But you've seen her, Pearl. Look at her power around men. They can't keep their eyes off her. I've seen grown men turn right into putty. At ten years old, when some of my men friends came over, I swear, I just turned my back for two minutes and Trudy was in the man's lap."

"That's not power! Them grown men were bothering her, Joan! She told me about your *men friends*," Pearl said knowingly.

Joan glared at her sister but let the comment drop. And the big thing they weren't saying finally came up, like the spins after a night getting smashed.

"You shouldn't have thrown her out," Pearl scolded her sister. "Trudy's too damn young to be out on the street."

"Bullshit, you and me were out at sixteen." Joan flicked the tall flame from her shiny gold lighter. "Trudy's twenty. That ain't hardly too young."

"Being out was a helluvalot different back then," Pearl said.

"Shoot, when you kicked Johnny out I didn't say boo! I let you handle your business. That was your son."

"I wish you'da said something." Pearl sadly stuck her hand in a big bowl of chips. "He's been locked up in Chino ever since." Pearl hated this subject. She'd tried to bring it up before but Joan cussed her and hung up the phone.

"Why are you tripping? Trudy's only been gone a few months."

"It's been well over a year and I'm worried about that girl. She's gravitating to the wrong kind." Pearl angrily munched on her chips.

"Look, she's grown. My job is finished. Why are you jumping in stuff when you don't have the facts?"

"What facts?" Pearl asked. "What the hell did she do?"

Truth was, Joan knew exactly why she'd made Trudy leave. Trudy was in her way. She blocked what Joan really wanted. See, Hall told her he'd leave his wife once Trudy was gone. But Joan couldn't tell Pearl any of that, so she decided to fabricate a story.

"She was stealing!" Joan said. "I caught her red-handed myself. The police were bound to be knocking on my door."

Trudy was stealing, but Joan didn't know that. Pearl quietly poured them both drinks from the pitcher of margaritas and shook some more chips in a bowl.

Joan opened her compact and patted her heavily made-up face. "Greedy folks always get caught left and right. Some folks can't work next to all that stuff. Thieving fever sets in. If I've seen it once, I've seen it a hundred times. Oh, they get away at first. Steal a few things; let their friends shove a pair of pants in the bag. But they always got caught. Greed caught their ass in the end. I remember this guy. Oh, man, was he crazy. He kept filling bag after bag after bag. Talking all the time about how easy it was. But that fool couldn't stop. It was never enough. That Oriental rug was where he crossed the damn line. You can't steal a thousand-dollar rug and not expect red flags to go up. They took that fool boy out in handcuffs." Joan sat perched on her stool like a queen and took a neat sip from her glass.

"I remember that guy. He took you to nice west side restaurants."

"Had the nerve to ask me for three hundred dollars. Fool wanted me to come bail his ass out," Joan said dryly. "Only thing he got was a piece of my mind."

"That was that rich fella lived over there in Hancock Park, right?"

"Rich, hell. He wasn't doing nothing but fronting. Had the

tiniest house on the whole fucking block. Told me he couldn't bear to tell his mama he stole. Skinny, stuck-up boy with big Coke-bottle glasses. Bragging all the time 'bout his argyle socks, like anybody gave a hot damn!"

"You were stealing, too. You used to get lots of stuff."

"The hell I was!" Joan snapped back. She crushed her butt in the ashtray.

"Thievin' fever has always run in this family." Pearl slowly stood up and emptied the ashtray. "No use tryin' to deny it with me."

It was never really talked about, but all of them did it. Switching tags, grabbing an extra pair of shoes. All of them came home with bags. "Oh, I got this or I got that," someone would say. No one asked where or ever asked how. All they saw growing up was price tags getting ripped off with teeth late at night or burned loose with cigarette lighters in cars so they could wear the clothes right away. Their mother claimed it was because they were all born on that new stolen bed. She got the bed hot out the back of a Beakins moving van. Some roughnecks had robbed the big furniture store and their mama, the neighborhood bookie at the time, heard about it and asked for first dibs.

"Uh-uh. Don't point your finger at me. I know what you're thinking, and you're out of your mind. Trudy didn't get none of that stealing from me. You and Sonny was doing it. That was you all. Don't put me in the middle of that mess." Joan sat up and re-crossed her shapely legs tight.

"Me and Sonny was doing it! Well, ain't this a bitch. Girl, that hot comb musta burnt what was left of your mind."

Joan snapped her compact and pursed her tight lips. "That was you all. That wasn't me, I remember. That was Sonny and y'all."

"Well, I remember when Mama had to drive across town." Pearl picked up a chip and munched it right in Joan's face. "Picked yo' thievin' ass up from the West L.A. station."

"That wasn't me, that was Sonny and them."

"That was Sonny and *you*! I remember that night. You and Sonny thought y'all was slick in that Italian man's store. I know you remember that little turquoise suit, don't you? I bet that shit's still in your closet."

Joan stared at her drink and slowly stirred her red straw. "That was only one time. I wasn't bad like you guys."

"Shoot, I remember that and some other times too. Like me and you in that new jewelry store off Third. Slid that gold saffron ring right inside your big jaw. Mashed it inside that wad of gum you was always chewing on back then." Pearl slumped her large body back against her chair. "Wore that ring and that gold kitty necklace for years. Only stopped 'cause your neck got fat when you got pregnant."

Joan couldn't argue but wasn't about to be outdone.

"Oh, and what about you? Think you're so high and mighty. Miss Dee had some pretty nice fur coats at her house. What the hell happened to them?"

"Miss Dee was my friend. Me and her was tight. Besides"—Pearl looked down and gave a pitiful smile—"I'm sure she'da liked me to have 'em."

"Liked you to have 'em. Don't that beat all! You just up and helped yourself! That's what yo' thievin' ass did." Joan grabbed the bottle and poured herself a long shot. "Probably got 'em shoved inside that armoire of Mother's."

"Why you gotta bring up that armoire again? You know Mama gave the armoire to me. You got the china cabinet. Got the butcher block too. Why you gotta bring up the armoire?"

"'Cause you took it! You know Mama said it was mine!"

Pearl didn't like being backed against the wall. "Well, at least I know where to draw the damn line. I don't steal other folks' husbands."

"I didn't take him!"

"Yes, you did!"

"The fuck I didn't!" Joan swore.

Pearl raised both her eyebrows and stared Joan down hard. "Then how do you explain Mr. Hall?"

"I didn't take him! I had him first." Joan stuck out her jaw and took a bite into her chip. "As far as I'm concerned the woman gave him to me. Holding out on sex is like taking a man's plate. Even a dog's got to go and eat somewhere." Joan downed the rest of her drink and threw Pearl a naughty smile.

"Amen," Pearl said, taking a handful of chips too. She was glad to reach some kind of truce.

Pearl got up and opened a tall wooden cabinet. She was rummaging around, peering deeply inside when Trudy walked into the room. Joan saw her come in and quickly stood up. Pearl shut the cabinet and frowned at her sister, holding her arm for her to stay. She wished Joan and Trudy could get along better. She didn't like her young niece living in an apartment alone. Especially in the beat cockroach street where she stayed. There were too many hoodlums hanging around. She worried more about Trudy each day.

"Hey, Trudy," Pearl said, trying hard to break the ice. "Come and give your ol' auntie a kiss."

Trudy'd been listening inside the club the whole time. She liked to eavesdrop on her mother when she talked. She was desperately searching for some kind of clue as to why her mother hated her so.

Trudy eyed Pearl and glanced quickly to her mother. She thought about what Vernita had told her in the car. She would try. She would at least try to talk to her mother. Maybe by now she'd calmed down.

"Hello, Mother. I got you that fragrance you like." Trudy opened her purse and pulled out a blue bottle.

"My Sin! Oh, girl, yo' mama loves that scent." Pearl smiled hopefully at Joan.

But Joan stood still. She didn't even flinch. So Pearl rushed up and grabbed the whole bottle. "Ooh, look at it, Joan, even the bottle looks sweet." Pearl tried to put the blue bottle inside Joan's hand. But Joan moved away and wouldn't take it.

"Come on, Joan. Smell it, it's nice." Pearl tried again to hand it to Joan, but Joan snatched her hand away so fast, the bottle crashed to the floor. The whole room filled with its thick floral scent. Trudy stared down at her shoes.

"Joan! Oh my goodness, what's wrong with you, huh?" Pearl frowned at her sister. "This stuff ain't cheap." Pearl tried to save what was left in the bottle.

"That's okay," Trudy said meekly. Her lids began to well, so she bit on her tongue and squeezed the thin handles of her lime leather purse.

Joan picked up her clutch and tucked it under her arm. Her eyes rested at Trudy's large chest. Joan shook her head like Trudy's breasts were disgusting. Joan's own breasts were lifted to unimaginable heights, supported by a phenomenally large padded bra.

"Why do you like wearing all those godawful braids? You look like Kunta Kente." Joan jerked her keys out of her purse. A giant Mercedes emblem hung from the chain. It was scuffed on one side, like her car.

"Come on, Joan, they look nice. All the girls got 'em now." Pearl tried her best to get her sister to stay. "You don't have to go, rest your feet a hot minute. Happy hour's about to start. I'll fix us a nice little snack." Pearl stopped rummaging in a drawer and pulled on her apron.

When Joan drank, she got angry and lost her poised speech. "Stay for what? Some shriveled-up pigs feet and ribs? Shit, ain't nothing at this bar but some common, loud-mouthed bitches and hustlers looking for marks. All of them have butcher knives for hearts."

Joan checked the gold watch on the inside of her wrist. She took a deep breath and regained her composure. "No, I have to go," Joan calmly told them. "I've got to take my three o'clock bath." She glanced at Trudy, then quickly away. "I like to keep mine nice and fresh."

When the floor creaked, Pearl slammed the drawer closed with her hip. Tony strolled into the room. He was holding a beer and an Oreo box. He looked at Trudy, then Pearl and a long time at Joan, like he'd finally found his true target.

"It smells like a got damn whorehouse in here!" Tony twisted the black cookie and licked off the white frosting. "Well, I'll say, Miss Thang came to pay me a visit." Tony let his gaze roam over

Joan's pulled-tight blouse. "Your ass always been nice and fresh to me."

Joan stared at Tony like he was a stray dog. To her he was nothing but cheap, lowlife scum. Speaking to him was hardly worth the effort.

"What? You can't speak? You too high-toned to talk? Well, I remember a time when you wasn't."

In a drunken moment long ago, Joan had gone home with Tony. It was a night she steadfastly denied in her head.

Tony's eyes never left Joan's tall, shapely frame. "Your baby girl's packing 'em in here each night." Tony licked the rest of the sweet white from the cookie. "I told 'em she learned from the best."

Joan sneered at Tony's hideous face. She glided across the room like a high-fashion model. But before she reached the door she stopped and turned around. "How's Flo?" Joan boldly asked Tony. She grinned as the pain began to weigh in Tony's face.

"Oh, that's right." Joan smiled more broadly. "I'm sorry, I forgot. Pearl, what's his name? You know, the postal worker, the well-built, super-fine, young-looking one? The one who knocks the hot breath from your lungs."

Pearl smiled at Joan. She knew exactly what Joan was doing. "Oh, yeah, that's right, pretty boy, gorgeous fellow. Make a woman want to pee when she see him." Pearl glanced at the ceiling as if she were thinking. "Let me see what's his name? I think it starts with a C."

"Oh, that's right." Joan smiled brightly. "How could I forget—Charles. The Lord didn't make many like him. Flo's with Charles. Yeah, that's right. They make such a nice couple. She's a little older, but hell, I tip my hat to that girl. She knows how to keep a man happy." Joan watched the small muscles in Tony's face tighten. Her own face changed into a savage, cruel grin. She threw her scarf around her neck and left.

Tony looked at Trudy and quickly at Pearl before taking his cookie box upstairs.

"What does Tony know about Mama?" Trudy asked.

"Nothing. Tony's just talking." Pearl started wiping the tabletop clean.

"Mama used to steal?" Trudy asked her point-blank.

But Pearl was uncomfortable talking about Trudy's mother. "We was all young fools back then, baby."

Trudy looked at the bar's colorful bottles of liquor. "I remember a time I saw Mama take something."

Pearl turned around and walked toward the small closet. She didn't like talking to her niece about that mess. Some things were best left unsaid.

"It was right when Mama first started seeing Mr. Hall."

"Hall ain't nothing but a fuckin' loan shark. Gave everyone credit." Pearl grabbed a broom and started sweeping the floor. "Then he sucks out the blood on those month-to-month notes. Look what he done to your mother."

"I remember the collectors kept calling all the time."

"Yo' mama went through hell way back then, baby. Lockheed shut down and your daddy lost his aerospace factory job. When he died, the state took the house."

"We moved to that tiny liquor store apartment upstairs. Mr. Hall would visit. He'd give Mama credit. All day and night our phone would just ring. She told me don't answer it, used to cover it with pillows, but one time Mama just couldn't stand it no more. She put on her black pumps, grabbed my hand and her purse and we went to go see Mr. Hall." Trudy sat down and picked up a chip.

"She was driving so fast, I really got scared. Cussing at the traffic and slamming the brakes. When her nylons got ripped she stopped off at Rite-Aid and helped herself to a new pair of queen-size pantyhose. She shoved the thin package inside my pink sweater. I was young and didn't know why she put them in there. So when we got to the door, I pulled the stockings back out and said, 'Mommy, we still have to buy these.'"

"She told me 'bout that." Pearl laughed as she swept a bent broom across the floor. "Your mama was fit to be tied."

"I'll never forget that hard look on her face. When we got to the lot, Mama pulled off one shoe. She whipped me right there, right between the parked cars. I had heel marks on my legs for weeks."

Pearl put the broom down. She'd hadn't heard that part.

"Your mama was under a lot of stress, baby." Pearl swept without offering anything further.

"I waited in the receptionist area and could hear them arguing inside. They stayed in his office for hours. When she came out, her lipstick was smeared and her dress was all twisted but her fist clutched a handful of bills."

"Your mama been slick like that from day one," Pearl said.

Trudy picked up a chip and snapped it in half. Trudy remembered when she'd started taking things from Mr. Hall's office. When she took things she felt like she was paying him back for taking the good part of her mother. She'd take quarters and all of his really nice pens, anything she found in the drawer. One day she even took Mr. Hall's family picture. She took it right out from its shiny gold frame. She folded it up in her white lacy sock and buried it in the yard when she got home.

"As soon as we moved here, everything changed. Mama got mean. She hated everything I did."

"Mr. Hall moved y'all but kept his other whole family," Pearl said. "I think that just about killed your poor mother. That and seeing you in his lap."

Trudy bit her lip. She shifted her purse on her arm. "I was fourteen," Trudy said, trying to hide a weak smile. "Hall wanted to know how much I weighed." Trudy remembered that day well. She'd felt a delirious sick pleasure. She'd had both her thick arms around Mr. Hall's neck. She could tell he was scared. She could feel his legs twitch. But for a split second she'd finally beaten her mother at something. She knew it was mean and it was only one time, but for a moment, while she sat, watching her mother's pained face, it was the most triumphant time of her life.

"That just about blew your poor mother's mind. She sat right in here and drank back-to-back shots of bourbon. And you know what she thinks about Dee's."

"I think Mama thinks he touched me, but the lap thing was it. He came every Sunday, right after church, and from then on I stayed in my room. He took Mama and me to church when his wife was on trips. Those church ladies looked like they might gash out our eyes. They never spoke once. Didn't invite us to nothing. If they saw Mama first they would always cross the street."

"Sometimes church can be a good place for evil to hide," Pearl told her. "Y'all wasn't missing too much."

"Mama tried to act like she was better than those ladies. She tried to dress expensive, pretended to be rich. She slaved over her clothes to keep them all looking perfect."

"Looks like you got that in common," Pearl said, smiling.

Trudy smoothed out her tight lavender skirt.

"Your mother was something else back when we was both young. Had the finest legs walkin'. Brothas used to line up. I was the short one. Had my few stragglers." Pearl smiled and fanned herself with a menu. "But your mama was tall. She could have been a star. Had a smile that could melt hard candy right in the jar."

"Well, what happened? How'd she get so mean?" Trudy bit into a chip. A few crumbs dropped to her lap.

"She ain't mean. Yo' mama just picked the wrong man. Wanting the wrong thing can ruin yo' life." Pearl stared at the club's water-stained ceiling. "If you walk with your head stuck in a cloud all the time, eventually you bound to trip and fall. Your mother stumbled on Mr. Hall."

Trudy thought her mother was the biggest fool on earth. "Why doesn't she leave him? What does she see? Everyone knows that he's married!"

"Her heart don't know yet," Pearl said, lowering her eyes. "Love is like gin. It's so clear, you can't see it. But Lord, you can sho' feel its heavy, hot taste. If you forget that bottle, or leave off the top, eventually it evaporates away. Yo' mama spilt her bottle a long time ago. I never liked Hall, used to call him Alaska. I never met a soul that damn cold. Old Hall stripped all the warm fire from yo' mama. Each time she sees him he sucks out more blood."

"All I know is she picked Mr. Hall over me."

"She didn't pick you or Hall, she was picking herself. Your mama was one to want things. Always loved her possessions.

Even when we was young she had to have the best. Hall lets her have whatever she wants but won't give her what really matters."

"Well, I'm taking my shit. I'm not waiting for no man. Come slap me if I ever end up that dumb." Trudy went to the dressing room and slammed the small door. She swore she'd never be anything like her mother. Her mother was weak. People laughed behind her back. She was a home-wreckin' sneak taking three o'clock baths. Trudy would never mess around with another woman's man. Trudy had standards. That's why she had a plan. But even the greatest of plans had to make some exceptions. Sometimes you didn't cross it but got close to the line. Like taking something once but then putting it back. Borrowing it like you might do a library book. Not stealing, just holding it for a hot minute. Trudy's hot minute was Charles.

8

Charles and Tony

Big Percy, a former boxer, manned the gambling door at Dee's. He was refrigerator-wide, with one crazy, wandering eye and a birthmark across his top lip. Once you entered Dee's doors, the first thing you saw was Percy. If you wanted to gamble, he led you behind black velvet drapes, hiding a large heavy gate, which led to a narrow flight of stairs. Percy would slowly click the latch on the metal-caged door. The door made an awful grating sound when it opened. He'd pat you down fast. Pat, pat, pat. Shoulders, waist, thighs, then he'd yell back to the boys inside, "Coming in!" You had to be real careful in a gambling house. You didn't want any cops or rowdy fools wearing guns.

Charles ran upstairs and took a spot at the table. It wasn't really a table but a large piece of plywood, covered in olive-green felt. The room was smoke-filled and dense with loud-talking men. A fan blew the dead, boozy air in his face. Charles was so anxious to win, his whole back was broken out in sweat. He tossed down two hundred and took a gulp from someone's bottle. In six minutes, Charles lost over four hundred dollars. When he crept back downstairs and went inside the club, he hoped Tony would give him a scotch on the house.

Tony spotted Charles sitting at a table alone. In the fifteen short minutes Charles had been at Dee's Parlor, he'd already lost all his money.

"I gotta cool game upstairs, man, if you want to sit in. Some high-rollers just came through the gate."

But Charles didn't have anything to gamble with now. The quarters he had on him danced a sad, empty tune with the few loose nickels and dimes.

"No, man, I'm cool." Charles looked away from Tony. "But I need to talk to you a minute."

"What's the matter, bro, y'all have a midnight spat?" He slapped Charles's back and laughed real loud, his throat wheezing like he had asthma. Tony eyed him sidewise as Charles was shifting in the seat. Tony could see Charles had something on his mind.

"Hey, Earl! Bring me one of them bottles for my boy here, and don't let Stan go behind the bar." Tony put his arm around Charles. They were sitting at a small table close to the stage. A trio was playing John Coltrane.

"Flo wearing you down, man? That's all right, son. Here. Have some of this." He took a deep swig, wiped his mouth with his sleeve and poured the dark liquid inside Charles's glass.

"Now see, that's why I don't live with no damn woman now. Who wants to see the same raggedy ass every morning? I like having me a stable myself. I got this one chick got a husband work thirty years for Pac Bell, says he's boring as hell. She be out there every morning with a worn housedress on, smiling while handing him his lunch bag. I creep over there 'bout an hour after her ol' man leaves. She be all dolled up to see my butt too. Shoot, I don't have to take her to lunch, dinner or nothing. Bring my own flask and take it back home. Don't nobody bother me for shit."

Charles downed the rest of his drink and held the empty glass in his hand. His mind was consumed with his looming gambling debt. He avoided looking in Tony's eyes.

Tony poured them both another stiff round.

"Flo's been tripping out lately," Charles said, steering the subject. He didn't want to bring up the subject of money. Charles had gotten himself in a mess. Charles loved cash like young girls love clothes. Though he borrowed, he never paid anyone back.

It's not like he couldn't. He definitely made enough. His postal job paid him a nice hefty check. And his benefits were the best in the state. But Charles always wanted something. He shopped all the time. He liked stereo equipment and forty-inch screens. He liked appliance shops and outdoor furniture sets. He didn't buy any of these items. Charles wasn't a hoarder. He just admired all these things when he saw them in stores.

See, Charles wanted a house. He was saving his money. He only window-shopped, dreaming of what to put inside. He saved all his money with a fiendish conviction. He cringed if Flo asked him to give up a dime. To him, giving money was like peeling off his skin. Their apartment was a sparse nest of wobbly chairs and lamps you had to bang with your hand to turn on.

But everything changed when he started betting at Dee's. Charles had never won anything before in his life. He wasn't a gambler. Gamblers were weak. They were slick toothpick types with gold teeth. To this day, he couldn't say why he drifted to the room upstairs. Maybe it was the men whooping wild or the clanking of bottles and the sound of people having big fun. Charles couldn't remember the last time he'd had a good time. The monotony of his postal job stripped the fun from his life, like the sun did his faded gray pants. The next thing he knew, someone handed him the dice. People smiled as he rattled the dice in his hand. He spun them hard, letting them dance across the smooth green. He didn't do it once, he did it time and again, and each time the crowd roared and cheered in his ear. He was winning. Charles could barely believe his eyes. In no time he had a huge stack of chips. There was nothing in life close to how good he felt then. He came day after day trying to feel that good again, but in no time he owed Tony thousands. But Tony didn't sweat him. He even let him play on credit. That's why he sat and endured Tony's bad breath. That's why he let Tony drape his arm around his shoulders. Maybe Tony would forget. Maybe he wouldn't have to pay him. It killed him to think of giving his savings away. Charles sloshed his drink across his straight, perfect teeth. Tony's breath stunk but Charles just sat there and took it. Making Tony his friend might erase his bad debt.

"Damn," Charles said, following Tony down to the bar. "Lady Luck ain't with me today."

"Nigga, please, you don't have to tell me. Lady Luck is just like any other kind of woman. Love 'em; leave 'em, none of 'em any good. I swore off them hags a long time ago. That's why I steal all of my pussy now. I don't have to hear no nagging or nothing. Nobody asking me to take the trash out or mow the damn lawn." Tony tapped out a Winston and jammed it in the side of his mouth. He leaned back in his chair and his shirt rode up his gut, which brimmed massively over his pants. "The onliest thing I hear when I walk through that door is the smack of my screen, the gush of me pouring myself a shot and the click when I hit the remote.

"Listen," Tony said, edging his chair closer to Charles's shoulder, "let me peep you some game on how to get Flo right." Tony leaned in toward Charles. Got right in his throat. The blue light in the room gave Tony's face a monstrous glow, and his silhouette bounced across the back wall of the stage.

"What you *need*, what you *want*, is a side woman, son. A side woman's known to cure all problems at home." Tony gulped down his drink and flicked his long ash. His Winston was down near the filter. When he exhaled the smoke, Tony started to choke. He wheezed and coughed hard for such a long time, Charles wondered if homeboy was dying. "Mark my words, son," Tony said, holding in his smoke. "Competition'll make any woman stop and take note. A side woman will drop Flo back down a few notches. Watch. You gotta know how to play the game, son." Tony's grin revealed a row of giant buckteeth, sporting plenty of juicy pink gums.

When Charles didn't say a thing, Tony changed the subject.

"So who you got for the fight coming up, man? Everybody in town say Liston'll have him down in five, but Jones ain't no city-boy neither. I hear them country fools box all the mules and mares down there. He's liable to do some real damage to Liston. Odds say he'll go down in eight."

"Man, I haven't been following it much," Charles replied, casting his eyes to the ground. He didn't want to talk about gambling. He was way down already. He swallowed the few drops that were left in his glass and dabbed his face with his napkin.

Charles avoided Tony's eyes. He tried to act upbeat.

Tony studied Charles for a very long time. "I can go ahead and place what you owe if you want," Tony said. He glanced over at Percy, who nodded his head.

Charles looked up. So Tony did remember the debt. Charles looked like someone standing in oncoming traffic.

"Don't worry, Youngblood, you'll get it to me," Tony said, smiling. He patted Charles's back and abruptly stood up. Tony talked to Big Percy, who nodded again, watching the club and guarding the gambling door with prison-guard eyes.

"Oh, it's cool," Charles, said, dabbing his brow. Shoot, if need be, he would have to take the money from savings. That's only if Tony sweated him, but if Charles played him right he might not. Charles couldn't see the heat in Big Percy's stare.

Suddenly the lights dimmed into one beaming ray. Maybe Tony was right. A side woman might be just what he needed again. Something to take off the pressure and stress. He watched Trudy glow under the single white halo, and like a platinum lighter she shined in Dee's haze. When she smiled she looked like she was smiling at him. Oh, he'd seen her before. Seen her a whole bunch of times. But tonight she looked different. She sparkled somehow. Tonight she looked something like hope.

9

Charles and Flo

It was a month and two weeks since Charles had flung that bottle. And as Trudy planned her scam, Charles's gambling reached the brink. But Flo didn't know any of that. All she remembered was the loud, violent crash. In fact, the very next day, Flo went straight to the bank and drained every cent they had. She knew what she wanted. Had already been to the dealer. She wanted a cool, ice-blue, chrome-rimmed Camaro. The dealer told her he'd hold it. He said he'd Teflon the seats, tint all the windows and throw in Lo-Jack in case it got stolen. Flo knew they were supposed to use that money to move, but when that glass bottle crashed all over her head, Flo went straight to the bank and said, "Fuck it."

"Fool better know not to mess over me," Flo said, seething. She flashed everyone in the bank line a cold, evil eye. She didn't want to chitchat or have to fake smile. All Flo wanted to get was that money.

See, that Jack Daniels bottle was Flo's final straw. Glass in her hair and all through her clothes. No, Flo's mind was made up. She didn't rip up his shirts or burn the hems of his pants. She didn't put sand in his shoes or white salt in his tank. No, this time Flo headed straight to the bank to take every cent they had out.

"Get his money," her grandmother said about Charles. "You want to stab a man smack-dab in his heart, go mess around with his cash."

See, it wasn't really the bottle that led to Flo's wrath. The bottle only ignited a simmering rage. An anger so bitter it was hard to keep down, and it burned like a Malibu fire.

Flo took Venice to Midtown where it hits San Vicente. It was hot, but luckily she made all the lights and in no time her tires were at Wilshire. She turned left and hooked another quick right, pulling into the Bank of America's opulent lot. The lot was packed. It was brimming with new, gleaming cars. Porsches, Bentleys, Mercedes-Benz, Range Rovers and Town Cars with drivers. Flo got out, giving the parking attendant her keys and taking the elevator up to the lobby. When she got inside the door, Flo took a deep breath. The air conditioner's full blast cooled down her skin. Flo walked in holding her purse snug against her arm. It was a large bank with huge murals and expansive marble floors. The tellers sat behind gold inlaid counters.

Flo stood there until the bell tone signaled her turn. Flo was digging in her purse for the tiny bank book when she looked up to the teller's glass window.

"May I help you?" Trudy smiled at Flo.

Flo just about dropped her purse.

"Yes . . . yes," she stammered. "I need to make a withdrawal. I'd like to close out this account." Flo pushed the yellow bank slip under the glass and pretended to study her own shoes.

Keeping her head down, Flo fiddled with the bank teller's pen. She felt uncomfortable looking Trudy in the face. She knew she worked at the club, and there was a good chance she knew Charles. She didn't want her to ask any questions.

"Is this a joint account?" Trudy asked.

"No," Flo told her flatly.

But on the computer screen, Trudy saw Charles's name. "Well, you'll both need to come in to close this completely."

"Why?" Flo asked point-blank. "My name's on it too. I don't see why there's a problem."

Flo stared at Trudy. She felt nervous and worried. *This bitch is trying to fuck with me, I know it.*

"I'm sorry," Trudy said, typing something on the screen.

"This is a trip—you take my money when I come in alone but

you need both of us when it comes to getting it back out." Flo glanced at the people waiting behind her in line. She felt anxious. Something about this felt wrong. Maybe Trudy knew something; maybe she didn't want her to have the cash. Trudy picked up a receiver and started to dial. Maybe she was calling Charles right now on that phone.

Trudy hung up the line and smiled at Flo. "You can withdraw, but you need to leave some of it in so the account is not totally closed."

"Well, how much do you need me to leave?" Flo asked.

"The minimum is five dollars," Trudy said coolly.

Flo was the one who smiled this time. "I think five dollars is fine."

Flo pushed another yellow withdrawal slip through the opening with the new amount as $7,995.

Trudy stared at the computer screen again. She put a small slip inside a miniature printer. She wrote something down on a ledger.

"How would you like it?" she suddenly asked.

Whoa, Flo breathed out. She was getting the money! Flo smiled again while nervously watching the door. If Charles came in she surely would be busted. She wanted to hurry up and go.

Flo unzipped the side pocket of her purse to get it ready. "Big bills," Flo quickly said and looked down. Flo kept her lids down. She watched Trudy's hands. Trudy opened a drawer, pulling a bundle of hundreds. She skillfully counted out each thousand-dollar stack. When she reached seven, she moved that whole stack aside. Then she counted out nine hundreds and moved that stack too. Then she opened the drawer again and got out four twenties, one ten and one single five. She put the whole stack in the bank teller slot, and Flo took it before Trudy let go of it good.

"Is there anything else I can help you with today?" Trudy asked, smiling.

Flo smiled too, but she didn't mean it. It was the kind of smile you gave someone you didn't like. "Yeah" Flo wanted to say, "stay the hell away from my man."

"No, thank you," Flo told her, zipping her purse closed. "I think this will be fine."

Flo turned and quickly walked toward the bank door. She looked back and saw Trudy's tongue race across her glossed lips. A white, tan-suit man now stood in her line. Trudy grinned at the man, flinging her braids across her chest. Flo smacked the elevator button and went down.

Flo couldn't believe how easy getting the new car was. In no time at all she was in the front seat. The smile on her face was real this time as she watched the salesman wipe off the fender and side mirrors.

As soon as her tires left the lot, Flo felt a hell of a lot better. When she got to the freeway she felt like a star. The new car made her feel she had finally arrived. Like she'd risen above Charles's trifling behind. She wasn't somebody you tossed liquor bottles at either. She had worth. She deserved something clean and expensive. The car told the world she was someone with value. That she was the one in the driver's seat now. That Flo was the only one calling the shots, even if she stopped twice to pull over and cry.

Because even as she drove the new car toward the beach, as its dazzling paint battled with the burning hot sun, as its gleaming chrome rims beat against the black pavement, Flo felt a sadness creeping in through the vents. A sadness she'd been masking from last year to now. It smothered her heart, drained the blood from her face, like a fog hovering over a grave.

See, from last year to now, everything went down. This time last year, everything changed. That's when a boiling flame engulfed her. It scorched her whole heart. That's when Charles went and fucked him that white girl.

Last year, Flo showed up unexpectedly at Charles's job. He always took his lunch break at the McDonald's on Western. Flo borrowed a friend's car to surprise him there. When she walked in the restaurant, she didn't see Charles at first. Then her eyes found a table way toward the back. There was Charles, but he wasn't sitting alone. Both his arms were wrapped around this big, garish blonde and he was grinning like some Uncle Tom slave. Flo never in her life felt a raw hurt like that. When Flo walked over, the blond girl leaped up and ran. Charles sat there and smiled, didn't try to deny it. He just looked at her with a sick little smirk on his face, saying, "Baby, I wish you'd a called first."

Lord have mercy, Flo never knew she could hurt bad like that. A white girl. Charles went and got him a Barbie! A fucking white skank ho and Charles. Well, Charles might as well have just stabbed her right there. 'Cause it sure killed something way deep down in Flo. Something that gnawed at her, tore at the core of her heart. Something she never got back.

In fact, after that day, they were never the same. She remembered how she felt before she walked through that door. She was beaming with pride. Had a sweet secret present. Flo had come to his job to tell Charles she was pregnant. It was supposed to be a surprise. But when Flo saw that white chick wrapped up in his arms, saw him stroking her long hair that hung limp like a skunk, Flo never said nothing. She never told Charles at all. She walked out the door and drove straight to the clinic. She paid four hundred dollars and lay on a white sheet. She watched the doctor's pink smock as she counted back from ten, and the next thing she knew, the whole world went black.

No matter how hard she tried, things were never right with her and Charles. Day after day she hated him more. And sometimes she'd lie up in bed late at night and think about slicing his throat. She became meaner inside, her head filled with cruel thoughts, and sometimes she'd do those things too. Last month she stole her co-worker's purse. It was something Flo never would have dreamed of before. But there the purse was in her drawer.

Heather kept her purse locked up in her desk with the small key dangling from her neck. Flo noticed one day that the drawer was slightly ajar. She looked around fast to see who was around and then scooped up the purse, slipped it inside her fat *L.A. Times*, sliding it back under her desk. At the end of the day, Flo watched Heather cry. Her blond hair stuck together in thick gooey chunks. She kept saying over and over, "It's gone, oh, my God!" Sobbing, with her head on her desk.

The company assumed the cleaning crew got it or the Xerox man snatched it. No one ever suspected her. When Flo got home she examined the purse's contents. She smiled to herself as she smelled the fine leather; she played with the keys and touched the tortoiseshell comb, running her fingers across its neat teeth. She twisted open the pale Clinique lipsticks inside; they were all the same dull shades of mauve. Sometimes when Flo had the whole house to herself, she'd take the purse out, touch the items inside and then slam the purse back in her closet.

Flo gripped the new steering wheel in her hand. There weren't two ways about it. She had to get this car. She deserved it for enduring all that awful hard pain. Besides, if she didn't do something about this bursting feeling she had, someone was bound to get hurt.

10

Tony and Flo

"My, my, my, Miss Flo. I always said you was a fine woman and can do some serious damage when you put your mind to it. Goodness!" Tony said, watching her pull in. "Car looks good on you, gal!" Tony pushed his gold sunglasses farther down on his nose.

Tony was sitting on the step waiting for her on her porch. He stood and tipped his brim hat as she parked.

Damn. Flo thought, slamming the car door shut. *What's this damn dog doing here?*

Flo passed by Tony and rolled her eyes.

"Whaz hap'nin, baby? Charles home yet? I knocked." Tony didn't step aside, and Flo's full body had to brush across his gut to get by.

"Not yet," she shot back, shifting a bag to her hip. She could smell the booze eating through his skin.

"Oh, well," Tony said, smiling. "It's kinda late, ain't it? Post office must be backed up again."

"I guess Charles will get here when he gets here," Flo snapped again, not inviting Tony in.

"Hee, hee, that's if he comes straight home. You know some mens like to make a pit stop first, but I'm sure Charles ain't one of them. Oh, no, I wouldn't think he was." Tony gently sucked his thick bottom lip. "Shoot, if I had all this peach cobbler waiting on my porch, I'd punch out and race home every day."

Flo rolled her eyes at him again. She didn't like Tony. She didn't appreciate him coming around behind Charles's back, trying to flirt with her and act like he was Charles's friend. Flo had never told Charles about Tony and her. It was a long time ago and they weren't together long. Besides, Charles didn't need to know another thing he could throw in her face. So Flo skirted around Tony whenever he came by and told him to keep his mouth closed.

"Didn't I tell you not to come around here?" Flo reminded him.

"You worry too much, girl! Don't you know me yet? I'ma take that shit to the grave." Tony looked at her legs an extra-long time. "But you and me got history. That ain't gon' change. Just 'cause you don't want that nigga to know don't mean I'ma forget." Tony smiled looking deep in Flo's dark, lovely eyes until she had to look down at the steps.

It was just like Tony to bring it up every time. Acting like he got extra privileges because they shared this secret. She didn't appreciate Tony coaxing Charles out to the club either. All that gambling mess and carrying on. Showing up in the middle of the night to collect.

One time Tony knocked on their door real late.

Flo was in her slip. It was what she liked to cook in on hot summer nights. The kind of night all your windows were slung open wide trying to catch a slim breeze. Where you opened the freezer to knock the heat from your skin. That night, Charles and Flo were sitting in the kitchen. He was watching her while listening to Sunday night slow jams. They were talking about their day. Having a glass of wine or two. Charles pouring her a glass. Her pouring his. The oven on and the radio crooning Al Green. The kitchen. Yeah. It was real cozy back then. The kitchen was always the heart of the house. She'd like to sit at her table with one foot on the stove. Bite into a peach; leave the juice on her cheek. She loved the sheer warmth of bread, happily soaking up butter. The dark, simple quietness of a drawer full of spoons. The hunger of forks trying to rest on their napkins. The glass melting wet in her hand.

It was one of those nights she and Charles were messing around in the kitchen. Charles was at the table rolling a smoke, watching her mix the batter for a pie. He liked the way her breasts would shake ever so slightly as she kneaded the dough and how her nipples stood so firm in that satin. Charles got up and squeezed her soft, ample waist.

"Boy, you better quit. I'm trying to cook here," Flo said.

But when Charles saw her pressing that dough he couldn't help it. He stood up and circled her waist from behind, lavishly kissing her shoulders. He spread her across the flat kitchen table like Flo was hot margarine on toast. Next thing she knew the Crisco bottle spilled over and Flo felt the warm wet running way down her back, pooling inside her tight thighs. Charles grabbed the bottle and poured it over her stomach. He started kneading her breasts just as she had done the dough.

"You feel so good, baby," Charles moaned in her ear. Thrusting real nice and easy, the way he knew she liked it. "I could just swallow you whole."

Flo bent her knees way up to her chest and Charles went deeper inside. She rubbed Crisco on her hands and massaged his wide back, squeezing and kneading his skin. Charles was well-built and caramel, with a wide chest and strapping arms and a six-pack twisted as tight as a radiator cap. Flo had never in her life had a man that damn fine.

Charles pounded her harder and the table rattled so loud Flo was sure it would snap right in half. But she didn't care. She could feel the raw heat working up from her toes, lingering between the skin in her thick inner thighs and then raging on up toward her gut.

"Wait." The word barely escaped from her lips.

Charles tried to slow down but it was already too late. He had turned to pure steel; there was no stopping now. Once he got to this point there was no turning back. He was thrashing so strong the table skipped across the floor and smacked against the back wall.

Well, it was right then when they heard a weak knock at the door. Truth was, Tony had been out there for quite a good while.

He crouched down and peeked into the window when he saw that the lights were off in all the rooms except the kitchen. He saw Flo's big legs dangling over the table and Charles standing between them. Tony lit a cigarette and took a gulp from his bottle. He tossed the bottle in the street and it crashed at the curb and then he banged real loud on the door.

Charles threw water on his face and answered the door. Tony saw Flo pulling her robe back together.

"Evening, everybody," Tony said, walking back toward the kitchen.

"Oh, y'all been making a pie!" Tony looked at the oil dripping down to the floor. "I sure hope I get a piece when you're through."

The way Tony said it made Flo suddenly look up. Like maybe he wasn't talking about no pie at all.

So when Flo saw Tony today she blocked Tony's path. He was always coming around, sniffing for crumbs. Like a cat you once threw a chicken leg to and now couldn't get off your porch.

"I wish you'd come down to the club sometime, baby. Trudy been packing 'em in left and right."

Flo ignored him. Wouldn't look in his face.

"Charles been catching all her shows. I don't know what he see. She don't do nothing for me, but I wouldn't let my man loose with that chick on the stage." Tony's eyes twinkled. He let that sink in. He eyed Flo's hips and studied her breasts. "But she don't hold a candle to you."

Flo didn't wait for him to say anything else. She went in and double-locked her front door.

Tony stared at the door for a real long time. He lit the burnt stub of his halfway-smoked Winston before stumbling back to his car. He stared at the moon and then at his shined shoes.

"As sure as I'm standing up out here tonight"—Tony blew the thick smoke back toward Flo's door—"I'ma have that damn heifer spread-eagled one day and calling me Daddy again."

11

Trudy and Ray Ray

"Hey, fat back."

"Hey, pig meat."

"Gimme them big suck-me titties."

A small band of teenage boys lined the sidewalk. They followed her fast strut down the street.

"Trudy with the booty. Come gimme some, girl!"

Trudy tried to walk fast but they circled her body. She had to struggle to keep moving down the block.

"Look at 'em move."

"Do fries go with that shake, baby?"

"They look like a batcha grape Jell-O!"

The boys gathered tightly around her firm frame.

"Move!" Trudy said, but only a few of them budged.

"Oooh, see, she mad!"

"Look, watch 'em jiggle."

"Come on girl, we just want to suck 'em."

The boys busted up laughing and started nudging each other. Some of them had her nude videotape in their rooms.

"That movie's a'ight, but it ain't got shit on yo' ass in the flesh."

Trudy struggled her best to get past the boys. One sucked a Blow Pop. One held an apple. All of them had big, gaping grins. Two women watched from the safety across the street; one blew a giant pink bubble.

"Leave me alone!" Trudy screamed loudly. She struggled against them. Her nylons got snagged. A seam busted on her tight dress. But she flung out her purse like it was a weapon, swatting their heads until a few scattered back.

She'd almost broken free, but somebody tripped her and she landed facedown on the sidewalk. The boys made a knot around Trudy's body. Someone grabbed her ass. Someone else twisted her nipple. A slimy tongue entered her ear.

"Get off me!" she screamed. But the boys pinned her down.

Ray Ray stopped his Lincoln in the middle of the street. He sliced through the crowd of boys with his razor-blade eyes. One boy ran off. The others leaned back on their broomstick-thin legs.

"Hey, Ray Ray!"

"What up, cuz!"

"Nigga, when'd you get out, Gee!"

The boys looped around Ray Ray's muscle-bound body.

Ray Ray scowled at them all. He stared hard at one.

"Ain't you Smokey's little brother?" he asked him point-blank.

"Yeah," the short boy said proudly.

Ray Ray reached down and pulled Trudy up from the ground. He glared at each boy and lit a match to his Newport. He stuck the cigarette way back in his teeth and blew the smoke out real slow. He pulled a leather cloth out the back of his khakis and unwrapped a long steel blade. It shimmered in the cruel, blasting sun. He smacked the Blow Pop out of one of the boys' mouth. He knocked the apple from the other boy's fist.

"Pick it up!" Ray Ray said to another.

The worried boy put the apple in Ray Ray's hand.

Ray Ray started peeling the green apple with the silver blade. He never looked up. He just kept on cutting. He skinned the apple until it was totally clean. The curled skin dropped dead on the ground.

"See, this here's my homegirl." Ray Ray pointed with his knife. His steely eyes cut each boy down. "I bet' not catch one y'all muthafuckas messin' with her again. Fool around and yo' mama's gon' be pickin' out caskets."

The neighborhood boys had fearful respect for Ray Ray. He

was an O-G. He'd been to the pen. They all wanted to be Ray Ray's friend.

"It's cool, man," one said.

"We didn't mean nothin'."

The boys slowly drifted away.

"You better walk away!" Trudy shouted at their backs. "All y'all can do is try to hijack some pussy 'cause no women with any sense gonna touch ya!"

Ray Ray smiled at Trudy. Homegirl was a trip. Wasn't but five-three but talked mega shit if you crossed her. He loved sexy bitches like that.

Fact was, Trudy was the only one who'd written when he was in the pen. She didn't write often. And she didn't write much, but those letters were what kept Ray Ray together. Kept the monotony of bar after bar from closing in. Kept him focused on doing his time and getting out. No, she didn't write often but what she did write he read over and over again. Memorizing every word. Rolling over every curve of each letter with his finger. Mumbling each phrase with his lips.

"I appreciated your letters."

"No problem." Trudy smiled, pulling her braids from her face.

"A kind word from the outside can take a brother a long way." Ray Ray brushed a torn leaf off the back of her dress. She looked so good, his whole body ached just to watch her. He wanted to feel her smooth skin against his hot, scalded face. To taste her long braids between his teeth. Ray Ray looked at Trudy deeply, breathing out slow. "Your letters are what kept me alive."

Trudy didn't know a lot about his life in prison. Whenever he wrote, large parts were blacked out. But one thing came through remarkably clear. Ray Ray was smart. And he cared for her deeply. He would hide little messages inside the lines. His metaphors gave her a glimpse of the harsh world inside. They were a telephone line to his soul. That wasn't blacked out. The jailers never found those. CALIFORNIA STATE PRISON was stamped on each letter in red, but Trudy was proud when the postman handed her a letter from Ray Ray. She would spread across her bed and read them alone.

"Girl, I loved seeing my name on those envelopes you wrote." Ray Ray smiled at her again. "That alone was hope. They made me feel like I mattered. Most of them dudes don't never get shit. Nobody writes. Nobody calls. Them letters kept me from going off and hurtin' somebody. I saw brothas snap, every single day." Ray Ray broke a small branch from a tree. "Yesterday's gone and you can't swallow tomorrow." Ray Ray smiled broadly at Trudy again. "But I could reread your words. They always calmed me down. I'd stop thinking how I fucked up and ended up like this. How I did all this shit to myself."

Trudy cupped his cheek. He wanted to kiss her hand, but he didn't. Trudy dropped her hand from his face.

"I wasn't ready. I had no idea how fucked it was. It was lonely and loud; dudes were always banging their cells, screaming from that four-by-six box. I hated the blackness of 'lights out.' All those roaches and sick food." Ray Ray threw a rock toward the gutter.

"Damn." Trudy didn't know what to say. She wanted to touch him again but kept her hand at her side.

"I don't want to talk about the shit. That shit made me sick."

But Ray Ray did talk. He was just like a faucet. All the words just gushed out like water.

"Norco separated the prison based on the amount of time served. The hard dudes were all housed at the top. Those were your murderers, multiple rapists and crazies. People doing triple-life and shit. The middle levels held the felons, one-time killers and drug dealers. The lower levels, where I was, were all recently popped. Car thieves, small-time crooks, domestic violence stuff. All of them down there were doing short time, anything six years or less."

But in California, the prison population had quadrupled overnight, thanks to the new "Three Strikes You're Out." Jails were brimming. Prisons had filled to capacity. Some facilities resorted to using old army barracks to deal with the mad overcrowding.

"I remember them first few months at Norco. They housed me and the other guys in a large abandoned army barrack. That old barrack was huge, with bunk beds squashed together. Looked

like a Boy Scout lodge, if you didn't look close. But we had windows you could see through. There was a grassy area with trees.
I'd watch birds and squirrels play all the time."

Ray Ray remembered their early-morning chirps. He'd wake
up, keep his eyes shut, lay there and listen. With his eyes closed,
he would pretend he wasn't in prison anymore. Free from bars
and the wild, hellish nightmares inside.

"In Norco, the Mexicans and blacks had a war going on. As
soon as I got in, a Mexican bashed in my face. Another one
caught me and broke my left thumb. But the guard was a brother
and had one guy transferred. The other one bunked two beds
down the way. I waited half the night working the good hand I
had. I ripped a piece of metal from under the bunk. I sanded it
back and forth on the rough redbrick floor. I crawled to the guy's
bed on my hands and my knees and jammed the metal piece in
his eye. Everybody heard that Mexican guy scream. They took
his ass out on a stretcher."

Trudy winced, but Ray Ray kept talking.

"But, man, that barrack shit didn't last long. One of the in-
mates tried to escape. There was a mad gunshot hunt that lasted
five days. The whole place was flashlights and bloodhounds. But
they got him. Found the man way down the interstate, panting
underneath an old Monte Carlo. The next day they hacked all
those tall redwoods down. Bulldozers came and killed all the
bushes and grass. The guards said it impeded their ability to see.
The next thing I knew, the whole place was concrete. The birds
were all gone and there was nothing outside except barbed wire
and chain-link for miles. The nightmares came then. And the
constant fighting for your life. I didn't think I could make it."
Ray Ray shook his head but looked up and smiled.

"But that's when I got your first letter."

Trudy couldn't help but smile back at Ray Ray. She and Ray
Ray went back. Ever since the eighth grade. He was a knuckle-
head even back then. If he wasn't reading, Ray Ray was doing
something to get her attention. Always giving her things. Ball-
points, big giant Frito-Lay bags, Snickers and Milky Way bars by
the fistfuls, and wallets with other people's I.D. His candy-bar

skin had the prettiest dimples. Flashed her his naughty-boy smile whenever he got caught.

Back in the day, Ray Ray's whole family was crazy. All six of 'em shoved in this one-bedroom unit. Mashed in there like some rats. His daddy drove semis, was gone half the time. Nobody was home to control 'em. One brother was gangbanging; another sold crack. Their mama loved to sit in the car with her daughter and talk shit all day and smoke weed. But the streets took a toll on Ray Ray's whole family. His father fell asleep at the wheel one night and died. One brother was found knifed in a vacant apartment. The other brother got popped and was doing back-to-back life. His oldest sister OD'd on a bad batch of smack. Ray Ray's apartment, which had always been the loudest part of the street, was as quiet and still as a morgue. They were all gone, everybody, except for his mama, who sat up all day like a zombie. But Ray Ray took care of her. Brushed her thin hair and cooked all her food. Some fools might have left. Couldn't deal with the trouble. But Ray Ray stood by. He took care of his mother. Trudy had always admired that about him.

But she knew he was wild. Completely untamed and totally street. With that burn on his cheek, he was still super fine. Crazy and sexy as hell.

"Thanks for getting those guys off me," Trudy said, clutching her purse to her chest.

"No problem," Ray Ray said, averting his eyes. He could feel the mild warmth from her bronze, even skin.

Trudy shyly let her braids fall into her face. "So how you been doin'? How's it feel to be out?" Trudy could feel the warm-oven pull too.

"Feels like I don't never want to go back!"

"I heard that," Trudy said. It felt good being with Ray Ray. With him she could be her natural free self. He was easy and clear as cool water.

"How's your mother gettin' along?" Trudy wanted to know.

"Same ol' same ol'," Ray Ray told her. "Moms and me still kickin' it. We doing our best to stay up." Ray Ray flashed her one of his rarely seen smiles. "I appreciate you stopping by to see her sometimes. That meant a lot to me, girl."

When Trudy smiled back, Ray Ray's whole body throbbed. He strained against the strong urge to grab her and kiss her. But Trudy used to be Lil Steve's woman. Lil Steve was his friend. It meant she was off-limits. So he held in his feelings. Kept his emotions in check. He stayed as cool as a Canadian lake. In prison, you learn quick not to show your emotions. If you did, those fools used them against you.

"You tell me if anybody messes with you, girl," Ray Ray said with a hint of mad dog in his eyes. But when he looked in her face, his hard eyes went soft. His thick lashes fluttered back toward the ground.

"I will," Trudy said, looking away. She could feel the soft pull of his eyes on her back. But Trudy knew how to cover her emotions too. She could be as calm as a mannequined window.

"Just lay low, Ray Ray. You're out, so be cool. Don't do anything dumb. And stay the fuck away from that fool Lil Steve."

"Lil Steve's all right. You know that's my boy."

"He's a punk," Trudy shot back.

Ray Ray threw another rock to the other side of the street. He never liked that Trudy was with Lil Steve. It cut him. It tore the pink meat of his soul.

"Why you so worried about me and Lil Steve?" Ray Ray asked sharply. He studied Trudy's face. "At one time you had no problem dealing with blood," Ray Ray reminded her.

"Dealing with him was the worst thing I did in my life. I didn't know how jacked he could be."

"So you deal with folks before you know who they are? And the ones that you been knowing for years, those the ones you choose to leave alone." Ray Ray was smart. He was trying to trip her up. All he ever wanted was for her to want him.

"Lil Steve's so to the curb. You don't need to hang with him. Damn, Ray Ray, he lives in his car. Homeboy ain't going nowhere but down."

"Shit, many a fool's a paycheck from living in a car. Shoot, if

Tony don't cut me my paycheck soon, I could be out there my-self."

"But he doesn't care where he is, Ray Ray," Trudy pleaded.

"And where are you going, girl?" Ray Ray wanted to know.

"I'm leaving. I'm getting out this skank town."

"That's why you doing this bank job with him?"

Damn, Trudy thought, *he already knows*. Lil Steve is obviously planning to use him.

"Ray Ray, don't trip! He can handle it himself."

"You got to have two. It's a two-man job, baby. One hits and one drives the car."

Trudy stared at the brown summer lawn, squeezing her braids in her hand.

"Why you acting so scared? You didn't used to trip like this." Ray Ray pulled some of her braids with his fingers. "You used to be fearless. A one-woman bullet. We used to clean up at Fedco, back in the day. You sure there ain't something you want to say?"

Trudy was stuck. How could she tell him she was setting Lil Steve up without blowing the whole fucking scam?

Ray Ray had his doubts, so he just put it out there.

"Why you doing this, huh? Why'd you pick Lil Steve?"

Ray Ray was suspicious. She had to say something quick to make him believe she was on the up-and-up.

"Look, Ray Ray. All I'm trying to do is protect you. You just got out. You need to walk a straight line. The only reason I picked Lil Steve is because he's the best. Of all the players in town, he's never been popped. Even white people like him. They don't even look at him twice. Shoot, the brother is as smooth as a kindergarten slide. I'm just doing this one thing so I can pack up and step. All I'm saying is just watch your back, okay?"

"Lil Steve's my homie, nigga been had my back. Besides," he said, playing with a handful of her braids, "I'll walk a straight line as soon as you do." Ray Ray mildly touched a few soft fingers of her hand but Trudy gently pulled them away.

"You need a ride?"

"Naw, I'll be okay."

Ray Ray watched her thunderous strut down the street. In no

time she was at the end of the block. But she stopped and looked back when she got to the corner. She stood there for a moment, holding his gaze, before slowly turning the corner. He noticed one of Trudy's long braids lying on the ground. He picked it up, fingering its length. The knotted end held a tiny smooth shell. Ray Ray shoved the braid deep inside the well of his pocket. Some folks you never get over.

12

Trudy and Lil Steve

Trudy had a smile on her face after seeing Ray Ray that day. She came home, peeled off her dress, left it there on the floor and tossed her snagged nylons in the tall kitchen trash.

Billie Holiday sang from the transistor in the corner.

Her apartment was small but it glowed from assorted candles. She had an old couch with a king-sized sheet hiding the ripped stuffing. There were artwork and beautiful coffee table books, small statues and hand-painted ashtrays and bowls. Almost everything in there was stolen. The outside of her apartment might be covered in bars, but the inside looked like a museum.

But the smashed–beer can life was right outside her door. Wild cursing and gunshots leaked under each screen. Trudy crushed a cockroach with her shoe.

Trudy had wanted to hit the tan-suit man for a while. Had watched his balance shoot up fifty grand in two weeks. The man put twenty-five grand in every week like clockwork. He was as regular as the *L.A. Times*.

She remembered the first time she'd seen him pull into the lot. He drove a spanking-new Lexus, an LS400, one of the best-rated cars in the world. It had a moonroof and beautiful tan leather seats and drove so quiet it must have felt like riding on air. That's what Trudy wanted. Real long money. Not to just look like she had some, like her mother. Not to have to check the price tag of every damn thing she picked up. She was sick of counting every red cent every time she got it. Sick of penny-ante schemes that brought in a few bucks. Trudy wanted real money so she could finally get out. She wanted to get away from all those reaching and touching men. All the long, knowing looks as she walked down the street. Even at work, that mess didn't stop.

Once this white teller reached over and yanked a fistful of her braids.

"Wow," he said, smiling. "I just had to touch 'em. I was wondering what they felt like."

Well, Trudy would have let him feel her hand whack his pink cheek but the big boss happened to walk in right then.

Trudy got smart after that happened. She learned to flash folks a cold, evil eye. People left her alone then. They didn't talk to her at all. Oh, she knew they thought she was stuck-up, had some chip on her shoulder, called her a "nigga bitch" and shit behind her back. But so what? Shoot, she didn't care. Trudy would stop in her tracks, flip a hard, crowbar stare, and most folks left her alone.

All Trudy wanted now was one final haul. At twenty, she was perfectly content at being alone. A nice, fantastic heist could get her way far away. Big money could buy her a brand new address. A newly paved place on a clean, tree-lined street. No more "Trudy with the booty" thrown up in her face. No more heels snapping off as she walked down the block. No more men trying to touch her or fondle her breasts. She hated the cracked, filthy streets and those helicopter nights and the wild screams of sirens going off all the time and bums always begging for money. New clothes didn't feel good walking up the same broken-down steps. One giant haul was all Trudy wanted. And to finally pay Lil Steve back.

Trudy had learned lots of schemes while working at the club. Car thieves and men doing repo-man scams, or chicks passing bad checks in stores. While working at the bank you always heard stories too. Her all-time favorite was Donali. Donali came to work wearing Prada or Armani and drove a cute white convertible Jag. Of course, he shouldn't have done that because that's how they got him. His salary didn't cover that shit. But his scam was unique and didn't take much effort. See, Donali used to switch the signature cards. His friend would come in and make great big withdrawals, and since Donali switched the cards his friend's signature always matched. For months they ran that scam, making off with large dollars, but the nice car and clothes got the camera pointed on him. The next thing Trudy knew they were taking him out in cuffs.

But Trudy had a plan that removed her completely. That's where the tan-suit man came in. Oh, there were others but he seemed the most reliable. Always friendly. Always her line. Always the same big deposit. That's why Trudy got the job at the bank in the first place. She didn't want to rob the bank. She wasn't a fool. She didn't want to end up like Donali's dumb ass. No, the bank was the place to find out who had money. To the dime, she knew exactly how much people had.

After watching the tan-suit man for months, Trudy went to the DMV. It was right after the tan-suit man made his eight large deposits. She spotted an older male clerk working off in a corner. Trudy waited in his line. When she got to the front she unbuttoned her top button. Her cleavage rested right on the ledge. "Excuse me," she said, making her voice sound troubled. She wiped her eyelash for effect.

"Are you okay? What's the matter with you, sugar?" The clerk got real close to Trudy's face. And although he tried hard to watch her pitiful eyes, he stayed latched to the deep wedge in her chest.

"This chick tripped out and keyed up my ride."

The man gave Trudy a fatherly nod. "You best not fool with them married ones, honey." He heard stories like this all the time.

"He's not married. His ex was just crazy. That skank followed me all the way to my house. Poured nail polish all over my brand-new waxed paint and deflated all four of my Pirellis."

"Well, call the police, honey. They'll put her in line." His thumb wanted to rub Trudy's skin.

Trudy started to pout. She batted her lashes. She leaned down to show the deep meat of her cleavage and stuck out her glossed bottom lip.

"I don't have anything. I just have her plate numbers."

"Well, give them to me, honey. We'll catch that heifer. I had a few hellions trying to ruin my life once. I'd be happy to get one off the street."

Worked like a charm. He was eager to help her. He gave Trudy the name, address and phone number of the car. He gave Trudy his phone number too.

"Be safe, young thang," he said to her as she left. "Give me a call if you just want to talk." The man said it like talking was the last thing on his mind. He smoothed his tie over the arch of his stomach as she left.

Trudy drove to the tan-suit man's house in Beverly Hills.

She had to park a block away so she wouldn't be seen. She let her seat fall all the way back so she was lying flat and looking out of her sideviews. She saw the man go into a large gated mansion. Two men followed him back out to his car. One of them was a brother in a black SUV. The tan-suit man handed him a large manila envelope. Another man popped open the trunk and laid a plastic bag inside the tire. The tan-suit man got in his car and took off. The black SUV took off too.

Dealers, she thought. *Just what I figured.*

Trudy lifted her seat back up and switched on the ignition. She thought for a long time on the lonely ride home.

"Dealers. How do you hit dealers? How do you get that long cash and not get caught?"

Then it hit her. You don't. You get some dumb lowlife fool to do the shit for you.

When Trudy got home, she dialed Lil Steve's bootleg cell phone.

"You busy?"

"Trudy with the booty? Girl, is that you?"

Trudy cringed, holding the phone slightly away from her ear. She hated being called that.

Lil Steve didn't notice the silence on the other end. He clicked the volume down on his portable TV and popped the seat up in his car.

"Damn, baby, how did I get so lucky?" His legs were spread wider than a hawk's wings in flight, and his hand massaged the seam of his jeans.

He couldn't believe Trudy had called him. She didn't speak to him last week when he saw her outside Dee's. In fact, he didn't think she'd ever speak to him in life.

Lil Steve popped a forty-ounce from the ice chest in the back-seat. He sure was enjoying this moment. "So how ya doin'? How's Tony treating you at the club? That clown still won't let me come in."

Trudy didn't want to talk about that. She wanted to get down to business. She knew Lil Steve was interested now. Vernita had casually planted the seed the other day at her shop. Lil Steve had come in to boost some hot roller sets, and Vernita had ended up giving Lil Steve an earful of information, as well as a touch-up and trim.

"Yeah, your girl spilled her guts. Man, that chick can't hold water. Telling her is like passing out flyers." Lil Steve thought he'd wiggled the information from Vernita. He didn't know she was setting him up.

Trudy dipped the tiny brush inside the bright bottle of polish. She slowly stroked each toe an ambulance red.

"Hey, I'm sorry to hear about your mother." Lil Steve's mother had passed last year. Her death was a shock to them all.

"Yeah, life's fucked up," he said, staring at the split in his dashboard. A panhandler worked his way toward Lil Steve's fender. Lil Steve held a gun out of his window. The panhandler jumped back and fell off the curb. "Seems like we got that in common," he said.

"But it doesn't have to be. Not if we focus."

Lil Steve leaned up farther in his seat.

"I got my eyes on bigger prizes," Trudy said.

"Does the prize got to do with your job at the bank?"

Trudy smiled and poured herself some more Alize. Lil Steve always thought fast.

"I got a little something something I think we can work on."

Lil Steve thought Trudy was trying to be cute. He always thought he'd taught Trudy how to steal. Took pride in the fact. Like she was his protégé and whatnot.

"I really need your help to pull this thing off. And it's easy. You can do the whole thing alone." What she really wanted to say was please don't use Ray Ray. But Trudy couldn't risk Lil Steve being suspicious.

"Look, if we do this, you and me split it fifty-fifty." Trudy knew that Lil Steve would be holding all the money. She reminded him why he needed to give her a share.

"And remember, there's the security tape at the bank. You don't want to give me a reason to go canary. You're way too pretty for jail." Trudy sugared her voice, stroking the hairs of his ego. Trudy knew which side her bread was buttered on. If you want a man's help, you got to give him his props. "You're the best, Lil Steve. I need you to make this work. You're the first person I thought of," she said.

"So you want me, huh, baby?" Lil Steve asked, smiling. He held the cell phone real close to his mouth. His hand rubbed the inseam of his jeans once again.

"Oh, I want it." Trudy let that sink in too. She wanted Lil Steve to focus on that. She had to make him think that she wanted him too.

Trudy poured a glass of Alize and sang along with Billy . . .

"God bless the child that's got his own."

13

Charles and Tony

The next day Charles went to gamble at Dee's.

"Come on, double six. Come home to Daddy." A man held the dice tightly in his fist. He brought the two dice right up to his lips. He blew on them slow, then shook them both wildly, tossing them with all his might, and let go.

"Woowee! That's what I'm talking about." The double six paid the man thirty-to-one. His ten bucks turned into three hundred.

"Gimme a double tray, the hard way, y'all hush yo' mouths." The man rattled the dice in his hands. "If I hit this bitch, all y'all drink free."

Charles watched the man like he was transfixed. Everything the man called came up. But Charles wasn't ready. He held a fistful of bills.

"I'ma let this ride," the winning man said. "I can *feel* my point coming in again."

The man looked at Charles. "Don't be skeerd, boy! You best get in this game and make some money in here, son. Lady Luck is red-hot tonight!"

Charles put his crumpled stack of bills on the table. He placed it down like he didn't want to let it go.

"Hey, cue ball!" The man laughed at Tony's bald head. "I'ma take your ends and make some for your poot-butt friend too."

What Charles didn't know was this game was fixed. The big

man and Tony had a system working against Charles. They let him win a few bucks just to keep him playing, but there was no way he'd ever win big.

"You putting all that down, son?" Tony asked Charles, examining the stack of bent twenties.

"Shoot, you know that's the only way to make serious money." The man with the dice winked knowingly at Charles. Charles smiled meekly back. He needed to win. He had to recover his losses. He'd dug a deep hole with Tony already. Luckily for him Tony hadn't sweated him yet.

Charles studied the man holding the lacquered red dice. The man was so lucky. Won boo-coo chips already. A thick stack of bills sat at the man's waist. Charles carefully placed his wager on him.

"You hot today," Tony said, pouring the man more scotch.

It was three o'clock and Charles was gambling on his lunch break again.

The man grabbed his suspenders. He stood wide-legged and grinned. "I'm just a squirrel in your world, trying to get me a nut. Now stand back and watch me work magic."

"Well, go 'head," Tony said. "Shoot your best shot."

The man threw the dice toward the back of the table. The dice rolled over the dark fabric and dropped. Both red squares added up to seven.

"Oh well," Tony said, quickly raking in the money. He raked all of Charles's cash too.

The man with the suspenders grabbed his billfold and hat. "Luck's just like a parking meter, son. You better get before your ticker runs out." The man smacked Charles real hard on the back. "Tony!" he roared before walking down toward the door. He handed Tony some bills as his cigar smoke lingered in the room. "Until you're better paid," the man said.

Charles had been gambling heavily for at least three weeks straight. Each check he brought home was smaller than the next. There was no use stalling around anymore. He owed seven grand now. He was going to have to get the money he had saved at the bank.

He picked up his leather mail carrier's sack and walked back out to his truck. He always bought a pint at the liquor store on Stocker. It was way off his route and no one would spot him. He put on a long coat to hide the uniform he wore; he couldn't risk some damn snitch turning him in.

Trudy followed Charles to the liquor store and waited for him to come out. She watched his reflection in the liquor store door. Charles was caught at the light right there off Stocker. She had just palmed some gum at the Liquor Barn on the corner, and even though the light had already changed, Trudy rushed out against the flashing red hand so she could cross right in front of his truck. That's why she threw an extra bounce in her step. She wanted to bait him. Reel him in. Give him something to make his mouth water.

When Trudy stepped off the curb, she swung her wide hips. She pulled down her V-neck and thrust out her breasts. Immediately horns started to bark.

"Damn," Charles said out loud to himself. He slammed on his brakes and made a U-turn into the mall.

Trudy glimpsed his broad frame in the mall's store windows. Charles was fine and linebacker wide.

Trudy remembered what Vernita told her one day.

"Girl, you ain't had no love until you had wide-man love." Vernita had licked the chocolate icing off her fork. "Lay on 'em just like a futon. Put your drink right in their shoulder blade, honey." Vernita smacked the chocolate from her tongue.

Trudy planted herself near the mirrored perfume counter. That was always the first thing you saw in a store. Trudy wanted to be easy to spot.

"Trudy with the booty," Charles mouthed under his breath.

Trudy pretended to examine the Lancôme lipstick.

"You like that shade?" Charles asked, pressing up.

Trudy twirled the burgundy tube until the dark lipstick slid up. She didn't even look at Charles at all. She gently stroked the tip back and forth across her lips and then carefully smoothed the burgundy all over her full mouth.

Charles stood mesmerized. This was one sexy freak. He waved the salesman over.

"Could you please ring this up for the lady?" Charles asked.

The salesman was a little swish with dark walnut eyes. He boldly gazed over Charles's wide brick-wall body. "Man-oh-man," he mumbled under his breath.

"Thank you," Trudy said. "But you didn't have to do that."

"I wanted to," he said, pulling out his credit card, hoping the small purchase would go through. He sighed, relieved when the salesman came back.

Trudy smiled at Charles. But he didn't know what to say. "You sing at Dee's, don't you?"

"Yeah," Trudy said. "But I work at a bank. Singing is just my side gig."

Trudy's warm smile made him tingle in his thighs.

"I wanted to talk to you for a minute." Trudy rubbed her lips together. "I hope you don't think I'm out of line."

Charles felt flattered. He couldn't believe she was talking to him. He let his mail sack slip to the floor. He carried his bag in case a co-worker saw him. He could always say he was delivering a package.

"I saw your girl at the bank this past Friday."

"My girl." Charles hadn't told her about Flo.

Trudy saw the question marks flash in his eyes. "Look, I don't know her, know her. She gets her hair done at the same salon. I've seen you guys out a couple of times."

Charles just waited. He didn't know what was coming.

"She came in today. She got in my line," Trudy continued.

Charles immediately became concerned. His eyes darted around the store. He was nervous and quickly hiked his bag up his back. It was four o'clock and technically, he was still on the job; a co-worker might turn him in.

"I'd like to talk to you about it alone if I could," Trudy said. "Do you have a card?"

Charles didn't want her calling him at home. Flo might pick up the phone. And even though he'd never owned a business card in his life, he peered in his wallet like he did.

"Looks like I ran out," he said sheepishly, digging both hands in his pockets.

"Here." Trudy handed him a matchbook from Dee's. "I'll be there tonight. I go on at nine. Maybe you and I could talk later."

Charles gently touched her fingers as he took the book of matches. "I guess I'll just wait until then."

Trudy waved and gave him one last farewell wiggle, making her way to the escalator upstairs. She felt great. Charles was just who she wanted. Everything was turning out fine. She felt so good she didn't even steal the pair of silver earrings she'd hidden in her hand the whole time. The earrings had turned her left hand into slime. She placed them down in the shoe section and left.

Charles went back to work and finished his shift. He couldn't wait to get back to Dee's Parlor that night. He asked for another advance on his check.

"That's your last one," his supervisor told him, annoyed.

But Charles didn't care if his money ran thin. Tonight he was going to meet Trudy at Dee's. Trudy with the booty wanted to meet up with him! The sun roared against his white teeth.

14

Charles and Flo

"What, you're not going to talk anymore?" Flo asked. It had been ten tense days since Charles had tossed that bottle.

Charles yanked a beer from the refrigerator door. He drank it while watching T.V. It was night but it was hotter in the house than outside.

Flo was nervous about Charles finding out about the car.

She secretly parked the car around the corner and walked so Charles wouldn't see the car when he got home.

When Flo stood right in front of the set, Charles went back into the kitchen.

"How long you going to be mad?" Flo asked him direct.

"I ain't mad," Charles said.

"Yes, you are," Flo shot back. She tried to touch his arm but Charles snatched it away.

Charles avoided Flo's eyes and swallowed more beer, squeezing the cold bottle in his hand.

Charles walked from the room, took off his clothes and got in the shower.

Flo quietly sat on the living room couch. She heard the beating of water. She flipped through a few channels, got bored and turned it off, and walked back into the kitchen to check the stove.

Flo had rushed home so she could beat Charles from work. She had hurried home to make a huge dinner for Charles. Cooked everything he liked. Cabbage, meatloaf, mashed potatoes and gravy. Kind of a peace offering for the sour week they'd had. For the nine days she'd had the car Flo felt nothing but guilt. She was sad about spending all their money and even tried to give the car back.

"Sorry," the dealer said. He told her it was too late. "Once the wheels leave the lot, lady, it's yours," the man yapped.

Flo wanted to tell Charles about the car but it was never the right time. Since she didn't want him to find out by seeing the car in the driveway, Flo pretended to ride the bus and parked the car around the block.

Flo stopped mashing the potatoes and watched Charles get dressed.

Charles and she hadn't been speaking much lately. They mumbled the occasional "pass me the salt" or "did anyone call?" Just your day-to-day small talk.

She wondered how long he was going to stay mad. Flo couldn't stand this horrible dry silence. She wanted to start over. Start the weekend off right. Have him be sweet to her again. She didn't know if Charles knew if she bought the car or not. If he did, he didn't say. But she knew she'd fucked up by spending all their money. The dream of owning a home was completely gone now. Flo mashed the potatoes with passion.

Charles got out of the shower and tied the towel around his waist. The water rolling down his glistening calves made a small puddle on the wood floor. Dripping a trail to the bedroom, he stood at the door of the closet, thumbing through all his good shirts. Those were the ones he wore when he went out. They still had the dry cleaner's plastic around them.

Flo sat quietly. Her eyes searched his back. She watched him take out the pressed shirt from the plastic. Watched him squeeze the baby oil and rub it over his firm body. He looked at his triceps in the mirror a long time and flexed before putting on his shirt.

Charles walked back to the bathroom again. Flo's eyes followed his skin.

Charles couldn't wait to get out the house tonight. He sprayed a heavy layer of cologne against his throat. When he caught Flo looking at him in the mirror, he closed the bathroom door with his foot.

"Damn," Charles said, blowing a kiss to himself. "You definitely one fine-looking brotha!" Charles clicked the bathroom light off and walked toward the living room mantel. He couldn't wait to get to the club and see Trudy tonight. He took his car keys out of his pocket.

It was one of those hot, blazing L.A. nights. So hot you had to drag out those cheap metal fans and run them full blast. Yank all the shades down to keep the cool in. Keep your freezer stacked full of ice trays. And even after that, the dead heat crept in just the same. But the funny thing was, no matter how hot it got in each room in their apartment, it sure was chilly between Flo and Charles.

Lately all Charles wanted to do was get out the house. He came home later and later from work and as soon as he did, he was itching to get to Dee's.

Flo sat down again on the couch. She hadn't been feeling so well lately; must be some nasty bug. She had cooked all that food but didn't want to eat. She clicked the TV on, nestling one hand inside a bag of Doritos. The bag made a horrible rustling sound every time her hand jabbed inside.

Charles's black shoes sounded extra loud on the cold hardwood floors. He carefully buttoned the front of his shirt and then picked up his wallet.

"You're not going out again?" Flo asked.

Charles didn't speak. He picked up his brush and stood by the mantel, smoothing his short hairs back down.

"I thought maybe we'd spend some time together tonight, go see a movie or something," Flo said. "I made all this food. You ain't even going to eat?"

Charles kept brushing away at his hair. He felt an urgency to leave. Trudy was waiting for him already.

Flo tried again, tried to sound more upbeat. "That scary movie looks good. You like scary movies. Maybe we could go and see that?"

Charles pulled his black sports coat from the closet.

Flo tried harder. "You know Freeman's in it. I know you like him. We could go to the eight o'clock show." Flo tried to kiss his shoulder but Charles pulled away. He shoved his wallet inside his back pocket.

"Well, go on then," Flo said. "Just see if I'm home." Flo sloshed more Coke down her throat.

Charles smiled to himself after Flo spoke. Yeah, she'd be home wearing her scrunchy pink curlers. Her robe riding over her large stretch-marked stomach, sound asleep, snoring loud on the couch.

Flo couldn't understand why Charles was being so hard. They usually made good love after those horrible brawls.

Flo and Charles would lie side by side like two old junk cars. And then one of them would roll or turn over sudden. And she'd touch his flesh, feeling his warm, juicy skin. Then the room would heat up like a fierce, roaring engine. Like a hot match against the black asphalt. He'd seize Flo and she'd please him any way he wanted. Charles would tug her warm frame hungrily, sucking her neck. Licking and pawing and gnawing her body until the deep moans escaped from her throat. Entering her so fast, so urgent and deep that Flo didn't have the chance to get up sometimes. And her diaphragm sat on the cold tile smiling. Waiting inside the pink case. But Flo couldn't stop the rocket fuel heat. She couldn't ignore her body's aching need. The wild, seething need to hold on to something. Hold tight even while her entire world sank. Even though a dark sadness had lodged in her body. A sadness that clamped down and wouldn't let go. Seemed like the only time she felt alive was when they were fighting like dogs. Clawing and gnawing away at each other. Trying to feel something while sinking in sand. They only got close after horrible drama. After chairs were knocked down and clothes were snatched off. Scratching for something that slipped away each day. But just like those gray, heavy waves at the beach, one minute you're up to your ankles in wet and the next you're just standing in sand.

See, Charles and Flo had hit a dry season. After Charles's affair, Flo began holding back on sex. She wanted to take something. Something to really make him suffer. So she slept on the narrow, slim edge of their bed. She lay breathing hard under the single tight sheet. She lay rigid, never letting a leg bend or arm dangle over to his side. She wanted to teach him. Keep his body near starving. And Flo, who'd always worn nightgowns to bed, began to sleep naked to torture him more. She'd stroke her own body, left one hand between her legs, but she never touched Charles's waiting flesh.

But now Flo was the one who waited hour after hour. She wanted Charles to seize her but he never turned her way. When she finally reached for him, Charles let out a snore. When her fingers grazed his biceps he jerked back his arm. When she tried to spoon his skin he refused to roll over. Eventually, Flo stopped trying. She lay quiet on the sheet, while Charles quietly pleased himself.

There was nothing worse, Flo thought, staring at the chipped rotting ceiling. There was nothing like lying right next to your man. Nothing like wanting him, wanting him to reach out and touch you. Having him so close you can feel his warm, steamy skin. Lying there blazing under sizzling covers, listening to your own violent, lonely heart scream. Being so close, so damn close to the one thing you wanted and not being able to touch it.

Flo got up and threw some cold water over her face.

No, Flo didn't know where she and Charles had lost it. But as sure as she was standing barefoot on the floor, she knew sure as hell it was gone.

"There's got to be someone," Flo thought to herself. She paced back and forth across cold bathroom tile. "There's no way he can lay day after day and not touch me." Flo splashed some more water, which ran down to her toe. "There's got to be somebody else."

15

Ray Ray and Charles

"Look-a here, look-a here." Big Percy tapped Ray Ray's shirt. Trudy walked to the front door after singing the first set. Vernita was supposed to meet her at ten.

Big Percy smiled his sloppy-mouth grin. Even though Trudy had been working at Dee's for months, Big Percy stayed up in her face.

"Well, if it ain't Trudy with the booty," Percy said, blocking her path. "Bet that ass tastes just like a Hershey's."

Trudy rolled her eyes and just kept on walking. A bum hit her up before she got to her car. She jabbed a few bucks in his hand.

"God bless you." The bum smiled from his black, deep-grooved face. Trudy smiled but kept walking. Her Honda was parked in the dark lot. She opened the hood and quickly un-hooked the cables. She shut it and walked back toward the club's door.

Percy's eyes ran up and down Trudy's body. "So, you too good now, huh? Can't talk to a brother proper?" Percy talked with the thick lisping tongue of a man who'd lost all his front teeth. He stood over Trudy like a solid brick wall. He was six feet and almost as wide.

"Could you back the fuck up?" Trudy said irritated. She waved when she saw Vernita coming up the walk but Big Percy still blocked her path.

"Ohhh, well excuse me, queen!" Big Percy said mockingly.

"Ain't this about a bitch. Ass all on Front Street, spread all over the whole damn town and we got the nerve to act uppity."

Vernita popped her gum but didn't say a thing. She'd been doing hair all day and wanted a drink. "Come on, Percy, I'm thirsty. Just let me in and quit trippin'"

"Oh, hello, ofay lover," Big Percy turned toward her. "Still sucking the white man's dick?"

Vernita had dated Carlos a little while back. He was half Mexican and Chinese but Big Percy didn't care. To him anybody nonblack was white.

"And who do you think's on the other end of that welfare dick yo' mama's been sucking ever since yo' ass been old enough to hold a food stamp?" Trudy snapped back.

Ray Ray came from the black drape and smiled at Trudy. Homegirl sure was something. Percy was glaring down her throat but Trudy still didn't care. She looked like she'd whup him right there like his mama.

"Be cool, man," Ray Ray said, watching Trudy's hot eyes. "Come on, man, let 'em come through."

Trudy kept her head straight and walked in strong and tall. She couldn't stand Percy. He had an ignorant side. His overgrown body and dead, eaten-out mouth looked like something you dragged out for Halloween. He was always tasting himself too. Sucking his own lips and wagging his tongue, which was real long and rough and always hung out, like you best watch your young boys around his big nasty ass.

But Trudy couldn't help but smile back at Ray Ray. She could feel that soft pull weight against her back.

"I'm glad you never stooped low to go with that brother," Vernita whispered to her once they both got inside.

Trudy didn't say anything. She'd always liked Ray Ray. If he hadn't grown up in a house so damn crazy, things might have turned out different for them.

"A woman like you could have straightened my ass out," Ray Ray used to tell her all the time. But some things were so crooked you couldn't get 'em straight. All that stabbing and stealing. All them hoodlums with guns. All the cocaine and heroin and crackheads strung out. All them 'hoish type women who hovered near his door—shoot, Ray Ray's road was mapped out.

Ray Ray leaned against his old tailpipe-dragging Lincoln, blowing low trails of smoke from his Newport. His dark, rusty skin glowed under the moon. The right side of his face was totally smooth; the left side was ravaged with scars. The burn mark resembled a slab of grilled ribs, left too long on the flame. Ray Ray scratched the burnt side of his face.

He walked inside Dee's and fed ten quarters into the cigarette machine and waited for the green and white box to drop out. He lit a cigarette and scanned the smoky, dim room. Charles was sitting at a small table near the wall. He was talking with Tony. Ray Ray opened the pack and walked over.

"Whatchu say, Ray Ray?" Tony's upper lip rose way over his gums. His wet smile was glistening with spit.

"You got the winning hand," Ray Ray said, rubbing the huge scar on his face. He walked close to Tony and got near his face. "Man, I been here over three and a half weeks. When I'm s'posed to get paid?"

"Boy, please, don't be bothering me tonight. The fight's in a few days and I got a lot on my plate."

Ray Ray stayed by his side, kept clocking his back until Tony stopped in his tracks. "Jailbird like you is lucky to get any work. You'll get paid whenever I say." Tony lit a half-smoked Winston, daring Ray Ray to comment, then boldly walked back toward the kitchen.

Charles smiled when he saw Ray Ray come into the room. Ray Ray was one cocky, cold-blooded fool. Charles was older, but he remembered him from high school.

"Zap'nin," Ray Ray mumbled to Charles. Ray Ray was fuming because Tony had given him the runaround again. "That overseer nigga. I ought to kick his fat ass. He turned around and gave Charles a pound.

"Man, I'm glad you came and sat next to me. I'm dodging Tony myself. I owe that sucka some money."

"You owe that fool and the nigga owes me. How much you in the hole for?"

"Seventy-nine hundred." Charles took a large gulp from his drink. His eyes rolled away toward the black, empty stage.

"Damn, man! How you let yo' shit get outta hand?" Ray Ray asked.

"Tony's been letting me gamble on credit," Charles said proudly. He wasn't real worried yet. He smiled in Ray Ray's hard face. "Man, I got money." Charles rubbed his chin, bragging. "If I wanted to, I could write a check for the whole amount now."

"Oh, yeah?" Ray Ray said, chuckling to himself. Charles talked like all of them other small-time gamblers, trying to act like they never needed cash. "Well, I wouldn't borrow none of that punk ass's money. The interest alone is a bitch and a half."

"He don't charge me interest." Charles smiled triumphantly.

"I work for the brother. He charges everyone interest. If he ain't charging you interest, my man, then you must got something his funky butt wants."

Ray Ray was tripping, Charles thought to himself. He was a broke jailbird who didn't own shit. He didn't understand money like him. Charles ordered another beer on credit.

"I guess he just likes me," Charles told Ray Ray proudly.

Ray Ray looked away from Charles's dumb face. "So how's Flo?" Ray Ray asked him. He turned the chair backward and straddled his seat, sprawling his thick thighs open wide. He pulled a sharp blade from the back of his pocket and sliced open a new pack of Doublemint gum.

"I don't know, man. Flo don't move me no more."

"That a fact?" Ray Ray said, scanning the room, barely listening. He folded the gum over his tongue.

"She's making it really hard for me, man. All I do, all day long, is deliver folks' mail. Working overtime hours so we can get our own place. Get up out that hollow apartment." Charles shook his head. He wanted sympathy from his friend.

Ray Ray pulled on his Newport and held in his smoke, blowing it over Charles's head. Charles had been the same stupid fool since grade six. Never satisfied with shit. Whining about this, crying about that. Eyeballing everything that lay across the street. Thinking everybody's grass was always greener than his. Forgetting both sides had to be mowed. Shoot, where Flo and Charles sat looked like paradise to him. Brother never knew what he had.

"I don't know. I'm thinking of firing Flo, man. All she cares about is herself," Charles said.

"Shit, dog. That's how most people is." Ray Ray stroked the small hairs of his well-groomed goatee. He didn't know why Charles complained all the time. Flo was in-house pussy that could cook and looked sweet. "Don't slip." Ray Ray smiled at his friend. "Another muthafucka be up in there like ice."

"So what? I'm bored with her, man. Used to be she waited for me after work. Used to have on some lipstick, a little perfume too. Now when I come home her hair's all rolled up, nubby legs poking out from her robe. I don't even like being in the same room with her no more. Everything I thought we had changed."

"I guess she don't know what's out here for you, brotha." Ray Ray scanned the dark club. There were only a few women left. One was heavily made-up in a red, garish dress. Two others bulged way over the rims of their stools. And one sat with her head slung over the bar.

"That's what I'm saying, man! Pussy be up in yo' face. Shit, you should see some of them 'hos I get on my route. Half of 'em come to the door with no panties. How you gonna keep yo' nigga from straying all the time if you don't take care of business at home? And I'm huffin' up and down the street all day long, delivering past dues and coupons. Breathing gas fumes and running from wild, unchained dogs. Thinking of ways we can get something decent."

"Dig it."

"All I wanted was a place where my woman's about me and I'm about her. Working together. Like we used to do."

Ray Ray ordered a Tanqueray mixed with sugary lime juice. He gulped almost half of it down.

"Was y'all working together when you fucked the white girl

too?" Ray Ray smiled at Charles. "Oh, my bad. I'm sorry about that, man. I don't mean to bring up yo' past." Ray Ray laughed.

"How do you know about that, man? You were locked up back then."

"Brothas in prison know more about the street then y'all. All we did in that bitch was pump iron and talk shit. Some of those O-Gs know Flo. Homegirl still got it poppin'. Brothas will always keep track of nice ass."

Charles ignored Ray Ray and stayed with the story.

"But, man, the worser the fight, the better the pussy. I make her wait so damn long she's ready to hump on my thigh." Charles laughed so hard he choked.

"I feel you, nigga." Ray Ray nodded in his glass.

"Man, sometimes I take her down on all fours."

"Nigga, please." Ray Ray thought Charles was a trip. Half the women he knew liked it like that.

"It's funny," Charles said, more to himself, "it's like she wants it. Like that shit turns her on."

"Probably does."

"It makes me sick, though. It makes me hate her more." Charles sat back, draining the rest of his glass. "No matter how fucked I get, bashing glass and shit, the next thing I know, baby girl's sucking my dick."

"Not all of 'em are like that, dog," Ray Ray told Charles. He didn't like men who put their hands on their women. Punk men like Charles made him sick.

"Aw, nigga, don't trip. I might throw a bottle at Flo, or rip off her dress. But I never really hurt her. At least not on purpose. I never once used my fists."

"Mm-hmm," Ray Ray said, taking a long drag from his Newport. "You gotta be careful. Not all of 'em play." Ray Ray leaned back in his chair and just laughed.

"What?" Charles asked.

"Man, I had this one trick. Now she was a stone freak." Ray Ray looked away from the stage. "But homechick was my regular shit."

"Yeah, so what happened? Where's she at now?" Charles asked.

"Oh man, it was crazy. But that's what I get for messin' around with stone freaks." Ray Ray put his gum inside a napkin. "But a shit-talking bitch has always been my weakness."

Charles couldn't understand Ray Ray sometimes. Why would he want some ol' filthy 'ho? Charles thought Ray Ray was crazy.

"I had this one chick, man. It was tight, all right. Had one of them snappin' pussys. Pi-ya! You put your shit in and that pussy clamped down like a fat rubber band, you understand? Man, I was sprung. Moved in after knowing her one day. Man, I was only in the eleventh grade. I was on and off the street selling nickel bags to get by. Baby just came up on me one night. Big meaty chick with thick legs talking smack." Ray Ray smiled wide. He rubbed his iron-pumped thighs. "Woo shit! Nigga, now you know that's my type. Her pimp had just busted her bottom lip open. Said she was skimmin' off the top. Told me she was, but it wasn't nothing big—nothing none of the other 'hos didn't do. Shoot, everybody in the game got to take care of themselves, right?"

"Right," Charles said, nodding.

"So we move in and play Mom and Pop and apple pie, right? She's selling pussy and I'm slinging 'Caine. Had plenty money all the time. Ate great every night. You know them thick sloppy joes they sell off 63rd? We was eatin' plenty of them and drinking apricot brandy. Man, everything was just gravy."

"You ain't afraid of getting no disease or nothing, man? Pussy been in everybody's ass on the street!" Charles looked at Ray Ray, disgusted.

"That's just it, cuz." Ray Ray leaned closer into Charles's face. "That's the whole thang. You got to be clean to be a 'ho. All them 'hos is like that. Get their shit checked like clockwork. All of 'em use condoms. 'Ho's don't go raw no time."

"So what happened to paradise, man?" Charles asked sarcastically. Ray Ray was always telling him some ghettofied story. But his scarred face made him sick. And his back teeth were jacked. Charles wished Ray Ray would get to the point.

"I broke off the leg of the dining room table. All the nails and shit were hanging all out. I clutched that leg like a club. I swung at her once but I missed. I wanted to beat her, but I couldn't. I held that table leg and froze. But the girl freaks out and runs and falls two flights of stairs. She was stuck in a hospital bed at County for months."

"Damn, man! You're lucky she didn't die. They'd have put your ass away for life." Charles opened a pack of gum and took a piece out. "Why would you even mess with a nasty bitch like that?"

"For love, man. I trusted that 'ho. Gave her half of all my cash. Laid up in the cut like a baby." Ray Ray took a deep drag and blew the smoke out real slow. "I would have stayed with that fuckin' freak for life."

"What'd she do?"

"Well, you know I still had a bad wound from a dog bite on a robbery that went bad. Shit never did heal right. Had to go to County all the time to get it checked and guess what?"

"What?"

"The muthafuckas do an AIDS test on my ass."

"An AIDS test for a dog bite?"

"Told me it was routine and shit. Said they checked everybody. So I say, 'all right, okay. Do the shit, right.' But guess what?"

"Naw, man. You lying, dog." Charles looked straight into Ray Ray's burnt face.

"The muthafucka came up positive," Ray Ray whispered low.

"Damn," Charles said, leaning farther back.

"But wait. Trip this, dog." Ray Ray took Charles's pack of gum and shook a stick out.

"So I get home, right? I'm pissin' bullets, see? I know this bitch musta went raw on some dude or showed me some fake-ass medical report, right. So I get home, but I'm cool, right?"

"Right."

"So I ask her."

"What she say?"

"Said she was straight. Said she never went raw no time."

"I said, 'What about us?' She said it was just me. Said she loved me. Asked me why was I tripping out now."

"But, I'm thinking naw, you a lying-ass trick. And I got the paper to prove it, right?"

"Right."

"So she said, 'No baby, you wrong.' She goes to get her paper. Shows me one and a few others too. 'I'm clean, Ray Ray! I been clean, baby. You know I don't mess around.' So she's pleading now, right? Beggin' and shit. But I don't give a fuck, right? Homegirl fucked with my life. Man, you should have seen the hurt in her eyes. She was begging me, 'Please, Ray Ray. Please, baby, don't,' and I'm holding the leg of the table like Willie Mays.

"But I didn't want to hear that shit, okay?" Ray Ray looked out toward Sonny's trio. Sonny was playing a sad black note solo.

"All I thought was this bitch done killed my ass, okay. That AIDS is a mutha on your mind, dog. For real. That shit ain't no muthafuckin' joke. Shit'll eat your whole fuckin' brain up alive." Ray Ray picked at his teeth and put the toothpick behind his ear.

"So what happened?" Charles asked. He knew Ray Ray was crazy but this shit was deep. He couldn't believe what he was saying.

"Man, I took all my shit and moved out that night. But guess what?"

"What?"

"Some undercovers get me while I'm trying to cop. I get sent back for parole violation. So them muthafuckas test me again. Test everybody that's sent up nowadays, dog. They separate all the AIDS folks from them other muthafuckas. They don't want that shit to get outta hand up there, man.

"So they do the test, right? I even tell 'em I have it. I don't care now. I figure I'm half dead all ready. But guess what?"

"What?"

"The shit comes back negative."

"Naw, dog!"

"Man, I even tell the doctor I got it. Beg 'em to do the test again. They do the shit and it's negative again, man. I don't have it. Never did."

"So what's up?"

"The County fucked up. I did half the eleventh and twelfth grade behind an AIDS test that went bad. Baby showed up in court in a new suit and all her 'ho friends too. Homegirl coulda got an Academy Award for all the boo-hooing she did for that judge, unbuttoning her blouse and showing him those deep ugly scars. But damn, I couldn't even look at her, dog. I never felt so bad, so damn wrong in my life. If I hadn't come at her she never would have taken that fall. Next thing you know, I'm in lock-down. I had some folks on the outside try to talk to her, dog, but she wasn't checking for me. Man, I tried everything to get out. I just wanted to talk to her, tell her I'm sorry. Say I had made a mistake. But I learned the hard way, you just can't go back. Jail gave me a long time to think about that shit. I was fucked up, man. I was totally wrong. Sometimes you cross the line, and love or 'I'm sorry' don't change a damn thing. You can't dog a woman like that and think you can come home. I heard her pimp is still looking for me. I can't even go up in Hollywood no more."

Ray Ray rubbed the huge burn mark with the palm of his hand.

"It was one of her friends threw that lye in my face." Ray Ray lit up a smoke and blew it out toward the bar. The hideous scar rippled from the flame. "I done crossed the line, fool. It's as sim-ple as that. That shit changed me, nigga. I look at life different. You can knock all you want on yesterday's door but that gone bitch will not let you in." Ray Ray stood up and rubbed the cross at his throat. "The only one I trust now is God."

Charles looked at Ray Ray as he walked away. He was so cool in high school. Girls went crazy for his ass. But you'd never know it by looking at him today. Half his teeth jacked. Big scar on his face. He was wearing a suit, but you could see underneath. Under-neath was twenty miles of bad road.

16

Trudy and Pearl

"You think this dress makes me look fast?" Trudy scrutinized herself in the tall, scratched-up mirror. She'd picked this dress especially to lure in poor Charles. It clung to her, hung on her womanly parts. Like a wet chicken breast dredged in flour.

Vernita was sitting on the dressing room counter, watching Trudy get ready for her set. It was a dingy room with a few stools, a sad row of square mirrors glued to the wall, and a long, wooden, broken-down counter. The counter was filled with ashtrays, curling irons, lipsticks and beads, fake lashes, eye shadow, gobs of foundation, wigs and a big plastic box stuffed with long, colored feathers. The feathers were used when the girls didn't have time to go do their hair or comb a wig out. They just greased their stuff down and picked a few feathers to match their clinging sequined outfits. There were lots of leftover clothes for last-minute changes. You never knew when a button would pop or a zipper might bust or some crazy drunk fool spill some booze on your dress.

"Fast? Girl, please. You worried about fast in this crusty-ass bar? Girl, you better just go on out there and sing to these fools while they still got some loot in their pockets," Vernita told her.

"So we straight?" Trudy asked. "You know what to do?"

"Girl, I done tol' you, I got it."

Vernita grabbed a blond wig and pulled it over her head. "All I got to do is play Miss Anne, huh?" With the blond wig and her freckles, Vernita easily looked white. Vernita held out her hand like it was a gun. "Gimme all yo' big money, man!" Vernita and Trudy broke into peals of laughter but Trudy's smile dropped when they heard the door handle twist. Vernita yanked the wig off just as Pearl pushed her way through the dressing room door.

"Hey, Miss Pearl," Vernita said. "Whatchu know good." And to quickly change the subject she added. "Trudy thinks that dress is too sexy."

Pearl smoothed her shimmering buttercream dress. Although Pearl was the cook, every now and then she raided the stage. "Ain't nothing wrong with showing how the good Lord done blessed you." With that she adjusted one of her massive bra straps, which lifted her big breasts to a cliffhanger point, jiggling against the dress like they just might bounce out and roll onto the floor.

"Come on, honey, let's get out and work. Sonny come in here awhile ago and said the place was packed. Y'all know what Friday means. Paydays and men who had fights with they ladies and a whole lot of pockets full of cash."

Vernita walked out. "I'll see you out there."

Sonny's combo consisted of Sonny on drums, a soft-spoken man with a slurry lisp. He drank Mickie's Big Mouth beer but didn't talk much. Paid too much attention to his red, wavy locks he had done in a slick, gummed-down process. But he was always respectful, called Trudy "miss" all the time. Never once stepped out of line. Then there was Stanley on bass, a skinny young cat who wore slim suits and dark shades. On top of his head sat a white skipper's hat. He said the hat made him look rich. The piano player looked like he could be eighty, a happy dark-skinned man everyone called Mr. Wade.

Trudy came out and held the microphone until Sonny gave her the nod. Then she walked to the center of the stage. Lots of men's chairs rimmed the edge of the platform. They all leaned back in their seats.

Charles couldn't take his eyes off Trudy. Her eyes were always pointing his way. Like the song she sang was for him. Tony came back and leaned in to tell him this old nasty joke, but Charles never heard him; his eyes never left the stage. He shook Tony's arm from his back.

"Damn, man. You act like you ain't never seen her. Booty been all over the town. You don't want to fool around with that heifer. Head's all messed-up already. Her own mama don't have nothing to do with her. Girl's got her ass so high off the ground you'd think she was the Empire State—"

"Wait a minute, man, she's about to sing another one," Charles said, leaning closer to the stage.

Tony sank back and stubbed another Winston in the ashtray.

Truth was, he had tried to hit on Trudy himself, but Pearl had caught him and loud-talked him in the middle of the room.

"Baby girl don't want to mess with no drunk ass like you. She's my niece. She's a singer. You hired her to sing. She ain't one of them boozy sluts you bring up in here. Got to pay most of 'em just to look at yo' ass. You best sit down and keep drinking that cheap liquor you serve and stay out that chile's face." Pearl stood her ground. The whole place got quiet. Trudy was family. Tony was out of line. The bar waited to see what Tony was going to say. But all Tony did was walk out.

"Someday, I'ma hafta hurt that gal," he said to himself.

Tonight Tony tilted way back in his seat. Charles was sitting at the edge of his. Couldn't take his eyes off that sweet, scratchy voice and her smooth, luscious curves all dolled up in sheer royal blue.

Homeboy's gone, Tony laughed to himself. He smacked Charles across the back, got up and went to sit with a well-dressed man at the far end back table.

When Trudy finished the last set she slipped back inside the dressing room.

Trudy sat down and unzipped her blue gown. She was just about to peel it off when she heard rapid knocking at the door.

Bap, bap, bap.

"Who is it?" Trudy yelled out. Damn. Can't a girl get out her dress good before some hound comes sniffing for crumbs?

"Miss Trudy," the voice said through the thin wooden door. It was Sonny from the band.

"Miss Trudy, there's a man out there in the front row gimme ten dollars to hand you this paper. Said it was real important you got it." Sonny was hoping he could get in the room and have a look around. He hadn't been inside the dressing room before.

"I'm sorry, Sonny, but I'm not dressed just yet. Could you slide it under the door for me, please?" Trudy said through the crack.

She could hear the fumbling around outside, then saw the white flap of a crumpled sheet appear under the door. She didn't hear anything for a while and imagined Sonny still there on his hands and knees, breathing through the slim keyhole.

"Is that it, Sonny?" she said.

She heard a rumbling and a mild cough.

"Oh yeah, Miss Trudy, that's it. Thank you, ma'am. I'll tell the man you got it all right," Sonny said.

Trudy could hear his heavy feet sanding the hallway's floorboards.

Pearl laughed. "Girl, that boy loves your dirty drawers. He is so proud to be doing you a favor, he don't know what to say. I bet he'd hold your panties back to let yo' ass pee."

"Stop it, Pearl," Trudy said, laughing herself and unfolding the note.

"You know it's true. You ought to pay that boy some mind. Nothing wrong with getting a man who loves you more than you love him. Man who loves you more is sure to stay at home nights. Nothing wrong with him being a little on the ugly side neither. An ugly man would be so happy to have you. Wouldn't be pushing you over trying to get in your mirror like these pretty boys do. Ugly'll treat you right. Treat you like royalty. I've had two myself, so I know." Pearl smeared on more red lipstick.

But Trudy wasn't paying attention. She was reading the neat handwriting on the tiny note while sipping a glass of red wine.

"What's it say?" Pearl asked, trying to read over Trudy's shoulder.

"I'm not telling," Trudy said coyly. She crumpled the note and dropped it in the trash.

Shirley jerked open the door and hurried through the dressing room door. She'd been listening outside and saw the note on the floor and picked it up and read it out loud. "Dear lady in blue, please join me . . ."

"Don't be so nosy." Trudy snatched the note back and ripped it all up.

Shirley had a small cocktail apron over a black, clinging dress. She had already spotted the man in a well-tailored ivory-colored suit. She watched him scribbling a note and handing it to Sonny. She had come back in the dressing room to find out what it said. She had hated Trudy from the first day she'd come on. She felt she did most of the work around the club. Trudy didn't have to do nothing but stand on the stage and be cute. Besides, all the men wanted to talk to her now. She was squeezing out all Shirley's action.

Shirley peeked out a small hole drilled through the dressing room wall. You could see the whole club through the tiny peephole. Tony had it done so he could come down and look at who was in the club without them knowing he was there. She saw Sonny making his way back to the table with a man with dark shades and a diamond pinkie ring. The man thanked Sonny and placed a bill in his palm.

"You don't see many high-class niggas like him up in here," Shirley said, rapidly popping her gum.

"Let me see." Pearl looked out the peephole herself. She saw a handsome man in a beautiful woven suit. He sat in one of the red vinyl booths. He was smoking a thin Tiparillo, and his pinkies were all filled with diamonds. The man nodded now and then to people passing his table.

"Well, I'll be. He's all grown up, but that sho' 'nuff's him. All this damn time and he still ain't no good. Look how he's holding his spoon," Pearl said, disapproving.

Shirley looked at Pearl like she'd lost her damn mind. "Y'all act too suspicious sometime. Go on and keep yo' ugly-ass men if you want. I likes mine pretty and I likes mine rich. All I gotta do is swish my big ass. Nigga'd be paying my rent by the end of the week." Shirley popped her gum three times in Trudy's face and smiled.

Trudy looked at Shirley and smiled cruelly back. "That big ass of yours ain't been getting you much."

Pearl smirked and leaned farther into the mirror, dousing her bosom with powder.

"You be acting too uppity lately." Shirley sneered at Trudy and then turned to Pearl. "Why you got to be so hard on the brother who got money? What'd he ever do to you?" Shirley asked Pearl.

"Oh, Cashflo be in here now and then, flashing them nice clothes and pretty-boy smile. Having his whispered conversations, big money changing hands, sending for champagne bottles and junk," Pearl said.

Trudy peeked out the hole to look too. Ah shit! she said to herself. That sure was him, sitting right there in front. The same one she'd seen in the black SUV. The one with the tan-suit man. What was he doing here?

Trudy dabbed her face and took a quick swig of water.

"What's wrong with you?" Shirley asked. "You look like you're sick."

"I hope you didn't snack on none of them wings before they got done." Pearl peeked out the small hole again. "Men like him make me sick too. The only thing a man like him cares about is money, and he ain't too concerned how he gets it. Your best bet is to stay put. Leave him alone. A man that high-class got to be dealing dirt. Oh, he'll take you whereever you want to go, as long as it's on his way."

"Maybe he got lucky and hit Lotto," Shirley added.

"Lotto, my ass. It's crack, if you ask me. He makes money sucking blood from the good folk in our community. I've seen many a mama sell her own flesh and bone just for one last hit. Dope man has no soul but the dollar bill, girl. You don't *even* want to go there," Pearl said, disapproving.

"You don't even know him and now you got him selling dope. Black folks are the most suspicious folks on earth." Shirley placed her hand on her hip.

"Trudy'd be better off with somebody like Ray Ray," Pearl said, still dousing her large bosom.

Trudy kept her eyes down toward the floor. Everyone knew Ray Ray had just come from jail.

"I know he looks rough. But that's a real man, honey. Always respectful. Had yo' back from day one. He made a mistake but he paid for it, baby. I swear that young man done changed."

"Ray Ray?" Shirley laughed right in Pearl's face. "That black jailbird bum? That burned ragamuffin? Who in holy hell would want him? All that boy is is a black walking scab."

"What the hell do you know about picking a good man? All you've had was something a gype dog drug in or what an old mangy cat wouldn't touch if it was drenched in nip. Now hush and just let me finish."

Shirley popped her gum loudly but sat down and remained quiet.

"We had this girl named Peaches, used to be at the club. Came by to help clean up and cook. She married this fella who drove them old tow trucks. Was always dragging some dead car around." Pearl laughed to herself and fanned at her bosom. "Black handsome man stood about six-foot-five, with some thick, wavy stuff he brushed down. Peaches would crack us up about that man's appetite." Pearl lowered her voice and looked around the room slyly. "And the girl wasn't talking about food." Pearl fanned herself again, smiling at the mirror. "Had two pretty babies. Two big fat, juicy boys. As cute as they wanted to be."

"Who cares," Shirley said, angrily sawing her nails. She was bored unless the conversation revolved around her. She'd heard enough of Pearl's backyard gossip.

"Now hold up, wait a minute. I'm fixin' to tell it." Pearl held up one of her hands. "Peaches showed up one day and Jimmy was there. That's his name, Jimmy. I recognized his slick gait a mile away. Pimp-walking, soul-stealing wannabe chump. His mother didn't want him down in San Diego no more. Dropped him down here every summer. He was five-and-dime then, a little street sucker who sold nickel bags and scratchers. So one day he starts flirting with Peaches at work. They were about the same age, and he'd wait for her on the sidewalk, talking while she swept outside. Next thing we know, she does a no-show the next morning. Nobody knew where she was. Her husband called up about ninety-eight times. Came on down here, holding a kid in each hand. Never did see her. Got turned out is what they say."

"You mean she never came back? You didn't see her again? You guys didn't file a police report or nothing?" Trudy asked.

"Yeah, she came back. Three and a half months later but I swear it wasn't the same girl. Face all broke out. Big gashes and scars. She used to have the smoothest complexion back then. Came back with her hair matted, wearing some worn, torn-up spandex, turned-over shoes and no socks. Yeah, she came back all right, long enough to get her poor husband's VCR and TV. Haven't seen hide nor hair of her since."

Trudy finished her makeup and looked back at Pearl.

"Well, what happened to that fine-ass husband of hers?" Shirley asked, interested now.

"Jail," Pearl said. She studied her lap. "I sure miss cooking for that overgrown boy. Man could sit up and eat hisself twenty-eight pancakes. But after what happened to Peaches, he was never the same. Losing poor Peaches shook the man to the bone. Poor thing was never the same. Spent most of his time in that truck hunting for Jimmy. But he'd never gotten a good look at Jimmy's face. He was going by build. Judging by type. Every fast-talking, game-runnin' punk made him sick. Lotta folks got whipped down that summer. But Jimmy didn't feel like duckin' and dodging no more. So he made a friend call saying he needed a tow, told the friend to use his name. Peaches's husband don't say nothing. Pulls up to the curb slow. Shot that boy point-blank in the face."

"But that wasn't him! Didn't somebody tell? Obviously he shot the wrong man."

"Hell, yeah, they told, but so what? It's too late. And then Jimmy, who hadn't shown his punk ass in months, strolls into Dee's Parlor that very same day, sits there and orders a steak."

"Well, damn, Pearl," Shirley said, "it was clearly a mistake." Shirley licked her finger and held it to her thigh. She made a sizzling sound through her teeth with her tongue. "And when he gets out I got something for him." She smiled.

Pearl shook her finger in Shirley's dumb face. "That boy's serving hard time for murder, you fool. Your hot little ass gonna have to sit there and rot 'cause he ain't getting out again, honey."

Shirley spun in the stool like it was a ride. "Oh, like every man y'all had was a nice slice of pie. Pearl, you ain't exactly no Catholic schoolteacher." Shirley smiled at the other two women. "Shoot, I seen a lotta y'alls men. Y'all pickin' off fleas just like everyone else."

Trudy stood up and got in Shirley's smirking face. "If I was as silly as you, I swear I'd bite my own tongue."

Pearl rolled her eyes. She patted her stomach. "Don't worry 'bout Shirley. She don't bother me none. Y'all know I didn't get this old being dumb."

Pearl turned back to Shirley and adjusted her breasts. "Don't envy my mornings if you don't know my midnights. You ain't never once danced in my pumps. Hell, yeah, I had my share of ragamuffins and whatnot, but that's not what we're talking about here. I seen that shit buried down deep inside mean folks' eyes. Now maybe yours ain't used to spotting shit yet, but after working in nightclubs for over twenty-odd years, I'd say I was a better judge than yo' skinny tight ass. See, I watch eyes, baby. Eyes'll tell you everything you want to know. Teeth might be smiling, hands counting out money, but them eyes. Humph. Lord, chile, them eyes, they don't lie. Just as evil and mean as you please. See, the wave always goes back into the water and the devil's ready to sucker punch you again. I done already carried my own share of sorrow. Had two husbands I already done put in the ground. My first one, Lord, girl, we fought every night. Tearing up shit like wild cats and dogs. Rolling on the rug, him pulling my hair and me trying to scratch out his eyes. But I thought my sweet would rub off on him. Shoot, all I ended up with was rug burns. Girl, that man gave me hell, from Monday to Sunday, I'm talkin' H-E-L-L, *hell*! Man put the 'me' in *mean* 'cause that's all he was, mean to me. Finally gave me some peace when he keeled over and died."

"That has nothing to do with—" Shirley tried to interrupt again.

"Then I met Mr. Jefferson, my second husband." Pearl smiled up at the ceiling. "Sweet as potato pie. Happy all the time. Didn't have much money, you understand, but he always helped out. Kept our place spic and span, painting and planting those fruit trees we got. And I didn't find him at no church Easter Sunday."

No one knew where Pearl had met her last husband. There was a big patch of time missing out of his past. He'd done some time upstate but she'd never told anyone that. He was good now and that's all that mattered. And there were some things with Pearl you just didn't ask, and she didn't plan on telling them now. "See, some men's don't have much but a whole lot of heart. That's what I'm about. I don't tangle with mean, honey. Uh-uh, nosirree. Don't got nothing to do with cruel. You better keep them eyes peeled and watch your back, honey. Them slick ones might grin and they wallets be bulging, but their hearts, girl, are blacker than tar."

Trudy looked out the peephole again. Two big, burly men sat, flanking each side of Jimmy. She'd have to be careful. Watch each step she made. Pearl might act real country sometimes, but she wasn't one to be lying. But with fear easing in, Trudy was still determined. She wouldn't change her plan out of fear of one man. She'd handle him, was all. Like she handled the others. Flirt a bit but stay noncommittal. There was no way she'd turn into somebody's dumb junkie. All she wanted was money. A chance to get out. She wasn't taking much. She wouldn't be greedy. Trudy studied the man's coal-black eyes a long time. He was a hurdle. No bones about that. But he'd definitely be her last.

17

Trudy and Jimmy

When Trudy finished her set she pulled through the bar. It was like trying to get off an overstuffed bus.

"Let me buy you a drink, precious."

"Can I ask you a quick question?"

"Come 'ere, gal and sit on Big Papa's lap."

Trudy mildly smiled as she wiggled through tables. Finally she found Vernita's table. Vernita was sitting between two older men. She'd been in the bar for less than ten minutes and had them both eating out of her hand. One bought her a drink and the other hooked his arm around her chair while she stroked the fine hair on the back of his neck.

"I told you, go bald," Vernita whispered inside Trudy's ear. Vernita's hair was less than a quarter-inch long. "Girl, you pull in a whole different man."

"Watch," Vernita said, standing up. "I'ma fool around and dance with 'em both." Vernita got up, and both men stood too. They looked like they'd follow her right into the ocean. "He-ey," Vernita said and batted her eyes. "If I gotta go play a white girl tomorrow, I might as well be ghetto tonight!"

Trudy laughed watching Vernita dance on the floor sandwiched between two happy men. She'd never seen nothing so raunchy.

Vernita was one who could ignite any party. She was a flare on a dull, dusty road.

All Trudy needed now was to square things with Charles. Her eyes skimmed around the dark edges of the room.

A tall man in black sunglasses approached her chair.

"Excuse me, miss. My friend over there wants to know if you'll join him." Trudy glanced over at Jimmy. He smiled and lifted his glass. Tony was sitting beside him.

"Well, why can't your friend come and ask me himself?"

The man seemed annoyed at Trudy's response and walked quickly back toward his table. He whispered in Jimmy's ear. Jimmy looked up and nodded. He stood up, gliding toward where Trudy sat, shaking hands and giving pounds along the way.

"Look at that," Pearl whispered to Shirley. "What'd I say? Everybody knows the dope man's name."

"So what?" Shirley sneered. "All I see is money."

"Hello," Jimmy said to Trudy. "May I join you for a moment?" His two boys sat at a table nearby and he moved his chair close to her shoulder.

Pearl walked by and looked down at him hard.

"Evening," Jimmy said.

Pearl just ignored him and disappeared backstage.

Jimmy waved for Shirley to bring a bottle of champagne.

Shirley sat the bottle down a little too rough. She scratched her giant hair and left.

A burly man sat down at the table a moment. He whispered something to Jimmy and then got up and left too.

"Looks like you lost your friend," Trudy said, looking back at the man.

"Looks like I found me a new one." His smile showed a row of dazzling-white, straight teeth. His shoulders looked like you could build homes on them. There was something else she saw too, something deep inside his eyes. It was as if he looked right through her, right into her bones. Trudy quickly looked away.

"I'm sorry," Trudy said, standing up, "I was on my way to see my friend." Trudy looked around for Vernita.

"Just sit for a minute and talk to me. Please." Jimmy was mildly holding her arm.

Trudy had never met any rich men in Dee's Parlor before. Oh, there were plenty of those who acted like they had cash. Tommy and Edmond, Darren and Shaun. They all dressed expensive. Went to restaurants and stuff. But none of them knew a job if it knocked 'em upside the head, and half of 'em still lived off their mamas. Nobody had real money. Not no deep-pocket cash, and they sure never gave any to her.

It was so loud in Dee's Parlor that Jimmy put his lips to Trudy's ear to speak. She could feel his warm breath on her neck. She was praying Charles didn't walk in and see her like this. Trudy nervously watched the front door.

"So you're Trudy," Jimmy said, smiling, leaning back in his seat and opening his legs wide. "I thought you were a church girl singing like that up there. I'da sworn up and down it was Sunday."

Trudy licked the cherry she picked from her glass. She noticed his purple silk tiepin, covered with diamonds and a giant diamond and sapphire ring.

"My name is James, but everybody calls me Jimmy. I got your name from the drummer over there. Had to give him ten dollars for the privilege. But," he said, gently squeezing her wrist, "I'd say it was money well spent."

"So tell me," Trudy asked, stroking the length of his tie, "how do you make yours?" She was never afraid to ask a straight question. It kept people on the defensive.

"Oh, so you one of them types likes to know everything?" Jimmy said.

"I just like to know who I'm dealing with, is all."

"Oh, we dealing already?" he said, opening his eyes wide and smiling. "Then I guess it's okay if we dance."

Before Trudy could protest, he stood up and pulled her hand.

"Shit," he said under his breath as he watched Trudy's hips weave through the tables toward the dance floor.

Trudy felt his gaze, but hell, what could she could do? Besides, there was something about him she liked. There was sureness about him, a confidence too. Like he was used to silver spoons and linen napkins. That casualness rich people had.

So when Trudy felt his honey-brown eyes ease into her backside, she dipped her hips some, winding them real nice and slow, giving him something to make his mouth water.

Oh, God, she thought, *don't let Charles come in and see me now.*

He circled Trudy's waist and she placed her arms around his neck. She could feel the heavy fabric of his jacket under her hands. Hmmm, she said to herself. This was cashmere. From all the clothes Trudy stole, she'd learned a few things about fabrics.

"So are you going to tell me, or do I have to beg?" As much as this man felt good next to her stomach, Trudy wanted to see if he'd say what he did. She knew he dealt dirt. She knew asking was dangerous but she wanted to watch Jimmy squirm.

Jimmy gripped her firm waist a little more snugly. "You seem like a woman who knows what she wants." He ever so gently tugged a handful of her braids until she had to stare up at his face. "But just tell me this"—his lips grazed her throat—"how bad do you want to know?"

Trudy pulled her braids out of his hand. "Don't you think what you do says a lot about who you are?" She was playing with fire, but damn this was fun.

"No," Jimmy said flatly. "Uh-uh, not really. Not unless you're the type that judges people by their jobs. The kind of person who puts a price tag on somebody's back." There wasn't nothing Jimmy liked better than messing with people's minds. He loved to throw nosy folks off his track.

"Listen, baby, I found you in a club, right? You sing, okay. But I'm pretty sure you're a helluva lot more than that."

Trudy smiled. *Yeah, fool. I work at the bank.* She wasn't about to say that.

"Oh, it's okay. I know you want to play twenty questions so you can try to define me. Try and pigeonhole my ass. Listen, I'll make it easy for you, okay? I'll just come right out and say it. I'm in the commodities business, baby," Jimmy said directly. "Stocks and bonds. Transactions and shit. You know, buy low, Dow Jones, all that drama." Jimmy stopped dancing and straightened his tie. "Satisfied?"

"You play the stock market game?" Trudy asked as he pulled her to him again.

"Yeah, and that's just what it is, a muthafuckin' game." He was grinding against her, pulling her closer to his chest. Trudy could feel the raw heat radiating from his skin. Just then a burly man came behind Jimmy and tapped him on the shoulder. He leaned over and whispered something in his ear.

"Listen, baby," Jimmy said to Trudy, "I have to handle some business. Is it okay if I call you later?" He still had both arms wrapped around her waist.

Trudy usually didn't like men who called her "baby" right away. Pearl said men used "baby" so they didn't have to remember names. All Trudy knew was her mother called her man Mr. Hall and that sounded like he was her boss.

But Jimmy said it so low and it sounded so sexy, Trudy didn't mind at all. Trudy didn't make a habit of giving out her number either. In fact, she had a rule against it. She dated this one fool named Roger who started to stalk her. After that she had to be careful. But there was something about this man. His wide, cocky smile, the way his eyes speared her body. His elegant, well-groomed demeanor. But there was something extra, too. That little touch of ghetto. That faint taste of street. That hard, manly edge that she loved. Vernita used to call it an addiction.

"Your thug-life men gonna get your ass twisted," Vernita said all the time.

She remembered how hard it was to get rid of Roger. She had to get call blocking on that freak.

Trudy was smiling, with Jimmy's hands trying to creep to her ass, when she suddenly saw Charles walk in.

"Follow me," Trudy said, leading Jimmy down the hall. She didn't want Charles to see her talking to Jimmy at all. She smiled at Jimmy and then opened her purse, taking out a matchbook and pen.

"Here," he said, turning all the way around. "You can write on my back."

Trudy placed the small cardboard against his broad shoulders. She could feel Jimmy's thick muscles underneath his cream coat. She wanted to caress his huge, bulging neck but instead slowly scribbled her number. She knew it was dangerous having this man get this close. She knew she was playing with a whole box of matches. But there was something about him Trudy couldn't resist. Maybe she could have some hot, quick fun for a minute. He could be her last taste before she left town. Like a mint you sucked right before steak.

18

Trudy and Charles

Trudy waved to Charles to come near the cigarette machine. She hoped Charles hadn't seen her talking to Jimmy. See, Charles was the main hinge in Trudy's bank-robbing scheme. Charles was the mail carrier on the Dee's Parlor block. She would watch his gray pants and large leather satchel. Charles was perfect. His occupation played an integral part in her plan. She couldn't do the job without him.

"Come on," she told him. "Let's talk outside."

"It's kinda dark outside," Charles said, following her feet.

"That's okay," Trudy said, walking ahead, her stilettos tapping the concrete.

Trudy jumped into her gray Honda and twisted the key. The car revved but it wouldn't turn over. Trudy tried it again. She gave it more gas but this time it didn't even catch. There was enough juice in the engine for the car to rev once but now it only clicked and went dead.

"You probably flooded it now," Charles said, peering in her window.

Trudy frowned. She pretended to be upset. "Really?" she said, making her voice disappointed, but inside she was just as pleased as pie.

"You have to wait a few minutes before you can start it."

Trudy banged the steering wheel hard for effect.

"Pop the hood," Charles said. He looked inside the engine, but he didn't have a clue about cars.

Trudy sat nervously in the front seat. She hoped he wouldn't see she'd unhooked the cables.

"Might be your alternator." Charles shut the hood. He was anxious to talk to Trudy about Flo. He wanted to know what she knew. Then, suddenly, two loud voices came bursting from the club. Their laughter filled the whole lot.

It was Percy and Ray Ray. Trudy pulled the lever on her seat until she was almost lying flat in the car.

"Maybe it's better if we talk away from here," Trudy said.

"Yeah," he agreed. "I can give you a ride if you want." Charles could hardly believe his good luck. In a second she'd be in his car!

Trudy looked at him like she was uneasy. Then she grabbed her purse from the backseat and got out.

"That's okay, my friend can come get me," she said. Trudy walked over to the pay phone and pretended to call Vernita. She knew Vernita had left the club to see Lil Steve. "No use wasting all this good liquor," she'd said when she left.

A vicious smile had slithered across her lips, as Trudy watched Vernita leave. Vernita was going to meet Lil Steve and give him the when, where and why. Everything was working out fine.

Trudy slammed the receiver and walked back to Charles.

"You sure it's no problem?" Trudy asked, fingering her long braids. She covered one breast with a handful of hair. The other breast loomed huge in the moon.

Charles held the door and Trudy wiggled into his Buick. He watched the seat belt dive into her chest. As soon as he turned on the car he started asking questions.

"So what do you know," Charles asked her point-blank.

Trudy pulled Charles's hand to her lap. "Look, I'm not trying to get in your business, but I saw something last Friday at the bank. Something I think you should know."

"What?" Charles said, smiling. What could this cutie-pie have seen? His hand tucked in hers, Charles wanted to touch the rest of her body.

Trudy gently brought his palm to her lips. "I work at the B of A on Wilshire, okay?"

"So," Charles said, smiling. "What's that supposed to mean?" Charles had no idea what Trudy was going to say, so he still continued to joke. "What, you want me to open another account?"

Trudy held his hand close. "When Flo came into the bank, she got in my line."

Charles wrinkled his face. He pulled back his hand. "So what are you trying to say?"

"Look, don't be mad, I just thought you should know. Flo came in and withdrew eight thousand dollars."

Charles bit the inside meat of his hand. "Wait a minute. What are you talking about?"

"Flo came to my line. I gave her the money."

"All of it? Most of that money was mine!" Charles banged his hand real hard against the dash.

"All but the five bucks the bank makes you leave to keep the account open," Trudy said.

"Fuck!" Charles yelled, banging his hand again. "I'ma get her, I swear!"

"No!" Trudy said. "Don't be dumb, Charles. All you'll end up doing is going to jail or at the emergency unit at King Drew."

Charles scowled hard. He was too mad to talk.

"Look, I know you owe Tony."

"Day-am!" Charles said. "You know all of my business!"

"Tony has a big mouth." Trudy pulled back his palm. She placed his hand over her breast. "Look, I know you have a good heart. I see you work hard. And I can help if you let me."

Charles was a hurricane of emotions. He'd never been so pissed off in all his life, but he was touching Trudy's amazing body and couldn't stop squeezing her fresh-melon breasts.

"Dammmmn," Charles said again, but it was more like a moan, and the car windows steamed from his breath.

"I can help you," Trudy said, tracing her thumb along his thigh.

"Yeah?" Charles said, trying to get on top of her. "What can you do for me, huh?"

"Why don't you start by turning on your engine and taking me home," Trudy said.

Charles started the car and she rolled down the window. She watched the small stars in the sky.

"I have a plan," Trudy said.

"Really?" he said, squeezing her thigh. He couldn't wait to get her home. He drove down Venice like a fiend. "I hope your plan includes me."

"It's about getting some money, that's all I can say."

"Is it dangerous?" Charles had an aversion to crime. Too many of his old friends were now doing time.

"No. Not the part you have to play. Drop me off here—that's where I stay." They were already at Western. Trudy unlocked the door. "I'll call you and tell you more tomorrow."

"Why can't you tell me all about it right now?" Charles pulled over. He wrapped his arms around her waist.

Trudy let him squeeze her before opening her car door.

"Can I walk you up?" Charles asked, hopeful. He was upset with himself for letting an opportunity pass. He tried to grab her arm and clung to her blouse. He heard the faint sound of a tear.

"Hey, wait a second. Let go," Trudy scolded him now. "Tomorrow we'll have plenty of time."

Trudy turned around and flashed him a generous grin. She cupped his chin in her hand. "Give me your number and I'll call you tomorrow."

Ripping an envelope in half, he scribbled his number, handing her the torn paper. He knew giving Trudy his home number was risky but after what Charles had heard tonight, he just didn't care anymore.

Trudy waved and waited until Charles took off. Then she walked the short block to the end of the street and went into her real apartment across the street. She didn't want anyone to know where she lived. She quickly went in and bolted her door. She didn't want Charles. She knew he was Flo's. All she wanted to do was tease him. Float him along. Get his mind right so he'd help her with her plan.

Poor Charles. Some men where such dumb Chihuahuas. Half

of 'em would do backflips if you'd just let 'em smell it. Lord knows that boy's nose was blown open wide. He was desperate for cash and had weak, roaming eyes. He was going to work out just fine.

But Charles had certain ideas of his own. He smelled Trudy's cologne on the back of his hand and drove home with a brand-new ambition.

19

Flo and Charles

When Charles left home that night, Flo paced the living room floor. She kept looking out the window and walking back and forth.

"I know Charles is up to something," she said out loud to herself.

She watched TV for a while and then clicked it off, tossing the remote across the floor.

"Dammit, I feel it. I know something's up. That asshole's backsliding again." She walked to the kitchen and popped open a Coke.

"If I could just catch him," she said to herself. Flo finished the Coke and squeezed the can with her hands. She fingered the new car key with her thumb. Having the car made Flo realize she wanted something more.

"If I could just catch him in the act." Flo grabbed a sweater and the rest of her keys. She was determined to go see what was happening at Dee's. The screen door slammed loud when she left.

In the heart-attack section of L.A. they stayed in, there was only one club worth putting your foot in. That was Dee's Parlor off Washington and Tenth.

Flo ran down the street, jumped in the car and drove down to Dee's like a dope fiend. She clicked off her lights when she got close. She didn't want anyone to see her pull up. And she sure didn't want Charles to know she had sunk so low as to trail his fucking punk ass. She'd seen those dumb women showing up at clubs. All of them looking beat-down, torn-up and sad, screaming "Leroy! Ty-rone! I know you in here." Flo'd never give Charles that satisfaction.

Flo kept her lights low until she could see the pale neon floating in the dark, murky sky. There happened to be a little side street sitting directly across from Dee's Parlor. It was the perfect spot to watch who went in and out. That's where Flo parked. Her car was only three away from the front, but the street was so tree-lined and the night was so black, no one could see she was there. Flo spotted Charles's raggedy car in the lot. Percy and Ray Ray were talking outside. She definitely didn't want any of those who-rahs to see her. They looked too gangsterish for her.

It was starting to get cold. Flo wrapped a sweater around her shoulders. No matter how hot L.A. got by day, it could get down-right freezing at night. She scooted down in the seat and kept her eyes on Dee's door and her rearview mirrors. This was not a very nice street. She didn't need any surprises.

Flo watched the steady flow of folks coming out the door. Working stiffs in uniforms, a few suits and ties and some stumbling drunks glued to hoochies wearing Band-Aids as skirts and big, lumpy, stiff push-up bras. They laughed or talked serious and lit their smokes while panhandlers hounded them for dimes.

Flo sat parked on the dark side of pain for two hours. After a while she started rolling her hair. She had to be at work early in the morning, so she'd brought her rollers in a plastic grocery bag. Besides, stupid Charles would never suspect she'd been out if her hair was all rolled up already.

Finally she recognized Charles's build at the door. She eased farther up in the seat to make sure. Yeah, that was Charles, all right. He was waiting by the pay phone next to this big-ass chick in a skimpy, low-cut top. The girl turned around and Flo looked right into Trudy's face.

"Well, ain't this a bitch!" Flo said under her breath and sat even farther up in her seat so she could see. She watched Charles help Trudy get in his car. "So she's the one got Charles's nose open wide." She watched Charles and Trudy drive off.

I knew it! I knew he was stepping out again.

"That bitch ain't got no shame at all," Flo said out loud. She watched Charles's taillights fade to black.

"Well, hell, I guess it's every damn woman for herself." Flo didn't even bother to buckle up when she pulled off. Her tires skidded away from the curb.

"If her mama helped herself to a damn married man, that shit must just run in the family."

As Flo followed them, her heart began to beat fast. She was so mad she could barely sit there and think.

Charles took Adams all the way down to Western.

Probably going to the Mustang Hotel, Flo said to herself. She knew about the Mustang from going with Tony. There were lots of hourly rate motels in L.A. Lots of them lined LaBrea Avenue near the Number 10 Freeway. But nothing compared to Mustang. The Mustang was huge. It was a three-story structure that took up the whole block with giant mirrors glued to the ceiling and walls. Flo was so distracted with these thoughts, she almost hit the car stopped in front of her at the light. She was panting so loud the sound filled her ears. Flo lingered back when she saw Charles's car stop.

"Oh," Flo said, "they must be going to her place."

Flo looked at the apartment across the street. It was nasty and its lawn was filled with trash.

Flo watched Trudy wave to Charles by the curb and then dash across the lawn and to an apartment farther down the street. That place was fifty times worse than the first.

Flo had to run a few lights to beat Charles home. She parked her new car down the street under some trees. She threw on her robe and kicked off her shoes. She turned on the TV and opened another bag of chips just before Charles pushed through the door.

"Oh, so Mr. Backslider decided to come home." Flo didn't say that, but that's what she thought. She sucked her teeth while pulling her robe over her gut. Her foot was flung over the set so she could get better reception. Charles noticed the hair on her knees.

Charles walked past her. He stopped in the kitchen. He opened the fridge to get a cold beer, drinking the whole thing while leaning his face on the ice tray.

In the freezing cold, Charles's whole body still blazed. He

couldn't believe Flo had taken their money. He stayed in the kitchen, waiting in the dark, drinking some Johnnie Walker straight from the bottle.

Flo couldn't take the cold silence anymore. "You paying the light bill this month," she yelled to Charles.

"You the one got every damn light on in here. Got radios going in rooms you're not even in." Charles walked through the apartment, flicking switches and yanking the cords from the wall until all that was left was the cool, icy blue of the TV. Charles yanked the set right from the wall. "You got a lot of nerve talking to me about bills."

Flo knew Charles might know something. But she wasn't sure what. All she knew was that she had just seen Charles with Trudy and she was steaming inside just like him.

He snatched off his shoes and yanked down his pants and tore into the bed with his boxers.

Flo never said another word. She was too plain disgusted. She brushed her teeth and fell into bed. She couldn't shake this flu and was getting more and more tired. She didn't have the strength to fight—besides, what could she say? All she saw was Charles giving Trudy a ride. But her anger still burned. She was frustrated and upset. What was he doing with Trudy? Why did he need to give her a ride? Flo lay under the covers but just couldn't take it. She tore off the sheet and sat up in bed. Finally, she had to speak up.

"I saw you," Flo said, clicking on the bedroom lamp.

Charles said nothing. He rolled to his side. He breathed in and let the air out slowly. He did not want to kill anyone tonight.

"I saw you. I saw her get into your car."

But Charles said nothing. He breathed deeply under the sheet. He was straining not to rip it in half.

Flo stared at his covered-up, muscular body.

Flo shook him. "Hey, I'm talking to you, boy. I know you hear me, Charles. Stop trying to pretend you're asleep."

Charles sat up, yanking the sheet to his waist. "You got a lot of fucking nerve," Charles told Flo, rolling the tight sheet over his head.

But Flo grabbed the sheet and yanked it back down. "I saw you with Trudy. I know it was her."

"Oh, you're spying on me now? Ain't this a trip. You steal all my money and now you're spying on me too. Don't say shit to me, you damn thief!"

Charles boldly sat up. He stared at her hard. He wanted to see what Flo had to say.

Flo looked down. She fixed one of her loose rollers. "Answer me first," she said quietly, looking down.

"What? What the hell do you want to know? I saw the girl. Her car broke. I took the chick home. Shit, I'm here with yo' ass. Get the fuck off my back."

Flo's scowling face looked plain without makeup. Her globe head was lumpy with curlers. She really felt bad; she felt nauseous and sick.

"Now answer me something!" Charles yelled in her face. "What the fuck did you do with my cash?"

Damn! He found out. She was in dangerous water. She didn't know what else to say, so she clicked off the light, but Charles clicked it right back on.

"Hey, I'm talking to you, huh!" Charles violently shook her. "God damn it, Flo, that was our down-payment money. What the hell did you do with it, huh?"

"So the bitch fuckin' told you. I knew that she would." Flo was so sick with anger, she almost threw up.

"Where's the money, Flo, huh? What'd you do with my cash?" Charles started tearing up the room, pulling out drawers. He knocked over a lamp and it crashed to the floor. "What did you do with it, huh?"

"Your money?" Flo screamed. "Some of that was mine!"

"Where's the money, Flo, huh?" Charles knocked over a cabinet. It crashed like a 6.9 earthquake.

Flo couldn't stand watching the room turn into a disaster.

"I spent it!" Flo yelled.

"What? Spent it on what?"

"You wouldn't have done anything but gamble it away!"

"What did you spend all my money on, huh?" Charles face was twisted with rage.

"You would have spent it too!" she said defensively. "Besides, some of it was mine!"

"You know most of that cash came straight from my check!" Charles grabbed her shoulders. He started shaking Flo hard.

It was late. The man upstairs banged his broom against the floor. "Would you country fools shut the fuck up!"

"What did you spend it on, huh?"

"A car!" Flo yelled back, trying to square up her shoulders. "I went out and bought a new car!" Flo said it loud, like she was proud of the fact, but inside, her body felt like a rag.

Charles wanted to bash his fist into her face. Instead he slammed his fist into the wall over the bed. The plaster broke all the way down to the wood, and huge chunks fell over their pillows.

"Well, where is it, huh? If you're so righteous, then why are you hiding it, huh?"

Flo stared at the ceiling and said low, "It's not hidden. It's parked in front."

"No, it isn't. I didn't see shit when I pulled in. You knew you were wrong. You knew this was foul. Because if you were right you would have parked the thing right in the driveway!"

Flo stared down at the floor.

Charles wondered what he'd ever seen in Flo in the first place. Then he remembered. It was her hair. Thick, black, gorgeous hair that was so bold and bouncy. Bobbing like it had a mind of its own. Just like Flo. It was that wild hair he noticed first when she'd stepped off the bus that one morning. He couldn't even see her face, just that springy mop covering her eyes as she threw her purse over her shoulder.

When she finally did look his way she had the wildest flashing smile set in the smoothest black skin he'd ever seen. Charles had pretended to be examining some letters, waiting for her to get closer.

"Good morning," she'd told him as she walked down the street.

"Good morning," he'd said back, watching her open her gate.

"Girl, you got a million-dollar smile," he'd told her.

Charles remembered when Flo curled her hair to see him. Big

shiny black curls with the sweet smell of Murray's or the slight hint of coconut oil.

Charles loved it when Flo got her hair done. Smiling all pretty, looking sexy and proud. Back then, it was all for him.

That was a long time ago, Charles thought to himself. And although she'd stuck with him after he'd had the affair, after he'd called her and begged her to please take him back, looking at her now in this awful, messed-up room, he could not for the life of him think of why he wanted her now. She had gotten a lot fatter since he'd moved in with her too, with them pies and cakes she made all the time. But he never imagined she'd take their money. He never thought she'd go that low.

Charles looked over at Flo's thickening waist. And that hair. Always rolled up. Always pulled tight. He rarely saw it out of them curlers no more. Charles glanced at Flo's hairnetted skull. She looked like an astronaut from hell. Only time he thought it really looked nice was when she stepped out the door to go to work.

Saving it for them white boys at her job, Charles thought. *Never lets me touch it.* Even making love she fussed about it all the time.

"Don't touch it so rough."

"Don't mess with my rollers."

"Hurry up, or you'll sweat out my 'do."

Every morning when he woke, Flo was lying next to him in those old dried-up curlers. By the time he got home, she had already changed from her pretty work clothes and her whole head was rolled, wearing some old, sloppy sweats.

Charles smashed an old empty beer can against the headboard and tossed it right on the floor. Flo got up and went into the bathroom. He could hear her softly crying. That made Charles sick to no end. He tore off his boxers, stretching naked over the mattress, staring at the hairbrush on the nightstand. The dense smell of hair drenched in coconut oil completely filled the whole room.

Flo stayed in the bathroom for a real long time. When she came out she quickly slipped into bed.

Charles never looked Flo's way. He couldn't believe she'd spent their money. Taking that money killed his dream of having a house. It eliminated his cushion, the breathing room he thought he had.

Having that money gave him some slack. He held it in but almost cried. What about Tony? What if he demanded his cash? His teeth gnawed the inside wall of his hand. What really ate him up was that Flo had gotten it first. This burned his skin to no end. Charles swiped the hairbrush down to the floor. He lay in the dark, watching Flo's heavy stomach slowly rise up and fall down.

Flo wore an orange lacy teddy; the panties had no crotch, and her large breasts tugged at the fabric. She hoped Charles's seeing the teddy would distract him a bit. She had held out, but now she really wanted to make up. If they made love, maybe they might be able to work something out. So even though the straps cut her arm and the seams felt too tight, Flo laid quiet, taking small mini breaths, dangling one leg daringly over the edge, hoping Charles would roll over and notice.

But Flo didn't know the depth of Charles's rage. She didn't realize how deep in debt Charles was and how much trouble that debt put him in.

Charles lay in bed blazing. He bit his whole fist. He felt like he was boxed in a narrowing cage. He decided to give her a taste of her own medicine. He wanted her to crave it, make her starve for his body and then lie there and not give her nothing. The same way she had done him. He saw her through the small space along the bathroom door. He saw her lotion her body and douse it with fragrance and put a silk scarf over her hair. But Charles never budged; he ignored her completely and kept his eyes glued to the cracked, peeling ceiling, and eventually he drifted off to sleep.

Flo watched Charles sleep near the edge of the bed. She'd never seen Charles this angry before. She rolled all the way to her side and slept in a tight little ball.

In the morning, Charles looked at Flo with disgust. There was only one thing stuck in Charles's mind. Trudy's breasts, the arch of Trudy's dark nipples. Charles's body began to thicken, and his muscles grew taut. The warm fluid between his legs began to stiffen. Finally he just couldn't take any more. He seized Flo and rolled on top of her body. He parted her legs with one knee between her thighs. He drove into her body again and again, until her frame hung way off the bed.

"You want some of this, don'tcha?" Charles plunged more deeply. Her rollers wildly shook to and fro. As he rammed the bed, some of Flo's curlers fell to the floor.

"You like it, don't you?" Charles said, squeezing her breasts. Flo wanted to yelp but she bit her own tongue. She didn't want to complain; she didn't want to stop him. All she felt was guilt over taking their money. If she gave him some maybe he'd stop being so awful.

But Charles was crazy. His lust was inflamed. Finally Flo had to complain.

"Slow it down, baby. Don't be so rough."

But Charles wouldn't go slow. He got even rougher. His hot body surged, he was full throttle now. With each wild stroke he was paying Flo back. A heart-attack madness ran through his veins. He was dizzy with rage and boiling on top. He was struggling against the desire to grab at her throat and choke the life out of her frame. The money, he thought. All his money was gone. He wanted to strike her, to gouge out her eyes. The thought of having no money made him want to break down. But the anger dried the wet from his eyes.

There was a deep pleasure he got from being so completely vile. Like a drunk beating his kid when he got smashed. And just when he thought he couldn't take any more, just when he believed he could kill with his fury, he came with a force that knocked the wind from his lungs. He came with an evilness he'd never felt before. And like a broken racehorse before that final shot, Charles slumped to a stony, dead heap across Flo's chest.

There were only two things on his lunatic mind. Two crystal thoughts that stayed lodged in his body. All he wanted to do was get Trudy like this and get his hands on a whole bunch of money.

20

Trudy and Tony

Trudy was about to sneak out when the handle turned and Tony pushed his way in.

"Lord have mercy! It's hotter than a whore's pussy after midnight out there. I swear I barely got out of Miss Williams's place alive. Good God almighty!" Tony dabbed his bald head. "Woman had on one of them long see-through numbers . . . whatchu call them things? Negga what's—neg ga leys thangs. What's that shit called, again?"

"Negligee," Trudy said without looking up.

Along with singing, Tony hired her to do light work in the bar's office. He liked having something pretty around while he worked. Besides the club, Tony had a side business lending money.

"Yeah, one of them nice neg-la-shays. Mercy. All that black meat, all spicy and hot. Woman had no drawers to save her natural-born life." Tony dabbed a handkerchief around his damp brow. "I know it was there, just as sweet-smelling and ready." He dabbed his head again and took a big gulp of water, smashing the white paper cup in his hand. "I couldn't see it, but I know'd it was there. I could barely hold the paper for her to sign." Tony's large body sat heavily on the couch. "I swear I'm getting too old for this job."

Tony stared at Trudy and lowered his voice. "The owner of the liquor store across the street has been sobbing all morning.

Seems like somebody broke in his building last night. Stole that poor man's place blind."

Tony looked at Trudy. His eyes locked on her face.

Why the hell was Tony looking at her like that, Trudy thought. She didn't have a thing to do with that liquor store robbery. But Trudy still felt guilty. She avoided Tony's eyes. She felt the creeping dead weight of those heavy-lidded eyes. Guilt lived inside Trudy's veins every day. Guilt loomed even when she hadn't done the crime. She still felt responsible. She felt like everyone knew it was her. It was one of the symptoms of stealing so long. You lived life feeling just like a suspect.

Suddenly a police officer pushed into Tony's small office.

"Ma'am?" the officer said. "I need to ask you some questions."

Trudy was worried. Why did they want to talk to her?

"Were you here yesterday morning?" the police officer asked.

"Yeah, she was here," Tony chimed in.

The officer glared at Tony and looked back at her. "Did you see anything? Any suspicious-looking people?"

Trudy was trying not to look suspicious herself. "No," she said, looking in the officer's eyes.

He was a thick, blond-haired man in a tight uniform. The black shirt and pants were so snug around his body, the uniform looked painted on his skin. In L.A., the cops don't play. You can wave, say hello, but you won't get no answer. They all have the flat, expressionless face of a statue.

"I didn't see a thing." Trudy told the officer. "I only work here part time."

The officer scribbled something down without looking at Trudy. He took out a business card from his breast pocket and, using his pointer finger he pushed it across Trudy's desk. "Call me," he said, "if you remember anything at all." He stared at her awhile before clicking in his pen.

The officer's sunglasses slipped and she could see his blue eyes.

Trudy breathed deeply and took a sip of water. She fanned herself with some papers when the cop left.

"What's wrong with you, huh? You know something about that robbery?" Tony opened his sagging briefcase, took out a handful of papers, picked up the phone and started dialing. Trudy stayed at her desk and pretended to be busy, keeping her back toward Tony's face.

"Any calls? How's your mama? Everybody all right? Lord, Mr. Hall don't know what he got, um! If I had a mind—Hello, Miss Wesley. Yes, I was there this morning. . . . What did Sharon say 'bout the house?"

Tony went into his routine of mindless chitchat, but it always ended with the same exact line: "So when can I pick up my money?"

Tony let a few locals drink a little bit on credit but he always came by to get paid.

Trudy listened to him talking to one of his old drinking friends.

"I tol' you not to marry that woman, Eugene. You'd only seen her in the club lighting, man. Don't never marry no woman you ain't seen in the sun. I tol' you that woman was old."

"Trudy," he hollered out, "I'm leaving now. I got to get over to Miss Jenkins's place today. Tell yo' mama I said hello."

"Tell her yourself," Trudy said, not looking up.

Tony walked back into the office and leaned against her desk. He was struggling to get his short, beefy arm into his way-too-small jacket.

"Girl, why you got to be so ugly this morning? Your mama's good people. Got a nasty tongue sometimes, but that's 'cause she got a huge chip on her shoulder."

"Why? What did the world do to her?" Trudy slammed a file drawer hard with her hip.

"It's Hall. He's been selling her wolf tickets for years. Promising her he'd leave his wife and he ain't never gonna do shit. Poor woman wasted her life on that fool."

"Poor woman! Tony, please," Trudy said. "Don't go sugarcoating it for me."

Tony looked at Trudy like she was a kid. The kind with hot-fire emotion but didn't know jack.

"Now, listen here, girl. I was there too. Everyone thinks your mama stole Mr. Hall. But your mama was Mr. Hall's woman first. Way back when Hall only worked as a clerk. Hall hovered over your mother when your daddy passed that year. Brought her candy and magazines and big jugs of ice cream and all the scotch whiskey she could drink. You weren't but two when y'all lived over in Watts. Stayed in a tiny unit over his store, and even though your apartment was small, it was stuffed full of everything he stocked."

Trudy bit a hangnail off her thumb. She knew this already. She sat quiet and bored. Tony wasn't saying nothing new.

"But Hall's business started to boom. He opened up another liquor store over off Vernon and that big one he got over off King. Your mother's sharp mind helped Hall buy them stores. But lots of things change when folks start tasting money. As Hall became rich, he saw your mama less and less and for three weeks he didn't come over at all."

"How do you know that?" Trudy asked him point-blank.

"Back then, me and Hall was good friends." Tony laughed. "Man, that was one crazy cat. Glory me! We used to play Spades in the yard every Monday. That nigga talked more shit!" Tony dabbed his forehead with his hanky. A cloud passed over his face. "But money changed Hall. He didn't have time for his friends. Naw, Hall's eyes only had dollar signs in 'em. That's when he started on this church girl cross-town. Joan pitched a fit when she found out about that gal. She wasn't very pretty. Not no looker like your mother and was definitely not as good in the sack, 'cause he told me."

Trudy pushed the rusted-out file cabinet hard. This talk about her mother made her sick.

"But that church girl had something that Hall really wanted. Her daddy owned that big, giant furniture store, and that girl was his last living kin. All hell broke loose that hot summer, girl. You remember the Rodney King beating and them riots in '92? Well, a year before that, a Korean woman blasted a girl in her store. Shot that black chile in the back over a bottle of juice. When that gung-ho bitch only got probation for the crime, a lot of places got fire-bombed and burned. That church girl's father got killed defending his store. Hall married the girl and never did tell your mother. Six months passed before she found out. Yo' mama was a wildcat. Fit to be tied. Joan ripped up the clothes she kept for him in a drawer, called him all kinds of bastards and took you and moved. Hall shoulda come clean. Told Joan the truth. But Hall wanted his cake and eat it too."

"Well, why didn't she leave him?" Trudy asked, interested now. "He sounds like an asshole to me."

"Oh, she tried. One time she even stayed with me." Tony smiled at himself. He was almost embarrassed. He'd never told anyone he'd been with Joan. He always felt Joan was out of his class. He didn't want any of his friends to clown him. "But your mother was hooked. Couldn't pry herself loose. But there was something else too. Downright pitiful, if you ask me. See, Joan used to like messing with Hall's wife. She knew people at General Electric and had them cut off the woman's lights or disconnect her water. Bullshit stuff like calling her and hanging up late at night. She used to laugh this insane laugh and tell me about it. She told me it felt like she was stealing something valuable from that woman, but I could see underneath. Saw the lines in her face grow. I could see underneath she was dying."

"And after six years she's still on the creep," Trudy said.

"And it eats at your mother a little bit each day. I tell you, she ain't the same woman I knew. Your mama used to be the sunniest thing walking. Men used to line up just to see her. She was fine and carried herself proud. Any man would have been happy to have her."

Tony's wide smile slowly turned into a frown. "Ol' girl got a serious chip now."

Tony was right. Bitterness had turned Joan's injured heart to stone. She'd been longing for Hall for over seventeen years. The last six aged her the most. When he married that church girl, Joan felt stabbed in the gut. But even in anger, Joan stayed determined. She'd been waiting so long, so when Hall promised her he'd leave his wife as soon as Trudy was grown, Joan couldn't wait to get Trudy out.

"And after all this waiting, she's got a new worry now. She's afraid Mr. Hall's eyes will stray."

"Shoot, she doesn't look too worried to me. Besides, Mr. Hall gives her everything she wants. You'd think she'd be happy, not some mean, stuck-up rake."

Tony closed his eyes. Shook his head at the ground. "Junk food, whiskey, a blouse or a dress, a house down the street from a bar! Hall gave her everything but dignity and respect. He cheapened your mother, if you ask me." Tony gathered his papers and walked toward the door. "There were plenty of men who'd have given her that and a hell of a lot more." Tony looked out the window a real long time. "Your mama sold herself off too cheap."

"She's mean," Trudy said. "That's all I know."

"She ain't mean. She just mad at herself. You was just the only one there."

Well, I'm getting out, Trudy said to herself. She glared at the ripped couch and the old crates that served as his shelves. "I'm glad I'm not like her. I'm totally different."

Tony let his eyes roam over her dress. "Y'all act the same, if you ask me."

Trudy couldn't see any similarity at all. She didn't notice they both sashayed when they walked. Strutting down the street like a loud, blaring siren. Looking fearless, like they wore a bulletproof vest, parting the street like a sharp fine-tooth comb.

She was definitely on the same path as her mama, unless she did something different.

Trudy fingered the police officer's card in her hand and then ripped it up, tossing it in the trash.

21

Trudy and Vernita

Trudy watched Tony walk down the street with slumped shoulders. A homeless man peed against the graffiti-filled wall. Tony stepped right in the wet.

Trudy picked up the phone and dialed Vernita.

"I thought I could leave early, but Tony busted me this time."

"Girl, yo' ass be taking some chances. You know I talked to Earl when I picked up my car. He told me his brother Junior got shot the other day."

"Junior! That quiet old man? He never bothered a soul."

"Earl said Junior was closing and a man driving a big black SUV wheeled up and blasted Junior's face."

"Damn. Junior was cool. That's exactly why I'm leaving the state."

"I know. It's the fucking Wild West, chile. These fools out here don't play," Vernita said.

"That's why we got to gank them fools first. Now listen. I got a hundred. I'll bring another over later. Keep picking Lil Steve's brain and planting them seeds. I want to know everything he's thinking."

"Girl, don't sweat it. I'm on the job." Vernita never had so much fun making money. She thought Trudy was crazy for paying her to be with Lil Steve. She'd have fucked that fine brotha for free. "Guess what that boy told me the other day about Ray Ray?"

Suddenly the second line rang. "Hold on," Trudy told Vernita. "Dee's Parlor, I mean, Tony's," Trudy said, answering the phone.

"Hello, songbird. How did you sleep last night?"

Trudy recognized Jimmy's deep, resonant voice.

"I just wanted to know one thing," Jimmy said and stopped.

Trudy's heart skipped a beat. Does he know something already? "What?" Trudy said, holding her breath.

"Is the sun shining on your street like it's shining on mine?"

Trudy smiled while holding her mouth close to the phone. "It looks real good from down here," she said.

"What time do you get off, baby?"

"My friend's supposed to come pick me up but I have a couple more things to finish first."

"Tell your friend you have a ride. I'll be there at three-fifteen."

He hung up the phone before Trudy could protest. She went back to the first line.

"Dang, you have people on hold a long time," Vernita said when Trudy clicked back. "Who were you talking to so long?"

"This guy I met at the club."

"The club? Girl, I thought you learned your lesson last time."

In the ten months Trudy had been on her own she'd already had a nice share of guys.

"This one is different. He's a tad on the thuggish side but he's hellified rich. You'd be jealous as hell if you saw him," Trudy said.

"He ain't the brother from the other night, is he?"

"You saw him? I thought you'd left."

"I was half out the door when he asked you to dance. Girl, Pearl pulled my coat about that crazy-ass brother. I know you're not trying to tangle with no drug-dealin' fool! Don't act crazy. Homeboy's in a whole 'nother league, hear? Yo' ass is bound to get played."

"Not unless I play him first," Trudy said back.

But Vernita was worried. She sucked against her teeth. "Girlfriend, stop trippin'! You're bad at judging men. 'Member when Baxter was after yo' ass?"

"Yeah." Trudy laughed at the memory. "He gave me those thigh-high suede boots."

"They were used!" Vernita reminded her friend. "Probably snatched 'em off some other chick's legs."

"Baxter was cool, just a little eccentric."

"Eccentric? He left a dead cat at your door! I know you didn't forget about that! Listen, girl, I'm telling you, homeboy's no joke." When Trudy didn't respond, Vernita kept talking. "I know you hear me. Look, don't be no fool. You ain't been on your own for that long. You had a couple of silly-ass boys and suddenly you think you're grown."

Although Trudy was living alone and taking care of herself, Vernita thought she was getting too fast. "This here's a full-fledged grown, drug-dealing man! Please tell me he's not in this shit you pulled me in. That boy's a heart attack walking."

Trudy didn't tell her he was part of the bank plan too. "You worry too much. Can we please change the subject?"

"Change the subject? Girl, you about to change your whole life!"

"All right, all right! Don't get so excited. I'm just playing with him, that's all. Teasing him a bit. I'm telling you, he doesn't know shit, Vernita. He doesn't even know that I work at the bank. He'd never suspect it was us."

"Us? I'm about to be out this bitch now!"

"Come on, Vernita. Just listen a minute. We ain't the ones that'll be doing the work. That's Lil Steve's job. He handles the drama. All we do is hit him."

Vernita was quiet. She didn't like this at all. "That's what I was about to tell you before you put me on hold. Lil Steve was the one who turned Ray Ray in."

"What?" Trudy asked, amazed. "Are you telling the truth?"

"He gave him up to avoid going to jail himself. Damn, girl, now you know that shit's cold. I told you these fools are treacherous. Don't think they're not; they just ain't aimed their big guns at you yet," Vernita said. "I'm telling you, I really don't know about this job. This shit's getting a little too deep."

Trudy thought long and hard about what Vernita said. Now

she was really concerned about Ray Ray. But it just made her more determined than ever to pay Lil Steve back.

"Look, don't you want your shop? Own the whole thing outright? Don't you want to kick backstabbing Keesha to the curb?"

"I'd rather kick yo' ass for taking dumb chances."

"Vernita, please don't trip. Our part is safe. Besides, you'll be wearing a disguise."

"I'd rather be alive in my rusty-ass shop than die because my silly-ass friend got too greedy. This man is dangerous, Trudy! Didn't you hear what Pearl said? You gonna fuck around and end up like you did in March."

Trudy knew what Vernita was talking about. Two months ago, Trudy had dated Roger, a boxer. She still couldn't sleep on one side.

"I'll be safe," Trudy told her. "My friend at the LAPD can have him checked out. You just worry about Lil Steve."

Trudy remembered what the cop told her when she had him look up Roger.

"Listen," the cop had said, studying Trudy's young face. "If you have to come down and run a make on a brother, you must be messing around with the wrong one."

22

Trudy and Jimmy

Jimmy slammed on his brakes and hung his head out the car. "Get the fuck out the street, you broke muthafucka!"

A wino had stumbled out into oncoming traffic. He did a knee dance near the edge of the curb and just laughed.

"I can't stand them fools!" Jimmy said loudly at the man. "Raggedy-ass bums make me sick!" His twenty-inch rims lapped against the low curb. The bum had to leap to avoid the SUV's tires and fell feet first in the street. Grimacing, the bum cursed them as they drove by. Trudy lowered her eyes and studied her hands.

Jimmy turned off Crenshaw traveling west from Leimert Park and started the slow climb up the hills. Trudy watched as they rolled along through the Dons. Don Felipe. Don Miguel. This was all residential. Stucco homes with pools and well-cared-for lawns. Baldwin Hills was the Beverly Hills of black Los Angeles and was immaculately groomed compared to where she lived.

They pulled in front of a Spanish-style home with a beautifully tiled roof and stained glass windows.

Jimmy jumped out and opened her door.

"Who lives here?" she asked.

"I do. Come on in." Jimmy opened the heavily locked door and entered a six-digit security code on a small panel right inside the door. As soon as Trudy stepped in, dogs were barking like crazy. There was a loud, angry chorus of harsh, ferocious growls and claws scratching over wood doors. There was a banging sound, as a dog broke loose from the room. He viciously raced over to where Trudy stood.

"Prince, Prince, stop!" Jimmy yelled at the dog.

Prince was a large Rottweiler with a heavy, wet jaw. The dog paid Jimmy no mind at all. It bolted past him and went straight for Trudy's legs. It jumped at her and then shoved its snout inside her crotch, growling while showing fanged teeth. Trudy screamed wildly and dropped her purse to the floor.

"Prince! Got damn it, Prince, stop!" Jimmy cussed at the dog, socking its face with his fist. But the dog was too forceful. He darted back and nuzzled right inside Trudy's thighs. Trudy screamed again, frozen in her tracks.

"Prince!" Jimmy hollered again, grabbing the dog by its black studded collar. He took a golf club out of the bag near the front door and beat the dog down. Beat it in the legs, the rump and the head. Beat it so bad it lay down on its back, whimpering with its hind legs pointing up toward the ceiling. Jimmy grabbed the dog's collar, dragging him across the smooth floor, shoving him in a room and slamming the door.

"Shit!" he said, wiping dog hairs from his suit. There was a small trail of blood on the marble. "I told Lemont not to leave the animals in the house. Sorry about that, baby. You going to be all right?" Jimmy gently placed both hands on her shoulders. "I didn't mean to scare you like that."

Trudy felt that horrible old feeling of dread. Like someone was playing the black notes of a song. Her breathing became labored. She started to wheeze. She cupped her hand over her mouth and breathed her carbon dioxide back in. She hadn't told anyone about these panic attacks. Trudy's whole body felt woozy.

"What's wrong?" Jimmy asked, seeing her horrified face. "Come on, girl. You'll feel better after you have something to eat."

Jimmy led her to a dining table elaborately set with fine china and long-stemmed glasses. In the center was a beautiful bouquet of fresh flowers.

"Those are for you, songbird." Jimmy held her hand and Trudy managed a weak smile. She took a large gulp of her wine and fanned her face with her hand.

Breathe, she told herself. *Breathe deep and don't panic.*

"Look, baby, don't trip. Them dogs ain't nothing but protection. I been hating on dogs since I was seven."

Jimmy buttered his bread and took a huge bite. "I used to walk to the store for my mama to get eggs and junk. Used to be a German shepherd stayed locked inside a chain-link fence next to Grady's store. Me and Cabbage would toss Coke bottles over the fence and run. Man, that was fun. When them bottles would crash, that dog went mad. Dog lost his mind trying to get back at us. We messed with that hound every day. Growling and barking, tearing up the yard. Man, we both laughed till we cried." Jimmy wiped tears of laughter from the corner of his eyes.

"But one day Grady left that gate open." Jimmy stopped laughing and leaned up in his chair. "We couldn't tell 'cause it was one of them kind of gates that opened off to the side. When me and Cabbage threw the bottle that day, all we saw was molars and fur. Cabbage took off, but the dog got my jacket." Jimmy took off the cuff link on his left sleeve and rolled it up. He showed a thick, rough row of pale, jagged scars.

"We didn't have no doctor money, so mama dipped a rag in some Dr. Tichnor's and kept it covered, rubbing cocoa butter until the skin grew back."

Jimmy dipped a large shrimp in the horseradish and bit. "Ol' Grady never did find that dog."

Trudy sat quietly. She watched him chew his food. His light brown eyes held her gaze until she looked away. She scanned the huge room. All the furniture was ornate. It looked like a lavish hotel lobby.

"I see your eyes popping behind that wine. You think I'm some kind of baller, huh?" Jimmy laughed.

Trudy looked at Jimmy. She was beginning to feel okay. "Stock market must be good, or do you just have nice friends?"

Jimmy ignored her and poured more wine in her glass. His

eyes went stony. He stared out the window. "You ask too many damn questions."

Trudy studied his hard face. He reminded her of her mother. Cold-blooded eyes. A harsh, ice-pick stare. An anger that was always right there. The agonizing silences she endured during dinner. The awful slow chewing of food. Trudy had become expert at judging Joan's moods. How she got out of the car. How fast she washed her hands. If she walked in yelling, "Why isn't there any food on this stove?" Trudy would have holy hell to pay. When her mother got mad there was no bad word she wouldn't use, but her all-time favorite was "slut." If your bed wasn't made, you were an ol' lazy slut. If the dishes weren't done, you were a filthy ol' slut. Anytime Mr. Hall said he couldn't come by, her mother flew into a rage. Trudy looked at Jimmy and smiled again. She was glad he didn't ask about her family.

"Come on," Jimmy said, tossing his napkin on his plate. "Let's go out for a ride."

It was five in the afternoon and Trudy had some packing to do. "I have to get home," Trudy said, standing up.

But Jimmy grabbed her hand like he hadn't heard and strolled back out to his car. He walked strong, like a man sure of where he was going. His head was held high. His feet moved with purpose. He walked like he owned the whole block.

"Do you have to leave now?" he asked, pressing her against the car, leaning her over his hood. "You got anything like this waiting for you at home?" Jimmy stretched her arms back against the hood. She felt vulnerable but could feel Jimmy's muscular body. It was a strange mix of fear and desire.

The only thing Trudy had waiting at home was a big, bulging stack of pink past-due bills and a sink brimming with dishes. But she wasn't any fool. This was a dangerous brother. But something about that was incredibly attractive. Her body fought hard against her good sense. Every vein was yelling, "I want him to touch me. I want his big hands on my skin." His silky shirt revealed hard, chiseled abs, and his biceps stood out like grapefruit. It wasn't like she couldn't. She'd done it before. She'd gone home with

Billy last month after knowing him for as long as one slow song, but Jimmy was different. Jimmy was rich. Rich boys were used to getting what they wanted. She had to make him wait. Make him beg for it first. Trudy could hear Pearl's voice in her head.

"Girl, you got to hold out, make 'em beg for it first. Let 'em sniff some bone before slicing 'em some meat!" Pearl had smacked her own ass for effect.

"You don't fuck no first date unless you a paid trick. Dick needs to be teased or it don't take you serious. You make him wait and a man starts thinking he's special. Thinks you saving it up just for him. Besides, you need to find out who some of these fools are before you lay down with 'em, chile! Men'll tell a whole gang of lies just to get in them panties. Once they drop, watch how fast they clam up," Pearl would say.

"I have to get home," Trudy said, pulling away. "I'll give you a call tomorrow."

But Jimmy was forceful. Even his eyes didn't blink. His hard body had her wedged over the car.

"Don't go yet. Come while I make this quick run. It'll only take a minute, I promise." Jimmy held her arms tight and would not let go. She wanted to say no but he was so damn aggressive. And when he kissed her, all down her throat and almost to her breasts, her body was winning the fight.

Jimmy stopped and pulled back before it got too far. "Let's go," he said, opening her door and letting her into his car.

Jimmy took her down Stocker, past the oil fields off LaBrea. Trudy watched the sad rigs slowly bend toward the ground, like an old field hand picking cotton. They turned and traveled west, until they hit Culver City. They pulled in front of this old-looking tract home. Some of the shingles had come off.

He knocked on the door for a real long time before someone turned on the porch light. A small face peeked out from the window.

A white man who looked like he was in his late fifties slowly opened the door. He stood firmly on the porch and didn't let Jimmy in. Even though the man smiled, he didn't look friendly. He looked like he was trying to explain something important.

But Jimmy kept pressing, kept inching up until the older man called out to someone in the house.

A younger man, about Jimmy's age, appeared at the door. The older man disappeared into the back. The younger man looked like the older man's son. He wore big, baggy shorts and an oversized T-shirt. He wasn't wearing any shoes. Jimmy asked him something and the younger man shook his head. Now Jimmy was the one who smiled but didn't look happy. Jimmy stepped real close to the young man's body. Trudy could see something change in Jimmy. It was barely visible. It was more in his movements. He stood very close and was whispering something serious. The boy's movements changed too. His body seemed to stiffen, like a chill ran down through his bones.

Suddenly the father came out again. His face was as tight as a mason jar.

Without looking at Jimmy the older man opened his wallet. He peeled off some bills. He handed them to Jimmy. Jimmy stared at the bills until the man peeled off a few more. Jimmy smiled and put the money in his pocket. He patted the young boy on his back, turned around and came toward the car.

Trudy watched the man and son look toward her.

Jimmy jumped in and angrily backed out the car. He made a sharp U-turn, and the giant SUV felt like it might tip over.

Trudy sat silently in the passenger side. She felt stupid coming with him now. But there was nothing she could do.

Jimmy ran through a stop sign and drove dangerously close to the parked cars. He looked determined and never once looked at her. "I have to make one other stop."

Trudy shrank back as his tires dared another red light.

"Slow down, baby. What's the big rush?"

Jimmy sat staring straight ahead.

Trudy was getting more and more nervous. He had already run two reds and was edging someone else off the road. A yellow truck honked angrily at them as they passed.

Jimmy pulled up next to the man. He rolled down his window and screamed from the car, "You want some of this, you no-driving punk?" The truck driver quickly sped away.

Jimmy drove to a residential area in Beverly Hills. Trudy looked out the window. "Ah shit," she said to herself. It was the house of the tan-suit man she'd followed home from the bank. Jimmy leaned out and rang the buzzer until the metal gate slowly opened. Trudy scooted way down in the passenger seat. She didn't want the tan-suit man to see her face. She was glad when Jimmy didn't invite her in.

"I'll be right back," Jimmy said, closing the door hard.

But he wasn't. Jimmy was gone a long time.

Trudy sat in an orangey haze for almost an hour. And when the sun ducked behind a house and the street immediately turned gray, she yawned, putting her palm across her mouth. She was bored looking at the same manicured front yards and clicked opened the glove compartment and began rummaging inside. She saw a crumpled map and a pair of black gloves. She saw an envelope from the DMV. She pulled it out. It was the registration for the car. Trudy pulled the paper all the way out. The name on the outside of the envelope wasn't Jimmy's. The car was registered to somebody named Zeno. Then she saw a little black notebook. Trudy flipped it open. It was a list of deposit amounts and dates. She saw a flowered organizer shoved way in back. The organizer looked girly, like it belonged to a woman. Trudy pulled it out and unzipped both sides. Inside was a large metal gun. Trudy heard a door close and looked quickly up. Jimmy and the tan-suit man were closing the trunk of a Lexus. They lifted a tire and put something inside. Now Jimmy was coming. The tan-suit man came too.

Oh my God! Trudy thought. *He'll recognize me.* She zipped the flowered case but the zipper got stuck. She tugged at the zipper but it wouldn't go any more. She saw the tan-suit man at Jimmy's side. They both were almost at the black SUV's door. Finally the zipper broke through the snag and rolled around the case. Trudy shoved the case inside the glove box and shut the small door. She pulled on the seat latch until she lay completely flat. She peeked and saw Jimmy two steps from the car. Trudy closed both her lids just before he opened the door, pulling her sweater up close to her face.

"What, you asleep?" Jimmy asked, shaking her a little too hard.

Trudy pretended to yawn and opened her eyes. Jimmy placed a small satchel behind his front seat.

"Let's roll." Jimmy wiped his nose a few times. He kept sniffing and talked fast but was driving even faster. He drove over toward Dee's Parlor, and along the way they passed Vernita's shop. Trudy thought about asking him to drop her off at Vernita's. But it was late. It was almost ten now and although Vernita was known to do a few heads after hours, nobody would be in her shop now. Trudy could see the metal row of hair dryers gleaming through the window like plastic jack-o'-lanterns.

"Girl, I feel like a million bucks next to you." Jimmy leaned over and rubbed his hand on her thigh. "So where do you stay?" Jimmy asked.

"I'm right down here. Turn left when you get to the end of this block." Trudy showed Jimmy where she really lived. She knew he'd find out if she didn't.

He pulled up in front, unlocked her latch and walked her to her front porch. It was nothing like Baxter, her in-between stash. Trudy saw him when the nights got too lonely. Baxter drove his daddy's old beat-up Voyager. Its hubcaps were just as pitted as Baxter's skin. When he dropped her off he'd lean across her lap and flip the latch for her to leave, stopped right in the middle of the street. He'd be gone before she stepped on the curb.

Jimmy grabbed her waist and pulled her to him. He kissed her like he couldn't get enough. On her mouth, on her cheek, sucking her lips.

Trudy was trapped in a mixture of pleasure and fear, panting like she couldn't catch her breath.

"So when can I see you again?" Jimmy asked. He had one foot on the step and his hand on the knob, like he was waiting for her to ask him in. But suddenly he stepped back and opened his wallet. He peeled off three bills and gently tucked them in her bra.

"What's that for?" Trudy asked, kissing him back. It was strange, but he flared up a daring kind of passion. Her good sense told her to put bars on the door but her body begged him to come in.

"I'm just paying you back," Jimmy said, stroking her braids, "for showing me a real good time." Jimmy kissed her slowly, rolling his tongue over hers.

Trudy cracked her door, easing it open slowly. She wanted him to come in. As her hands rubbed the muscles in his back, a moan escaped from his lungs. But Jimmy pulled away and turned toward his car. The next thing she knew he was back at his fender. "Girl, you going to have a hard time getting rid of me."

He waited until she was all the way in the house and Trudy flashed her porch lights like they were already tight.

When she got in, Trudy pulled the money from her bra. There were three fresh hundred-dollar bills.

"Well, I'll say," she said out loud to herself. This was the first time a man had given Trudy money. Her mother could always pull change from Mr. Hall. She worked Hall like a damn ATM machine. She'd sit in his lap, whisper in his ear with her tongue. Begging for small things she wanted.

Suddenly she heard a sharp rap at her door. She tiptoed to see. Her breath became labored. Was this Jimmy again? Did Jimmy suspect her already? She edged toward the peephole and stared through the slot. It was the landlord. He looked like he was about to use his key.

"Yes?" Trudy said. "What do you want?"

"Your rent's three weeks late! I need to get paid." The man stroked his beard. His hands were in his pockets. "Unless you want to make other arrangements."

Trudy didn't have her rent but she opened the door. She offered one of the hundreds to the man. "Will this hold you until next Friday?" she asked.

Today was Monday; that gave her less than five days.

The man's eyes rolled up and down Trudy's body. He loved his new tenant. He watched her every day from his porch. She was better than anything he saw on TV.

"Sure, that'll hold me. Uh-huh, Friday'll be fine." The man took a long time leaving her door.

Friday is fine, Trudy said to herself. She planned to be long gone by then.

Trudy unfolded one of the hundreds, smoothing it all out. She took out some scissors and a stack of newspapers. She held down the bill and traced around the edge, then began cutting up newspaper to the same size and shape.

She noticed the red light flickering on her machine and pushed Play.

"Trudy, it's Vernita. Me and Lil Steve's straight. Hit a sista back, you ol' stayin'-out-late hootch." Click.

"Hey, bootylicious! I got your number from Tony. Call me if you want some good dick." Laughter, click.

"Hi, Trudy. This is Charles. I've been thinking about what you said. Call me when you get this message." Click.

Trudy picked up the phone and dialed Charles's number.

"Hey, Trudy," Charles said. His voice sounded nervous and low. "I was wondering if we could get together and . . . ah . . . ah, talk?" His eyes darted around the room for Flo. He could see her reflection in the large bedroom mirror. Flo was rolling her hair.

"We have to meet tomorrow," Trudy said quickly. She looked at the newspapers covering her floor. "Why don't I come over there?"

"Here?" Charles hadn't planned on Trudy coming to his house. He lowered his voice to make sure Flo couldn't hear him.

"You want to meet *here*?" Charles put his hand around the mouth of the phone.

"I wish you could come here but my place is being sprayed." Trudy's floor was littered with newspaper shreds. "I'm going to be gone for three days." Trudy used her slow, husky voice while she lied. "I don't know, baby. Maybe it's me. But I felt something deep that night when we talked. It's crazy but I've been thinking about you all day." She could almost feel Charles swell through the phone.

"Yeah, I have been doing a lot of thinking too." Charles watched Flo put the rollers in her hair. The upstairs neighbors sounded like they were pushing furniture across the floor. "Come on over. Tomorrow is fine."

Trudy hung up the phone and took a long, nice, warm bath. While lying on her bed, she smelled a hint of male fragrance. Picking up her blouse from the floor, she brought her sleeve to her face and took a deep, strong whiff. Yeah, that was it, masculine and clean. It was the wonderful scent of Jimmy's cologne. He was right in her shirt, lodged there in her sleeve. Trudy dropped the whole blouse over her face, inhaling the deep male scent while laying in bed. She dreamed of him holding her and gently touching her face. She looked like a child, rubbing the silk against her cheek, and even though she had orange nail polish on, Trudy started sucking her thumb.

Trudy opened all the windows in her apartment. Whenever she got panicky she got hungry. She placed a thick slice of chocolate cake on a napkin and took the piece with her to bed.

She thought about the dog growling low in her crotch and that man and his son looking scared on the porch, and the long time she waited all alone in the car and the long, knowing smile of her landlord. But mostly she thought about wild, hungry sex and touching Jimmy's rock-hard biceps again.

Suddenly Pearl's voice came into her head. "It takes a smart woman to pick a good man. Don't be dumb, honey. Life can be short. You could lose your whole life picking wrong."

But Trudy had her plan and was well on her way. She knew Jimmy and the tan-suit man were connected and that the Lexus was carrying a really big stash. Trudy inhaled the sleeve deeply. She wanted Jimmy. He could be her last taste of L.A. before leaving. So what if he had a slightly dangerous side. Who didn't? He hadn't done anything to her. She was already used to maneuvering herself around men. She'd handle him just like she handled her mother. She wouldn't be here long. She was leaving town soon. He'd be her last juicy swig before Vegas.

I'll be careful, she thought. *Look out for signs. Won't be nobody's fool.*

But see, that was the funniest thing about fools. They were always willing to be fools again.

23

Tony and Lil Steve

Everybody's got needs. Everybody's got wants. Lil Steve's was like hunger. Like going days without food. He could always feel that tight, awful pull under his shirt.

While Trudy was sleeping and dreaming of Jimmy, Lil Steve wandered the street in the dimly lit moon. It was one of those huge orange-hued moons, hanging so low you could touch it, like a flat pancake sopping in butter. He moved easily down the street. He passed the blurred neon of Dee's Parlor. He unrolled a bag and popped open a forty, taking huge swigs as he moved. He was almost there now. He downed the whole can and left it on top of a mailbox. There it was. The house he grew up in. Right down the street from Dee's Parlor. The grass was overgrown and the paint job was trying its best to hang on, but it still looked pretty much the same. The fig trees were there and the jasmine bush, too, and the low hedge he used to jump over.

No matter how late it was, Lil Steve would wind up walking or driving past his old house. Something kept pulling him back down this street, even though he hadn't lived there in years.

This was her house. It belonged to his mother. He remembered the steak, and heaping plates of steamed cabbage, and those warm, sudsy baths in the green tiled bathroom. But that was way back, when they all lived together. Before Daddy left for work and never came back and his mama hadn't learned how to drink.

Something changed in Lil Steve once his daddy was gone. Nothing he could put his finger on, but the change was still there. He didn't care much for school or model airplanes anymore. He just hung from his windowsill night after night, watching folks go into Dee's Parlor. He liked seeing the men in their nice shiny cars. Dudes with good clothes and nice rides and plenty of money, holding fine chicks with Jolly Roger smiles.

See, Lil Steve's mama had stopped smiling a long time ago.

"Heathens," she'd say, sweeping away at her porch. She'd suck her tongue hard at the short-skirted women, slam the screen door if a man tipped his hat. But as time passed, she'd stop and watch those folks too. The next thing Lil Steve knew, she was coming home late and the jasmine that stayed in her hair all the time was replaced with the foul smell of cigarette smoke and her breath held the tense scent of gin.

Lil Steve watched the house for a real long time. He looked in the window. The kitchen light was on and the front room glowed blue, and the TV blared from the barred metal door. Earl never could hear good. Lil Steve saw his foot. It was flung over the couch and his snoring oozed through the windows. He remembered when Earl had put the metal door up. How he covered all the windows with cold steel bars and the pretty yellow curtains that blew in the wind were replaced with the black grid of metal.

Lil Steve kicked a rock and moved farther down the street.

His mother thought Lil Steve had just messed up his life. She couldn't understand why all his good friends were hoodlums and thieves. Why he spent all his time in the streets. But his homies were the only ones he could really count on. The only ones who ever stayed loyal. Ray Ray was never gonna not be his boy. They had stolen lawn mowers and cars and had grown up out there together. He was the only one Lil Steve trusted. Besides, the people in the street were all just like him. Nobody had shit. Nobody was nothing. All of 'em hustlin', just trying to get over.

There was only one time Lil Steve felt like something. Only one person who could make him drop his cold-blooded guard. Make him look at life serious or lay back and laugh mighty. That was the short time that he was with Trudy.

Lil Steve kicked the rock farther down the dark street.

Yeah, Trudy was the best, and Lil Steve had had plenty. She was pretty and smart, with a criminal streak, and she treated him like he was special. But Lil Steve had fucked that up, like most things in his life.

"Besides, she'd have left me," Lil Steve said out loud. "She'da drop-kicked my ass once she saw I was nothing."

He picked up the rock and threw it up at the moon. Lil Steve lied to everyone he knew about Trudy. He called her lazy and fat and ugly and cheap. He couldn't bear thinking of her with anyone else.

"Yeah, she'd have left me. I'm damn sure of that." He opened the white pack and shook out a Salem. "Eventually, most women do."

A crow flew from one of the juniper trees, shaking tiny dead leaves to the ground. The sound startled Lil Steve and he crossed the street toward Dee's. The neon lights shone even when it was closed. He sunk his hands deep inside his front pockets and kicked a glass bottle across the street.

He gave Ray Ray a pound when he got to the door. Tony was inside wiping down the bar. It was well after one in the morning now, and Dee's would be closed in an hour.

"What are you doing in here?" Tony asked.

Lil Steve lifted his pant leg and pulled a fresh hundred from his sock. He handed it to Tony. He'd just gotten that bill from Vernita the night before. Now he and Tony were straight. Even if he couldn't gamble upstairs anymore, maybe Tony would let him come in for a drink.

"All right. Okay. Can I get you a beer?" Tony put the hundred in his pocket.

"Yeah, man," Lil Steve said, putting the beer to his lips. "We want to talk to you about the fight next Friday. You taking the odds for Liston?"

"You know I got the odds on anybody fighting these days." Tony looked at Ray Ray real close. He was standing there shifting nervously back and forth on each foot.

"What's up brotherman? You gotta take a leak or something?"

"Naw, man, but we do need to talk. I wanted to know if you had my check." Ray Ray avoided looking in Tony's eyes. He didn't want him to see how bad he needed the money.

"Your check? Nigga's always wanting to get paid. You lucky I gave you a fuckin' job, boy!" Tony kept rubbing the bar. He didn't look up either. "You'll get paid when I say. Didn't I tell you that already? You about to piss me off out of a job." Tony waited. He wanted to see Ray Ray's reaction. Percy watched Ray Ray close under his dark tinted shades. Ray Ray gritted his teeth but he didn't move, and Tony chuckled out loud to himself.

Lil Steve stepped up this time. "Is it cool to talk, man? Are you busy right now?"

Tony threw down the towel; he filled an iced glass with gin. He smiled at Ray Ray but not Lil Steve. "Yeah, it's cool. Y'all come on upstairs."

Next to the gambling room upstairs was a tiny separate space where a couple of folding chairs kneeled against a wall and a leather chair peeked from a desk. Tony led them up the narrow wood staircase near the back. The stairs moaned and creaked under his weight.

Ray Ray and Lil Steve stood in the room. A hanging bulb swung over the ceiling.

Tony pulled the chain. He looked right into Lil Steve's face. "So how can I help you, Mr. Slick?"

Tony never had liked Lil Steve. He had seen him take one too many card games, and some of the regulars claimed he had a system, but Tony hadn't figured the 411 on that yet. He watched him, though. Watched that ready smile and smooth handshake. Yeah, he was watching him steady. "Why don't you boys sit down, take a load off your feet?"

Tony jammed his body into a ripped leather chair. He put one of his feet on the desk.

"What can I do you for, Ray Ray? You look like a hound that hasn't found the right tree to piss on yet." He cracked up at his own joke and slapped Ray Ray's back. Ray Ray shrugged his hand off his shoulder.

"Listen, Tony, we want a cut on some of the odds on Jones," Lil Steve said.

"Oh yeah?" Tony said, raising one eyebrow. He took out his red pack of Winstons and lit one up.

"And what makes you boys think y'all can get in? That's a man's game, son. You got to have more than a few chips. I'm talking double digits, boy."

Lil Steve stepped forward. Tony didn't mean shit to him.

"Look, Tony, I know you got this card thang, and it's cool. You the man. I'll give you that, but who can we talk to about fronting some long money on this fight you got coming this Friday?"

Lil Steve was smooth. He knew Tony didn't trust him. He had to come correct. That's why he paid Tony up front, as soon as he came in. He had to pretend to give Tony his props. Respect in the hood was all some brothers had. But it was hard for Lil Steve. The hardest thing he ever did in life. See, Lil Steve couldn't stand Tony's pasty black ass, after what had happened that night to his mother.

Lil Steve didn't know the whole story. But the parts he did know were hard. All he knew was his dad had left, and his mama took it bad. She used to wait every day for Lil Steve's father to return. She'd wait until sunset, until the streetlights came on, sitting on her front steps watching Dee's neon lights burn the sidewalk. After Lil Steve went to sleep his mother would watch Dee's doors. She hated the club but didn't mind watching all the people go by, like a child does a carnival ride. Tony would always wave for her to come over, but his mother always shook her head no.

Well, one night Lil Steve's mother was watering the lawn and Tony crossed the street with a drink in his hand. He'd garnished the rim with pineapples and cherries; a green monkey held an umbrella. Tony winked at her and left the tall drink by her screen. His mother waited for Tony to get all the way back inside Dee's before she picked up the drink and took a sip. The liquid was sweet but it burned going down, so she spit the drink out and splashed the rest across the grass. But she saved the small monkey and fingered the umbrella while looking at Dee's from her porch. And one long, lonely night after twisting in the sheets and biting her pillow, she bolted straight up, knocking her water glass to the floor. She smeared on her lipstick and crossed the dark street toward Dee's.

Tony had two old-time hard-drinking friends. One was an out-of-work drunk named Stan and the other was a jackleg mechanic named Earl. They were the kind of men who preyed upon middle-aged women. Women with pensions and old, roomy homes. Places they could live free and eat.

Earl started coming over and forgot how to leave. Like a mouse you couldn't get out your house. His mother acted different whenever Earl was around. She fawned over him. She spoke high-pitched and phony. Laughing too loud when stuff wasn't funny. Wearing extra makeup and heavy perfume. Saying all the time, "Earl, you kill me."

Lil Steve couldn't see what she saw in that fool, but the next thing he knew they were married. Ol' nasty Earl with his mechanic fingernails that were permanently black and that large retarded daughter of his. The first thing Earl did was put bars on the windows. He killed the front lawn with the gasoline jugs and dented car parts he stacked all over their grass.

But the worst was when his mother gave that retarded girl his room. Just gave it away like he was nothing. Made Lil Steve sleep on the couch.

Lil Steve tried his best to make his bad feelings heard. He stared Earl down, flashed him cold, evil eyes, calling Earl "son" even though Earl was thirty-nine years older, anything to make Earl mad. But Earl didn't care. He just laughed all the time. All he wanted to do was play dominoes or checkers or drink with his buddies. Yelling for Lil Steve's mother to bring his greasy ass a beer. Like his sloppy ass ruled the whole house.

In one swig his mama wasn't his anymore. The family life he'd known was a memory now. It had slipped through the cracks like a black row of ants. His mother stayed so busy with cooking or cleaning or drawing the girl a bath. Earl and the large girl both lounged around all day while his mama waited on them hand and foot like a slave.

He couldn't understand why she gave them so much. Why she sacrificed her life for two total strangers, just so she could say she had her *a man*.

One day Lil Steve just asked her point-blank, "Why you let that ignorant nigga pimp you like this?"

His mother stood there with both hands on her hips. "Boy, a woman has needs, a woman has wants. There are some things you can't understand."

Lil Steve couldn't stand watching her act so damn stupid, so he packed up and moved into his car. It was just after high school, so not many of his friends knew. He parked that car all over, traveling all over town, from Crenshaw to Compton, to Venice Beach or Pacoima, staying with anyone who'd feed or let him crash on the couch. He kept a gym membership so he had a place to shower and keep clean or to park for long hours without worrying about all those signs saying NO STOPPING.

But the simmering hate and street life scorched his heart. He started smoking crack to black out his brain. He started hustling full time to make money to eat. When his money ran low he broke up with Trudy and sold her nude video for cash. After that, he only dated honeys with money. He didn't like it but it gave him time to spy on his mother. Make sure she was all right.

But as much as Lil Steve hated Earl, he hated Tony more. He blamed him for what happened last summer to his mother. But Lil Steve didn't even know the worst part of the story. If he did, Tony wouldn't be breathing today.

See, last summer, Lil Steve's mother had gone over to Dee's. She was looking for Earl, who was having trouble finding his way home lately.

Tony blocked her path when she got to the door.

"Hey, girl, how you doin'?" he said, leading her away from the giant black gate that led to the gambling room upstairs. "Come on, have a quick drink on me."

Tony was always trying to get Lil Steve's mother to drink. He always stayed after her about it.

"Come on, sugar, it won't hurt you none. It's real nice and sweet. Guar-an-teed to make all pain go away." Tony poured her a white creamy piña colada, garnishing it with a dead-looking pineapple wedge.

"Now, Earl ain't doing nothing but gamblin' some. A man's got to do what a man's got to do. You don't want to chase him away." Tony knew about Lil Steve's father leaving. He knew where to put in the knife.

As the night wore on, the liquor set in. His mother started to sway back and forth in her chair. The warm room was beginning to spin.

"Come over here, girl. Give ol' Tony a kiss." Tony circled her waist with one of his arms. His other hand rested over her knee.

"Earl don't want me," Lil Steve's mother slurred.

Tony slid another drink in front of her face. "Pretty as you is, that's hard to believe." Tony let his hand roam farther up her thigh. "Shoot, I bet every man in here wants you."

"I know I do." Tony's friend Stan laughed. He was holding his fifth whiskey, sitting on her left side. Lil Steve's mother's breast kept grazing his elbow. He was having himself a grand time. But when he noticed Tony's hand creeping up her thigh, Stan started feeling uneasy.

She smiled and rolled back into Tony's warm arms. "Where's Earl? Did you tell him I'm over here waitin'?" She almost fell from her chair.

"Whoa," Tony said, sliding her back up. "Girl, let's get you some fresh air."

Tony stood up. He started to guide her outside.

But Stan stood up too.

"Man, don't mess with her. Can't you see she's sick?"

"So? What difference does it make?"

Stan's lip began to tremble. He struggled to get the words out. "That's Earl's woman, man." Stan said the words low. He hated to contradict Tony.

"Listen," Tony said, taking a step back toward the bar, "you like that drink?"

"Yeah."

"Whiskey taste okay?"

"Uh-huh."

Tony handed Stan the whole bottle but didn't let go. He leaned right inside Stan's wrecked, plastered face. "Then sit down and shut the fuck up."

Sweat began to drip from Stan's desperate brow. He worriedly glanced at Lil Steve's mother. She was swaying back and forth under Tony's whale arm. She had a tormented look on her clean, pretty face, like a puppy about to be gassed at the pound. But Stan was a drunk. His right knee was shaking. He couldn't pass up a free liquor bottle like this. He grabbed at the bottle but Tony snatched it away. Stan's sorrowful eyes pleaded. His mouth started to water. His shaking hands reached for the bottle again. Tony slammed it down hard on the table.

"You got something else to say?" Tony asked him again.

"Uh-uh," Stan said, sitting back at the bar.

Stan never looked back. He drank heavily that night. He drained the whole bottle and kept his bloodshot eyes glued to his glass.

Out back from Dee's was a cluster of trees. A mountain of cardboard boxes hid an old, beat-up mattress. Tony would some-times sneak lonely drunk women back there. The old mattress reeked of cheap booze. There was a cat laying at the mattress's frayed edge, Tony kicked the cat with his boot.

He laid her down gently. He lifted her dress.

"Wait, Tony. Sto—-op it. What we doing out here?" Lil Steve's mother squirmed but she was too drunk to move.

"Earl may not want you," Tony's gut straddled her body, "but I been wanting you for months."

Lil Steve's mother struggled, but the liquor had made her weak.

Her twisting body got Tony more excited. He stuck his tongue out and licked her whole cheek. She squirmed underneath him, but his giant girth held her firm. Tony's sandpaper tongue slid in-side her mouth. The whole world spun fast. She felt dizzy and sick. All the trees began to fly past her eyes.

Earl found her later, passed out on the mattress. He didn't know what had happened and tried to wake her up, but she wouldn't budge. He poured the rest of his beer in her face.

Lil Steve was on his way home to his mother's house that night. He was only a mile and a half away.

Earl and Lil Steve's mother stumbled out into the street from Dee's bar. Earl was walking way ahead of his mother. She was trying to keep up, teetering on spiky black heels. Her dress was a mess. Her hair was on end. She was arguing with Earl and he was waving her away. She suddenly stopped and got sick on the lawn. Earl got in his car, slamming the door hard, and she got in, slamming hers too.

Now, Tony swore up and down she was driving that night, but Tony was damn good at lying for his friends, especially when they were running from their wives.

Earl and Lil Steve's mother used to fight in the car in front of their house so his big lazy daughter couldn't hear. Fussing until way after midnight sometimes. But this time, Earl revved the car's engine. He backed out the driveway, crushing the hedge on their front lawn, gunning down the street like some nut.

Everybody living heard that hard, deadly crash. The wild screech of brakes. The crashing of glass. The horrible twisting of metal. Folks rushed out their homes in house robes and socks. They came out of Dee's Parlor in droves.

Lil Steve heard the crash too as he skidded around the corner. He jumped from his car, leaving the door open, and ran right up to the wreck. When he got there, the car was completely turned over. The passenger side was horribly smashed. The whole front window was gone. His mother had been tossed straight through the windshield. Glass was all over her arms and her legs. Earl stumbled out and cried on the curb, drooling like some idiot boy.

Tony lit a Winston and sized up the damage. "What a waste of a Regal," he said, blowing out his smoke. "Shoulda bought that bitch when I had the chance."

And that's how Earl got Lil Steve's house. Everything his mama owned was all Earl's now, and there was talk going around that his big retarded daughter wasn't no real daughter at all.

It gnawed on Lil Steve awful to see Earl living in his house. It made all his insides bleed and feel raw. He struggled each day to not bash someone's head. To not pick something up and smash it back down. To just rip up something to shreds. He bit his own fist just to shift off the pain. But nothing made it go away. Sometimes he did shit to just mess with Earl's mind. He'd dump out their trash, spread it over the lawn, or let out the air in all of his tires, steal his rims or take off his gas cap. Sometimes he'd just pee on their grass. But whatever he did, Earl was always unfazed. When Lil Steve dumped the trash, Earl left the trash there. When his hubcaps were gone Earl didn't replace them, and he stuffed an old rag in his tank for a cap.

Lil Steve's only satisfaction came from cheating Tony out of his money. He used every card-playing trick to break Tony's bank. He hated his smug face and nicotine breath. How he dogged out Miss Dee and stole her club and her money. But nothing was worse than how Tony did his mother. Lil Steve knew some, but not the worst parts. If Tony hadn't given his mother her first drink, she'd still be alive. He could barely stand to look at him now.

"See, my man here will have five Gs on Friday," Lil Steve went on coolly. After the bank job this Friday they'd have plenty of money. "We have an anonymous investor." He smiled at that statement. They all did. Tony was listening. He didn't mind where folks got their Ben Franklins, as long as they could be recognized at the bank.

"We just want to place a little wager. Everybody saying Jones is going to take him in the seventh."

"You can have Liston to win or Jones if he goes eight." Tony took a small pad from his coat pocket, scribbled on it and tore the sheet off. "So where's the money at, boy?" Tony asked.

"We don't have access to all the funds now. We'll have it all to you by Friday." Lil Steve glanced at Ray Ray and back at Tony again.

Tony took a long drag and smashed it out in the ashtray. He'd heard so much yin-yang about money, he could hardly keep track. He smiled at the young junior flips and stood up. "Yeah, well, until you get your investor together, don't come in here and waste my damn time." He crumpled the paper and tossed it in the trash.

Big Percy came upstairs and followed Lil Steve down.

"You boys need anything else?" Tony asked, waiting.

"No, man, we cool. We'll be back." Lil Steve nodded.

"What them fools want?" Percy asked Tony when they walked out.

"Just some young-ass bullshit. I don't know, hell. Probably be calling someone's mama tonight to bail their punk asses out."

24

Tony and Flo

Tony walked to the kitchen and spit in the sink. His buddies Earl and Stan were sitting at a card table in the living room. It was afternoon, when the club wasn't open yet; Tony liked to play cards at home with his friends.

"Probably serving that skinny nigga right now," Earl yelled to Tony. Earl loved instigating shit.

He sneaked himself a quick shot of gin while Tony was in the kitchen and drank it down before Tony came back.

"Charles, you know that fool, the one who took Tony's woman. They say he owes Tony a whole bunch of money." Stan snuck himself another quick shot too and poured more in the flask he kept inside his jacket.

Tony stumbled back into the living room, where the other two men sat at a tiny card table.

"I saw Flo," Tony told his old drinking buddies.

Earl and Stan nodded their heads. They'd heard this sob story so many times, but they never complained. They always agreed with everything Tony said. The drinking was free, the ham sandwiches too. Shoot, he could talk as long as he liked.

"I will say this," Tony said, blowing a long trail of smoke out his nose. "That girl knew her way around a kitchen, man. Nothing like these honeys today."

"All young girls want to do is go out all the time, and the small ones can eat just as much as the big ones." Earl eyed the pickle jar Stan was holding.

Stan filled his sandwich with thick slabs of meat, carefully layering the pickles on top.

"All womens is the same." Earl made his voice go real high. "'I'm not really hungry, I just wanna taste.'" He bit down and spoke with a mouth full of food. "Women'll sit there and wolf down a whole four-course meal and have the nerve to start eyeing yo' plate."

"Damn straight," Stan agreed, wiping his bread in the juice. "When the time come to cook it's some nasty-ass meat or some fake mashed potatoes, some canned peas and cheap Gallo wine." Earl laughed so long that he choked.

"None of 'em like Flo." Tony shook his head and studied the rug. "Flo could throw down in the bed and kitchen. Black-eyed peas, collard greens, pork chops or chicken . . ."

". . . rum cake, peach cobbler or sweet potato pie," Earl said.

"Coconut pralines and pone," Stan added. They both knew the story by heart.

"You know it was one of them cakes she threw at me when I pushed her."

"Yellow cake with thick chocolate frosting," Earl said without looking up. He was licking the mustard off both of his hands. Tony told this story whenever he got drunk. Must have heard it nine hundred times.

"I came home late after that six-hour streak. You remember, Earl. I tore the place up. Nobody could touch me that night!"

"You were a firecracker, all right." Earl poured them all another round.

"Won thirty-six hundred in two fuckin' hours. Bought the whole room a round, everybody had doubles, even that three-piece-suit nigga who lost." Tony scratched his wide belly and looked at the ceiling. "Man, I was so happy. Been trying to bust that punk ass all week. You was there, Stan. You know I was rollin'."

"You couldn't hit nothing but sevens."

"I come home yelling, 'Flo, look-a here, come here, gal. Look what yo' daddy done brung you.'"

"That's when you kissed her and fell flat on yo' ass." Stan was trying real hard not to bust out and laugh. He bit down deep into his sandwich.

Tony drank two shots and shook his head back and forth.

"She hauls off and calls you an ol' sloppy drunk, didn't she?" Earl said, holding his smile underneath his hand.

"Shouldn't have said that," Tony said sadly.

"It wasn't yo' fault. She shouldn't have called you that, man. Women need to learn how to give men respect." Earl gulped his drink and belched loudly.

"Next thing I know, she started packing her clothes." Tony almost cried, then wiped his face with a napkin.

"Um, um, um," Earl said, barely listening to Tony. He was holding a knife and a new slice of bread. He spread some more mustard on it slowly.

"So she walks out the room, huh? Earl, it's your move, man." Stan wanted him to play. He nudged Earl's elbow. Earl took his turn while Stan poured more liquor into Tony's empty glass, then he poured more into Earl's and his own.

"Man, I stormed toward her. I was so mad I wanted to rip off her clothes. I say, 'Woman, you better talk to me, girl!' I grabbed her head and pushed it against the kitchen wall. 'Don't you ever walk away from me, bitch.'"

"Called her a bitch, did ya?" Earl said it like it was the first time he'd heard it. He sucked on each finger and then moved his checker. "Boy, I bet she was mad."

"'Talk to me,' I screamed, but she stands there all quiet, just blinking her big eyes. 'Talk to me dadgummit,'" Tony screamed again. He leaped from his seat and knocked over his glass. "She ran but I grabbed her and slammed her against the cabinets. All them damn glasses rattled like mad."

Earl and Stan didn't look up anymore. Stan took a napkin and wiped up Tony's drink. There were only a few checkers left.

Tony was standing and twisting his napkin.

"'Always quiet,' I yelled, 'ass always out of whack. Speak up, I know you got something to say.'"

But Flo hadn't said nothing. She had looked at Tony with this sad, heartbreaking stare, like a hound you done whipped on too long."

"Your move," Earl said quietly to Stan.

"So I grabs her neck. I try to make her talk," Tony said, twisting the napkin inside both fists.

"She says 'Stop, Tony. Stop, I can't breathe.' "

"I bet she was breathing all that liquor on your breath," Earl said, mocking.

"Sucking a mint woulda helped," Stan added, smiling.

Tony's face was scowled up, like he smelled something burning.

"Nigga, we both know how you can go off." Earl and Stan both laughed in Tony's pained face.

"Veins be all bulging out the side of his skull." Stan grinned.

"Nigga looked just like Godzilla," Earl said.

Tony swayed on his feet, both fists twisting his napkin.

"So I let go, but not without ripping her robe. I tore the thing off her. Ripped the whole thing to shreds." Tony violently tore the napkin to bits. Greasy shreds fell to the floor. He slumped to his chair and downed his whole glass. "I should have treated her like royalty," Tony said.

"Queen me." Earl nudged Stan's hand.

Stan crowned the queen and put two fingers in the jar. He plopped a sliced pickle onto his tongue.

"Never bothered getting dressed. Flo just stood there, knifing the icing on slow. Oh, she had it so nice. I couldn't wait for it to be done. Nothing like having something warm from the oven, and Flo's yellow cakes with their thick chocolate frosting were the best I tasted in life."

Earl put the checkers inside the can. Stan folded the worn board in half.

"We always made good love after a blowout. The girl was real good at that too."

"Never saw that cake coming," Earl said, shaking his head.

"No, I never did," Tony answered back. "She must have thrown it straight from the kitchen. The glass pan hit the wall and crashed down my back. Cake bits splattered all over my shoulders; chocolate was all on the wall.

"She grabbed a big bottle of whiskey and busted it against the sink. 'You put your hands on me for the last time, god damn it!' She held up the neck like it was a mallet."

"Got her voice then, didn't she," Stan said, getting his jacket.

"Oh, Flo got her voice—got her coat and her car keys too. Good thing, 'cause I probably would have killed her that night, the way I felt after that cake hit. She moved the next day. Cleared everything out. Next thing I knew, she had Charles." Tony slumped his large body down to his chair. Just saying Charles's name made Tony sick.

"I'm going over there now!" Tony leaped to his feet and grabbed a gun from a drawer. "That fool better give me my money!"

Earl and Stan both held Tony back down.

"Don't be no chump. Right now he don't know nothin'," Earl said.

"Keep playin' him, man," Stan added mildly. "Keep giving him chips, make him feel like he owes you. Percy'll do the dirty work for you."

Tony struggled free, but he tossed the gun back in the drawer. His face was pure rage but he never said a word. He'd pretended this long to be Charles's friend. But he hated him, hated that cocky half-smile, hated that young, confident strut. He hated that Charles had Flo.

All Tony wanted was to get Flo to come back. He'd love to snatch Flo behind Charles's back.

Tony got up and spit in the sink.

25

Charles and Trudy

On Tuesday morning, Charles got dressed and left the house early. He and Flo lived downstairs in a backyard apartment. It sat on a very deep lot. When Charles backed down the driveway and got to the street, he saw Percy's powder-blue Regal circle the block. Charles parked by the pay phone way down the street and told his boss he'd be out sick today. He sat and watched Flo get in the new car and drive off. He tailed her all the way to the freeway. He made sure she got on the 10 heading west before finally doubling back to the house. When he came back he saw Percy had parked. Percy was inside his car, holding a mug to his lips. Some dumb fool must owe Tony some money. Tony hired Percy to beat down the deadbeats. Charles was glad Tony cut him some slack. He rushed in and changed both the pillows and sheets and made a tall pitcher of sweet lemonade. He pressed two fat, ripe strawberries into each glass and left them to chill in the freezer.

When Charles peeked from the window again, he noticed that Percy was gone. Charles scanned the small living room once again. It was filled with old crap Flo dragged back from thrift shops. There were wobbly tables and odd chairs that didn't match. Horribly ruined bureaus with doilies on top. It looked like it belonged to an eighty-year-old maid. Charles liked chrome, black lacquer and glass but he was too cheap to ever go buy any of these things. That would mean he'd have to give up some cash. He'd never cared or noticed how the living room looked before, but he'd never had another woman in his house.

Charles socked the smashed pillows, thinking of Flo getting that car. No, he'd never brought a woman to his home before, but things had dramatically changed.

Every time a car passed, Charles immediately looked up. He couldn't believe Trudy was on her way over. But having her here was taking a chance. Someone might see her. A neighbor might tell.

Trudy rang the bell at ten-thirty sharp. She wore a snug aqua dress with a blond slender fringe that licked her thick calves as she strolled. It was an eye-candy dress. She wore it to get Charles's attention. She wanted to get in and explain the whole plan. She had no intention of having any sex.

But Charles had different ideas on his mind. He grinned and took a swig from his lemonade glass. His was swimming in gin.

"You got something for me to drink, honey?" Trudy wickedly smiled. She crossed her big legs, hiking her dress five inches farther up her thigh. She looked around the apartment. It smelled clean and looked homey. Trudy felt bad being inside Flo's place.

Charles offered her a chilled glass.

"You're wearing that dress, girl. Can I come sit next to you?"

Trudy hated that he asked. Begging her for permission. She'd have respected him more if he grabbed her right there and threw her down on the orange shag. But as soon as Charles sat, Trudy stood up. She walked across the floor to the mantel. There were three beautifully framed photos of a couple in different poses. All were of Charles and Flo. One at the beach. One in front of a church, another at a large backyard party. Charles saw them too and wished he'd taken them down. Trudy frowned when she saw them. Charles and Flo looked so happy. She began to feel sick to her stomach.

Charles saw her mood change and turned the stereo on. But the blues Etta sang only made her feel worse. It was the same way she felt right after she stole. Dumping the sad, wrinkled bags on her bed. All that stuff didn't mean nothing. It was just junk piling up. Much of it sat with the tags still intact. In fact, having it only reminded her of who she really was. Someone who takes things. Someone who lives in the cracks. No new outfit could ever shake off that bad feeling. When she stole, all she wanted was to get her foot out the door. Feeling that wonderful first lung-filling breath of escape. Having made it out the door and turning the corner, that was the real true thrill. But she hated living life looking over her shoulder. Wondering when and if she was going to get caught. Trudy looked down at her manicured nails. But how do you control your own reckless hand? How do you trust your fingers when they've failed you before? Trudy was twenty and had stolen for almost ten years. If only someone had stopped her, way back when she was young. If only someone had come up and snatched back her wrist, maybe her life would be different. All she wanted was to do this last final haul so she could stop stealing for good and finally start fresh.

Charles guided Trudy back to the couch. When he put his arm on her shoulder Trudy knocked it back down. When Charles pecked her cheek, Trudy wiped off his kiss. When he reached for her leg she leaned farther away.

Charles was nervous but his roaming hands wouldn't stop trying. Every car going by made him want to leap. The fear of getting caught knotted his stomach, but the excitement made him squirm in his seat. Besides, since Flo went out and bought the new car, Charles felt like she owed him. He was just getting his share. It was time for him to get paid.

"Baby . . ." Trudy said, facing him, placing one hand around his neck. Her thumb stroked the bone in his collar. She hated to touch him. Her fingertips ached. She didn't want Charles. She wanted his help. She glanced at the pictures on the mantel again. All Trudy felt now was scummy. This was Flo's home. She was here in her house. Trudy's eyes fell to the floor. Here she was sneaking around the back like her mother. Everything about it felt wrong.

"What's wrong with you, girl?" Charles laughed nervously. He wanted to get her inside the bed. He hoped she wasn't having second thoughts.

But Charles was sitting there scared stiff himself. Each screeching car made his arm hairs curl up. Each little sound made his head turn around. He was waiting for Trudy to make the first move. If she wanted him, he wished she would hurry.

Trudy had to act fast. There was so little time. She hiked her dress farther up the meat of her thigh. She couldn't be squeamish. She had to speak up. She could see he was waiting for something. He was teetering between satisfying a hot, aching need and wondering if he should get up and run.

Charles tried to act cool. He did not want to blow it. He didn't want this fine chick to get up and leave. So he clutched his wet drink in the palm of his hand. He let the sweet taste of gin wet the back of his teeth and roll all the way down his throat.

Charles leaned closer. She didn't resist. But when a car honked its horn they both sat there frozen. They waited until the car sped away.

Trudy let his mouth kiss her, but it was nervous and stiff. She tried to relax while his hand tugged her dress. She felt totally detached as he unhooked her bra. It didn't feel like she was really there at all. It was like she was at the show, in the dark, watching a movie. Like her body no longer belonged to her. When his hand made its way down the length of her spine Trudy cringed as she stared out the window. She felt awful. She didn't want to go any further. A lone leaf blew listlessly across the dull lawn. It rolled over itself again and again and then stopped in a harsh field of weeds.

"Baby?" Trudy said, pulling him off. This was it. This was the time. She had to ask Charles now.

"What's wrong?" Charles asked, wondering why she made him stop.

Trudy breathed deep and exhaled slow.

"What? What is it?" Charles pulled her face toward his. He was anxious to get back to business.

Suddenly the doorbell chimed through the still-silent room.

Trudy pulled her dress on and Charles peeked from the drapes. He saw his neighbor on the porch.

"Damn it," he said under his breath before going to the door. "Yeah?" Charles yelled without opening the door up.

"We're leaving," the neighbor said, looking out toward the street. "We were wondering if we could borrow five dollars." The man wouldn't look at Charles. He looked ashamed to be asking. Charles dug inside his pocket. He counted his money. He held it close to his body so the man couldn't see. He had six twenties, three tens and nine folded ones. He cracked the door open and gave the man a dollar. "That's all I got on me," Charles lied to the man. "I'm kind of busy right now." The man had caught a glimpse of the money Charles had. He also had seen Trudy slip in the front door and knew Charles lived there with Flo. So the man stood there. He adjusted his feet. He looked back at Charles with a slight knowing smile. He put his hands in both pockets and waited. Charles put a ten inside the man's hand and angrily shut the front door.

Trudy stared outside at the savage backyard. A chain-link fence separated the backyard from the garage. The garage was a very old, large, run-down shack. The roof was caved in. Assorted car parts and what looked like a million dented paint cans were in there. All kinds of cans, all stacked together, old gummy colors running down the front, pooling around the bases of the cans.

The people upstairs were making a whole lot of racket. Their apartment exploded with loud, crashing bottles and the rough, angry sound of people told to move out. Charles hated living there. He craved his own place. It stabbed him when Flo went and spent all their savings. How could he ever get away from this now?

"Charles." Trudy smiled and stroked Charles's hairy chest. She didn't want to touch him, but she forced herself on. She wanted him interested enough to want to do the job. "I got a plan to make us both plenty."

Charles was listening but his mind was focused on something else. He pulled Trudy close. He circled his arms around her waist, letting his hands roam across that magnificent ass.

"I'd help any woman who had all this." Charles let his hands roam across her silk panties. "How much money are we talking about?"

"It's one-hundred-thousand dollars in cash. That's fifty thou' each. I'm willing to go fifty-fifty."

"One hundred grand. Who's got that kind of money?"

"This man I see up at the bank."

"I ain't down for hitting no bank."

"We ain't robbing it, Charles. Your part is easy."

"So why'd you pick me? What can I do?"

"Nothing you don't already do every day. Just deliver the mail at the bank where I work."

"But I'm Dockweiler, baby. That's not my route. That's Beverly Hills you're talking about."

"Look, don't worry. I got this worked out. Our regular mailman doesn't come until one o'clock. We'll be done way before homeboy gets there."

"That's all?"

"That's it. I got it all timed. All you got to do is make sure you're early." Trudy looked down, studying her hands. "But really it's not just the money I want."

"Oh, really," Charles said, pulling her chin toward him again. Charles said this last part slightly mocking her. He liked watching them big titties shake while she talked. He pulled her on top of him again.

"When Lil Steve snapped that picture, he changed my whole life." Three real tears rolled down Trudy's face. "I want Lil Steve. It's his ass I want." She struggled to pull herself together.

"Look, baby, don't cry. I'll help you out." Charles felt so good to be needed as a man. Flo didn't need him. She got her own stuff. Didn't ask him to take her to work anymore. He missed those long rides on the 405 Freeway. He'd roll along the coast chasing black-lava waves. The radio blaring. A cinnamon roll and black coffee, licking the sweet off his hand as he drove. One time he pulled off at an OPEN HOUSE sign on his way back from taking Flo to work. He didn't get out. Didn't want to talk to nobody. But he sat there admiring the house from his car. It wasn't the best house but it was cared for and clean. Straight fence, good paint and trimmed grass. That's what Flo took. The down-payment money. He glanced at the dishes stacked up in the sink. Flo got what she wanted. She didn't need him. Charles opened his thighs and grabbed Trudy's body, driving her down to the couch. Trudy struggled against Charles, but he had her pinned down. His left leg was wedged between hers.

Just then, Trudy and Charles heard the front door lock click. Both of them shot up and sat completely still. They heard the door handle turn and the creak of the screen.

"Quick!" he said, handing Trudy her purse. "Get in here."

Trudy jumped inside the closet while Charles grabbed the two glasses. He looked around fast, wondering where he could hide them. He heard the front door open. He tried not to panic. He put the two glasses in the oven.

Flo walked inside the house and threw her purse down. She got sick on her drive into work this morning. She picked up the phone and dialed her office, telling them she wasn't coming in. Flo went to the stove and turned the flame on high. She opened the cabinet and took out some tea. She figured while she was home she could rummage through Charles's clothes. She was more determined than ever to catch him.

"You forget something?" Charles said, walking into the kitchen.

Flo almost screamed.

"Hey, ah, no, no, the freeway was jammed," Flo said, looking away, walking out toward the porch. "Figured I'd come home and wait." Flo actually had gotten sick and thrown up by the road before doubling back to the house.

Charles looked at her good to see if she knew something. She looked at him to see if she suspected her. The sun was out now. It warmed the whole porch. Flo looked really pretty standing out there today. He usually saw her getting ready for work, and by the time he got home she'd changed into old clothes. He felt really bad for the first time in his life. He kept his head down. He couldn't look in her eyes. He hoped she wouldn't stay long.

"What about you?" Flo asked, glancing at him. "What are you doing here?"

"Mail carrier strike," Charles casually lied. "Only the scabs worked today."

Trudy could hear Charles and Flo talking. She tried not to breathe when their voices approached her. She could see Flo through the slits in the door. She was coming toward the closet. Trudy's heart raged. She prayed Flo didn't pull on the handle.

Charles stayed up front. He didn't want to appear suspicious. He grabbed the sports page and pretended to read, but his body was as stiff as a crowbar.

Something is different, Flo thought to herself.

Charles tossed the paper. He anxiously stood up. He leaned on the living room mantel. He could see most of Flo in the gold beveled mirror. *Don't open the closet! Don't go in there!* He hoped she didn't see the changed sheets.

When the teakettle yelled, Flo and Charles both leaped. Charles hurried to the kitchen and turned off the flame.

Flo frowned when she finally walked out of the room. She didn't notice the sheets but she did notice something. It was the faint hint of flowers from a woman's perfume. She looked at Charles hard when she left.

Charles avoided Flo's question-mark eyes. But he watched while she threw the new car in reverse. It left skid marks on their long driveway.

Charles sighed deeply when he slid the closet door open. His rib cage expanded and collapsed with each breath. From Trudy's position he could see her red panties. He knelt down and pinned her right there on the floor.

"Wait a minute!" Trudy said, shoving against his dense weight.

But Charles held her arms. His body was determined. He wanted something to erase the look on Flo's face.

"Come on, girl," Charles said. "Don't make me beg." Her standing, firm breasts looked like two juicy melons. He wanted to bite them. Let his tongue graze each tip. He tried to hook off her panties with his thumb.

But Trudy twisted and turned on the shoe-laden floor. She didn't want sex. She wanted to go but Charles pushed her back down.

"Stop . . ." she said louder. "Get off me, Charles!"

But Charles was blazed from the lemonade gin. The thought of almost getting caught turned his burners on high. He wanted some of this. There was definitely no question. He was risking too much to get nothing.

"Wait . . ." Trudy squirmed. This was not what she'd planned. But Charles ignored her and pulled down his pants. Trudy felt his belt buckle digging into her leg. "No!" Trudy yelled, trying to push Charles up. Trudy's frantic eyes shifted around the dark floor. She grabbed a leather shoe from the back of the closet and slammed it with all her might across his head.

"Are you crazy?" Trudy said, ripping herself up. She got out of the closet and left the room. She smoothed down her dress and walked into the living room again.

Charles tried to stroke her arm with his finger as she passed, but as soon as he touched her Trudy jerked it away.

I ruined it, he thought. What was he doing? He'd never pulled a stunt like that before. He looked down at the carpet, avoiding her eyes.

"Look," Trudy, said jabbing one hand on her hip, "let's get this job done. Then we can play house. Besides"—Trudy mustered a thin veiled smile—"getting done on a junk-closet floor ain't no date."

Charles kept his head down. He felt totally ashamed. He didn't know what else to say.

"Just be at the bank like I told you, okay?" Trudy handed Charles a blue vinyl bag. "And make sure you bring this in your satchel."

"What's this?" he asked, unzipping the bag's top. The bag was stuffed with newspaper stacks cut down to the same size as money. Each stack had a real bill on top. "Hide this in your satchel and bring it tomorrow. All you have to do is be there at ten and pick up the mail from my line."

Trudy walked down the steps and hurried to her car.

"Ten o'clock!" Trudy yelled from her window.

Charles watched her car race down the street. A snail worked its way under a bush.

The two glasses clanged when he took them out of the oven. He carried them both to the sink. Trudy's strawberry was still jammed on the thin crystal edge. Charles put the whole strawberry inside his jaw and bit down. He licked the sweet tart from each of his fingers. A line of red juice ran down his chin.

26

Flo

Don't nothing make you feel your race more than putting a perm on your head.

The god-awful burning.

Those horrible sores.

That foul-smelling chemical stink.

"You so quiet, girl. You ain't yo' same peppy self," Vernita said to Flo in the mirror.

It was Wednesday. Flo had a hair appointment at two. Flo sat there while Vernita sectioned her hair. She watched while she mixed a batch of white, putrid stuff. The short, chubby tub, the small plastic spatula she used, the hospital gloves on her wrists. The room was so warm, Flo had to sip some water. The toxic fumes mixed with the dank, angry smell of hair sizzled to the root were slowly making Flo sick.

Truth was, Flo was fuming herself. As the lye began eating the first layer of her scalp, all she could think of was Charles.

Charles was fucking up again. Now she was sure. Flo sat there remembering how bad she felt last time. How he begged the next day, how he called the girl "dog food," some co-worker whore, then he swore that he'd never stray again.

"Dump him," her grandmother had said when she called. "The dog that bites once bites again."

Flo felt that first tingle, knew there wasn't much time before the sting started working her brain. All she could think of was burning hot ovens, barbecue pits filled with piping-hot coals, cayenne that burned the first layer off your tongue, and Charles out fucking up again. She sat perfectly still while her tender scalp blazed and the searing rage blistered her heart.

There was definitely nothing fun about getting a perm, unless you were washing it out.

Flo left the shop and got back in the car. The new car had lost all appeal for her now. She felt tired, and this flu feeling would not go away. She stopped at the drugstore down the street. She bought some Theraflu and some Tylenol PM, but as the man rang her up she bolted from the line, racing to the feminine products aisle, and picked up a pregnancy test.

When she pulled in her driveway, Charles was nowhere to be found. Flo got out, clutching the brown paper sack with the pregnancy test and a rustling bag of barbecue chips. She'd bought the chips to hide the pink pregnancy-test box from those nosy folks standing in line.

She ripped the package, peeling open the instruction sheet.

"Please, Lord," she said out loud to herself, "please don't let me be pregnant this time. Don't make me go through all that madness again."

Flo squatted over the toilet seat and peed in a blue cup. She put the cup on the sink and stuck in the wand. She paced the floor for the ten endless minutes the test took, while the test rested on the sink's counter. Finally it was time to pull out the wand. But in her eagerness she accidentally knocked the plastic cup over. Flo bent to her knees to wipe up the mess. She prayed before she looked up again. But at the tip of the wand, there was definitely no mistake. A dark blue plus sign had appeared at the tip. Big and clear as the day.

Positive! Oh, God! It can't be positive again. Flo tossed the kit in the small bathroom trash. She laid some tissues on top to hide it.

It can't be positive. Please, Lord, not now! I can't be pregnant again.

Flo jumped in her car and drove halfway across town to the free clinic on the west side.

She waited. Her face was stuck inside a magazine, but Flo

wasn't reading at all. She was studying the other women who sat in the clinic. Women with two or three children already. Young ones with boyfriends parked out in front. Older ones sitting there staring straight ahead. Most of them looked scared. Their faces etched in worry. Like they were all waiting for some terrible lottery that half of them were guaranteed to win.

Someone came out and called Flo's name.

A woman in a peach doctor's coat brought her to the back room. Technicians were testing the clear yellow liquid. One of them stopped and looked up.

"It's positive," the woman said. "If you'd like to make an appoint—"

Flo turned and ran quickly back to her car. Her hands gripped the steering wheel so hard, her knuckles turned pale and went numb.

It can't be positive, she thought. *Not now, not like this.*

There was a time when Charles and she had discussed having a child. It was when his hand cupped her face under the cool steel moon. When he'd whisper and tell her he wanted a daughter. A little girl who'd look just like her. He would hold Flo so tight, bring her close to his chest or nibble against her plump stomach.

But all that seemed like a long time ago. Now when Charles got in the bed, he just pulled all the covers across his muscular back and the next thing she knew he was snoring. And that last time! Well, that was so awful that Flo had silently cried herself to sleep when it was over. Her eyes welled just thinking of it now.

Flo drove with the radio off and all the windows rolled down. She couldn't stop feeling nauseous. Her stomach did flips. She felt like she was stuffed on an over-packed bus with fifteen aggressive perfumes stealing what was left of the air.

Damn, I'm pregnant, Flo thought. *I'm pregnant again.*

Even though Charles was her man, Flo felt it was over. Deep inside Flo could feel he was already gone. She drove, half-conscious, until she reached her long driveway. She parked and walked inside the house. She saw the light blinking on the message machine and pushed play.

There on the box was the high-pitched voice of a female she didn't recognize.

"Charles," the voice said low, "be there at ten." The message clicked off after that.

Whose voice was that? It sounded familiar. Flo played the message over and over again, standing in the kitchen, right next to her knives.

Finally it dawned on her whose the voice was. Trudy! So he was seeing her! That bitch had the nerve to call Charles at home? Where the hell was his trifling ass at?

Flo'd been watching Charles these last few days, before he left the house. The way he dressed, the way he smelled, the way he paid extra attention to his hair and teeth. Humming to himself while he ironed his pants. It was the way he took his time, never once looking at her. Blind to Flo standing there grinding her teeth.

It wasn't easy watching your man get ready to go see another woman. It felt like all four burners on a stove set on High. It made tears leak like lava from her red, bloodshot eyes. She felt vicious, a lot more animal inside. Like she wanted to break something or bite down really hard, or rip something up like a stray does your trash.

Flo stood in the kitchen thinking of gunshots and skid marks on the center divide, but mostly she thought of revenge.

27

Ray Ray and Lil Steve

Lil Steve woke to fingernails tapping his car. He was sleeping good from a half-hour shower at the gym he'd taken real early that morning.

"Good morning," Vernita said, peering at him through the glass.

Lil Steve squinted while rolling down his car window. The cool air killed the hairs on his arm. L.A. was a desert. It could be one hundred degrees by day and drop to forty in the wee hours of morning.

"Get in," he said. "It's too chilly to keep this open."

"No, baby, I gotta go." Vernita pointed to her car. "I just wanted to talk to you a second."

"You always gotta go. Why don't you break a brother off proper?"

Vernita smiled and slipped into the passenger's seat.

"Can you braid my hair, please? I need to look corporate." Lil Steve always snatched whatever that person was selling. Whatever they had, he wanted it for free. "And zigzag one side and tuck the ends when you finish."

Placing his back on her seat, Lil Steve leaned his head over and Vernita skillfully plaited his hair. The only reason she was there was to make sure Lil Steve was ready. This was Friday. Today was the day. Trudy told her to come early. She wanted her to make sure he didn't get high and forget.

"So what up, baby? Tell me what you need." Lil Steve smiled, rubbing his hands over his wide-open knees.

Vernita examined his neck. He smelled nice and looked clean and was as scrubbed as a Catholic-school nun. She braided his hair with speed and finesse. All she had to do was fake a quick question.

"I just wanted to know the hot picks for tonight's fight." Vernita didn't want to bet. She hated losing money. But it was the perfect reason to tap on his door.

Lil Steve loved attention. He drank that shit up. He'd give a big long speech if anyone asked him a question. Truth be told, not too many folks did.

Lil Steve scratched his head, like he was pondering the question. He studied the birds on the telephone line. Unzipping a toiletry bag, he pulled out a fine-tooth comb and a tiny black handheld mirror that was cracked. He carefully began combing down his mustache.

Vernita watched his eyes in the tiny mirror and smiled.

"Jones. Put your hair money on him." Lil Steve rubbed his goatee and pushed black glasses over his eyes. "Liston swore he'd knock Jones out in three, but I wouldn't trust Liston. Always running off at the jib. The smart money's going against him."

Vernita finished his hair. She looked into his eyes. "Okay, you're all set."

Lil Steve got up and pulled an Armani suit from the trunk. He ducked in the backseat, expertly changed his clothes and rose from the seat looking like a stockbroker.

"Damn, you look like you're going on a job interview, honey." She rarely saw him in anything but head-to-toe Nike gear. That brother had more Air Jordans than the law allowed. He polished his Gucci sunglasses and pushed a C-note inside his sock. He'd boosted two Compaq laptops that morning at the gym. The rest of his money slept under his car mat. His trunk was a stock room. It was filled with boxes, stereos, radios and speakers for your car, laptops and digital cameras. Leather coats with security tags still on, mini vacuums, thirteen-inch television sets and a whole row of new tennis shoes.

"So are you ready?" Vernita asked.

Lil Steve sidestepped this question. He knew Vernita knew about the job but he didn't know how much, and he was never one to show his hand.

"I stay ready, baby." Lil Steve smiled, pulling a gun from under the seat. "Y'all better recognize," he said as he put the gun back.

Seeing the gun immediately made Vernita nervous, and she hurriedly got out of his car.

"Wait. Can you give me a ride to my partner on 39th?"

Vernita managed a weak smile. That brother sure was something. A real pretty boy. A handsome thug with cut features. Lil Steve didn't have much, but you'd never know from how he dressed. And you sure wouldn't suspect that he lived in his car. He always looked so fresh and clean.

It was too bad she wouldn't be hanging with Lil Steve anymore. It had been fun planting seeds and pumping him up with information. Oh well, she said, gliding the key into her car door. This life was about to be her past.

"I appreciate this, baby." Lil Steve hopped into her 5.0 Mustang. "My transmission is starting to slip."

Vernita roared her big V8 engine and let the top down. The car was a dark turquoise green that sparkled in the sun, with chrome rims and a white convertible top.

Lil Steve admired Vernita's new car. "Damn, girl, you got the freshest ride in the streets. Riding down the street witcho brains all blown out."

"Brains blown?"

"That a convertible, girl! Damn, I sho' love these five-ohs."

Vernita rolled down Crenshaw Boulevard until they hit 39th. "Goin' Back to Cali" shook her woofers and tweeters. Biggie Smalls had just been gunned down that year.

"Turn here," Lil Steve told her.

Vernita glided her Mustang into the driveway. "This it?" she asked, leaving the ignition on.

The apartment had a few dead cars on the lawn; a washing machine was left on the front porch and there were some rose bushes that looked like barbed wire.

"Baby?" Lil Steve kissed Vernita's hand. His lips pressed the fake diamonds she had drilled in each pinkie. "Can I borrow a yard 'til tonight?" He smiled and brushed his palm across her warm cheek. Lil Steve clocked a whole lot of loose cash like this. He'd been unsnapping purses all over town. Beauticians were notorious for carrying lots of money. Fixing hair has always been a cash-friendly business. He knew plenty of men who macked the hell out of beauticians just to get next to them ends.

Vernita sighed mildly and opened her wallet. She knew Lil Steve's thing was milking honeys for money. She took out a five, holding out the crumpled bill. "Sorry, babe," she lied, "but that's all I have." Shutting her purse tight, she put the car in reverse and held the brake until Lil Steve hopped out of the car.

Lil Steve scowled but he shoved the bill into his pocket. He didn't have time to mack her down and get more. He watched her roll back her car.

"Hey, wait!" Lil Steve screamed. "Call me, all right? Don't make a brother wait so long, either. You know that shit ain't right." He smiled at himself and combed his thin mustache. He may have gotten only five bucks today but there was definitely going to be more. Watching Vernita's shaved skull leave, Lil Steve's tongue licked his lips. It was only a matter of time.

Vernita glided her car into Drive. As she started to pull away she saw Ray Ray come outside. Ray Ray had that hard penitentiary look. The sun showed the hideous burn mark on his face. He had a coffee cup in one hand and wore black low-cut socks and a pair of worn corduroy house shoes. Damn, she thought, pulling off. Ray Ray sure was a mess. How could Trudy think that hatchet face was cute?

"I don't know why she's messing with your sorry ass." Ray Ray grinned. "She's a little too high-class for you." Ray Ray took a long swig from the hot fluid he held, flashing a wide, knowing smile at Lil Steve. "Got a nice looking 'Stang under her ass, though."

"Woowee!" Lil Steve rubbed his palms together. "Fool, that's my new shit. Don't give me no trouble. Don't ask for no cash. All she wants is my black juicy dick."

"You wish, homie. A bitch like that has more than your monkey ass on her mind."

Lil Steve frowned. Truth was, he didn't know Vernita. The only thing he knew was Vernita did hair. He'd really seen her only a handful of times. It was always real early, always at his car, and she always went home right away. She just showed out the blue, parked next to his car and asked for help putting oil in her tank. They never had sex, but he didn't tell Ray Ray that. He let him think all women wanted him bad.

"Let's go, Romeo." Ray Ray walked into the house.

While following him into the bedroom, Lil Steve saw Ray Ray's mother. "Hey, Moms," he said. "What's going on?" But Ray Ray's mother never looked his way.

Lying on the bed was a gray .45, a black Smith & Wesson and a short-nosed, pearl-handled, cute .22. There was a switchblade and two boxes of bullets, some handcuffs and two cans of Mace.

"Shit, we ain't robbing the muthafuckin' bank! Why we gotta bring all this shit?"

"Protection, brotha. Just take your piece and chill." Ray Ray strapped on his underarm holster.

Lil Steve had a gun but just used it to flash. He didn't even have any bullets. He leaned down and picked up the pearl-handled one.

Ray Ray picked up the Smith & Wesson and snapped in the clip.

"Damn, man, where'd you get this shit, dude? It's sweet." Lil Steve admired the steely weapon.

"I just got it, all right?"

"It's cool, nigga, but what's up? You gonna Mace the dude and shoot his ass too?" Lil Steve laughed. "That Mace'll fly back in your own got damn face," he told Ray Ray. "You ain't never had that shit, have you, man? You'll be coughing so bad and your eyes'll be crying. You'll be begging for some Primatene mist but can't have it. Why we gotta be strapped?"

"Just in case," Ray Ray said, serious.

"In case of what?"

"In case he gets wild and starts trippin'."

"You gonna shoot him?"

"Listen, I'll shoot the fool if I have to, but I ain't in it like that, G. Besides, I got priors. I ain't tryin' to get me no strike. If the shit don't look right, it's all off, okay? I ain't getting my ass faded 'cause some raggedy shit went crazy."

"For real," Lil Steve said, fingering his gun.

"I done did my time on some whack shit already." In tenth grade, Ray Ray had gone to juvenile hall. He wasn't the trigger man but wasn't about to scream on no OGs. He did four months and kept his mouth shut. The brothers in the 'hood respected him for that too. It was one of the dudes from the set who kicked him down with the arsenal. But he wasn't about to tell Lil Steve that. Lil Steve didn't claim no gangbangin' shit. He was a hustler. Took cuts from both sides. Made money from anybody who wanted to be in the game. Not like Ray Ray. All his people were Crips. And although he didn't claim in a color-line way, in his heart he wore nothing but navy.

"You ain't gonna use that, dude. Listen, if there ain't no money, we out, right?" Lil Steve said this last part real slow. He wanted to make sure Ray Ray understood this.

"Right, right." Ray Ray nodded his head, throwing his robe off on the bed. Pulling a black T-shirt over his hard, bench-pressed body, he put on the rest of his gray pinstriped suit. He hooked a silver-chained cross around the back of his neck. He brought the cross to his lips and kissed it.

"Come on, Moses, let's go." Lil Steve buttoned his Armani.

Ray Ray mumbled a quick prayer to himself.

"You the most religious psycho I know."

They both strolled outside into the loud A.M. sun. It was a clear day for a jacking. The sky was completely clean. You could see the Hollywood sign straight from VanNess Boulevard.

Lil Steve and Ray Ray went to Winchell's doughnuts first and ordered a couple of glazed before heading down Wilshire to the bank. They parked the Lincoln and waited across the street.

Ray Ray spoke after sitting for almost an hour. "Where's he at, dog?"

"Chill out, G, we early." Lil Steve finished his last bite of doughnut and popped open a new pack of Kools. "You don't want to just drive up and do this shit, man. We got to see what the dude looks like first."

"Trudy's going to point the dude out when we get there. All we do is wait for that damn fool to show. Said he never comes in before eleven."

"You got your fake ID?" Ray Ray asked him.

"Yep."

"Okay, so you go on in and I'ma be—"

"Nigga, you don't have to tell me my business. Listen, I'ma walk in, right. I'ma ask a few bullshit questions. I'ma wait at that skinny table and pull out these checks like I'm filling the amounts on these slips. You stay out here and wait. Don't bother coming in. They see two young black niggas in a bank and may trip. We don't want anybody gettin' suspicious. I'ma take my time, right, like I got a big deposit." Lil Steve unbuttoned his coat and took out a stack of loose checks. He got out of the car and looked back inside.

The car didn't have a backseat. It wasn't that long ago that Ray Ray had gotten the car. Looked like a piece of shit in less than six weeks. Brother was as hard on cars as he was on women and shoes. A rosary hung from the Lincoln's rearview mirror. Ray Ray's mother was Catholic—they never went to church, but Ray Ray never left the house without his cross.

"Remember, wait here. I'll be back in a minute." Lil Steve checked his Rolex and dodged across the street.

Ray Ray watched Lil Steve walk through the bank's large glass doors. He fingered the cross around his neck and turned his head from the blazing sun's rays.

Lil Steve strolled through the door. He paused for a moment. It was burning outside but the bank was near freezing. He buttoned his jacket, took off his Gucci sunglasses, wiping them off

and putting them back inside their case. Lil Steve boldly walked
toward the tall middle counter and started removing the stack of
checks from his billfold. Trudy watched him come in but kept
her eyes on her hands. The bank was mildly busy, but only two
tellers were open. Nine people were waiting in line.

Trudy almost smiled when she saw Lil Steve. He looked like
he owned a yacht in Marina del Rey. He had the tall, well-
groomed frame of a broker.

Lil Steve smiled at one of the ladies standing in line. The
white lady smiled back but quickly turned away. Lil Steve began
filling amounts on the bank deposit slips. He coughed and pulled
out a check register book as if he were cross-referencing amounts.

Trudy watched him closely from her bank teller's window. Lil
Steve watched her too but never straight on. He was watching
her reflection in the glass.

Just then, a short man in a beautiful tan suit rushed in through
the front door. He had a black leather clutch wrapped tightly
around his wrist, and his small tasseled shoes moved quickly
across the floor. He worked his way through the fat burgundy
rope and stood behind the last person in line. Ten minutes went
by. The line moved slowly. A man at one of the windows didn't
have the right ID.

Suddenly Ray Ray burst through the bank's glass front doors.
Both Trudy and Lil Steve looked up, stunned. Ray Ray looked at
Trudy and then at Lil Steve. He was tired of waiting outside in
the sun. It was taking so long he thought something had happened. He walked slowly around the bank, not really knowing
where to stand. He bolted to the bathroom in the back.

Trudy panicked. Vernita was in the bank's bathroom too. If he
saw her the whole plan would be ruined.

Lil Steve glanced at Trudy. She was busy with a customer but
she did look up briefly at Lil Steve. Her nervous eyes quickly
shifted toward the tan-suit man. She pulled a ballpoint pen from
behind her ear.

That was the signal. Lil Steve gathered his papers. But the
tan-suit man still had five people in front of him. He tapped his
small, impatient feet.

Lil Steve decided to sit down at the "new accounts" couch.

An elderly Filipino woman with thick glasses and salt-and-pepper hair sat in the chair behind a large paneled desk.

"Are you here for a new account, sir?" she asked, peering over her horn-rims.

"Sir!" Lil Steve sure liked that. Nobody had ever called him "sir" before. Lil Steve adjusted the tie under his collar.

"Why, yes. I'm looking for a new bank. I'm awfully tired of the people over at First Federal. They say they'll merge, you know, and I can just imagine the lines and impersonal service I'll receive there."

Deceiving came easy to Lil Steve. Lies would just float out over his caramel-toned tongue. His mama said he was born with the gift.

He could lie on the spot without blinking an eye. Lie about anything at any given time, and could speak white in a heartbeat if need be. Learned it when his mama had him bused to school in Granada Hills to keep him away from the gangs. He got out of the gangs but not the criminal activity. The white talk just came in handy. Used to get jumped for it before he started getting smart and switching back and forth between 'hoods.

He remembered the time one of his teachers caught him gambling in the boys' bathroom. The room was full of smoke and foul-mouth yelling.

Lil Steve was oblivious to the teacher's presence in there. He was caught up in a lucky streak that had him holding a fistful of ones, and his pockets were bulging with coins.

"Fuck you, punk-ass muthafuckas. I'ma spank you and have yo' mama sucking my dick. Who tol' yo' ass to roll a double six, bitch? Y'all is some dumb lunchmeat punks."

His teacher was shocked. Steven Williamson was one of his star pupils. "Come here, young man. Where'd you learn to talk like that?"

Lil Steve looked angry but quickly changed his face. He followed the teacher out into the hall. The teacher took him to the principal's office.

"Oh, Mr. Johnson?" he said, knocking lightly and then going

in. "Could I have a moment? Go ahead, Steven, talk the way you were talking a moment ago. Listen to this, Frank. This is going to be great." He knowingly nudged the principal's arm.

Lil Steve just sat in the wooden chair, staring.

"Go on, talk the way you were talking in the john. We just want to hear it." His teacher was trying to stifle a laugh. He was fidgeting away in his seat.

"I really don't know what you mean," Lil Steve said, keeping his eyes at the ceiling.

"Come on. Do some of that 'brother-man' stuff." Mr. Lawson nudged the principal again. "Watch this, Frank. Oh, come on," he said more excitedly now. "Talk that nigger talk you were doing in the bathroom again, boy."

A rush of heat flushed over Lil Steve's face. Like someone held an iron too close to his cheek. He was glad he wasn't no punk white boy neither, so none of them dumb fools could see.

Lil Steve rushed past them both and walked out the door and down the hall. He walked through the thick wooden doors to the street and went straight to the bus stop and sat on the bench.

It was not until the afternoon breeze of the valley hit his face, that he finally breathed deeply again. Lil Steve never went back to school. Oh, he left every morning at the same exact time. He got dressed, got his books and things, but he'd double back and kick it with all the hustlers and gangsters who'd stopped going to school long ago.

"Excuse me, sir," the Filipino lady said to Lil Steve. "May I please see your ID?"

"Oh, I'm sorry," Lil Steve said, reaching for his wallet and pulling out his ID and matching fake credit cards.

"Will this be a joint account?"

"Oh, no," Lil Steve shot back. "I've never had joint partners. I remember Father's friend Phillip split up his business." He looked away a moment, just for effect. "You can't drive a car with four arms."

Lil Steve set the stage and let his marks fill the rest. He watched Ray Ray out of the corner of his eye. He was standing at the thin table, by the long teller line, dangling the bank pen from its long metal chain.

Lil Steve took a leather billfold from his upper breast pocket, carefully removed the elegant Cross pen and began filling out the form the Filipino woman gave him.

Trudy kept her head down. She couldn't look at Ray Ray. She really felt bad he was there.

Ray Ray stayed at the table for a minute and looked over at Lil Steve, who was filing his nails while the woman typed his name on a blue vinyl book.

The tan-suit man was nearing the front of the line. He repeatedly tapped his small foot.

Lil Steve noticed Ray Ray and turned his back on him. He gave the new-accounts lady his full attention.

The Filipino woman slowly rolled the bankbook out of her printer.

"All right, Mr. Jones, you're all set. How much would you like to deposit today?"

Today? Damn it, Lil Steve thought. He had forgotten he needed to put money into the account. He looked down into his wallet at two crumpled fives.

"Well, how much do I need?" He saw Ray Ray raise his eyebrows at him. He wanted Lil Steve to come on.

The tan-suit man was now at Trudy's window. In a moment he would be leaving the bank and gone.

"The minimum is fifty dollars, sir."

Lil Steve fumbled around with his wallet. He tried not to panic but the time was ticking away. Trudy was already counting the huge stack of cash. He glanced at Ray Ray, who was mad-dogging him big time now, his face all scowled up and mean.

Fuck! Lil Steve thought. This was not supposed to happen. He wouldn't even be dealing with this shit if Vernita had given him some money. Lil Steve felt the wet drip down the length of his back. Ray Ray scowled at him again and Lil Steve glanced at the door. The C-note was the very last of Lil Steve's money. Reluctantly he leaned over and peeled it from his sock.

"One moment," the Filipino woman said, getting up.

Lil Steve was sweating now. *Hurry up, bitch.* If they didn't move soon it would be too late.

Ray Ray walked away from the table and stood near the wall, pretending to read the brochures in the stand.

The tan-suit man was still at the window.

Lil Steve leaned forward, anxious. Sweat was beading around his brow. "Where'd that damn bank 'ho go?" The tan-suit man was getting ready to leave.

The Filipino lady finally came back. She handed Lil Steve the small slender passbook. She reached out her hand for Lil Steve to shake.

"Thank you very much, sir. I hope you'll enjoy banking with B of A."

"I'm sure I will," Lil Steve said, feeling more confident now. "Especially if all the people working here are as beautiful and pleasant as you." He was handsome in that black Armani suit. His height and goatee made him look distinguished. He could charm women right out of their clothes.

The woman smiled, revealing a wide row of teeth surrounded in gold.

Ray Ray collected his papers and left. He walked briskly across the street and jumped into the Lincoln. Lil Steve let go of the Filipino woman's hand. Flashing everyone in his path his Cherry Coke smile, he walked casually out the front door. All they had to do now was wait for the tan-suit man to come out. Lil Steve brushed his sleeve and strolled to the car. It felt good standing there in the Beverly Hills sun. Even the parked cars sparkled like gold.

28

Charles and Vernita

Charles was waiting in a midget white mail carrier's truck. It was parked right in front of the bank. As soon as he saw Ray Ray and Lil Steve leave, he walked quickly inside. He was wearing his blue and gray postal uniform with a giant canvas sack strapped to his back. Charles wore a hat and dark tinted glasses. A fake beard covered his face. He walked straight to the back to a water cooler in the corner. No one even looked up. Charles knew that see-through feeling well. Uniforms were always equated with the help. He was the worker, the last rung of a ladder, as noteworthy as the fake ficus tree in the lobby.

Charles studied the room under his dark tinted shades. He poured a small cup of water. He tried to act cool. He took a huge gulp and crumpled the paper cup. He took deep breaths to clear his head.

The tan-suit man watched Trudy's hands. She was busy counting bundles of money. A strap was a fat roll of money in hundreds, but a bundle equaled ten straps. Trudy counted out five hundred Saran Wrapped bundles, exactly one-hundred-thousand dollars. A blue vinyl satchel rested on her desk. Trudy took short breaths through her nose as she slowly counted the money.

Don't panic. Stay calm, Trudy scolded herself. She could feel the rushing drum of her maniac heart. *Breathe deep! Take it easy. Don't panic now.* Trudy could feel the attack trying to close up her throat. She stopped and fanned herself with a bank teller slip. She wished she could go get some water.

Suddenly, Vernita whisked toward the other teller's window. She'd been hiding in the bathroom the whole time. She was wearing a light linen suit with a dangerously low-cut halter and six-inch black patent leather stilettos. The blond wig hung way down past her shoulders. It swung across her back as she walked. The contrasting dark sunglasses made her look like a star. The men in the bank began to stare.

Vernita went to the other teller's window. She held an old check in her hand.

"May I help you?" the bank teller asked Vernita when it was finally her turn.

Vernita pushed the check and her ID under the glass. "Cash this for me, please," Vernita said coolly. She took out a compact and began dabbing her lipstick. She looked whiter than a coconut pie.

The teller smiled at Vernita. She opened the cash drawer. But suddenly she stopped and held the check in her hand. "I'm sorry, but I can't take this. It's not made out to you."

"Just cash it, honey," Vernita said, avoiding the teller's eyes. She was watching the bank in the mirror of her compact. "Go on, I'm sure it'll be fine." Vernita watched the tan-suit man at Trudy's window. He was waiting for Trudy to finishing dealing his bills.

"I'm sorry, ma'am, but we can't," the teller mildly told her.

"Well, for heaven's sake. Who's in charge here?" Vernita demanded.

Trudy looked up and stopped counting the man's money.

"Now, really, I've been a customer too long at this branch to settle for this kind of crap!" Vernita put one hand on her hip. The blond wig shook with her loose, bobbing neck.

Charles stayed quiet. He crushed another water cup in his hand.

"Ma'am, we can't cash a check made out to another person." The teller talked to her low. She wanted to calm her back down.

"The hell you can't. I've been doing it for over ten years!"

The tan-suit man glanced in Vernita's direction and then motioned for Trudy to finish.

Damn it! Trudy thought. How were they going to make the switch if the tan-suit man's eyes never left Trudy's wrists? Her breathing became labored. It sounded much more staccato. She hoped the tan-suit man didn't notice.

"I'm sorry, ma'am," the teller told Vernita. "We don't honor endorsed-over checks anymore. There's nothing more I can do."

"You are sorry. Now go get the manager, please." Vernita glanced at her wrist. She wore a fake Cartier watch. "I really don't have time for this shit." Vernita rapped her acrylics against the hard marble counter. "Really, it's only nine hundred and eighty bucks!" Vernita slammed her purse so hard on the counter that a stack of brochures floated down to the floor.

Trudy finished counting the money and zipped it inside the bank's blue satchel. She was logging the money on her bank teller ledger. All she had to do was print the receipt.

The manager came over to the other teller's window. His horn-rims stared at Vernita's platinum head. He'd been playing Korean video games at his desk. He hoped this white snob didn't take long.

"We don't cash second-party checks anymore. Please, ma'am, calm down. There's no need for drama."

"Drama?" Vernita scowled. "Shit, this isn't dramatic. Dramatic is if I decide to leap over this counter and go upside your lopsided head." Vernita popped her gum in the manager's face.

The manager motioned for security to come over.

No! Trudy thought. *This is not good!* The guard moved away from the bank's large front door and now stood right next to her window.

"What? Am I supposed to be scared?" Vernita raised her eyes over her sunglasses.

But the security guard aggressively grabbed hold of her arm.

"What are you doing, you rent-a-cop punk?" Vernita struggled wildly to tear herself free. Her platinum wig shook like a big Christmas tree you struggled to get out of the house.

The tan-suit man glanced in Vernita's direction. But he looked back too quickly for Trudy to make the switch. He was anxious. He rapidly tapped with his foot. He wanted Trudy to hurry up so he could get out.

"Let go of me, fool. Leave me alone." Vernita was losing the fight with the guard. He was moving her toward the front door.

No! Trudy thought. She needed Vernita. Trudy was so outdone she could barely breathe now. She watched the security guard yank Vernita toward the front door.

Trudy printed the receipt for the tan-suit man and zipped it up in the blue vinyl bag with the money. There was nothing left to do but slide him the bag of money. Trudy hesitated but the tan-suit man looked so annoyed she knew she couldn't wait anymore.

"Let go of me, punk, I know Johnnie Cochran. Y'all done fucked with the wrong bitch this time!"

Trudy's eyes shot to Vernita. What the hell was she doing? She was talking way too ghetto for someone passing as white. The plan was for Vernita to create a mild diversion so Trudy could make the quick switch.

But it was too late. Vernita was captured. The guard firmly ushered Vernita toward the door.

"Excuse me," the tan-suit man said to Trudy. "Really, I don't have all day." Trudy had to give him the bag with the money.

Damn it! Trudy thought. The plan was all ruined. She handed him the blue vinyl bag.

But somehow Vernita managed to escape. She ran straight toward the tan-suit man's line, colliding right into his back. Vernita and the man stumbled down toward the floor.

It was Charles's turn now. He was waiting for this moment. He'd been moving closer and closer to Trudy's teller window. "Mail ready, ma'am?" Charles asked her fast.

Trudy handed him a stack without looking up. She'd slipped the blue bag inside the thick mail pile and handed it quickly to Charles.

Charles gave Trudy a mail stack too with an identical blue vinyl bank bag tucked inside. This bank bag was the same exact size and weight. Nobody in the bank even noticed the switch. In less than a minute Charles was back at his truck.

The manager helped the tan-suit man to his feet. The guard hustled Vernita out of the door. The tan-suit man was visibly upset. He smoothed down his suit and straightened his tie. He snatched the blue vinyl bag from Trudy's window and briskly walked out the front door.

29

Ray Ray and Lil Steve

Ray Ray and Lil Steve nervously waited across the street. They both saw the security guard walk out to the bank lot. He wore the mirrored sunglasses of a cop. Ray Ray didn't like cops or prison guards either; he kept his squinting eyes clocked on him. Suddenly a blonde in a white linen suit emerged from the bank's wide glass doors. She walked briskly down the street tilting her head toward the ground. The guard watched the blond woman too.

Then the tan-suit man came. He walked in a tight, quickened pace and hopped into his car. Ray Ray's Lincoln idled loudly; the whole inside shook. They watched the tan-suit man tool the champagne Lexus from its spot. He easily pulled his car from the bank's parking stall. In a few seconds, he'd be on Wilshire.

"That's him, homie. Let's roll."

Ray Ray slipped it in Reverse and then shifted into Drive. He floored the car when he took off.

When the tan-suit man drove out of the bank driveway, the guard nodded at his car. The tan-suit man left the lot.

"Fuckin' buster," Lil Steve said. "I hate muthafuckin narcs."

Ray Ray drove the speed limit behind the sparkling-clean Lexus.

They followed the tan-suit man two car lengths behind. He rolled his car mildly through the street.

"All right, man. Ease up next to his ass." Watching the tan-suit out the corner of his eye, Lil Steve said "That's right, homie, real slow. We'll take him on a residential street."

They were heading west down Wilshire Boulevard. The Lexus made a right on Beverly. They went another mile or so and made a quick right on Cherry. It was a narrow street lined with immaculately groomed palm trees. The kind of street you see on postcards saying "Greetings from L.A."

At the stop sign, Ray Ray pulled right next to the tan-suit man's car and then sped up and blocked the Lexus's front tires.

Ray Ray had a blue bandana tied around his nose and mouth. He took out the grey Smith & Wesson. Lil Steve stayed in the idling car.

Ray Ray leaped out. He ran to the man's door. He busted the window out with the handle of his gun and grabbed the front door open wide.

"Hand me the envelope, white boy, 'fore I blow your bitch-ass face."

The tan-suit man was shocked. It all happened so fast. He'd been playing Frank Sinatra's "Nice and Easy Does It," and now here was a gun in his jaw.

"What envelope?" he asked, his voice trembling hard. He was trying to reach the gun he had hidden under his seat.

But Ray Ray saw the tan-suit man reach for the weapon. He bashed his gun upside the man's jaw. Blood leaked down from his earlobe.

"Okay, okay! Please, dear God, don't shoot." He shakily removed the envelope from his clutch and handed it over to Ray Ray.

Lil Steve revved the engine for Ray Ray to come on.

"Shut up, and start walking down the street," Ray Ray said.

The tan-suit man got out and shakily walked away. He slowed down like he was going to turn around.

"Don't even think about looking back, bitch, or I'ma haveta grease this fuckin' curb with your muthafuckin' brain!"

Ray Ray leaped in the Lincoln and slammed the door closed. "Let's go."

"Naw, man," Lil Steve said, opening his door and leaping out. "I'm takin' the Lex, dude."

"Don't be no fool! Nigga driving a Lexus is bound to get noticed. You know Johnny Law don't allow no brothers to drive nice rides, especially in no got damn Beverly Hills!"

"Man, stop tripping. You startin' to sound like a bitch! Let's divvy up and meet at the crib in an hour."

Suddenly they both heard the loud scream of sirens. Ray Ray still held the blue envelope and his gun.

"I'm taking the Lexus. We got to split up. They'll be looking for two. Put that cash down on the fight like we said." The sirens grew louder. Lil Steve revved the car and did a 180. The car made a big skid mark loop in the street. Ray Ray watched him tool that big ride down the next street. That crazy-ass fool didn't need to take that car too. Nigga made a fuckin' mistake.

Ray Ray took off. He drove in the alleys. He wasn't about to get caught with all of this cash.

Lil Steve was flying. Racing fast down Wilshire. With one button, he had all the windows rolled down. The sunroof rays danced on his skin. He yanked off Sinatra and turned the radio knob until Tupac boomed loud from the woofers and tweeters.

He looked in the rearviews. No one was behind him. He found a half-smoked cigar and put it between his teeth, bringing the lighter up close to his face. He exhaled the smoke deeply, blowing it out the window.

"Now this is it," he said. "This is the straight-up high life. White folks sho' know how to live." Woowee, this was some cool fucking ride. He flicked the ashes out the car window just in time to see the patrol car pull up alongside him.

Lil Steve tried to look straight ahead, but the cop motioned for him to pull over.

Lil Steve froze.

He never saw the cop car coming.

"Fuck!" he said loudly pulling the ride to the right. He smashed the cigar butt back in the ashtray. Lil Steve heard a loud pounding sound inside his eardrums. His heartbeat thumped just like a bass line.

Lil Steve watched the cop car get closer and closer. Lil Steve never looked over. He opened his Kools, using his tongue to pull one out. When the lighter's pink head popped out from the dash, he slowly brought it up to his lips. He had to act cool. Had to manage his breathing as sweat began ripening in his armpits.

30

Lil Steve and the LAPD

He was sweating so badly, his shirt clung to his back like gum on the sole of a shoe. Lil Steve remembered the first time he got popped. It was Beverly Hills too. He and Flash were coming back from a party. They were riding in Flash's new cranberry Porsche. Flash always had the nicest, cleanest ride in the 'hood. He had a red 911, not one of those chump 914s; it was the baddest car Lil Steve had ever seen. They were just coming down Sunset laughing all loud when the red lights shined on their necks.

"Pull over now!" the loudspeaker barked.

The next thing they knew they were facedown on the concrete, fingers woven together behind their necks. The police kept their legs spread a whole forty-five minutes, while they called in to check out the plates. Said they had to wait because the computer was down. Them busters always said that. Kept them sprawled on the street. They never did no white boys like that.

Turned out all them cornfeds wanted was to watch some black flesh squirm. Johnny Law was liable to yank your card any ol' time he pleased.

Lil Steve remembered the cruel humiliation as the other motorists slowed down to watch. He remembered how he felt when the police finally did speak. How a policeman had yanked him up from the concrete with scorn, smashing his face hard against the wall. How their machine-gun questions kept blasting him like bullets. How their racism welled in their mouths and hit him like a big glob of spit.

"Where are you boys going?"

"Why are you in Beverly Hills, huh?"

"Let me see your ID."

"Where were you fucks born?"

"Keep your hands up," the fat cop screamed in Lil Steve's face. "I'm not done with you yet!"

"What's all this red?" the skinny one asked. "You boys banging or what?"

The fat one tapped his flashlight against Lil Steve's head. "Where are you black asses headed?" he asked. "There are no cotton fields around here, boy." They both got a real good laugh at that. The fat one's gut shook with joy.

"Just tell me," the fat one said, breathing in Lil Steve's face, "how can some black monkey-ass niggras like you all get a bitching car like this?"

"Must be dope money," the skinny cop added.

"Why'd you stop us?" Flash impatiently asked. "The registration's good. You got my license. What else do you want me to do?"

The fat one lowered his baton and jammed the tip in Flash's throat.

"Oh, so you're one of them talking Negros. So maybe you can tell me where you got this car from, huh?"

Well, the truth was, the car was legit. Flash bought a Porsche frame from a junkyard in Compton. He knocked the dings out and dropped in a Volkswagen engine. Painted the whole thing candy apple red. Flash had his Porsche cherried-out in no time. He liked fat rims and bright lacquer paint jobs. Hand-washed it himself twice a week. He wasn't about to get pulled over for some busted-taillight crap. Flash kept that Porsche sparkling. Everything on that car worked.

"Look man, he showed his ID. Why don't you leave us alone," Lil Steve said.

The cop slammed Lil Steve with his wooden baton. Blood oozed out over his tongue.

"Did I ask you to speak?" the fat one yelled in his face. Lil Steve felt the cop's spit on his cheek.

"Busters," Lil Steve mumbled under his breath.

"Oh, tough guy!" the fat one said, both his eyes gleaming.

"Larry, we got a tough guy over here," he told his partner.

Both the officers rushed over to Lil Steve and rammed him against the brick wall. The fat one grabbed him and put him in a chokehold while the skinny one held his Taser gun next to his forehead. They slammed him again and his teeth slit his lip.

"What's-a matter, tough guy?" the fat cop said, huffing against Lil Steve's jaw. He slammed his head hard against the wall.

"Lose your tongue, huh?" He held Lil Steve until his feet dangled off of the ground. Blood flowed out of his nose.

The other cop cuffed Flash and shoved him inside the patrol car.

"Man, we didn't do nothing!" Lil Steve screamed.

"Shut up," the fat cop said. "Get in the car, nigger."

They smashed Lil Steve inside the backseat. The officers checked for warrants, stolen plates, registration, any crimes that had gone down in the area. Nothing came up on their screen. The car and both of them were totally clean, but those assholes drove them all the way downtown anyway.

"Okay, let 'em go," the fat one told his partner, who walked over and uncuffed them both. Flash's sister picked them up and drove them down to the impound.

"Man, why'd they pull us over? We didn't do shit. You wasn't even driving fast or nothing!" Lil Steve asked Flash, still very much upset.

" 'Cause they can," Flash said, staring at the mountain of cars. "Because them muthafucks can."

But all that seemed like a long time ago. Flash had been dead for over two years now. He got shot when someone tried to steal his Porsche.

* * *

Lil Steve stayed focused. He had to be cool. He didn't want to get caught or go out like Flash. He was as cool as ice lying in the tray.

Lil Steve kept his head forward. The patrol car eased right against his side. There was no place to run or to hide. Ray Ray was nowhere in sight. Lil Steve removed the pearl-handled gun from his pocket and slipped it underneath the seat. "If they bust me, that brother'll get to keep all that cash and I'll get sent up for sho'."

The siren got louder.

Lil Steve stayed glued.

He kept his face straight. He clicked off the radio. He carefully placed his wallet on the passenger seat next to him. His movements were slow, methodical and measured. He didn't want 5-0 to ask him to do anything with his hands. He didn't want to give them an excuse and say he was reaching. Everybody knew how it went down in the 'hood. There were enough brothers who got shot by a cop who claimed they were going for a gun or a weapon, when all they were doing was rolling down the window or getting their wallets from under their seat.

The heat was not going to fade his black ass.

The officer got closer; his red and blue light soared. Lil Steve watched the green flashing arrow of his blinker as it loudly beat the leather-bound seats. But something made him pull his head off to the left. He saw the cop slow down and stare at him hard, then sped up and pulled over the car in front of him.

Mexicans! It was some muthafuckin' Mexicans they were after. Lil Steve blew out a huge sigh of relief. He watched the cop pull the Chevy truck over; three men were riding in the front.

"That's right," he said to himself. "Get them, busters." He zoomed down La Cienega Boulevard and hopped on the 10 Freeway and then took the 110 heading south. He took out his cell phone and dialed Reggie.

"Hey, man, I got one. Can I bring it by? Yeah, I'm riding in it right now. Cool. I'm coming right now." He pushed down the phone and put it back inside his pocket. He exited the 110, made a quick left off Gage and rode the rest of the way on back surface roads. He took out the cigar and pushed the ashtray back in.

"Damn, these rides is sweet," he said to himself. He opened up the glove compartment to see what was inside. There were some sunglasses and a black Donna Karan cologne bottle, designed to look just like a gun. He put both of those items in his pocket. Way in the back of the glove compartment was a tiny black box. He pulled it out with one hand and lifted the lid when he got to the light. When he looked inside, Lil Steve almost rammed the car in front.

"Got damn!" he said. Inside the black box was a giant pinkie ring smothered in giant inlaid diamonds.

Lil Steve licked his finger and jammed the ring on. It was tight, but it fit.

"Oh, yeah," Lil Steve said. "Y'all can say what you want, but look at Stevie-baby now." He smiled and hung his left hand out the window so he could see the brilliant diamonds hit the sun.

"Yep, this is some real shit here."

He looked back at the box and noticed the tiny edge of a piece of plastic coming out. Below the black fabric of the jewelry box was a tiny plastic bag with about 5 grams of cocaine.

"Well, merry Christmas, baby. We done hit the Lotto this time, nigga." Lil Steve pulled up to an old metal warehouse with a raggedy metal garage door that rolled up with a chain.

Lil Steve drove the Lexus inside while his cousin quickly pulled down the garage door.

"Hey, Big Time," Reggie said, smiling broadly at the new Lexus.

"Hey, Reg. Let's go inside the office a minute." Lil Steve walked in fast, looking suspiciously at the big, burly brother wearing blue overalls and no shirt.

They walked to the metal door of Reggie's office. It was a small room with a few folding chairs and a worn desk without any drawers. The only thing on the wall was an auto-mechanic calendar. Three big-breasted women in hot pants and bras were holding up wrenches and pliers.

Reg kept the place empty. He didn't want anything lying

around that might be used as evidence. Reggie could pack up and move his whole operation in a heartbeat if he had to. Had already moved three times that year alone. Word got out on a place like Reggie's. Hot cars coming in got people jabbing. The next thing you know, somebody's sniffing around the yard.

He had a few mixed-breed dogs in the back that watched the place twenty-four-seven. He called them Neckbone, Raw Meat and Kidney. They were some loud, rowdy-ass hounds that stayed on the lean side of mean.

Lil Steve walked behind Reggie and closed the door. "Listen, man, I got this out of the glove box. Whatchu think?" he said, showing him the ring.

Reggie squinted after taking a long drag on the indo joint he passed to Lil Steve, who waved it away.

"I'm straight, man, got business."

Reggie held the smoke in his lungs a long time and then let a long trail ease through his teeth. "I'ma tell you what I think in a minute."

Reggie studied the package a long time. "Gimme the keys."

Lil Steve tossed them across the table.

"Come on," Reggie said, rising up. "Let's pop the trunk and see what that sucker got inside."

Lil Steve followed Reggie to the trunk and watched him click the lock back.

There was nothing inside but a pair of golf clubs.

"See, man, homeboy don't have shit," Lil Steve said nervously.

Reggie removed the clubs and pulled back the mat lining the trunk and hiding the spare tire. Reggie lifted the spare tire and popped out the rim.

"Look what the hell we got here," he said.

Lil Steve stepped closer and saw a large package wrapped in black plastic with duct tape holding it shut. Lil Steve was about to take it out, but Reggie held his arm. Reggie picked up the tire and rolled it to his office, and when Lil Steve followed him inside, Reggie closed and locked the door.

Reggie looked at Lil Steve. Reggie popped a pocket knife

with his teeth. Inside were two plastic bags filled with coke. Lil Steve had never seen that much blow in his life.

"Listen, cuz, I don't know who dude was or what. Don't want to know. All I know is you got somebody's serious stash. Did they see you when you snatched the ride? Was you by yourself?"

"Naw. Me and Ray Ray jacked his ass off Wilshire, man. We had rags around our faces and shit."

"Whose ride was you in?"

"Ray Ray's."

"Did y'all kill the dude?"

"Hell, naw, man! Wasn't nothing like that!"

"Probably should have." Reggie put the small knife back in his pocket.

"Man, I ain't doing no murder time, dog. I'm still clean. I ain't never going upstate. No salad-tossin' bitches touchin' this ass! All we did was jack him. Ray Ray's holding the cash. It was the easiest shit we ever did."

Reggie shook his head. "Man, you don't understand. You and Ray Ray think you big-time players and shit. Y'all ain't nothin' but some muthafuckin' punks. Y'all fuck with somebody's stash like this and you get put on the short list of a drive-by. White boy probably running down Ray Ray's plates now."

"Don't go home, man." Reggie didn't know Lil Steve lived in his car. "You can drive my black Bug if you want. Don't even touch Ray Ray, man. You got to let that shit go." Reggie took a long drag off his fat indo smoke.

"Let it go? You must be sick. I ain't leaving without getting my ends."

"Fuck the money, boy. It's nothing but chump change anyway. You in some deep shit, fool. This ain't no credit card bullshit or some repo man scam. These muthafuckas don't play. How many folks know about this bank shit?"

"Nobody, man."

"Nobody?"

"Nobody but Trudy at the bank. You know that fine-ass sister I used to mess around—"

"You mean Trudy with the booty is in on this, fool? Everybody and they mama knows who that bitch is."

"Man, she didn't do nothing. That bitch ain't in it. She just IDed the dude, homie. Told us about them deposits."

"Man, that's the first place them jugheads gon' look. They know somebody at that bank knew about them deposits. And they know she, most likely, was the one that dropped the dime. Man, they probably at that bitch's house right now. Look, don't go home. Go stay at yo' lady's for a few days."

Reggie stared at the large bags of coke. "Here, gimme your coat." Reggie wrapped the cocaine bags in Lil Steve's jacket. "Take this bullshit witchu, man. I don't need no extra mess."

Lil Steve stared at the rolled jacket. "I'll sell 'em to you, man."

"Aw, hell naw, cuz. I'ma stick with cars. I don't fool with that bullshit, cuz."

Reggie unlocked the door and they walked to the main garage. Lil Steve had only been at Reggie's for ten minutes and two men had already stripped the Lexus down to the chase. All the parts were wrapped in huge pieces of plastic and stacked against the wall ready to be shipped to Long Beach.

Lil Steve walked between a blue BMW and a gun-metal Benz. He stopped at a '71 Bug and got in.

"Don't go home," Reggie said over the Bug's noisy engine.

Reggie took a long drag off his spliff. He watched Lil Steve slowly back out of the lot.

"Don't go home," Reggie said again.

31

Ray Ray, Charles, Trudy and Flo

Ray Ray decided not to drive home either. He went to Lil Steve's car. He waited across the street for more than two hours but homeboy never did show.

Damn, Ray Ray thought. Something must have went wrong. That fool never should have snatched that Lexus like that. He smashed out his Newport, pulled the gear from Park and glided the Lincoln down 10th.

Where could he go? Where should he hide? Ray Ray drove with the Lincoln's seat tilted so far back you only saw his neck in the car.

He suddenly thought of Charles. He was just down the street. Maybe he could go and just chill for a minute. He could get a cold beer, throw some water on his face and try to get straight before heading to the club. Ray Ray parked the car around the corner, between Edgehill and 11th, in front of a jacked California craftsman. He pulled the blue vinyl B of A bag from under the seat and stuck it inside his shirt. He dashed across quickly with his head slightly down and ran up to Charles's porch.

"Hey, Charles," he said, banging his car keys against the screen. "Hey, Charles! Man, are you home?"

Charles was home. He peeked at Ray Ray from the shade. "Fuck!" he said under his breath. "What's he doing here?"

Charles started to tiptoe away but then heard Ray Ray say, "Man, don't try and hide. I see your shadow through the shade."

Charles was barefoot and still wore his blue postal pants. His white tank was damp from the heat.

"Open up, man! Shit, I ain't got all day." Ray Ray looked toward the street hoping he wasn't seen. He banged hard against Charles's window again. The pounding shook the whole door.

Charles was just about to twist the knob when he caught a glimpse of himself in the mirror. He was still wearing the fake beard and mustache. Charles peeled it off and shoved the disguise in his pocket. A fan blew against the sheer drapes.

"Wait a minute," Charles said, rubbing his eyes, like he was sleepy. He opened the door but he was too petrified to breathe. He didn't even unlock the screen.

"You know Flo don't want no bullshit over here, man." He hoped Ray Ray would take the hint and go.

"Sorry, man, my bad, but I thought you was the man up in here," Ray Ray said this with a big, flippant grin. "Come on, nigga, stop trippin'. Let me in." Ray Ray turned around and looked over his shoulder. "This is serious business, dog. I got to talk right now!"

Charles slowly unhooked the top latch and let Ray Ray inside.

"So what's the rush, man? Why you so eager?" Charles tried to sound cool. He didn't know what Ray Ray saw. And even though inside he felt like he'd been sideswiped, outside he remained extremely low-key.

"It's Lil Steve, dog." With that Ray Ray crossed the floor and peeked out the front drapes. "You seen him today?"

"Naw, dog. I just got up. I haven't seen shit. Anyway, it ain't like that fool gonna drop by my spot. You know we don't hang. That's yo' homie, man. Me and him barely speak." Lil Steve had sold Flo a vacuum cleaner once. That piece of shit had worked once, then quit.

"Man, I need a drink." Ray Ray stood at the kitchen sink and doused his face with cold water. He wiped it off with a paper towel and laid his black gun on the counter.

Charles glanced at the gun. "I drank the last beer an hour ago." Charles didn't want to offer Ray Ray nothing to make him stay. What was he doing here now? Did homeboy know something? Charles glanced at the black gun again.

"You got a shot? I know you got some of that Johnnie Walker Black in the back room. Let me get some of that, man." Ray Ray wiped the sweat from his neck with the paper towel. "Shit, it's hot as a muthafucka out there, man!"

"Hey, let me use the phone right quick."

Ray Ray picked up Charles's phone and started to dial Lil Steve's cell.

"Shit, man. You want a drink, you want the phone. You gonna want my woman next." Charles came back with a bottle and one glass.

"Naw, man. Flo got that evil eye poppin'. I don't want none of yo' shit, dog." Ray Ray got up and looked out the drapes.

Charles walked to the side window. He peeled back the shade. He put his hand in his pocket and fingered the fake beard and mustache. He watched the lady across the street water her burnt grass. Sweat raced down the side of Charles's face. He couldn't believe Ray Ray. Why the fuck was he here? Any minute Trudy would be at his door. She'd already called to say she was on her way. He had to act cool and get Ray Ray to leave.

Charles took the bottle and downed a quick shot, then walked to the kitchen holding the neck in his fist. And even though this was the last of his very good scotch he drained the rest of the bottle in the sink. Maybe Ray Ray'd leave since the liquor was gone. Charles tried to steer him away. "Man, I'm tired. I got to get me some sleep."

"Straight up?" Ray Ray said, barely listening to Charles. He had already swallowed his Jack and was twirling the wet, empty glass.

"I want to get some rest before Flo gets home, man. She's been tripping big time lately."

Ray Ray got up and peered again out the drapes. He came back and shook the last drops from the bottle. "Damn, man, is that all you got?"

"I was fixing to go get a drink at the club. Besides, I got my eye on a honey up there."

"I ain't never seen no honeys at Dee's, man," Ray Ray said, looking at Charles. "Most of 'em just want someone to keep buying 'em shots and lighting the tips of their Virginia Slims." Ray Ray went to the kitchen and picked up his gun. "None of 'em got any heart."

Charles watched him put the gun inside a holster. "Whatchu know about heart?" Charles smiled at his friend. "You as ice pick as they come."

Ray Ray didn't even look up. He noticed a pack of gum on the dining room table. He handed a piece to Charles, folded a stick inside his mouth and then put the whole Juicy Fruit pack in his slacks.

Ray Ray massaged the bulge in his stomach. He wanted to go count the money. The blue vinyl bag itched inside his shirt. "Man, let me use your bathroom a minute."

Charles looked up, nervous. You had to go through the bedroom to get to the bathroom. His canvas mail carrier's bag with the money inside was laying on top of the bed.

But it was too late. Ray Ray stood up. He went to the bathroom and bolted the door. "Let me ride to the club with you tonight, dog," Ray Ray yelled out through the crack.

"Ride with me?" Charles sat chewing his gum fast and nervous. "What's wrong with yo' shit?" He had to get Ray Ray out. Trudy would be there any minute!

Suddenly there was a sharp rap at the door.

Charles sat paralyzed. He didn't dare move. Ray Ray seized up. He zipped up his pants. He took the gun out from his holster again. He hadn't unzipped the blue envelope yet. He peeked from the bathroom door and stared through the crack. *Lord*, he said, rubbing the flat metal cross, *please don't send me back to the pen*. He cocked his black gun and peeked through the crack.

"What's wrong witchu, man? Ain't this yo' house? Go ahead and answer the door," Ray Ray whispered loudly.

Ray Ray opened the bathroom door wider. He clicked off the light. He stood in the shadowy black.

Charles twisted the front door handle slowly and the heavy door creaked as it opened.

Flo stood there holding two bags of groceries.

Fuck! Charles said to himself. What was Flo doing here now?

She was supposed to be at work. All hell would bust loose if Flo saw Trudy at their house.

"Hey, Miss Flo," Ray Ray said relieved. He walked into the room. "Whatchu know good?" Ray Ray smiled, revealing a row of rough teeth; his gun was back under his arm.

Flo silently carried the bags to the kitchen. Lazy asses, Flo thought to herself. Neither one of them would think to offer her some help. She glanced at Charles quickly and then looked away. She was struggling with the big, heavy bags.

"See what I mean, man?" Charles said in a low tone. "I don't need that attitude up in my own place." He looked toward the door and raised his voice slightly. "People think they a queen 'cause they got a new car." Charles looked over and whispered to Ray Ray. "Let that bitch carry that shit in herself."

Flo poked her head back in. "I don't see your name on no-body's lease. Let the doorknob hit ya where the good Lord split ya." She let the kitchen door swing back shut.

"Shit, man," Ray Ray said, looking at the closed door. "If I had a nice woman coming home with groceries, my ass would stay home every day."

Charles grabbed his coat and a bottle of cologne. His keys jingled in his deep pocket.

Ray Ray nervously eyed Charles. He didn't want to drive his own car. He was afraid to go out in his Lincoln again. The police might be looking for it now.

"Hey, Charles, ol' Bessie been acting up lately." Ray Ray hadn't called his Lincoln Bessie in ages. "Mind if I ride with you?"

Charles didn't comment. He went to the bedroom. Charles wasn't worried about who drove or not. He had more important things on his mind. He shook the mail bag and the blue vinyl bag landed on the pillows. He wrapped it up inside his jacket. "No problem," Charles called from the door. "I'll be out in a minute." He watched Ray Ray walk to the front door and pause. "Go 'head, man. I'll be right there." Ray Ray peeked from the window and then stepped to the porch.

Charles was nervous. His stomach felt jumpy. He was worried about carrying around all that money. He wished he could leave some of it here. Not take it all to Dee's. He picked up a green glass bottle of Brut, spraying the cologne along his throat just to stall. Where could he put some? Where could he hide it? He grabbed the fat blue envelope and his coat and walked straight out the front door. But when he got to the curb he turned around and jogged back down the long driveway.

"Wait a second, man." Charles hollered at Ray Ray. "I forgot something. I'll be right back." Charles ran all the way back into his yard. He looked around quickly to see if anyone was watching. But he didn't have to worry. The upstairs people had moved out. Charles glanced around the yard. There was nothing but dirt. A worn-out sheet blew from the line. In the corner stood a falling-down garage. Charles pulled hard to get the old garage door open, knocking down the thick cobwebs with a stick. The old garage was stuffed with all sorts of junk. Broken-down furniture, bags of old soiled clothes and a whole lot of rat-chewed boxes. The kind of stuff people bagged up and shoved against a wall and never came back for again.

Charles eyes skimmed the dim, cobwebbed room. A wooden plank was brimming with paint cans. Using a pocket knife, Charles worked around the lid of the can and then pried off the stubborn round top. He dumped what was left in the can on the grass. Gray, gunky paint oozed over the lawn. He sprayed the inside of the can with a hose. Luckily the money was still wrapped in plastic. He jammed most of the cash inside the old gallon can. He took fifteen thousand and put it in the envelope in his pocket, shoving the paint can behind some others in the back and ran back down the long driveway.

"What's that?" Ray Ray asked, noticing the paint on his hands. "You planning on painting a house?"

Charles didn't respond. He wiped his hands on a napkin. He pressed on the gas, racing the car down toward Dee's Parlor.

Flo walked to the front window and peeked from the drapes. She watched Ray Ray and Charles drive away from the house, but as soon as their tires cleared away from the curb, Trudy passed by slowly in front of their driveway.

"Oh, I know this 'ho don't think she can roll over when she

wants." Flo grabbed the egg carton from the plastic grocery bag. She raced from the house. "He ain't over here, slut!" She sped down the steps and straight toward Trudy's car.

"Get the hell off my street 'fore I kick your cheap ass!" Flo tossed a fresh egg at Trudy's car and missed, but the other one smashed on and in her halfway rolled window.

Flo grabbed her door handle and tried to pry it open, but Trudy skidded off toward the corner.

"Oh, it's on now!" Flo said to herself. She fanned her hot face once she got in the house. So Charles and Trudy were trying to be slick. Having Ray Ray show up was obviously a decoy. Flo kicked the grocery bag across the floor in the kitchen. She picked up a box of Wheat Thins and the phone and dialed Tony. She sure hated to call Tony but she needed his help. This shit was getting dealt with tonight.

"That you, Flo? Flo Washington calling me? Must be my day. What's up, baby? That nigga showing his color at last?"

"Tony, can I come over for a minute?"

"Hell, yeah, 'cause I'm sure not coming to your house and getting my ass shot by your postal-working husband."

"We're not married, Tony."

"Might as well be. Y'all been shackin' forever."

"I just want to come over for a second, okay?"

"If you come, it ain't for no minute and you know this." Tony laughed a wild, evil, drunken wheeze, like he'd just told the funniest joke.

Flo didn't say a thing.

"What's wrong witcha, girl? Cat got yo' tongue?"

"I'll tell you when I get there." Flo hung up and plugged in the hot rollers and quickly got into the shower. She oiled her legs and combed out her hair until it flowed big and black against her shoulders.

She didn't want Tony. Hell, naw. Flo didn't want nothing to do with his nasty ass and foul habits. But Tony had something that Flo really wanted. See, Tony had a thing for guns. Had a whole arsenal over there. Had .350 Magnums and derringers too, snub .45's you could fit in your purse and old rifles you strapped on your back. You were supposed to surrender your weapons after 'Nam but Tony and his brothers had kept some. She remembered how Tony would sit in the living room for hours. He'd spread the newspaper out over their wooden coffee table and carefully oil each one. He'd check all the triggers, gut and clean out the shaft. Then he'd twirl the barrel fast, watching it spin, until it sounded like those big roulette wheels in Vegas.

Tony took real good care of his guns. Flo thought that if he had paid that kind of attention to her they might have been able to work something out. But no, Tony was from that old school of women being in the kitchen and not having opinions. No, all Flo wanted was what Tony had and the way she felt now after all that had just happened, she'd suck a golf ball out of a water hose to get it.

32

Trudy and Jimmy

Trudy rushed home and double-locked her door. Her phone was sirening loudly from the cradle. Her makeup was smeared and some of her braids were dripping with yolk.

"Hello?" she said, snatching up the receiver while rinsing her hair in the sink.

"What happened?" Charles asked fast. "Did Flo see you go by? I saw your car in my rearviews with Ray Ray."

Trudy didn't tell him what happened with Flo. "You're with Ray Ray? Does he know?" Trudy said low, even though she was alone.

"He doesn't know shit," Charles whispered back. "But I'm sweating bullets just being with blood. All I know is you wouldn't be talking to me now if Ray Ray knew we switched those damn bags."

Deep grooves grew across Trudy's forehead. It wouldn't be good if Ray Ray found out he'd been tricked. All Ray Ray had was a couple of hundreds, and newspaper cut down to size.

"What should we do now?" Trudy asked Charles. She was still a little flustered from Flo running to her car. She wanted her money so she could hurry and leave town.

"Meet me at the club. Just sit and act natural. We'll divvy it all up when you get here."

Trudy didn't like that Charles was in control, but she had to act cool, let him call the shots. He was the one with the money.

Trudy hung up and quickly tossed her things in a satchel. Everything she needed was in that tight little bag. She was leaving tonight. She wouldn't be back. Her plan was to settle with Charles, give Vernita her cut and get on the road tonight, but now she had to go to the club.

"Fuck!" Trudy said to herself. Fuck. Fuck. Fuck. Fuck. Dee's was the last place she wanted to be. Besides, it was dangerous now. She had just ripped off a drug dealer's money. She didn't want Jimmy to point his flashlight on her.

Trudy pulled a white dress from the back of her closet. She wanted to appear cleaner than water. She rummaged through what she'd already packed in the bag: two dresses, two pairs of pants, three blouses, a few T-shirts, a new pair of shoes, some Nikes and a white pair of socks. She folded the handgun in a black bandana. The gun was the last thing she'd stolen from her mother. When Joan threw Trudy out she'd smuggled her gun. She carefully placed the gun in her purse.

She popped in a Barry White tape to calm her nerves.

Suddenly the telephone rang.

"Whatcha doing listening to that old school stuff, girl?"

It was Jimmy! *Oh shit*, Trudy thought.

"Hey," Trudy said, trying her best to sound sleepy.

"Don't try to play like you taking a nap, baby. I've been waiting across the street. I saw you pull up. Now open this door and quit playin'."

Trudy panicked. Jimmy wouldn't just come over here, would he? How long had he been waiting? Why was he here? She walked over to the front window and peeled back the blinds. Jimmy's black SUV was parked right in her driveway.

"Why are you trying to sneak up on a girl?" Trudy said while shoving her satchel under the table with one foot. "Just give me five minutes before you come to the door. I've got to get myself together."

"I'm not waiting no fucking five minutes, girl. Open this damn door up now," he commanded.

God damn! Does he know? Why is he here? Trudy hung up. Her eyes flashed over her apartment. It was a royal mess. She had stuff all over the floor, trying to figure out what to pack. She picked up the little clothes pile on the floor and shoved it on the big clothes pile and carried it to the closet. Trudy pushed all her odd shoes and purses and belts under the bed. She yanked the comforter up and fluffed the two pillows. She took the dishes in the sink and put them all in a large plastic tub. She gathered the various cups and plates from around the TV and next to her bed and then carried the whole thing to the back porch and left it out there on the steps. She took all the brochures about Las Vegas and hid them under the rug.

Act cool, girl, Trudy told herself in the mirror. The doorbell rang. Trudy's eyes darted quickly around the room again. Everything seemed okay. Then she saw it lying out on the sink. It was her stash. Six thousand eight hundred bucks lay gaping from an open envelope on the sink. She'd skimped and saved, living on one meal a day, hoarding half of each check and surviving on Dee's Parlor singing and tips.

The bell rang again, longer this time. She opened a pack of Kraft macaroni and cheese and dumped the contents in the trash. She tucked back the flap and shoved the envelope inside. "Coming," she called toward the door.

Trudy zipped her snug dress and slipped some black fuck-me pumps on. Smearing gloss over her trembling lips, she gently opened the door.

Jimmy didn't say a word. He walked briskly inside. His eyes scanned her room and traveled over her body, and his breath was like an overrun horse.

"What are you doing dropping over out the blue like this, boy?" Trudy asked, smiling widely. She tried to keep it light.

"What?" Jimmy said leaning close to her face. Jimmy didn't smile at Trudy at all. "You trying to tell me what to do?"

"Shoot, I just asked you a question." Trudy threw her thick braids across her shoulder and walked away, but Jimmy grabbed her arm and yanked her back.

Aw, shit! Trudy thought. *Brotherman knows something. My ass is busted.* Her eyes went to the bag with her gun. But all he did when he pulled her was lean down and kiss her, sucking the length of her neck. "Don't ever keep me waiting outside like that, baby." He kissed her again, squeezing and rubbing on her body. Suddenly he pulled her away and stared into her eyes. "I don't play that shit, okay?"

"Sorry, I'm just tired. I haven't been able to sleep." Though she breathed out the faintest sigh of relief, inside she shook like a leaf.

"You have any Courvoisier?" Jimmy asked, skimming her meager liquor cabinet.

All Trudy had was one swallow of Cuervo, a dab of Alizé and a bottle of Merlot for show.

Trudy went in the kitchen and opened the wine. She saw a corner of the Kraft box and shut the cabinet all the way. She kicked her satchel farther under the table.

When she came back, a fat gun lay on the coffee table. Trudy's hand trembled when she handed him the glass. But Jimmy didn't notice. He was peering into his wallet. He spread five hundred dollars on her table.

"Who's that for?"

"You, girl. I take care of my boo." He took his glass from Trudy and pressed her hand to his lips. "Get your hair done, stock your liquor cabinet—shit, I don't care, baby, but make sure you got some Courvoisier next time. That's the only kind of shit I like."

Trudy sat down on the couch next to Jimmy. She tried not to look at the gun but couldn't help it. A cold fear started to leak into her body. Her blood warmed her face and her heartbeat sped up. It was just how she felt when she stole. Suddenly she could hear Pearl's voice clear as day: "Ain't nothing ever free in this world, girl. If ever you think you got something for free it just means they ain't figured what to charge your butt yet."

Trudy tried to shake those thoughts from her mind. She took the money from the coffee table and slipped it inside a book, just in case he decided to take the bills back.

Jimmy downed his wine and pulled Trudy to his lap. He was nibbling her lobe with his teeth when he noticed the black satchel on the floor in the kitchen. He scowled and looked in her face.

"You fixin' to leave?" Jimmy asked, puzzled. He pulled Trudy's chin toward his face.

"Oh, that's my Goodwill," she lied easily. "Nothing in it but junk. Every time I buy something I give something away. I'm taking it to the second-hand store in the morning." She hoped he wouldn't look at the contents inside. She figured it was best to change the subject.

Trudy took his drink and put it down on the table. She straddled his legs and bent over his chest and fiercely kissed him on the mouth.

"You bad girl," Jimmy said, holding her waist. "You know how to treat a man good."

Trudy was quaking with fear but lifted her dress. Jimmy's wool pants tickled the fresh skin under her thighs. Laying back, Jimmy allowed her to straddle his waist. Trudy usually liked sitting on top of men like this. Right in their laps. Staring down in their faces. It gave her a thrilling feeling of sexual power. But this time was different. She felt vulnerable and open. Like realizing you left the front door unlocked, or hearing a loud noise while taking a shower. But Trudy hid her fear. She learned how to fake it. She concentrated on Jimmy instead.

He was wearing suspenders with a blue oxford shirt. It was stiff like it had just left the cleaners. The tapered cut accentuated his firm, narrow waist. His wide shoulder blades spread for days. He was cut. There was definitely no doubt about that. The man was six-six and so damn big and strong, he looked like car alarms would go off when he walked by.

Trudy started unbuttoning his shirt in slow motion. With her red dagger nails she tugged on each button until the round circle inched out the slit. The blue shirt fell open. His wide chest rose up, revealing his clingy white tank. Those tank tops were all called "wife beaters" now, because every time you saw a cop show and there was a domestic brawl, the man they dragged out always had one on. Trudy yanked up the tank and started rubbing his chest. With one hand she unhooked his belt.

"What's the hurry, baby?" Jimmy asked smiling. "Relax, take your time. I'm not going anywhere, girl." Jimmy held her waist, like she was a valuable vase. Something he didn't want to drop. He squeezed her, then unzipped the back of her dress. He unfastened her bra and pulled it out from under each arm and began circling her nipples with his tongue.

Trudy was losing her mind. Her breath beat fast as propellers. Jimmy was doing things that shot all the way up her spine. But damn it! She didn't have time for this now. She wanted to be done. To be out the door. But his tongue seared her flesh. He excited her skin. With her nerves all on edge he was hitting a deep itch. She tried to resist. Her mind struggled to fight it. But in no time she was butter sliding across a hot knife.

"You act like you're starving," Trudy said with clenched teeth.

"I am," he said, looking at her hard, then slowly closing both his eyes.

"Why?" she asked, breathing in quick staccato. "Don't you get enough to eat?" Was she crazy? This fool could snap her damn neck. She had to get him out of the apartment.

Jimmy slid a wet finger along the length of cleavage. "Not quality." His hand explored her whole figure now, feeling her hips and that legendary ass.

"Now, aren't we aggressive," she said low in his ear. She loosened the belt on his black knife-creased slacks. She unzipped them with her teeth.

"I know," he said, skillfully flipping her over. "I kind of got that in spades." He reached up and clicked off the light. "But it looks like ol' Jimmy finally met his match."

Trudy laughed but a cold fear had lodged in her tonsils. She wanted him gone. She had to do something. If she gave him some maybe he'd at least go to sleep; she could sneak out the back door. She reached for the oil she kept under the couch next to a basket of condoms. Trudy rubbed her hands together until they were both piping hot and then massaged her warm palms across his thick, bench-pressed stomach. Jimmy moaned deep, and his breathing got heavy, the sensation made his massive legs twitch. Trudy ripped open the condom pack with her teeth, rolling it over Jimmy's skin like a new pair of stockings.

Finally, he just couldn't take any more. Jimmy held down both arms and began grinding her skin. Massaging her slow, mixing a warm ghetto roughness that made Trudy purr like a cub. This was good. But got damn, it was dangerous now. And even though his belt buckle dug into her skin, even though she tried hard to stay in control, the whole dam was broke; Trudy could not stop the flow. She began to glide right off of the planet. But her fear was what made the whole feeling exciting. Fear heightened her senses. It ignited desire. She was scared stiff but couldn't stop thrusting her hips. Her body betrayed her. It laughed in her face. His touch made her grunt, made her bite her own wrist. She felt full but still hungry. She felt thirsty yet wet. Her body had turned into one starved, sloppy sponge. She wanted to wipe something up. Though outside she tried to appear as cool as a freezer, inside she raged like a Malibu fire. His thunder, his fierceness was burning her up. He wanted her. All his ripped muscles told her that. His body said he wanted her bad. The fact that he could hurt her made her widen her legs. She knew she was crazy but her lust seized her mind. She dangled somewhere between sizzling bliss and the thought that tonight she might die. The panic grew stronger. It screamed in her veins. Her breathing was so intense the sound drummed in her brain. Did Jimmy know something? Did Jimmy suspect? She teetered on the edge of terror and desire as Jimmy's firm hands clutched the small of her back.

"Gimme that pussy!"

"It's your pussy, daddy!"

Her body kept responding. Her fear fueled her pleasure. When she moaned in his ear it was real this time. Jimmy's body rubbed her stomach in a maddening frenzy, and she met each stroke, arching her back, frantically gasping for breath. Trudy barely could stand it. She wanted him to stop, ease a bit some, but she heard her own voice beg for more. Her low moans had now turned to guttural screams. Her braids slapped against the hard wooden floor. The couch banged and shook the cold stucco wall. And just when she thought she couldn't take any more, just when she thought her pink lungs would explode, Jimmy stopped suddenly. He clicked on the light. He wiped her wild braids out of her sweaty, drenched face.

Jimmy glared down at Trudy with a menacing stare. His forehead was soaking wet.

Oh no! Trudy thought. What was he doing? Why was he staring at her like this now? *Oh my God, he must know!* Trudy nervously glanced at his gun.

A sinister smile spread across Jimmy's mouth. His curled lips revealed a row of white, violent teeth. His fists nailed her wrists to the couch.

Trudy was frantic. She struggled under his body but his rigid arms held her wrists tight. And just when she thought he would make her confess, as his razor-blade eyes sliced across her taut body, Jimmy slowly moved inside her again.

He was teasing her! My God, that's what Jimmy was doing. Trudy had held her breath for such a long time, she felt like she might pass out. Each time he dove in, her body went crazy, winding her waist like she worked at a strip club, thrusting her big hips and wide, juicy thighs. She wanted him to come. She wanted it over. The terror was too much to bear.

"Damn, your shit's good," Jimmy said, smiling again. "I keep pulling out to just make it last."

He tried to stop again, but Trudy wouldn't let him. She could see he was teetering right near the edge. If she raised her large hips and sucked one of his nipples, she knew she could bring him back down.

"Don't do that. Wait, girl. Wait, baby. Stop." But Trudy smiled this time and sucked even harder and used those extra-strong muscles buried way deep inside that she saved for special occasions. Jimmy tried to slow down but Trudy's hips pumped fast. He blew up and slumped over her stomach.

Trudy waited a long time for his breathing to get heavy. She watched him drift softly to sleep. Trudy gently rolled from under Jimmy's overgrown body and tiptoed away on the rug. She took the five hundred dollars out from the book and added it to her stash. She picked up his pants and took them with her to the bathroom and quietly locked the door. She put on her flowered silk robe hanging from the knob and rummaged through his pants pockets. Car keys, gold case lighter and cell phone. The other pocket had a few crumpled-up fives and ones and a business card to a dentist. The back pocket held his wallet. She examined his driver's license. That was his picture all right, but the address was an apartment in Inglewood, not the house in Baldwin Hills. She looked inside the billfold. There was eighteen hundred dollars. Trudy left that money alone. She didn't want him to wake up and think she had robbed him. That's how folks ended up shot. Next to the money was a folded piece of paper. Trudy unfolded it and found a picture inside. It was a young Latin woman in a bikini. Trudy turned over the picture and read the small print on the back. "Hey, papi, here's the picture you wanted. I miss you so much. Can't wait to see you. My eye is almost healed, you big bruiser. (smile) I'll call you as soon as I get back from San Juan. Love, Conchita."

Who was this chick? Had Jimmy hit her? Trudy flushed the toilet and walked back to the room just as Jimmy rolled over and opened his eyes.

"What are you doing up?" Jimmy asked from the couch. Trudy almost jumped out of her skin. She still had his pants behind her back.

"Where'd you learn to love a brother like that?" Jimmy pulled her back down to the couch.

Trudy stayed cool and let the pants fall silently to the floor. She began to kiss the fine hairs below his navel. "What about you? Your mama didn't show you those moves," she teasingly said.

"My mama didn't teach me shit." Jimmy shot her a dirty look. "Fuck her," he said.

Trudy watched him carefully. She didn't know what to say. Her own mother was a sore subject.

"Listen. You don't know a got damn thing about me. Where I'm from. How I was raised. What I had to do to live."

Trudy pulled back. She didn't know him at all. Here she was naked, just had sex with the man and she really didn't know him from Adam. The one thing she knew was she had to get out. He was dangerous. Trudy definitely knew that. She had to find a way to get away.

"She's my mama, but Hallmark ain't talking about her in them cards. Bitch had the nerve to call the cops on my ass. Said I pushed her in the street while driving my car. Ain't that about a bitch. I never touched her ass. She's the one who opened the door."

Trudy recoiled. "What happened to her?"

Jimmy narrowed his eyes. "Now there you go with your interrogation shit. 'What happened? What happened?' I'll tell you what happened. She dropped out and rolled and got pinned under a car." Jimmy smiled when he said that, his voice filled with pride. "Oh, she cried and carried on, put on a show for 5-0. Lied and said I was slangin' 'caine. I lost everything, all of my money, all my cars; I had all kinds of stuff. She said she wouldn't press charges if I left the state. After that, all I did was strongarm at clubs."

"You mean like a bouncer?"

"Yeah, but not like Percy or raggedy-ass Ray Ray." Jimmy looked at her like he knew something about her and Ray Ray. "Nothing like them nickel-bag fools around Dee's. All them niggas want is enough scrilla to stay high on. See, I branched out from that. Any time there was some real mess they beeped me. Used to call me 'QC.' Stood for quality control. Hired me to make sure the club always stayed tight." Jimmy suddenly sat up. "Say, what you got to feed a brother around here, baby?"

Trudy looked over her shoulder. She wasn't cooking this man nothing! She was hoping he would get up and go. She wanted him to leave so she could finally get out. She had to hurry up and meet Charles. Maybe he'd be happy with a bag of corn chips. She got up and went to the kitchen.

"So," she called out from way back in the kitchen, "ever get hurt doing that kind of work?"

"Not really," Jimmy said, rolling over, exposing half of his well-sculpted body. "This one fool tried to pull a knife on me once when I threw his ass out of this club." As she walked out of the room, Jimmy pulled down the blanket on the couch and showed Trudy an ugly jagged scar that ran down the length of his calf.

"I had him in a stronghold and he stabbed me straight in the leg. It was on after that. Nigga shouldn'ta never done that." Jimmy laughed. "He didn't come out too good, though."

"What happened to him?" Trudy said, walking back into the room.

"Snapped that muthafucka's neck, pi-ya! That's what the hell happened. Punk stay up in some halfway house now. Trying to talk shit from a wheelchair, damn buster. Dude used to drive this baby-blue Impala. Only wheels he got now are up under his butt. Could have killed him, they said. Just came that close. They taught us that shit in Desert Storm."

"You were in the military?" Trudy became more and more worried. This brother was a trained killer. He was hot-headed too. Jimmy was a clean and pressed sledgehammer walking.

"Yeah, but only for a minute until them tight blue suits tripped. Said I beat up an officer. Lied on me again. Didn't like all the cheese I made in that place. I used to lie in my cot and just count it at night. Had all them dead presidents in my bunk bed, baby. None of them dudes wanted to risk getting shot without getting their high on first. Some were even high-ranking officers. Shoot, they *had* to let me go. No black man can have that much power." Jimmy walked to the kitchen. Trudy took one step back.

"Girl, you sure know how to love a man right." He pulled Trudy's leaning-away frame and held her close. "I ain't never letting you out of my sight," Jimmy said.

"So," he said opening her cabinet, "what you got in here to eat?" He looked at the macaroni and cheese box, a large can of corn and three squat cans of sardines.

Trudy's heart raced. *My stash! Oh my God, please don't let him open the macaroni box.* Jimmy stared at her pitiful pantry for a long time. "You on a diet or something?"

Trudy hadn't bought food because she knew she was leaving. "I can make you a sandwich," she said, trying to close the cabinet.

"No, I like macaroni." He was reaching for the box when his cell phone rang loudly. He walked out of the kitchen and picked it up from the coffee table.

"That's okay, baby. Just bring me a can of sardines and a Coke."

Trudy got a Coke and peeled open the can.

"And put some ice in the glass," Jimmy yelled back.

He was putting his gold watch back on. "Yeah, Fresno, what's goin' on, man?"

"Jimmy, we got a little problem," Fresno said.

"What problem? Man, I ain't tryin' to hear 'bout no problems tonight. Tonight's the fight, man. I'm fixin' to head down to the club now."

"Man, somebody hit Wilson coming from the bank."

Jimmy stood up, walked over to the window and peered out. "Naw, I know you ain't talking about *my* shit getting robbed, dog."

"I'm trying to tell you." Fresno paused for a minute. "I'm trying to tell you it's gone."

"Wait a minute, wait a minute. Back the fuck up. What the hell do you mean gone?"

"Some busters jacked Wilson down the street from the bank. It's gone, man."

"What?"

"I'm telling you, they got him!"

"But that muthafucka was driving my Lexus, man. All of my shit was inside my ride. Where the hell is my LS400, man?"

The tan-suit man and Jimmy had the same boss. The tan-suit man made deposits. They used him to hide the cash. But Jimmy had a totally different kind of job. He delivered large stashes of coke for the mob.

"I told you already. Dude was crying like a baby when he came in today. They took it all. The money, the suitcase, the Lexus, everything. Said somebody at the bank must have tipped them off."

Jimmy snapped the phone shut and knocked over Trudy's houseplant. He watched her in the kitchen.

"Where'd you say you worked again?" Jimmy asked, cornering her near the stove.

"I work for Tony. I sing and do office work at Dee's three times a week." Trudy said it matter-of-factly, but inside she was dying. She could tell from the call Jimmy knew about the bank. She was trying her best to act natural.

"Naw, baby," Jimmy said, looking inside his jacket. He pulled out a small business card and flipped it toward her face.

Trudy recognized her bank business card. She hadn't given it to him. How in the hell did he get it?

"You dropped this inside of my car the last time we went out," Jimmy said, walking toward her.

Trudy sat quietly while her stomach did flips. She hoped Jimmy wouldn't notice her left leg was shaking. "I *used* to work there. I quit there last month." Trudy felt her satchel with the heel of her foot. Jimmy'd already seen it but might check it now. She scooted it farther underneath the kitchen table.

Jimmy got right in front of Trudy's face. "No, girl, I remember. You said you had two jobs, Tony and the B of A on Wilshire." He jammed her against the wall and Trudy's eyes skimmed her knife rack. She wondered if she could reach one without him knowing. He was holding Trudy's face when his cell rang again.

It was the boss. Jimmy covered Trudy's mouth with his hand.

"Jimmy, I heard some nasty shit went down. I need that shit handled now!"

He put on his clothes and threw Trudy her dress. "Get yo' shit and let's go!" is all he said, dragging her out to his car.

33

Tony and Flo

Tony picked up the used beer cans from around the TV and threw out the stacks of racing forms. He was pissed that he got stink-eyed and hadn't cleaned the place better, but when he unhooked the latch and saw Flo in all her glory, he felt like the Fourth of July.

"Well, well, well," Tony said, sucking his thick bottom lip. "Come in and make yourself at home."

Flo walked next to Tony and let her body gently graze against his plaid polyester pants. She flashed him a radiant smile.

"Hey, Tony, baby, got anything to drink around here? You know I like that pink stuff you used to make."

Do I have anything to drink, he said smiling to himself. Baby girl was trying to be cute.

"Those were panty-droppers, girl, Tanqueray and lemonade. Don't come in pretending like you don't remember. 'Cause I remember a time when you begged me for some. Now I might be getting a bit bald on one side, but that don't mean I'ma forget."

Flo got two glasses from the low bar in the corner, filled them and handed Tony his drink. She leaned, letting her healthy cleavage fall in his face. She knew what a weak fool he could be.

"My, my, my. I swear your steaks are still rare. And you ain't had no babies yet to knock them breasts down neither. Girl, you look good enough to eat." He swallowed that comment and downed the clear fluid, using his sleeve to wipe off the rest.

Always was a sloppy fool, Flo thought to herself. She got up and fixed them another quick round. She made his drink strong, pouring in tall Tanqueray shots. But in hers she used clear 7-Up. She lit one of his Winstons and took one deep drag. *I hope to God this don't take long,* she sighed low.

At thirty-four, Flo had known a busload of men. She'd had young ones, old ones, rich ones and fools. Most of them wanted the same fucking thing: some good sex and a nice place to eat and sleep. She smiled at Tony. She wasn't giving him shit. The only thing she was getting him was drunk.

But Tony had ideas of his own.

He was getting warm. He sprawled himself over the couch, unbuttoning his ripe polyester shirt until it fell and his gut poured over his belt like a half-harnessed whale.

I'm definitely getting me some of this tonight, Tony said to himself, rubbing his massive stomach.

Flo took the cigarette she lit and put it right in his mouth.

"I was wondering when you'd come to your senses, ol' gal. You finally see who the real man is." Tony tried to grab her arm but Flo smiled and squirmed away.

Shit, Flo thought, making his third drink. She was going to have to give this fool something to hold him off. Tony got up and rubbed her butt as she stirred her cold ice. Flo slowly buttoned the top part of his shirt and guided him back to the couch. Tony leaned over and started caressing her breasts. She let him rub them a long time while she watched the news. He tried to take her blouse off but Flo walked away, pretending to glance through his loose stacks of music.

"You got anything good?" Flo said, looking around.

Tony sat way back, sipping the rest of his gin.

So Baby wanted to take her time, he thought to himself. He watched her pick up Al Green's greatest hits and put on *Love and Happiness.*

Flo lit another cigarette and made Tony down the last of his glass, only this time she slipped in two of those yellow pills the doctor had prescribed for her nerves.

"Come on, baby," Flo said, unzipping the front of her blouse and tossing it down to the ground. "This is my jam, honey. Let's dance!"

Just looking at big-boned Flo got Tony excited. She wore a giant lacy bra and had full-riding tits and a nice pair of black skintight pants. "Whoa, shit," he said, sucking his whole bottom lip. His dick was harder than holiday candy.

"Yeah, baby, that's right. You still got them moves." He twirled her around as they cha-chaed over the worn carpet. "You ought to come down to the club sometime, gal. Them jitter skips would have them a fit, seeing you."

Flo slipped his fourth drink into his hand and said, "Let's toast."

"To what, baby?" Tony slurred. His burning ash sadly dropped down to the shag. He felt woozy. He sank both his hands into Flo's shoulders. Like he was in the deep end and didn't remember how to swim.

"To that big thang you got pushed against my stomach." Flo tried to sound raunchy, like she was really tipsy too.

"Damn," Tony said. It throbbed so hard it hurt. He couldn't believe Flo was standing here in his living room. He grabbed up his glass, swallowing the hot fuel so fast it burned a razor-sharp path down his gullet to his bowel. He raised his glass, swaying back and forth on his feet. He felt blurry-eyed and wild with lust.

"Let's make a toast to that mail-carrying chump."

"To Charles!" Flo said fast, throwing back her own glass.

"This is a new day. I finally got my woman to come back."

He threw back his head and drained his glass with one long, messy-mouthed swallow. He wiped his face and kissed her hungrily and wet.

Flo got seriously sick to her stomach.

She didn't want to have sex. She just wanted him out. But Tony was all over her now. She had to think of something quick.

All she had to do was stall him, let the liquor and dope kick in. Flo decided she would give him a little striptease show.

"Take your clothes off," she said. Tony started fumbling with his pants.

"I'ma give you a fast erotic dance," she told his mouth. Flo began to unhook her black satin bra. She removed both her arms from the sleeves. She let the blouse graze across her firm-nippled breasts. Flo pulled the blouse taut, like she was holding a rope, then pulled it back and forth between her thick, juicy legs like her blouse was a giant black horse she was riding. Flo smiled as she approached Tony's rippling gut. She unzipped his pants and then zipped them back up.

"You're killing me!" Tony screamed, but he loved the whole show. He'd never been closer to heaven.

Flo laid him flat and tied both feet with his belt.

"Girl, you always was a stone freak." He laughed. His head was rolling against the couch now and his eyes were completely glazed.

He started moaning to himself. His tongue hung to one side. Flo walked over and slipped her big toe in his mouth. Tony sucked it like he was a baby.

Tony's body jerked suddenly forward, and he grabbed her and held her firm with both hands. His whale body pinned her down firmly to the couch. She was barely able to breathe.

"I'm getting some, girl. You done played me too long. Now, gimme that sweet meat you've been savin' up, honey. You know it's supposed to be mine."

Flo let him rub but she wouldn't let him get it. Every time he got close she'd move left or shift back to the right, so he never could get near the door. Suddenly he lunged hard, like he was diving over water, and completely passed out on the couch.

"Finally," she said, quickly gathering her things. She washed her hands and face and buttoned up her top. Tony's face was sideways on the brown-checkered pillow, and one hand hung off the couch.

Flo went straight to the bedroom, remembering the giant saxophone box. That's what she wanted. That's where Tony stashed his guns. She looked under the bed and yanked out the case. She scanned the box and let her fingers graze the cool steel inside. She felt a chill run through her bones.

This is serious, girl, she thought to herself. And then she remembered seeing Charles in the car with that bitch and the smell of a woman's perfume in their bedroom the other morning

and the sound of Trudy's low-pitched voice on their phone and
Charles creeping in late again.

She picked up the Smith & Wesson "Chief's Special" PD. It
was the gun the police department used. It had always been Flo's
favorite weapon. It was a satin stainless steel, 9mm chubby-
handled gun, and it felt like a tank in her hand. It was a small
personal-protection gun and the one Tony had taught her how to
fire when they went to target practice together.

Yes, this would work. It fit good in her purse.

But where were the bullets? There weren't any inside the box.

She even removed the dark velvet that lined where the horn
should have lay. Nothing. She looked in the kitchen drawers and
closets and shoeboxes. Nothing. She was getting anxious about
Tony waking up.

She quickly tiptoed back into the living room, where Tony
snored loudly. He turned around and she felt her heart leap from
her chest. She had to find those bullets and get out of there fast!

Tony was not cool sober, a stone fool when he drank, he had
no problem putting his hands on a woman. Flo had to get out of
there quick.

Where were those damn bullets? Shit!

She pulled out his drawers and fumbled, threw the shambled
clothes inside. She heard Tony cough. She went back in the bedroom. She saw the small clock on the dresser clicking slowly
away. It was summertime, daylight saving time too, but it was already starting to get dark.

She looked at the phone books stacked under the table. She
went back in the closet and patted down his jacket pockets.

She heard Tony cough. She found a pack of cigarettes, a few
matchbooks and coins. A crumpled stack of bills totaling forty-
five bucks. She put the cash in her pocket and looked around.

Damn those bullets!

She went back to the bedroom again. She fumbled through
the closet. When she got to an old army peacoat in the back, Flo
found what she was looking for. The pockets on both sides were
stuffed full of boxes, heavy and rattling with the rough sound of
metal. She opened a box, shook out a few and dropped the rest in

her coat pockets. Flo took the 9mm, cocked it and loaded the barrel. She pushed it back until it clicked into place.

Flo remembered holding that gun. It had been fun going to practice. Sometimes she would stand and imagine her target, aiming straight between the eyes. At the range, no one shot to cripple or wound. The only word around there was "bull's-eye."

Flo decided to take the whole box and dropped it in her purse. She scanned the room one last time to make sure she didn't forget anything.

She looked at Tony snoring on the couch. One arm hanging limp from the armrest.

Flo aimed the gun at him and said, "bam," under her breath.

She grabbed her purse, clicked the light out and left.

Flo drove like a fiend while thinking about Charles. That old feeling crept back and lodged deep in her brain. It was just how she felt before flinging that cake. That hate building up, that wanting to do something. That wild thirsty lust for revenge. Charles was probably sitting in Dee's laughing, oblivious to Flo as she drove with the cold, steely gun in her lap.

34

Joan

Trudy's mother, Joan, finished ironing Mr. Hall's pants. She brushed them again with a lint brush. She watched the crowd forming a line outside Dee's.

"Crabs in a barrel," Joan hissed under her breath. Joan preferred to do her drinking alone. She watched the activity at Dee's from her big picture window and the velvet-drape safety of home. Those were lowlifes. They were not in her class. She wouldn't be seen in that rinky-dink bar. But the reality was Joan never went anywhere at all. She was afraid she'd miss Mr. Hall's call.

Mr. Hall sat and smoked in the dark living room corner. He examined the pants carefully before putting them back on. One by one he slowly buttoned the front of his shirt. He quietly strapped on his watch.

"What time are you coming back?" Joan mildly asked him. She trained her voice to not sound desperate or controlled.

Mr. Hall crushed his cigar back down in the ashtray.

Joan had long since given up on pushing to get an answer to that question. She'd see Hall whenever he got good and ready.

Mr. Hall took his coat. He checked the contents of his wallet. He shoved it in his pocket and gently put on his hat.

"What the hell's over there that you've got to get to so bad?" Joan's sullen face made her look at least fifteen years older. "All I see is some cheap government cheese–eating roaches. How can you be seen with those crows?"

Mr. Hall almost smiled. He took out his keys. He picked up his Bible and opened the door. He left a giant bottle of scotch on the dining room table and walked out toward Dee's neon sign.

"Well, go on," she said loudly once he got out of earshot. "Go and be with those cheap, lowclass wenches. All of those spooks make me sick." What really sickened Joan was the new crop of women. Young women. Young women with flawless, fresh skin. Women with hard butts and breasts and fresh, glistening hair. Women with bodies so firm they looked made out of rubber, like if you squeezed them they'd pop right back out. And the men, men her own age didn't glance her way now. They all wanted young bodies, wanted to touch those young spines. All of this rattled Joan to no end.

"Why can't these tramps stay with men their own age?" Joan yanked her drapes closed. She poured the scotch Mr. Hall had brought her. Once he left, she spent half the day waiting like this, wondering if Hall would come back.

As the crowd outside grew louder, the voices eased into her den. Curiosity made Joan pull the drapes open once more. The line outside Dee's swelled into the lot. She saw pink halter-topped women in black fishnet stockings. Their spiked heels looked like ice picks. Joan lit her smoke and exhaled slowly. *Yeah*, she thought to herself once again. Hall had his eye on one of them wenches. It was only a matter of time before one of them snagged him. Just like she'd done a long time ago.

Joan was about to close the drapes when something caught her eye. She put her whole face on the wide plate-glass frame. She saw Hall standing in line, but pushing her way through the pack was some scantily clad heifer. Her dress was half on and the men jeered as she passed. Joan followed the girl's backside, squeezing her eyes tight. It looked like Hall was following the girl too. He worked through the pack and almost touched the girl's arm. As the girl turned, part of her breast leaked from her dress just as she passed through Dee's door. Joan's eyes rose above the girl's neck and she sucked in her breath as she stared right into Trudy's young face.

"Slut!" Joan savagely snatched the drapes shut. "A whore for a daughter, that's all I got." Joan caught a glimpse of herself in the mirror. She scrutinized the lines in her neck and her forehead. Her eyes frowned at her tight bun and dropped down to her feet. They were warped from large, engorged bunions.

She flung what was left of her drink at the mirror. She grabbed all of Mr. Hall's clothes from the closet and violently ripped them to shreds.

35

Ray Ray and Tony

The telephone ringing was what woke Tony up.

He heard Pearl's shrill voice on his answering machine. "Where you at, man? I can't hold these folks back. They all want to place down their bets on this fight!"

Groggily, he got dressed and rode back to the club. The parking lot was almost packed. He knew he was late but had no regrets. He sucked his bottom lip thinking of Flo. No Tony didn't regret being late at all. His baby was finally back and tonight was the fight. He was going to make a killing tonight.

When he pulled up, some folks were already inside and more were outside standing in line. They couldn't wait to throw their money on Liston or Jones. The sports betting was a big chunk of Tony's income. Most of these folks didn't have cable. Shoot, cable lines didn't even come in some areas. But he had the hookup. Got all his stuff free—HBO, Showtime, all the pay-per-view he wanted, and plenty of slick nudey movies. And now with Miss Flo back in his life, all he had to do now was make money.

Pearl was rummaging through an old cigar box in the kitchen when Tony strolled into the room. Pearl dropped the box and pretended to be putting on her makeup when Tony walked up to the counter.

"I hope that extra cook in there is ready for the crowd we got tonight. And there's plenty more lining up outside."

Pearl rolled her eyes and kept painting her mascara. She wanted him to leave so she could keep looking through the box's contents.

"Can I take a bet for you this evening?" Tony said, leering over Pearl's bustline.

"Thanks, but no thanks. I keeps mines in the bank," Pearl said.

"No use letting it sit there and grow mold." Tony said it like he wasn't talking about bet money at all. He left the kitchen and lit a Winston in the hallway.

Heifer worked a man's nerves, Tony said to himself. But tonight was the big fight and Flo had come back. The cigarette glow revealed a smile inching out his mouth. Even Pearl couldn't mess with him now.

He walked into the restaurant to make sure everything was ready. He saw Charles and Ray Ray together.

"Hey, man, I need to talk to you," Ray Ray said.

"I'm right here. What's up?" Tony said, grinning at the tight crowd.

"Not here, man," Ray Ray said, looking around.

Tony looked at Ray Ray, who was nervously moving his weight from foot to foot.

"Well, let's go into my office, then, son." There was a small line waiting outside the gate now as people eagerly waited to bet. Tony unlocked the gate and walked up the stairs to the office and pulled the drawstring over the desk. Charles and Ray Ray both followed Tony's back and took seats in the two folding chairs. Percy came up too, wearing a long black leather coat. He waited outside the small door.

"So what's up? You guys finally got some betting money this time? Must be something." Tony grinned. He flicked off his ash. " 'Cause Ray Ray looks like he might piss any minute."

"You seen Lil Steve in here yet?" Ray Ray asked.

"Naw, man, I ain't seen him. But believe you fucking me. If I ever catch that skinny nigga cheatin' in here again, his ass is gon' be barred for life." Tony looked hard at Charles, like he was talking to him too. "So y'all ready to put some money on the table instead of talking shit this time?" Tony took a long drag and looked at Ray Ray. He brought one big leg over his desk.

Ray Ray started to pull out the blue vinyl bag.

"Wait a minute, Ray Ray. Let me go first," Charles blurted. He knew if Ray Ray unzipped that blue vinyl pouch he'd see he only had newspaper scraps.

"Look here, Tony. I know I been owing you. But I'm ready to settle up now." Charles pulled out an old envelope. It was stuffed full of money. Ray Ray's eyes widened but he kept his jaw tight.

Suddenly Pearl burst into the small room. "I knew I'd find you out. All I did was keep looking." Her narrowed eyes squinted at Tony like she'd caught him. She held a crumpled piece of paper in her fist. She glanced at Charles holding a big wad of money. Tony had his hand on his gun.

"Get out!" Tony said.

"But I—"

"I said get out!" Tony slammed his fist on the desk.

But Pearl smiled to herself as she walked back downstairs. She smoothed out the crumpled piece of paper in her hand. "The shit's done hit the fan now."

Tony scowled. He hadn't planned for Charles to pay him back. He wanted his debt to get way out of hand so he could have Big Percy break his back.

"Naw, man, it's okay. Go 'head and play. We'll square everything up next week."

But Charles had already counted out four thousand dollars. Tony's eyes bulged at the bag Charles was holding. The four G's only skimmed the top.

Ray Ray studied Charles and the money for a while. What was homeboy doing? Where'd he get all this cash? But Ray Ray knew better than to open his mouth. He stared at the money and stayed mute. Rubbing the burn scar with the palm of his hand, Ray Ray wanted to light his smoke but didn't dare move. He started to pull out his blue bag too, but Charles held his wrist back and stopped him.

"Wait, man," Charles said, nervously.

"Whatchu doin'?" Ray Ray said.

"Here," Charles said quickly. "This is what I owe you, too." Charles reached in and pulled out five neat stacks of hundreds. He handed the bundles to Ray Ray.

Charles leveled his eyes on Ray Ray. "Now we straight, right?"

Tony's eyes glowed big in the broom closet room. What were these two fools doing with all this dough?

Ray Ray knew Charles didn't owe him shit but he folded a grand and dug it into his sock. He took the money Charles gave him and gave it to Tony. "I'ma put the rest here on Liston." Ray Ray didn't even bother opening his bag. Where did Charles get his money? Ray Ray looked at him hard but decided it was best to stay quiet. Shoot, his bet was placed without him having to touch any of his own money. Everything should be gravy, but Ray Ray felt worried. Something was definitely wrong.

"So," Ray Ray said, "you gonna call the dude, or what?" Ray Ray stepped closer to Tony.

Tony smiled at the money and, for the first time, at Ray Ray.

"Don't have to. The man's on his way. I just hung up a few minutes ago," Tony lied. "I'll hold on to this till he gets here."

"Naw, dog. I wanna talk to him myself."

"Sorry, brotha, but we don't work it like that. If you want to place a bet it goes through me and I get mine. The man takes his twenty and you get eighty if your hit pays."

"Don't I get a receipt or nothing?" Ray Ray asked Tony.

Tony's smile broadened. "This ain't no grocery sto', Negro. Just sit tight, relax. Get something to drink; it's on me. Wait a minute." Tony opened a drawer and pulled out a bottle and removed the flask he kept in his jacket. "Here, I got something to hold you." Tony filled the flask with sticky peach brandy. "Go ahead and knock yourself out."

Two other customers waiting to place their bets came into the room and Tony motioned for Charles and Ray Ray to leave, slamming the door right in Ray Ray's worried face. Ray Ray stood there a moment before going back downstairs. He unzipped his bag and peered deep inside. On top were real bills covering each stack, but the rest was all *L.A. Times*.

"What the fuck?" Ray Ray said. He wanted to stand there and think, but Percy nudged him to go back downstairs.

Ray Ray didn't know what to do. Where the fuck was all the money? Had Lil Steve crossed him when he tossed him the bag? Had this been a scam the whole fuckin' time? Where the hell was the red nigga at? Ray Ray was mad. He rushed down the stairs. He studied Charles's back as they hustled back down. And what about Charles? What was this fool doing with cash? Last time they talked, Charles was singing the blues about owing Tony some money

"Hey, homes?" Ray Ray stopped Charles by the arm. "Where the fuck did you get all that cheddar?" Ray Ray stood in his face. He saw the lines in Charles's eyes. Charles sputtered and started to choke.

His brain was anxiously thinking of something to say.

"Where'd you get it, huh?" Ray Ray asked him again. "What's-a matter, cat got your tongue?"

The club felt so hot. Charles loosened his collar. The pre-fight was on. Two men were boxing. Their muscular brown bodies were glistening wet. One had a smashed, bloody face.

Ray Ray's face was so close, Charles felt his breath on his nose.

"Huh? I'm talking to you, man," Ray Ray asked him point-blank.

Charles fidgeted against the wall. One of the fighters fell down. A small Cuban guy knocked down a big pale Russian. Half the crowd in Dee's Parlor lurched up and screamed. Charles panicked. What the hell could he say? Where in the hell could he have gotten fifteen grand? But suddenly it hit. The lie floated through his teeth.

"I sold that bitch's new car."

36

Lil Steve and Vernita

A hot breeze blew a pack of Kools into the gutter off Western. Lil Steve scratched his neck and leaned against the cracked vinyl of the Bug.

"Damn, it's hot," he said, wiping his face with his sleeve.

He checked the Rolex on his wrist again. It was 7:55. Across town the Lexus had already been stripped down. The parts were shipped to Long Beach by now. He looked at the bag of cocaine. He had to hide this bag before Johnny Law saw him and pulled his card.

But Lil Steve had a jones or two of his own. He was real low-key. He didn't let it show. See, nobody knew he smoked coke. There were baby rocks he got off the street from time to time but he always went to the east side to cop. He only bought rocks off the *Cholos* in MacArthur Park or the *Eses* along Alvarado. None of the brothers knew he did blow. He smoked rocks by himself, all alone in the car. He never shared. He avoided all those crack-heads around Dee's. He didn't want none of them fools to label him a "head." Once it gets known you base, you in a whole other league. People start to watch you around all their shit. He couldn't have that. He needed folks' trust. His whole game was confidence and macking. He wasn't about to fuck that up. That was out of the question. So whenever he did lines or smoked some cocaine, it was always late at night by himself.

Lil Steve looked at the trash and liquor bottles in the street.

He peered down inside the bag. The last time he saw this much stuff was right before the battering ram busted Flash's door and hauled everybody down to County.

Lil Steve stuck a pen and made a small hole. He licked his finger and dunked it inside the powder, rubbing the white substance over his top gum and teeth. The low life was over. It was all gravy now. Lil Steve sucked the tip of his finger. He wasn't even worried about Ray Ray with the money. With this giant bag of coke, there was no telling how much he could make on the street.

There's got to be someplace I can do some of this. Suddenly he thought of Vernita.

He smiled to himself. Yeah, Vernita was cool. All them other skeezers he knew couldn't hold water. They'd drop a dime on him in no time.

He turned down Adams and headed toward 10th Avenue. He stopped at Johnnie Pastrami and got a couple of sandwiches. He saw the bright lights from her shop.

Vernita had one more customer in there. She was doing a short woman's hair. She hadn't gotten to the blow-drying stage, so Lil Steve just sat there and waited. He stared long and hard at the bag on the floor. A few palm trees swayed in the cool evening moon. The liquor store across Adams kept the grass littered with empties. Bent cigarette boxes licked the curb.

Lil Steve picked up the bag and brought it up to his lap. He carefully opened the case and looked out of his rearviews to see if anybody was coming. The black Bug had illegally dark tinted windows, so Lil Steve wasn't worried about anybody seeing him inside, but he didn't want any surprises. He carefully pulled back the duct tape that held the package shut. He took his car keys and used his knife to cut open the plastic bag, making an incision along the top so nothing would spill. Then Lil Steve closed the knife back in, pulled out the screwdriver tool and used the flat tip to dip inside the bag. He got a small portion of the white powder on the tip, brought it to his nose and inhaled deep. This was the first time he had him some serious powder. Everybody around there only did rocks.

He watched Vernita bring the curling iron toward the woman's scalp.

Lil Steve dipped the screwdriver in again.

He noticed the smooth movements of Vernita's hands. The way they worked and pulled the hair in strong, artful strokes.

He inhaled the powder real slow.

Vernita spun the chair around so she could do the woman's left side. Lil Steve lifted the wide-tip screwdriver back to his nose. He inhaled eight more times and saved some in the seat before folding the duct tape back over the small hole he'd made. He popped his pocketknife with his teeth and sawed along the cushion of the passenger seat. Pulling the vinyl seat back and removing some of the foam, he firmly pushed the plastic bag inside and folded the vinyl back down.

Lil Steve didn't realize how keyed up he was. He pulled the handle up and let the seat fall. He lay back so he could relax. Though his head barely rose above the window to see, he watched Vernita work in the large salon window. His heart began beating with speed.

He took a cigarette and pulled some of the tobacco from the top and put the cocaine that he'd saved in the cigarette tip. He noticed his hand started trembling a bit. His head felt like he'd sucked on a helium balloon.

He had the music up and was puffing the end of a Salem Light when the short woman finally emerged from the shop. She came right to the car parked in front of him, a beautiful burgundy Jag. Vernita sure did hair good. Had that plain woman looking Hollywood in no time. Waxy locks framed her soft, round face. Gold dolphin earrings screamed against her reddish-brown skin. The woman had a real pep in her step when she walked out of Vernita's shop door.

As soon as the woman pulled away, Lil Steve grabbed the pastrami sandwiches. He put a Raiders cap on and some wraparound sunglasses. He left his suit jacket in the seat.

"Hey, baby," he said, coming in and closing the door. "I got you something to eat."

Vernita was sweeping. She had her back to the door. She hadn't seen or heard Lil Steve come in and almost jumped when she saw his cocky smile in her door. Oh shit! What was he doing here? She planned to meet Trudy here at the shop. She didn't want them rough fools looking sideways at her. She spied the blond wig she'd worn laying in a chair and gently dropped a silk scarf on top.

"What do you want, boy? Didn't I take care of your hair? I know you ain't ready to be tightened again." Vernita tried to be glib. *Be cool*, she told herself. *Don't act nervous or he'll suspect something.*

Lil Steve pulled down the shades and clicked off the huge light that illuminated the shop. Only the lamp with the sixty-watt burned. Vernita picked up the broom and started sweeping again.

"Is that how you greet a man who came all the way up here to bring you some food?" Lil Steve yanked the shades on the other side of the room. "Besides," he said slowly, "I been missin' you, baby. Come here and give Lil Steve a kiss." He put a lot of sugar in that last line.

"Boy, please." Vernita eyed Lil Steve. He seemed more animated than his usually cool ice-tray self. Vernita felt something was wrong.

Lil Steve walked across the room and pulled the other shades down. The shop immediately grew dim.

"Why you got all these windows open in here all the time, girl? Ain'tchu supposed to be closed?"

"I guess I am now," Vernita mumbled to herself. "How come you're so worried about how I run my business?" Vernita tried to keep the conversation light.

"I'm trying to help you, girl." Lil Steve smiled. "You never know when someone might come in and jack you." Lil Steve looked dead into her eyes.

Vernita was sweeping more feverishly now. When she accidentally knocked the silk scarf to the ground, the blond wig drifted down to the floor. Vernita's heart skipped. She stood still as the moon. Lil Steve moved close to her knee. He picked up the wig. He looked at Vernita a real long time, fingering the platinum hair in his hand.

"Why don't you put this on for me, baby?" Lil Steve held it out for her to take.

"Listen, I don't play blondie for nobody, okay? You want a blonde, go to Huntington Beach." Vernita started quickly sweeping again. She put the last bits of hair in the trash.

"What's wrong with you, huh? Why you acting so mean? You weren't like this this morning."

Lil Steve peeked out from the shade and then closed it again. He narrowed his eyes on Vernita.

"I'm not acting like shit." Vernita tried to sound casual. "You the one coming in here trippin'."

Lil Steve loved the rush the cocaine brought on. Though his nerves felt like millions of ants on his skin, inside his skull sizzled and glowed. "Come on! Put it on!" He shoved the wig toward her, but Vernita brushed his stiff hand away.

Lil Steve rushed up on her. The wig dangled from his fist. His face was all twisted with hate. He tried to put the wig over Vernita's cropped head.

"Stop it!" she said. "I don't want to wear it!" Vernita tried to pull free, but Lil Steve held her arm.

"Why not?" he screamed. "Come on. Put it on!" His voice was loud but he didn't know why. He was taking fast, rapid-fire breaths. The coke crept up on him. It was tickling his brain. He held Vernita down hard but didn't know why. He didn't realize how keyed-up he was when he pointed his gun toward her head.

"Put the fucking wig on." Lil Steve was surprised at his own actions. Why in the world was he was talking like this? He knew he should chill but he couldn't stop himself. He didn't even know he'd cocked back the gun.

Vernita looked stunned as the gun shook in his hand. She pulled the blond wig on top of her head. In her nervous haste she put the wig on backward. Long blond strands hung over her face.

"Now see," he said. "Wasn't that easy? All a brother wants is a little variety now and then. Men are visual, baby. We like seeing new shit. We want something fresh from our women." Lil Steve grinned as the gun trembled in his right hand. He eased into a beauty salon chair.

Vernita stayed quiet, clocking his movements. She inched her left hand way behind her back, reaching for the large can of hairspray.

"Girl, I been driving around all day trying to figure out what's wrong, what's been missing in my life." Lil Steve stared into Vernita's light, concerned eyes.

"I've been thinking about you and me all damn day long. As soon as you left me this morning I knew." What the fuck was he saying? He never thought of her once. But his pimp side was recklessly now in full bloom. As he lied through his teeth, his lungs strained for air. The coke had messed him up bad. He recklessly dangled the gun in his hand. He pulled Vernita's body inside the salon chair, holding her flat against his quivering chest.

Vernita let one arm hang from the chair. She was holding the hairspray in the palm of her hand.

"There now, see? You made me come all the way over here and say it. All this time you done got a nigga sprung." He pulled on her neck, bringing her mouth close to his. He pulled the chair's lever until they were both lying prone. Her small body lay completely over his. Vernita watched his gun. She felt his frantic, quaking lungs. They vibrated like a helicopter hovering close to a house.

Vernita was trapped. Lil Steve held her tight. But she still had one hand dangling from the chair. She slowly moved her finger over the spray can's small nozzle.

Lil Steve kissed her mouth. The wig's hair fell in his eyes. He snatched off the wig, throwing it over his shoulder. He held Vernita's neck. "I want you," he said, holding the gun on her cheek. She could feel the cold steel resting right against her jaw. Vernita wouldn't kiss him. She moved her mouth from his lips but she smiled and ran her fingertip over his teeth. They were as smooth as a row of strung pearls. Lil Steve seized her body, gently nibbling her pointer finger. He licked her two fingers as she played with his tongue. Her fingers inched toward the deep grooves of his back molars. With his eyes rolling up and his mouth opened wide, Vernita sprayed the can deep in his throat. A gunshot blast blew the huge mirror into shards. A large fragment busted the overhead light, and the whole room went totally black.

37

Flo

Flo's headlights pierced through the dark anxious night. She raced down the street like a three-legged dog, hell-bent on biting a truck. No, Flo could not wait to catch Charles now. This was it. It was on. She was fit to be tied. She was definitely going to get him tonight.

As Jimmy was racing Trudy over to Dee's, Flo swerved her Camaro there too.

Flo flew through the greens, floored it on yellows and when she had to stop once at the blaring red flame, she took off before it changed back. At last, there it was, Dee's Parlor's rusty orange neon, laughing at her from the gloom. Flo slowed and pulled into Dee's gravel lot. There was a green awning over the large wooden door. The club did its best to look upscale outside but this hit-and-run parking lot said it all. Potholes full of old, stagnant water. Smashed cans of beer and miniature bottles of liquor. Bloated cigarette butts floating in dank, murky puddles like hundreds of tiny drowned bodies.

Flo eased in and rolled to the back of the lot. She didn't want to be seen by the huge wad of people choking the front door.

She rammed the brake down, put the car in Park and was dabbing her lipstick when she heard the grinding sound of wheels on rock. That was one good thing about the lot next to Dee's. You could always hear when someone pulled in. Those pebbles barked loud under your tires.

Flo slithered down a few inches and watched an older couple go inside. She wanted to get out of the freak clothes she'd worn for Tony and put on the jumpsuit she had in the trunk.

Flo got out of the car and inched her leather pants off. She opened the trunk, taking a black jumpsuit from a plastic cleaner's bag, and stepped one leg inside. Just as she was about to pull her leg through the hole, she heard the loud crunching sound of gravel. Flo ducked down behind her fender to avoid the headlights. A giant black Suburban pulled in and parked two spaces from hers. The headlights illuminated the parking lot so much that Flo had to press herself flat against the fender and door. A big man waited a long time before he got out. He looked like he was arguing with the person inside. Suddenly, the man looked over her way. But Flo was no fool. She stood still, didn't move. She held her breath until the man looked away.

Flo hurried her other foot into the other pants leg and zipped the suit up to her neck. She could hear angry shouting coming from inside the car. She slowly lifted her head and peeked over her hood to take a look. But before she could see, she heard a door open and slam, so she ducked her head down again. There was a crumbling-gravel sound of large heavy feet, and Flo peeked up over the hood to see.

The big man was yelling loud. He was furiously upset. His arms were hawked up and his huge chest was swollen. He ran over, yanked open the passenger side and screamed.

"Get out!" he yelled to the person inside.

A silhouette slithered out from the seat.

When the streetlight hit the woman, Flo could see her pained face. "Well, I'll be," Flo said, recognizing her now. It was Trudy. "I guess having my man ain't enough for her trifling ass. Them chickens finally came home to roost."

But when Flo moved to adjust her foot, which had fallen asleep, she accidentally dropped her car keys.

"What was that?" Jimmy said. "Didn't you hear something?" he said to Trudy.

Pulling out his gun, Jimmy started over toward Flo's car.

Flo didn't know what to do. She was shaking in fear. The man was almost at her car! Flo slithered around her fender, ducking lower than before.

Jimmy stood next to Flo's passenger side. She could hear him breathing. She watched him peer inside. He waited a long time before he finally put his gun back and turned around. While Jimmy was gone, Trudy inched toward the club's door, but Jimmy grabbed her arm like a hostage.

"Where the fuck do you think you're going?"

Trudy hung her head and froze.

Her dress slipped from her shoulder and Flo saw her full breast. It loomed large under the orange neon moon.

Jimmy grabbed her, yanking her hard through the densely packed crowd. Trudy tried to cover her body. Her dress flopped off one side. The zipper was all the way down in the back.

"Whatchu say, Percy," Jimmy said, giving a pound without smiling.

"You got the winning hand," Percy said, gazing at Trudy's backside.

Jimmy slipped him a fifty. "Keep an eye on her, man. Don't let her out of your sight."

"I don't mind putting in work for you, homes." Percy sucked his tongue until it smacked.

Flo quickly got back inside her car. She needed to catch her breath. She needed to think. Flo decided to move her car forward and park where she could watch Dee's busy front door.

38

Trudy and Jimmy

"Stick him!"
"Throw that right again, man!"
"Don't show that sucka you weak."

The club was filled up. People were packed to the rafters. The fight blared on three television sets: a big screen, a nineteen-inch over the bar and a thirteen-inch with no color left that sat by the cook in the kitchen. Even people who normally didn't go to Dee's Parlor were sitting there slinging back beer after beer, laughing and munching on chips.

The ring girl grinned big. She was all lips and thighs. No one could see the large wart on her hand.

Ed "Meatloaf" Jones and Billy "The Hitman" Liston stood glistening on the taut canvas floor. Glaring, they looked anxious to finish the assault. The referee stood in between.

Ray Ray's eyes were glued to Dee's Parlor's front door. He hadn't seen Trudy yet or Lil Steve either. He got up and skimmed the packed parking lot, then he walked all the way back to the kitchen.

At that moment, Charles saw Jimmy pull Trudy in. Aw shit, he thought! Trudy got popped. What could he do? He better sit and stay quiet. But when Jimmy ran upstairs, leaving Trudy alone, Charles pushed his way to her table.

"Is this seat taken?" Charles looked at Percy.

"Yeah," Percy said, mad-dogging him hard. Trudy flipped her braids and rolled her eyes up at Percy.

Charles stood by the table but didn't sit down.

"You all right?" Charles asked, talking low.

Trudy gave a quick shake "no." Charles stared in her eyes; they were red like she had been crying.

Jimmy was coming back downstairs again. He was rapidly talking to two well-dressed men. One of them started to shout. When Jimmy saw Charles standing next to Trudy, he stormed over to the table, knocking over a glass.

"Who the fuck are you?" Jimmy angrily screamed.

Charles looked down. He wished Ray Ray were there.

"I asked you a question. You mute, muthafucka?" Jimmy stepped up to his face.

Charles stuck out his hand. "Charles," he said fast. Charles didn't have a clue who Jimmy was, but he looked like a man you don't mess with.

Jimmy stared at Charles's hand but just left it hanging.

Charles put his hand in his pocket.

Jimmy abruptly snatched Trudy up from her seat.

Charles wanted to say something but he scanned Jimmy's wide body. It had already bumped the table and knocked down two chairs. The bar was loud, and the brutal fight had turned the crowd rowdy. Nobody noticed how rough Jimmy handled Trudy's frame.

Meekly, Charles quietly sat down and smiled at Jimmy. He wasn't no fool; he was the one holding the money. He drank from a flask in his jacket. Though he felt bad for Trudy, he didn't want any trouble for himself. He stared at the TV like everyone else.

It was already round three. Liston stuck Jones against the ropes. Liston's bloated glove cut Jones across his jutting-out maw. Jones' skull turned a horrible Merlot.

Charles silently watched Jimmy twist Trudy's arm behind her back. He sipped from his flask as Jimmy slammed her into the men's bathroom. Charles bit his lip. He could taste the peach brandy. He looked up at Percy. Percy smiled down at Charles, daring him to move. Charles looked back at the set.

Jones broke from the ropes and snatched the battlefield back. In a blizzard of hits, he nailed shot after shot. Liston did a strange dance, like his legs didn't know each other. He swayed in a dull haze and almost went down. The crowd jumped from their seats and flew into a frenzy.

"Stomp his ass, man!"

"Bash Hitman's teeth!"

"We want to see that punk bleed!"

Jimmy grabbed a whole handful of Trudy's thin braids. An elderly man quickly zipped up and left when Jimmy slammed her against the cold tile.

"Now, I'm going to ask you, and I'm only going to ask once." Jimmy breathed hot, angry air in her mug. "Where the fuck were you today?" His hand was balled-up, his neck muscles bulged and her braids were wrapped tight around his fist.

Trudy panicked. Her air passages felt closed. She took quick, panting breaths. Her eyes darted back and forth but no one else was in the room. She wished someone would come in and help.

Suddenly the whole place filled with loud, whooping screams. Liston left-hooked Jones in the rib cage and chin. Liston kept drilling Jones with heart attack jabs, hammering him with swift combinations to the head and the body. When a right jab caught Jones smack-dab in the eye, the weak tissue ripped and people went crazy. The cut man had a hell of a time stopping the ooze.

Jimmy's veins bulged like snakes slithered under his skin. His red face was tense with hot venom.

Trudy held her mouth shut. She decided to stay quiet. She was afraid if she said something, uttered one small wrong word he'd slam her face into the glass.

"Talk to me, girl! I asked you a question." Jimmy tightened his grip around Trudy's long braids. "Where the fuck were you? I drove by your place twice. Tony ain't seen you all day."

Trudy struggled not to cry. She had to think of some lie that would stop Jimmy's rage, but her whole brain was numb and her skull really ached from him yanking her hair. Her scalp felt like it was inflamed.

"You in this, huh?" Jimmy slapped her face hard.

Trudy shook her head no. Her lids brimmed with tears. She struggled to stop them. To not let one drop. This was just how she felt when confronted by her mother. Her mother would scream and yell right in her face while Trudy willed herself not to weep. She knew if she let one fall, let one single drop, her whole face would flow like an ocean.

Jimmy let go of her hair and took a step back.

Trudy took a half breath when she saw Jimmy smile. It took everything she had to try to appear calm while her insides raged on like a storm.

"Come on, baby, it's me, Jimmy. I wouldn't hurt you, girl."

Jimmy smiled at her cunningly while he pulled out his gun. He wiped the gun clean with a white satin cloth. He spoke to her softly, saying each word nice and slow.

"Now I'm going to ask you one time." Jimmy folded the cloth, putting it back in his pocket. He was standing so close she could count the lines in his eyes. Jimmy aimed the clean gun against the hollow of her throat.

"Tell me everything and you won't get hurt."

Trudy wouldn't speak. She just stood there silent. She tried to breath easy as her blood blazed with fear. She was losing the fight in trying to stay calm and was almost engulfed in full panic.

Trudy's mind flashed to the only time she ever got caught. It was two years ago and she hadn't stolen in weeks. She was desperately trying to stop. But before she left this store she saw a beautiful jacket. It was lavender suede with a furry fox collar. She looked around the store without moving her head. She quickly unlooped the big metal ring and pulled the chain out through the arm. She glanced around the store again. She slipped the coat on. She casually took the escalator downstairs while the fluorescent lights shined on her brow. She could see the front door. She saw the cars in the lot. When she finally got both feet all the way out and inhaled deep, someone violently grabbed hold of her arm. Trudy was shocked. The undercover came from nowhere. She'd never seen the man anywhere near her in the store.

"Come with me, miss," he said, holding her firmly. He brought

Trudy to a small basement room downstairs. A man behind a desk asked her all sorts of questions. "Who are you with? Where are your parents? Don't you know stealing's a crime?"

While sitting there still, Trudy unzipped her purse. Her body was rigid. She just moved her hands. Her fingertips searched through her purse for her wallet. When she found it, she lifted her pants leg with one hand and shoved the wallet inside her boot.

Trudy was eighteen. She did not want to go to jail. But taking a five hundred–dollar coat was considered grand theft. She had no choice but to lie through her teeth. "I'm only fifteen," she told him without blinking. "I thought you had to treat minors different."

"You're under age?" the man examined her hard. With her body and made-up face she looked at least twenty. "Hand me your purse." The man grabbed her bag and dumped the contents on his desk. There was makeup, a mirror, a Mr. Goodbar and sixty-five dollars in cash.

Trudy knew as a minor she couldn't be charged, but the manager was pissed. He didn't like losing a suspect. So he called the cops to come down to the store anyway and take her. They cuffed her and took her back to the West L.A. station. Trudy was petrified riding in that black and white car. One cop rode in the backseat with her.

"Tell us everything," the nice cop said, "and you won't get hurt." He smiled with the warm face of a father.

"She's a thief," the other one barked. "Don't waste your time. I can't wait to lock her up in a cell."

The police jumped right into their Mutt and Jeff routine. She ignored the hard one driving and looked at the one who stayed nice.

"Tell us everything," the nice one said. "We'll go easy on you, honey. Is there anything you want to say? Do you have more stuff at home? How long have you been shoplifting?" he wanted to know. "Tell us and I promise you won't get hurt."

Trudy shook her head no. She blinked tears from her eyes. She tried to create a look that mixed sweetness with sorrow. She knew about Mutt and Jeff, the good cop, bad cop routine. She knew it was best to keep her mouth shut.

When they got to the station she looked on the floor. There was a thick yellow line, two outlined feet and letters saying, STOP HERE AND FRISK.

Trudy was frantic. Were they going to frisk her right there? They would find her ID. They'd realize she was lying. Damn, she was going to get caught. But Trudy toyed with the cops, she asked them questions about their job, and when it was time to walk up to the frisk line and stop, the cops walked her right over the letters. They brought her inside the station. They joked with her more. Someone brought her a cold can of Sprite. They liked having this sexy young thing in the station and leered at her giant young breasts. She watched when they brought in a young-looking brother. He held her gaze for a second. They worked him over hard and threw him down inside a cell. Trudy watched the man standing, holding the dark steel bars. She was glad she'd kept her mouth shut. She'd always be grateful for what her mother did for her that day. Joan came to the station as soon as she got the call. Trudy didn't have to tell Joan she'd lied about her age. Joan came in and sized up the whole situation. In ten minutes she had gotten Trudy released. She scolded the cops for "handcuffing babies" and immediately took Trudy home. Joan never got after her about stealing that stuff. She thought getting handcuffed was punishment enough.

Trudy clenched her back teeth as Jimmy's gun pressed her neck. She knew one thing for sure: it would be worse if she talked. So Trudy did just what she did back then. She stood there and did not say one word.

When Jimmy realized Trudy was not going to talk, he cold-cocked her hard in the jaw.

Outside the bathroom door, the club went berserk. People were howling and screaming and hitting spoons against bottles. Jones left-hooked Liston in the ear. Liston looked stunned. He swung at the air. He tried to throw a right but his timing was off. He took a full swing but he missed and lunged forward, teetering back and forth on his water-hose legs. Liston was dazed, like someone who forgot where they'd parked, like any minute he'd be eating the canvas.

Trudy dropped to the floor. Her mouth tasted like salt. She could move her front tooth back and forth with her tongue. Trudy wished she could blast Jimmy's head with her gun, but her gun was in her purse on a chair.

Jimmy stood over her, putting one foot on her chest. "Look, I don't care. This can go either way. Just tell me where my cocaine is at."

He started choking her neck with his boot.

Just then Pearl burst through the men's bathroom door. Jimmy had one foot at Trudy's throat and aimed his gun straight at Pearl's face.

Pearl stopped in her tracks. She squinted hard at Jimmy. She was wearing a long, silvery, sequined gown. One fist was hitched to her thick, strong, firm hip, and the other fist held the neck of a long wooden bat. She glanced quickly at Trudy but held a steady gaze at his eyes. Pearl stood like he could shoot her nine hundred times and she'd still be posed the same way.

Jimmy held the gun, but he dropped it a few notches. "Oh, I'm supposed to be scared." Jimmy laughed in her face. "Come on," he said to Pearl. "Go ahead, take a swing. I'll even put my gun down."

Jimmy loved this. This was big fun to him. He loved taunting folks. To him this was pure pleasure, like a kid stabbing bugs with a stick.

"You need to be clocking some of these fools up in here instead of wasting your time messing with her." Pearl threw a glance over her shoulder toward the door. "I heard someone came in here with a *whole* bunch of money. You need to go see about them."

"Who? What the hell are you talking about?"

"Tony knows. Ask him. He been bragging to anybody who'll listen, talkin' 'bout he got big bank tonight."

Jimmy pushed past Pearl and peeked from the door. Tony was laughing, sloshing drinks into rows of shot glasses. Both fists clutched two expensive bottles.

Jimmy looked confused. He clicked back his gun and shoved it into his waist. He reached down and pulled Trudy up. "Look, I don't know what's up, but don't try to leave." Jimmy put his gun in the back of his waist. "You better stay put. I'm not done with you yet."

Trudy wanted to spit in his face.

Jimmy left the bathroom and went back inside the club. He told Percy to watch the bathroom door.

Trudy ducked inside the men's stall and pulled across the latch. She was so scared she almost peed in her panties. She watched Pearl from the stall's tiny crack.

Pearl hissed a sharp whisper when Trudy came out. "Girl, didn't I tell you not to tangle with him? That crazy fool don't need a reason to murder. That mean shit just runs in his blood."

Pearl narrowed her eyes as she peeked out the door. Jimmy and Tony were starting to yell. "Look, girl. I found it upstairs." Pearl handed her a wrinkled piece of paper. "I knew I'd find something if I kept snooping around."

"What is this?" Trudy said, scanning the sheet. "Looks like a receipt to a rest home in Barstow."

"Look at the name at the bottom," Pearl triumphantly said.

In tiny print at the bottom of the receipt was the small name "Miss Geraldine Dee."

"You mean Miss Dee's up there? She's been alive all this time!" Trudy could hardly believe it.

"That's just what it means, according to this. That no-good dog lied to us all." Pearl looked out the bathroom door once again. Jimmy was talking even louder this time. Another man knocked down an older man's drink. Some women were screaming for shots. "You best get the hell outta here, chile. I smell a riot up in this spot tonight. Better use the side door in the back."

Trudy nervously walked toward the dressing room door when Percy left the bathroom door to pat some man down. Charles raced up to her elbow. He handed Trudy her purse.

"What happened in there? I was scared to come in." Charles meekly dug both his hands in his pockets.

"Um," Trudy said, rummaging around the junky room. Finally

she found what she wanted. She took a hairy mass from out of a bag and shook the brown curly wig out. "Where's the money?" she asked Charles, watching him in the mirror. She shoved all her braids up under the wooly haired cap and slipped on some dark tinted glasses.

"I got some of it on me," Charles said, opening his jacket, revealing the blue vinyl pouch.

Trudy quickly yanked Charles's jacket shut. "Are you crazy? Keep that thing closed. That fool almost killed me a minute ago! And what do you mean 'some of it'? You don't have it all? Charles, where the hell is the rest?" Trudy stopped peeking out from the dressing room hole, staring Charles in the face.

"I couldn't let Ray Ray see I had all that cash. I hid the rest."

"Hid what?" Shirley said, bursting through the small room. She surprised Trudy and Charles. They stood totally stiff, like kids caught making out in the closet. Shirley grinned wide, popping her gum. "Ummmmm! Whatchu all doing hiding in here, huh?"

Trudy impulsively grabbed Charles's hand.

"You something else, girl. Ain't no shame in yo' game. Don't matter to you if he's taken or not. You want some, you get some, you treacherous skank." Shirley rolled her eyes up and down Trudy's body. She popped her gum loud in her face. "I ought to tell your ol' lady myself," she told Charles. Shirley grinned at the wig sitting on Trudy's head. "Oh, hello! Are we role-playing tonight? You trying to be Cleopatra Jones in this bee-yatch?"

Shirley reached over and tried to snatch the wig off. But Trudy caught her hand and slapped it away. She was shaken and angry about what happened with Jimmy. She reached in her purse and pulled out the gun.

"Touch me again and I'll blast your jacked-up face," Trudy said.

Shirley was stunned. Her mouth dropped completely open. She backed to the corner of the room.

Charles was stunned too. He didn't know Trudy had a gun. When she said, "come on" this time, he did what she said.

Trudy and Charles pushed through the tight crowd of people in the club. Shirley watched them out of the dressing room hole.

"I'ma get you for that, bitch. Don't think I won't." She blew a giant pink bubble with her gum.

"Walk slow but keep moving. Try and stay cool. We gotta get out of here fast!" Trudy's brown eyes slid across the dense, smoky club. It was packed with folks watching the loud, angry fight. "You go out front. I'll meet you in back." Trudy didn't see Jimmy. But Percy was there. He was obviously searching the room for her now. But Percy was looking for Trudy's long braided head; he didn't recognize her in dark lenses and brown curls. Trudy snuck out the back. Charles drifted out front. He trotted quickly toward his car.

Charles saw Trudy ease out the back door of Dee's. But she didn't rush over to Charles's car first. Instead, she raced over to a huge glossy black SUV and carefully sliced all four tires. Charles took another big swig from his flask, letting the warm liquor enter his skin.

Trudy raced toward Charles and jumped in his car. She gushed out a sigh of relief. Charles stroked her hair, touching the curls on the wig, which glistened in Dee's warm neon glow. Charles eased his brandy-stained mouth over hers but Trudy pushed Charles's face back.

"Uh-uh! Let's go! We gotta leave quick." Trudy breathed deep and exhaled out of the window. Homeboy was tripping, she thought to herself. She looked at Charles hard out of the corner of her eye. He was too scared to come in the bathroom to help her and she'd almost been shot in the face. Trudy cracked the window. She needed to breathe some cool air. Charles was testing her nerves.

"Where's the rest of the money?" Trudy urgently asked.

Charles's eyes shifted down the street. "It's at home. It'll be safe there."

"You left it at home? Where did you put it? How do you know it won't get stolen?"

"It won't. It's hid real good." Charles took out the blue vinyl pouch of money. "You want to have part of it now?" He could lie about what was left in the envelope now by saying the rest was at home.

"No, Charles, let's go. We can't do this here. We'll divvy it up at Vernita's." Trudy strapped on her seat belt.

Charles strapped his too. He decided not to say he'd given some of the money away. He was feeling euphoric. He'd paid Tony back. He was holding an envelope with some serious money and there was plenty more waiting at home. For the first time in a long time he felt like a man. He wasn't about to spoil his good mood by being honest. He tried to peck Trudy's cheek but she pushed him away.

"Let's go," Trudy said hastily.

That's okay, Charles thought. He drained the rest from his flask. He could definitely wait. He turned the ignition. He clicked the radio on and switched the headlights. He thought about the paint can with the money and smiled. He put his hand on the gearshift and adjusted his mirror. Trudy had the sweetest little worried look on her face. Like a child trying to figure out a difficult puzzle. But suddenly her face changed to horror.

Trudy screamed but before she could finish Charles heard the gunshots. Three loud, angry blasts. Trudy slowly sank into Charles's lap. Blood leaked all over her dress.

Flo stood at the car window. Her face was enraged. Her chest heaved up and back down again. The warm gun dangled limply from her wrist.

39

Ray Ray

When people heard those shots they started running outside. Trudy thought she'd been shot when she finally eased back up. She thought she'd see Jimmy standing next to the car. But Jimmy wasn't there. He wasn't anywhere around. She lifted her head slowly to look.

Pearl was out first. "Somebody call the police. Hurry!"

People began to get in their cars and pull away.

Ray Ray looked around wildly. "What happened?" he asked.

"Get out the club, man. Police'll be here any minute." Sonny was about to go. Even Big Percy hurried away.

Ray Ray wasn't leaving. He scanned the club's room. Chairs were turned over, bottles lay dripping. A large crowd of people tried to squeeze through Dee's door, like booze coming down through a funnel. But Ray Ray had business. He walked quickly upstairs. He wasn't about to leave the club without getting his money. He eased the door open to Tony's small closet office. Tony was stuffing something in a brown leather bag.

"Hey, Ray Ray, whatchu doing up here, man? Ain't you heard? A man down there's been shot. We got to clear out before the police gets here, boy!"

Ray Ray didn't move.

"Didn't you hear? Whatchu waitin' on, son?" Tony didn't even bother looking up. He hastily shoved some papers in a briefcase.

"Naw, man, I didn't hear nothin'. I got business up here. I ain't leaving without you giving me my money." Ray Ray's eyes locked on Tony. Tony's locked back on his.

"I done tol' you already, the man's got it. I passed it on to him. He got it now, got mines too. You saw him in here collecting all them bets. You give it to me and I give it to him, remember? I know you saw him. He came right over to where you and Charles was." Tony was talking real fast. He wanted to get his cash and get out.

"I didn't see shit," Ray Ray said flatly.

"Listen, man, Jimmy came in and took the bet money. We got to leave before the law turns the place out!" Tony stood up and tried to walk around Ray Ray's frame. But Ray Ray was blocking his path.

"I ain't leaving without my ends, man." Ray Ray took out the gun in his underarm holster.

"Come on, man," Tony said, laughing nervously now. "Don't do nothing rash. I'ma get you your money. You know I'm good. Don't I always come through? Didn't I treat you like a son? Wasn't I the one who hired your black ass when all of them other folks wouldn't have ya? Now put that gun down. Think about what you're doing. You don't want to go back to the pen."

Ray Ray walked closer. Tony felt his breath on him now. Ray Ray pressed the gun into his stomach. A ripple shook his gut like a rock tossed in a pond.

Under the small hanging light, Tony's worried face creased. His eyes darted around the room like a brown, scurrying rodent, hoping for some kind of opening.

"I'ma go in my pocket. Look, man, don't shoot." Tony slowly pulled a handful of hundreds from his pocket. "All right. See. Looka here. I got five hundred dollars. Take it. It's yours. You can have it all, son. Now come on, man, put the gun down!"

Ray Ray looked down at the sad wad of cash.

"You must be sick. Where's the rest of my ends, nigga? I played Jones to win. I ain't leaving without my eight grand." Ray Ray shoved the gun farther into Tony's fat stomach. Tony's whole face was dripping sweat now.

"Now, hold up, man, hold up! I done tol' you already!" Tony's eyes looked crazed. Sirens were blaring. He had to get out. "I ain't got it, I said! The man came and took all the cash. I know you musta saw him. I put it on Jones. Just like you said."

Ray Ray didn't say a thing. He raised the gun higher. Putting it right next to Tony's bald head, he pulled the safety way back until it snapped.

"All right, man! Okay!" Tony pulled a small briefcase from below the desk but didn't open it. He saw Jimmy coming up behind Ray Ray real quiet. "Let me get you your shit, before you act a stone fool." Tony unsnapped the case. It was stuffed full with money. "This is what I get hiring a damn convict." Tony slowly stepped back. "Here's yo' shit, man." Tony stepped further back. "Go ahead, take it."

But when Ray Ray leaned forward to reach for the case, Jimmy grabbed Ray Ray's throat and snatched back the gun, pointing it back at Ray Ray's face.

"Be cool, man. Don't move," Jimmy whispered. "All I want to know is where is my stash. They said brothers jacked my man this morning at the bank. Said one was a tall, thin, pretty-boy type." Jimmy grinned in Ray Ray's scarred, scowling face. "Now that sho' ain't you." Jimmy continued to smile. "Naw, cuz you as butter-black ugly as they come."

Jimmy rolled the gun over Ray's Rays large, gravelly scar. He stood in Ray Ray's face and continued to whisper. "But my man said the other one had a nasty burn mark peeking out under his scarf." Jimmy took out a knife and ripped open Ray Ray's skin. Ray Ray winced. Jerking back, he clenched his back teeth. Dark blood rolled from his keloid. Ray Ray stood there in pain as the sticky blood seeped over his neck.

Tony walked up to Ray Ray and spit in his face. "Yeah, it was him. Dumb stupid convict. Came in today with a whole gang of money. I bet he and Lil Steve been plotting this shit all week. Lil Steve probably snatched your cut, man."

Jimmy socked Ray Ray's gut and he doubled over. "Where's my shit, huh? Where the fuck is it at?"

Tony closed the brown briefcase and put it under his coat.

This wasn't his fight. He wasn't in it. He scurried down the stairs while the sirens grew fierce.

"Put both hands around your neck," Jimmy barked loud to Ray Ray. "Now, don't turn around or I'll blow your damn head."

"Open up," they heard the cops yell from downstairs. They were banging the wrought-iron door with batons, but they couldn't get the door to bust open.

Jimmy backed out of the room, aiming his pistol at Ray Ray. Jimmy didn't want to be caught at the club with the cops. He backed all the way out of the room and ran out the back door.

Tony didn't want the cops to see he had a gambling room upstairs, so he locked the gated door tight.

But the officers were prepared. Two of them held a battering ram. They hooked the ram onto the large steel door. With both of them holding the thick metal pole, they knocked the iron door off the hinge.

The police charged up the stairs with all their guns drawn. Ray Ray's eyes darted around the small closet he was in. He could hear their feet on the stairs. He couldn't go back to jail. He couldn't get caught.

"Please, Lord," Ray Ray said, rubbing the cross at his neck, "don't put me in that black hole again." Even though he was two floors up, Ray Ray broke a small window over a water heater with his gun. He said one last prayer and then jumped. His body was almost completely halfway out when someone grabbed his leg and dragged him all the way back.

"I got one," a police officer proudly announced.

Ray Ray was caught in a black uniformed knot.

The cops cuffed him quickly. His hands dangled in front. His silver cross glittered against his gray pinstripe suit. His dark suit was splattered with blood.

"That's him!" Tony said, walking back inside the room. He wasn't carrying the old briefcase anymore. He looked straight at Ray Ray. "Yeah that's the one who done it. I hired him to work. Didn't know he was a felon. He shot one of my best paying customers too."

"You a lie! You know I didn't shoot nobody!" Ray Ray said. He struggled to get free, but the officers held him firm. They dragged him downstairs and out the front door toward the blinking squad cars at the curb.

Ray Ray tried to resist, twisting and contorting his body. But once they got him on the sidewalk they beat Ray Ray down. Their batons smacked his arms, his rib cage and his legs. They beat him so hard on the back of his head, blood flowed from out of his nose. Jamming Ray Ray's dazed and doubled-over body into the backseat, they slammed the door hard and took off.

Ray Ray lay unconscious on the black vinyl seat while the car screeched down the dark street. His silver cross medallion dangled next to his face. It was a thick chain with a fat cross of Jesus. The officers didn't bother to take it. He was cuffed and inside the backseat metal cage. Ray Ray wasn't going nowhere but jail.

Ray Ray gradually regained consciousness. He opened his eyes. He looked around, trying to figure out where he was. The car was racing downtown. Ray Ray had trouble breathing. His ears were ringing loud and his nose was all caked with blood and he had to pry his face from the seat where Jimmy had opened his wound.

He looked up and saw the two officers' heads. They were cracking jokes and laughing and running red lights. They never once looked back at him.

Now, officers aren't supposed to handcuff in the front, but sometimes they get lazy. They let their guard down. Ray Ray knew one thing. He had two strikes already. He wasn't about to go back to the pen.

Ray Ray raised his cuffed fists and used the tips of his fingers to work the medallion he was wearing. The flat silver cross had four slender tips. He put one of the tips inside the narrow keyhole. He started fiddling the cross around and around with his fingers until he heard the gentle snap of the lock.

Ray Ray kept his head down. His eyes searched for an escape. But the backseat was as tight as a cage. He didn't want the officers to know he was awake or notice his free, uncuffed hands. He felt around the seat but came up with nothing. He checked the side windows but they didn't roll down. He looked under the floor mats and that's when he saw it. There was a dim light coming from the front seat.

There was an opening! A space wide enough for a shoe. Ray Ray dropped his whole head all the way down and saw the officer's boot on the ground. He stretched, reaching his hand as far as it would go. He grabbed hold of the foot and wouldn't let go.

The driver slammed the brakes hard but the car skidded toward the sidewalk. It jumped the curb and kept flying down the street, slamming into a dense concrete bus bench. The car dangled halfway on the curb and the road. The driver was knocked out and slumped over the wheel. The horn tortured the normally silent street. A Mitsubishi swerved and braked hard but couldn't stop. It smashed the police car with such a strong force it knocked the driver's door open. Ray Ray kicked his door window until he shattered the glass. He leaped out and grabbed the slumped officer's gun. He started running down the block. The other officer was conscious but dazed. He grabbed his gun and shot at Ray Ray but Ray Ray shot back. He clipped the officer in the shoulder.

Ray Ray raced down the street like a wild, rabid dog, hopping a fence and scaling two walls and then ducking into a beat-up apartment. He crept down into the apartment's garage and saw an old blue Ford pickup parked against the garage wall. Ray Ray popped the hood and examined the engine. He looked around the garage for a tool and spotted a mangled coat hanger on the floor. He wrapped his bandana around the end of the hanger. He touched the solenoid and the battery cable. The Ford engine roared to life. Ray Ray busted the window and leaped inside the truck. He sped down side streets until he reached the 110. Keeping his eyes on his rearviews, he opened the ashtray. He found half a butt and popped in the lighter, but Ray Ray didn't light up until he was all the way past Gage. Ray Ray knew one thing; he had two strikes against him and had just shot a cop. He'd best get out of the state. But as he drove, something gnawed him. It clawed at his gut until he couldn't shake that sick feeling away anymore. It was against his best judgment. He knew it was wrong. But Ray Ray made a U-turn and went all the way back.

40

Trudy and Charles

After Charles was shot, and before the cops arrived, Dee's Parlor was going berserk. People raced through the streets like they did during the riots. Some folks were screaming, and one man waved a toy gun. Others just went in and took what they wanted. They ran holding six-packs and bottles of gin. An elderly lady struggled with a big stack of plates. One dropped in the street but she didn't break her stride. She just hoisted the stack farther up her hip.

Trudy roared Charles's Buick down side streets and through alleys.

"Don't worry," Trudy told Charles's slumped-over body. "I'm going to take you to a doctor. We'll get you fixed up. Just sit tight and keep trying to breathe." But Trudy didn't take Charles to the hospital at all. She drove down the street until she got to her house. She wanted to pick up her black leather satchel and get rid of these old bloody clothes. But when she got near her block she made a U-turn instead. Was she crazy? It wasn't safe to go home right now. Jimmy might be waiting for her there. Charles's gas tank was on empty; the red light had come on. She couldn't keep driving for long. She parked behind a Dumpster in an alley to think. Charles's body slithered down in the seat. Flies were buzzing around the car on his side. Leaning him back up, Trudy sucked in her breath. The whole front of his shirt was drenched in red blood. Her white dress was splattered in rusty blood too.

Trudy was frantic. Charles was hurt bad. She found a water bottle in the backseat and tried to give Charles a sip but the water just rolled down his chin. She ripped part of her dress to make a quick bandage. But the blood wouldn't stop coming out.

"Damn it," she said, beating her fists against the wheel. "I've got to get you to a doctor." Trudy raced through back streets, hovering at stop signs. There weren't many emergency wards anymore. She'd have to go down to King Drew. Trudy raced to the hospital and parked in the red lanes; she struggled to get Charles's limp body out. Grabbing his arm all the way over her shoulders, Trudy dragged Charles through the large sliding glass door.

But as soon as she came through the Plexiglas door the alarm started screeching like crazy. Everyone stopped and looked at them both. Blood was splattered all over her dress. The bottom half was completely ripped off. Charles was so wobbly and weak, he barely could stand. Bright red blood soaked through most of his clothes. But it was late Friday night and this was "Killer King" Drew. The lobby spilled over with stab wounds and bullets. Some folks were worse off than them.

A security guard raced up to where Trudy was. Trudy panicked. Oh God, she was trapped. There was a guard waiting at the entrance to the lobby and a guard standing where she came in. She was captured inside a small plastic room. Everyone stared at her hard.

"Ma'am!" the guard barked. "Are you carrying a weapon?"

Trudy had forgotten about the gun in her purse. The gun had set off the metal detectors and the alarm brought out both guards.

"I have to take it, ma'am," the guard said, coming toward her. Oh no! Trudy began breathing hard. She didn't want to be arrested. What if they thought she shot Charles? What if they called the police?

"It's my husband's. He shot himself cleaning his gun. I begged him to not buy that thing. Please come take it away." Trudy kissed Charles softly on the cheek. "You'll be all right, honey. We're at the hospital now."

Trudy handed the officer the gun. He studied her awhile but eventually walked back toward the door.

A nurse handed Trudy a clipboard filled with forms.

"You got to see him now!" Trudy pleaded to the nurse. She wanted to get out of the room and away from the guards; they kept watching her from the front door.

The lady didn't look up at Trudy at all. She leaned over the counter and took Charles's pulse. She examined his wound. "He's breathing," she said. "The bleeding has stopped."

"He's bad off. You got to look at him now!" Trudy said.

"Honey, I got an arm sawed off, a drive-by that left eight people bloody and a hand ripped from fixing a disposal. Just take a number and please sit him down. I don't want no blood on my counter." The woman's eyes never left the chart she was holding. "We'll call you as soon as we're ready."

"A number? Is this a god damn butcher shop or what?" But when Trudy saw the hard looks of the other people waiting she quickly grabbed a number and sat down. There was a man whose hand drooped in a loose homemade sling. The fingers and thumb were completely chewed off. Blood caked in the folds of his skin. A pregnant woman twisted and turned in her seat. Her loud groaning echoed throughout the whole room. Trudy looked around the room for two seats together. A man with a gash in his leg moved down one. He sat next to a woman with a black and blue face.

When Trudy lifted Charles's jacket to cover him up, the blue envelope fell to the floor. Trudy opened the envelope to examine the contents. The envelope was more than three-quarters short. Trudy nudged Charles's slumped body.

"Charles, wake up," Trudy whispered in his ear. "Where is the rest of the money?" But Charles was groggy. Trudy shook his leg gently. "Charles!" Trudy said, more determined this time. Charles opened his eyes wide but then shut them slow. He groaned, folding his body in the seat. "Charles!" she said low, shaking his leg harder. The man with the gash looked at Trudy and frowned. The marred woman sucked her tongue and sadly shook her head.

But Trudy wanted to know. She had to find where he put it. "Charles, can you hear me? Charles, wake up!"

"Can't you see he's bleeding?" The man with the sling shouted. "Why don't you leave the poor fellow alone?"

Trudy crossed her arms on her chest and stayed quiet. She didn't dare say anything else.

"Ma'am!" the woman behind the counter calmly called. "The doctor will see you both now." A nurse came and helped Charles into a small curtained room. She swabbed his chest, took his temperature and left.

"Charles!" Trudy said, holding on to his arm.

Charles raised his head but then collapsed down.

The nurse rushed back in. "You'll have to leave, ma'am. He's lucky. It's only a flesh wound." She plugged in a monitor and thumped a syringe. "We'll let you know how he's doing," the nurse bluntly said. She yanked the curtain in Trudy's anxious face.

Trudy waited until the nurse left. She lingered way down the hall. When the nurse turned the corner, Trudy slipped back into his room.

"Charles!" Trudy whispered inside of his ear. "Where is the money? Where is it hidden in your house?"

Charles turned over. He opened his eyes. He started to mutter something but the morphine knocked hard at his door.

"Charles!" Trudy said, shaking his shoulder real hard.

"Get out," the nurse said sternly, rushing back in the room.

When Trudy refused to move, the nurse touched her arm.

"Charles!" Trudy said trying to hold Charles's shoulder. Charles was struggling. He tried to mouth a word.

"Paint," he said weakly. His lids fluttered and closed.

"Charles!" Trudy screamed at the top of her lungs.

The nurse tried to pull Trudy but she was frail and small. Her thin arms were no match for Trudy's big-boned girth. So she pushed a green button and set off the alarm. A buzzing sound consumed the room.

Well, this was it. This was her final, last-ditch effort. In a minute they'd be tossing her out the front door.

"Charrrrleees!" Trudy hollered. She let her voice roar. It carried

like a *Ma Rainey's Black Bottom* song, thundering way down the hall.

A male nurse came in and grabbed Trudy hard but not before these words crept from Charles's slurring tongue.

". . . back . . . yaaaaa . . . rrrrrrd," Charles said. One eye was shut. "Paint can in garaaaaageeeee," he muttered, then passed out.

Trudy smiled big when she heard these last words. Even when the male nurse tossed her out of the double lobby doors, she grinned all the way to the car.

Less than five miles away, Shirley grinned too. She had followed Jimmy trying to drive on four flattened tires. She pulled alongside his black SUV. Her dinged Cougar rattled and choked at the light. She looked like an old carnival ride.

"Your left tires are gone." Shirley gestured toward his rims.

"It'll be all right," Jimmy said unfazed. His tires were slashed but he could still drive. It was useless to put on his spare.

"I can help. I think I know who you're looking for, baby." She gave him a snaggletoothed grin.

Jimmy's black tinted window rolled the rest of the way down. He was angry as hell but smiled back at Shirley. He cracked open and lit a brand-new cigar.

"If you'da asked, I'da told you to not fool with that girl. Trudy thinks she's all that and a big bag of chips, but that girl ain't never been shit!"

Jimmy stared at Shirley. He wanted her to talk. "Where is she?" he asked her point-blank.

Shirley smiled and popped her gum for a minute. She wanted her last comment to sink in. The car parked behind started blowing its horn. Shirley waved the car to go around. Shirley rubbed her thumb and fingers together, gesturing she wanted money.

Jimmy stretched out his arm and handed her three new bills. Shirley rolled them and stuck the tube in her stuffed push-up bra.

"Thanks, sugar," Shirley said, chewing her gum fast. "If she's not home, then most likely she's down at Vernita's. It's a beauty shop off 10th, right on Mont Clair. I betchu that freak's over there."

Jimmy leaned halfway out of his large SUV. "How much you want for your car?"

Shirley popped her gum like a twelve-year-old girl. "I'll let it go for eleven hundred."

Jimmy peeled off more bills. "Here's five," he said hard. "Now get out before I take it for the three in your chest"

Shirley snatched the extra cash and handed him the keys. "Pleasure doing business," she said, popping her gum again.

Jimmy got in her Cougar and put it in Reverse. It clunked when he put it in Drive. But the Cougar was fast and it had a huge engine. Shirley screamed as he flew down the street. "Don't blink or you'll miss it," she continued to yell. "Lemme know if you need anything else!" She smiled as Jimmy's taillights faded down the dark block. Her cruel grin turned into a nastier scowl. She filed a few rough nails before walking down the street. "Serves that ol' skanky bitch right!"

41

Tony

Tony flicked the dead ash from his half-smoked Winston. His large walrus gut dug in the steering wheel he held. "Nigga shit," he said to himself. Tossing the cigarette butt out the window, he turned on Ray Charles and hummed. He kept glancing and checking and rechecking his mirrors as he drove the side streets back home. He pulled his Caddy up the narrow concrete strips of his driveway. In between the concrete strips was a long row of unmowed grass.

Tony carried his briefcase out toward the back porch whistling "Midnight Train to Georgia." He stopped and sniffed hard. Somebody was barbecuing something. He looked up and noticed the soft trail of smoke floating up into the black. Nobody could see inside Tony's backyard. It was completely covered with vines. The vines and trees grew in one dark, overgrown mass that twitched and screeched loud from the crickets and rats. Tony pried open the back step and lifted the plank up. With Ray Ray and Charles's money and the rest of the club's take he had more than eighteen grand in his hand. A grin inched its way from his thick bottom lip. "It's a crime to make this much scratch in one night." Tony laughed, flicking his Winston from his hand.

Before nailing the plank shut, he heard the Great Dane next door. It growled and barked through the hedge. Tony looked across the yard. It was totally dark. He could barely see past his own arm.

"Must be one of them opossums," Tony said to himself. "Always climbing across the damn clothesline and rooting through your yard." He hammered the one plank back down. If Tony had gotten up and examined it himself, he would have seen that the clothesline had been taken down.

When Tony stood up, someone hooped his fat neck. The cord choked him so hard, he couldn't get air. He struggled so furiously to get himself free that he kicked over a glass Sparkletts bottle. The Great Dane went crazy at the shattering of glass. It pounced against the thick chain-link fence and barked wildly. Tony's eyes bulged. His tongue was slung like a dog, a dog that's been run way too long. He wildly clawed against the tight fists that held him but the more and more he moved, the tighter the cord yanked until Tony's husky body went limp. His lungs fluttered once. His heartbeat slowed down. And his brain faintly played "Midnight Train" to him again before drowning in a galaxy of black.

Ray Ray unwrapped the clothesline from around Tony's neck. He took Tony's gun from his sack-of-rice stomach and dragged him to the fallen-down garage in the back. He put Tony inside an old trunk and locked it. He threw a thick rug over the top. People thought the smell was a hound that had climbed back there and died. It was months before anyone found him.

42

Trudy and Flo

Trudy hurried to Charles's car and jumped in. She studied the envelope with the money. She held the keys to Charles's house in her hand. She couldn't show up in Charles's car. Flo would recognize it in a minute. In fact, it wasn't safe for her to go over there at all. Flo probably meant to shoot her. Trudy ran to the phone by the hospital doors.

She dialed Vernita and listened to the phone ring and ring. "Vernita, pick up!" Trudy held the receiver to her mouth. "Come on, Vernita, be home!"

Suddenly the phone clicked. Someone picked up the line. "Vernita?" Trudy asked. "Girl, is that you?"

The person didn't say a word. There was only hard breathing.

"Vernita?" Trudy said in the receiver again.

"Hello," a voice said low. It was almost a whisper.

"Vernita, is that you? Why are you talking so low? I can barely hear what you're saying."

"Your boy's over here," Vernita faintly said.

"Who?"

"Who do you think? He's knocked out in my chair. I tied his hands with an extension cord. You better get over here quick."

Trudy drove to the shop. A black Bug was parked across the street. She searched Charles's car for some kind of weapon. She wanted something in her hand just in case. The only thing Charles had was a steering wheel lock. Trudy twisted the lock until the metal bar slid out. She lifted her dress and hooked the lock to her panties, letting the thick bar hang down next to her thighs. She couldn't see inside. The blinds were all drawn. Trudy gently knocked on the shop door.

"Vernita?" Trudy mildly called to her friend.

"Shhhh," Vernita said, unlocking the door. She held one finger up to her lips. "He's out but who the hell knows for how long."

Trudy looked by the rinse bowl and saw Lil Steve. He was snoring inside the salon chair.

Vernita noticed Trudy's stained and torn dress.

"Look, I don't even want to know what bullshit just happened. You're still breathing, so I guess you're all right. Just give me my share. I'm through with this mess. I'm not made for this kind of stress."

Trudy glanced away from her friend's pale eyes. "Uh-uh, not yet. I don't have it on me." Trudy studied the floor. She felt Vernita's piercing gaze. "We have to go get it from Charles's place."

"We? No, not me! I told you I'm done." Vernita pointed a manicured finger at Lil Steve's head. "That boy came here and held a damn gun to my head. I already helped you enough."

"But, Vernita, I can't go. Charles left the money inside his garage. Flo showed up at the club gunning for me and Charles. I just dropped him off at the hospital to get checked."

"See? That's what I'm talking about. I knew this would happen. This shit is foul. Look at you, you're a mess. You're covered in blood and Charles is at the damn doctor!"

Trudy broke down. She felt bad about Charles. Hot tears raced out of both of her eyes. Her frustration and the day's events finally took their toll.

Vernita handed Trudy a towel for her face.

"I knew it. I knew doing this wild shit was whack! Didn't I say this shit was crazy?"

Trudy struggled hard to pull herself together. "Vernita, I'm fine. Charles is okay too. The bullet went right through his shoulder, that's all. But I need your help. I just need a quick ride. I swear, I'll do all the rest."

Vernita frowned and didn't say anything at first, but her disgust made her yell at her friend. "That's all? Girl you must be sick! This is dangerous, okay? Your dumb ass could die! Have you been smoking chronic all night? This is idiotic shit. Look, I don't even care about the money. Y'all been shot at. Y'all coulda got done. Some of them gun fragments must have lodged in your head if you think I'ma still get in this fuckin' mess."

Trudy ignored her friend's sarcasm. She didn't have much time. "Charles told me the money is hidden inside a paint can. He hid the can in his garage. Look, I don't know why Charles put it in there but Ray Ray was with him. Charles probably had to hide it from him." Trudy held her friend's arm. She narrowed her eyes. "I got to get that paint can from Charles's backyard. All of our money is just sitting back there waiting. Vernita, we got to go before someone else gets there first."

"We? Haven't you heard what I said? Do I look like I got 'fool' written on my forehead?" Vernita's arched eyebrows rose high above her eyes.

"Come on, Vernita, please!" Trudy begged her friend.

But Vernita just stood firm. She didn't make a sound. Both hands were hitched to her hips.

"Come on, say something," Trudy demanded.

"I'm still thinking about that .22 glued to my jaw. I'm thinking about Flo tripping, getting a gun and shooting at folks. Why the hell would I want to go over there?"

"'Cause the money is there! Haven't you been listening at all? We got to go over there and get the shit back!"

"Naw, girl, I'm sorry. I'm not doing anything else. Guns, police, robbing banks, folks getting shot. And now I got this fool tied in my shop. This shit's way too deep for me."

Trudy stared at Vernita. Her deep frown was set. Trudy didn't know what happened between her and Lil Steve but Vernita was obviously scared. Trudy didn't dare say what Jimmy had just done to her. Vernita would never help if she knew the truth.

"Well, can't you just drive me over there, huh? I can't drive myself. I'm in Charles's car. Just drive me there. That's all I want."

Vernita sighed deeply. She wiped her hands on a towel. She

grabbed some hair out of a brush and threw it in the trash. She placed a clean pile of combs in a large plastic jar. She filled the jar with green disinfectant. Her eyes shifted back up to the huge broken mirror. "I'm sorry. I just don't think it's smart." She grabbed a broom and started sweeping up shards. "You gonna have to be dumb by yourself."

"Look, I'm begging you, Vernita. Please help me out."

Vernita had heard enough. She turned her back on her friend. She scooped the glass bits and dumped them inside the trash. Her lips were drawn tight as she shook her head. "No, Trudy. I'm sorry. I can't help you now. I'm done with all of this mess."

So Trudy played her trump card. She had no other choice. There was one thing that could stop Vernita dead in her tracks. But she hated to use it. She'd sworn never to mention it again. But Trudy was backed against a cold concrete wall. "Wal-Mart," Trudy said. She let the word fall.

Vernita stopped sweeping. She clutched the broom in her fist.

"I know you don't want to hear it. I'm sorry to bring it up . . ."

Vernita flashed her green eyes. The white part looked red. She glared like she wanted to slap Trudy's face.

"I stood by you, remember? You *needed me* back then."

Vernita clamped her back teeth. She dropped the broom to the floor.

Vernita had buried that memory a long time ago.

See, in their last year in high school, way before Vernita had her own shop, Vernita worked for a beautician off 54th and Vermont. It was a small bootleg shop operating with no license, run by a mean, callous woman with thin lips and a mustache. The callous woman came in demanding Vernita give her a perm. Vernita didn't want to do it. The woman's hair wasn't ready and it was dry and as hard as a broom. And on top of that, the woman had been scratching her head something awful and Vernita didn't want the perm to damage the woman's raw scalp. "Shut up," the woman said. "Just do your damn job. I'm not paying for your god damn opinion, okay? Just open that Revlon and start smearing it on. If you don't like it, then you can just quit!"

So Vernita got the jar from the shelf in the back. She told the woman to please have a seat in the chair. Vernita tied a smock around the woman's long neck. Vernita was careful not to get the harsh perm on the woman's skin, keeping the chemical just on her roots. But when she rinsed it, big chunks of hair came out in the comb and a whole lot more floated alone in the sink. The left side of the woman's scalp was completely skinned bald. When the woman saw her hair loss, she punched Vernita hard. Vernita got angry and slapped the bald woman back. But the woman went crazy. She tore up the shop. She cussed her; she pulled a razor blade from her purse, threatening to slash Vernita across the cheek. But just then, Vernita's young cousin Moon came in for a trim. Moon sized up the situation, which got immediately out of hand. A sea of tan khakis and white tees filled the room. Blue bandanas hung from their back pockets. "Lock the door, cuz," Moon said to his friend. A tan-khaki man bolted the door. Moon slammed the woman hard against the wall. The razor fell out of her hand.

"You want to cut someone, bitch?" Moon spat in her face.

The half-bald woman panicked. She tried to run from the shop, but they caught her and dragged her inside their car. "Don't worry, girl, we got it from here." Moon gunned the car and careened down the street. "We 'bout to go do some shoppin'."

"Wait!" Vernita screamed. But the Monte Carlo didn't stop. The next day they found the woman's body inside a Dumpster. It was in the parking lot behind the new Wal-Mart.

When the cops questioned Vernita, Trudy covered for her friend. She told them she was with her all day at the mall.

"All right," Vernita said, finally leveling her eyes. "I'll do this last thing. But after this shit we're even. Don't ever bring that mess up again."

Trudy smiled at her friend. "I knew you'd come through."

"Look, Trudy, I'll take you. But I'm staying down the street. Flo might recognize my hooptie too."

"What about him?" Trudy looked at Lil Steve.

"If you help me we can lift him and carry him outside," Vernita said.

Trudy eyed Lil Steve tied up in the chair. She waved her hand across his face to see if he could see. She saw the cocaine in his nose.

"You think he ODed?"

"Naw, he's all right. Just strung out from being too high."

Sticking her hand inside his right pocket, Trudy pulled out a small ring of keys. They were both engraved with the Volkswagen logo. "Hey, let's use his car. That Bug out there's his. You're right. Your Mustang's too flossy to hide. No one will ever recognize us in a Bug."

Vernita looked worried but she still grabbed her purse. She took Lil Steve's feet and Trudy held his hands. They dragged him across the floor and outside to the back. Vernita locked up the shop when Trudy walked out the door. They walked around the corner and got into the car. Vernita turned the Bug's engine. She told Trudy to get down. Trudy smiled at her friend as she shifted from first. The Volkswagen roared like a Porsche.

As soon as they left, Jimmy appeared in the alley. He saw Lil Steve outside the beauty shop's back door. Lil Steve looked like a drunk who'd passed out in a stupor. As Jimmy got closer, something glowed in the moon. Jimmy eased the car closer to Lil Steve's body. He recognized the ring immediately. It was his diamond and sapphire pinkie. Jimmy got out and dragged Lil Steve inside the Cougar, spreading him across the backseat. He noticed a baseball bat behind the seat on the floor and decided to drive to the dark corner of a lot.

43

Trudy, Vernita and Flo

Flo went home feeling numb. She was driving half-conscious. "Oh my God," she said, gulping huge tears. "I can't believe it. Oh my dear God! I just shot my man!" She was going to open the car door and toss the gun toward the curb when a police car pulled up from behind. Flo made a right turn inside someone else's driveway and waited until the cop drove away. When she got to her house, she pulled the car to the backyard. She ran inside and bolted the front door.

Vernita downshifted to second and coasted through the yellow, revving the car loudly down the street. Trudy felt a large bulge under her passenger seat cushion. There was a ripped, jagged slash on the side. When she got to the next light she lifted her butt and pulled a duct-taped bag out. Vernita looked at Trudy while holding the bag. It was filled with a powdery substance.

"Oh, hell, naw! I knew this was wrong. We're in someone else's ride, driving with a whole gang of blow. Shit, I might as well drive us to jail right now and save some damn cop the trip." Vernita didn't want to go to Flo's house, and seeing that coke made her nervous. Vernita started to turn but Trudy held her hand. Trudy knew this wouldn't be good.

"Look, girl, don't trip. We're almost there now. Just ease up and pull down the street real slow."

"This was a fucking bad idea," Vernita told her friend. "Somebody gonna get hurt."

When they were three houses away, Flo burst out the door. She walked quickly down the driveway and out to the street.

Flo had put the gun in the bottom of a bag and was going to drop it down in the trash.

"Duck down—hurry, quick. Flo just came out!" Vernita shoved Trudy's head way down in the seat. Flo walked down the path with a small paper bag. She buried the bag down in the can at the curb.

"Vernita, stay calm. I know what to do. If she says something, you just talk to her, that's all. I'ma be right back," Trudy said. Trudy left the steering wheel club on the seat and quickly got out of the car.

Trudy slipped from the door, ducking down between cars. She hid in a bush as Flo got to the sidewalk. Flo saw a Volkswagen idling a few houses down. She studied the driver. It looked like Vernita. What was Vernita doing driving a Bug? And why was she here on her street? Flo turned to leave but Vernita stuck her hand out and waved, so Flo walked, toward her car.

"What are you doing here?" Flo asked nervously. She didn't know if Vernita knew she shot Charles or not. But she knew Vernita and Trudy were friends.

"Oh, my nephew just moved in down the street, guurl. I was bringing stuff to help him move in."

Flo looked questioningly at the empty backseat.

"Oh, I ain't moving no boxes." Vernita held out her hand. "I'm not breaking any of my nice nails, chile. Naw, I'm just bringing that little fool his car." Vernita watched Trudy out the corner of her eye. "That boy got me gallivanting all around town. I didn't know you lived right here." Vernita smiled wide, faking surprise. She saw Trudy running down Flo's long driveway and wondered if Flo still had the gun on her somewhere.

Flo faintly smiled. She tried to look normal. "Where's your Mustang?" Flo asked, avoiding her eyes.

"It's back in the shop. Girl, it's always giving me drama. Cars are just like men, chile, some broke, some go too fast, all of 'em a pain in the ass."

"Well, I'll see you. I gotta get back in." Flo was eager to get back inside. Someone might recognize her as the shooter. She wanted to get off the street.

Vernita saw Trudy was just getting to the yard. "Flo!" she barked out.

"What?" Flo said, worried. *Oh no*, she thought, *Vernita must know something.*

"Girl, what in the world are you doing to your skin? I tell you your face is just glowing!"

Flo didn't feel like she was glowing at all. She did feel nervous. It made her feel clammy. But somehow she felt Vernita was bullshitting her now. She decided to bullshit her too.

"Girl, I don't buy none of them small expensive bottles." Flo grinned at Vernita. She showed all of her teeth. "All I do is just rub in some Crisco."

Meanwhile, Trudy was already inside the garage. It was an old cobwebby shack filled with all sorts of rubbish. Old coats and dead lamps and lots of beat-up boxes. A lot of odd paint cans were stacked on a shelf.

"Shit!" Trudy said out loud to herself. "How am I supposed to know which one it's in?" She started in the front, grabbing two of them down. But she had a hard time prying the rusty lids up. Luckily she remembered she still had her keys. Her house key was the longest. She pried around the can, but when she tried to lift the top it bent her key back.

Damn it! She needed something stronger. She looked in the garage. It was murky and dark. She moved one of the boxes and then stopped in her tracks. There was an awful sound coming from the corner in the back. Trudy bit into her lip. She held her frame rigid. The clawing sound grew more intense. The sound would stop and then leap into wild, full-fledged scratching. Trudy was suddenly aware of a harsh animal scent. It smelled like a dog that'd been caught in a storm. Trudy was frantic with fear. Her eyes strained toward the sound. *I got to get that money. I've got to get out! Even if this garage is teeming with rats.* Trudy kept still. She studied her foot. If the rat ran across it she didn't know what she would do. A box stacked with books sat next to her leg. Trudy grabbed the one on top. She threw it toward the sound.

The horrible clawing sound stopped. Frantically a small kitten flew out the garage door. Trudy breathed her relief. It was only a baby. She had to get a grip on her nerves.

Trudy opened a box, carefully sticking in her hand. But when she felt something furry she let go and screamed. The box dropped and all its contents fell to the ground. Trudy stood terrified against the spiderweb wall. The garage became murderously quiet. When she looked down she saw it was only a doll. The doll's long black hair spread out on the ground. Its dead blue eyes stared into hers. Trudy used her foot to kick the doll out of the way. She used her heel to sort through the rubbish. She was afraid to stick her hands into anything now. But next to the doll's gingham dress was another small box. It rattled with the hard sound of metal. The box was full of old tarnished spoons. Trudy grabbed one of the spoons and went back to the paint cans. She worked the spoon around the can and easily lifted the lid. But this first can was wrong. There was nothing inside but rancid liquid. The harsh smell stung the skin in her nose. Trudy grabbed the next can, but when she violently pried the sticky lid off, it dropped on the hard concrete floor. Trudy hoped no one heard the lid dropping sound. She waited, listening for the sound of someone coming. Trudy stared in the round can, determined to finish her search, but this one was filled with yellow two-toned gunk. "Shit! Trudy said reaching for the next can on the shelf but she stopped when she heard something, something like a twig snap. She stood mute. She was holding her breath. She peeked out the garage and saw the bedroom light on. Flo stood in front of the window. Trudy didn't move. She just stood quietly and waited. Trudy knew Flo couldn't see inside the dark garage. But she might decide to come out and check. When Flo clicked the light Trudy took a deep breath. She hurriedly pried the next paint lid. It easily slipped off. Finally, she found what she wanted. Glued to the white gunky can was a clear plastic wad. Inside the wad were thick stacks of cash.

Trudy emerged from the garage. She wanted to wash the paint from her hands, but the water hose nozzle was set to spray and the hose wet Trudy's whole face. She adjusted it fast, rinsing the slippery paint off and rubbing her hands on the lawn.

Flo was in the bathroom when she heard the sound of water. The old copper pipes started to groan.

Trudy ran down the driveway with the can in her hand. She didn't know if Flo was watching or not. All she knew was she finally had her hands on the money and she was getting the heck out of there now. As she ran down the street a lone car flashed its lights. She ran back toward the black Bug.

Flo got a flashlight and examined the backyard. Someone had been rummaging around in the garage and there was a white puddle of paint on their grass.

"Come on!" Trudy said. "Let's get out of here quick!"

Vernita had the engine going. She shifted to first. The Volkswagen skirted down the street.

Trudy started counting out money. She handed a large wad to her friend. "Here, girl. That's yours. This is your cut. I threw in some extra 'cause you really helped me out."

Vernita couldn't believe she was seeing all this cash. The idea hadn't hit until the money touched her hand. Vernita raced down the street with a smile on her face.

"Drop me off two houses down. Let's stay low-key. I don't want anybody to see me come in."

When she got out Trudy scooted into the Bug's driver seat.

"So you headed to Vegas now?" Vernita said to her good friend.

"Yeah. But I have to stop in Barstow a minute first."

"Barstow? What the hell is up there?"

Trudy showed her the folded-up paper Pearl had given her.

Vernita saw the words "Rainbow Tree Rest Home."

"Miss Dee's up there. Can you believe Tony hid her up there? I'm going to check on her on my way out of town."

Vernita hugged her friend. She rubbed her big wad of cash. "I must admit. I definitely had my doubts. Who'd-a thought you could really pull this fucking thing off?"

Vernita patted her stomach. That's where she'd put her money. Her panties held the wad snug against her warm skin. The thrill of having all this money began to sink in. "Woowee, this sweet cash sure makes me feel good. It was a lot of trouble but I guess it was worth it."

"I told you don't worry. Didn't I say it'd be okay?" Trudy grinned at her friend and her friend smiled back. "Hey, maybe I'll send you a postcard."

Trudy revved the engine. "I better get going." Trudy held her friend's gaze for a minute. "I'll never forget you helping me, girl."

"Well, let me know, homechick, if you need me again." Vernita smoothed the small hairs on the back of her neck. She looked radiantly happy. Her bright green eyes shined. She was relieved. This crazy shit was finally over. She kissed Trudy's cheek and teetered back to her house. Her high heels smacked the rough concrete. But when she got to her door her wide smile dropped. The fine lines of worry began inching around her mouth. What about Lil Steve? What was she supposed to do now? The money didn't seem to offer much protection from him. She wished Trudy had asked her to go away with her. Staying here alone felt dangerous now.

44

Vernita and Jimmy

Vernita pulled the wad out of her panties once she got in the house. While keeping the light off, she studied the small room, wondering where she could hide it. She settled on the ceramic water jug in the kitchen. Lifting the three-gallon jug up off the base, she drained half the water in the sink. Vernita laid the plastic wad of cash down in the base, placing the half-full water container back on top.

"Lord," Vernita said, "I'm glad this shit's done." She turned the hot water faucet on in the sink until it flowed nice and warm on her skin. Emptying a small amount of shampoo into the palm of her hand, Vernita began washing her short, spiky hair. Vernita liked to wash her scalp whenever she felt stressed. It cooled her down and made her feel refreshed. She took off her blouse and put on a light robe, laying a towel around her small neck. Lathering her head until her whole scalp was nice and foamy, she closed both her eyes, letting the warm water flow as she slowly massaged in the soap. The rushing warm water felt so good and relaxing. Vernita let the water beat the base of her neck. With her head under the spigot and her eyelids shut tight, someone suddenly seized her and held down her head.

A hand grabbed Vernita's mouth. Another held her crown. The sink basin rapidly began filling with water. Drumming her ears like a hot sloppy tongue, the warm water killed off all sound. Vernita struggled. She fought with all her might to rise, but the hands forced Vernita back down. The soapy water hurt her eyes. The soap stung her nostrils. But not getting any air inside of her lungs made Vernita's body twist wildly with panic. Though she fought and she strained, her arms flailing around, there was no way to get any air. The hand left her mouth and pressed her face against the bottom. Vernita thrashed away and screamed. The rising water surged with hostile bubbles. Vernita tried to bite the hand but it was clamped around her jaw. She twisted, she kicked the wood cabinets under the sink, but she couldn't get the hand off her neck. Vernita began to feel herself growing weak. Her rubbery legs started to buckle. The water in her nose seemed to ease into her brain. With her eyes open wide she could see only gray. Her arms dropped. Her heartbeat grew faint. As the gray world began to grow darker and turn black, the large hand lifted her back out. The hand pushed her against the washing machine. All the neatly stacked clothes dropped silently to the ground. Vernita began to choke uncontrollably loud. She ripped open her eyes and looked around the room wildly. Someone was holding her from behind. Jimmy stood a few inches from her eyes.

Jimmy took the moist towel and wiped Vernita's cropped head as the other man held her wet body.

"Thought y'all was slick." Jimmy said, glancing at the jug and then back in her eyes. "Where's Trudy, huh? Where the fuck is my stuff? What'd you dumb bitches do with the rest?"

Vernita was stunned. Water leaked from her lips. Jimmy held his gun while another man held her body. The man clutched her hard in a rib-crushing vice.

"You a cute little thing," Jimmy said, eyeing Vernita's slim frame. "I like a little more meat on, myself." Jimmy grabbed the back of her neck.

Someone held Vernita's arms tight, pulling them way behind her body, which lifted her breasts up a few notches.

Jimmy took a knife from out of her drawer. He cut the robe's sash, revealing a lacy turquoise bra. "It'd be a shame to mess up something as pretty as this."

Jimmy lit a cigar. He watched Vernita's worried face.

Vernita strained and the hand eased up a little. She could see the slight hint of a slender goatee. It was Lil Steve! His jawbone looked funny. The bottom looked unhinged, and it was horribly swollen and bruised.

Jimmy took the sharp knife and cut open Vernita's bra. Her small breasts now stood completely exposed. Jimmy ran the knife point across the tip of one nipple. He began kneading and squeezing the other exposed breast like a kid playing in wet sand.

Jimmy stopped, whispering inside Vernita's warm ear. "Tell me where your friend is and I swear I'll stop."

But Vernita stood mute. She didn't say one word. Her eyes pleaded with Lil Steve. Why didn't he do something? But Lil Steve couldn't look Vernita in the eye.

He realized she must have been working with Trudy. She'd tricked him, although he wasn't sure how. He couldn't even look in her face.

Jimmy forced her head back in the water again. He held her so long she felt like she was dying. Water enveloped her nose and her lungs. She frantically fought against his hands.

When she rose again, Vernita was sputtering badly. She choked but could not catch her breath.

Jimmy stared in her eyes. He wiped her face with a towel. "Now, I know you don't want me to do that again."

"I swear!" Vernita screamed. "She didn't tell me shit!"

Jimmy grabbed her head and bashed her face to the sink.

"Wait! Trudy took Charles to Watts. They went to King Drew after Charles was shot. I swear to God, that's all I know!"

But Jimmy wasn't convinced and ducked her back underwater, holding her face all the way to the porcelain base.

Vernita struggled and thrashed, bubbles rose to the top. Though she fought Jimmy desperately and strained hard to breathe, her brain was beginning to grow numb. Vernita watched the swirling water upside-down in the sink. She wanted to live. She tried hard to speak but all the words came out garbled. There was no way to talk underneath all that water. Everything turned a dull, scummy gray.

Jimmy stopped plunging and lifted Vernita back up. As she

rose she took in a lung full of water and suds. When he brought her up again, her skinny legs buckled. She fell to the cold kitchen floor and passed out.

Jimmy straddled her, pressing against her small chest and heaved, pushing the water back out of her lungs. He wanted her alive enough to get what he wanted. He blew in her mouth while pinching her nostrils. He jammed his hands against her chest again and again until her blurry green eyes fluttered wide.

"You like swimming, huh? Ready for round three?" he joked. A cruel smile creased the skin around the corners of his eyes. "But I don't know. I had trouble bringing you back. You may not wake up this time."

"Barstow . . ." Vernita muttered as water rolled from her nose. "The Rainbow Tree Rest Home in Barstow."

Jimmy grabbed the phone and dialed information. "Yeah, Barstow. You got a Rainbow Tree Rest Home over there?" Jimmy smiled and wrote down the number.

"Now see," Jimmy said, standing, "wasn't that easy?" He picked up his coat, keys and fat, steely Glock. He took the money from the jug and put it in his coat pocket. He stopped, taking one last look at Vernita. He picked up her purse and walked toward her front door. But when he got to the door Jimmy abruptly stopped and turned. He shot Vernita right in the stomach.

Lil Steve was sick. He couldn't believe Jimmy had shot her. He doubled over and vomited on the cold tile floor.

"I told you I'm getting to the bottom of this shit. The only reason you alive is I need you to get me Trudy and that ugly burnt fool you roll with." Jimmy lit his cigar and stood in Lil Steve's face.

"Here," he said, shoving Vernita's purse in Lil Steve's hands. "This shit may come in handy."

45

Trudy, Ray Ray, Lil Steve, Jimmy and Miss Dee

Trudy drove through the flat, empty desert for hours. She was hungry. Her red eyes were starting to burn. She desperately wanted to rest. The events of the day kept flashing through her mind. She had one last stop to make before escaping the state, and that was going to see Miss Dee in Barstow.

She pulled out the receipt and double-checked the address. She slowed toward an old beat-up, sloped-rooftop complex. RAINBOW TREE REST HOME, the crusty sign read. There was no tree in sight. The landscape looked vacant. The sad, aging building lacked any sign of color. From the fence to the stucco, to the old chipping trim, was the same moldy, trying-to-hold-on beige.

Trudy grabbed her purse and got out of the car. Her open-toe shoes lapped up the dry sand. It ground against her toes as she hurried to the front door.

Jimmy hovered by the side of the rough desert road. At ninety-eight miles an hour he'd made really good time. He parked Shirley's old Cougar near some Joshua trees. They leaned in the olive-dim moon.

It was three in the morning when Jimmy lit his cigar.

"There's the car right there." Lil Steve pointed to the black Bug. Jimmy blew the smoke slow and looked at Lil Steve. "Remember what I told you," he said, pulling the latch. "Do exactly what I said or I'll blast off your dick. I'm not fucking with none y'all no more."

Jimmy ground his cigar right next to the car. He pressed his face up to the Bug's dirty window, looking down at the empty vinyl seat. He looked around the lot until he spotted a huge rock. He smashed the rock into the Volkswagen's window, reached in and pulled open the latch. There were some old bloody clothes and a white empty paint can. Lil Steve said the stash was inside the seat cushion. Jimmy pushed his hand all the way into the ripped slit but didn't feel anything there.

"Where the hell is it? You said in the seat!" Jimmy slammed Lil Steve back against the Volkswagen.

"I don't know." Lil Steve said, scared. "That's where I put it. She must have taken it out."

Jimmy glanced toward the Rainbow Tree Rest Home's front door. He let go of Lil Steve and popped his suit collar. Pulling the Glock from his waist, he carefully clicked in the clip.

Peering inside the misty glass doors, Jimmy looked inside the small rest home's lobby. The lobby was empty. There was no one in sight, so he pulled the cold handle, opening the heavy door wide, and shoved Lil Steve inside.

As soon as he walked in, he wrinkled his nose. The whole rest home reeked with the dense smell of piss. It was mixed with the powerful, harsh scent of bleach and the godawful stench of rotten skin. Jimmy took a small hanky and held it close to his nose, examining each room lining the beaten gray wall. This had to be the worst rest home he'd ever seen. Old people lay still on raggedy cots. Some of the twin beds had two people crammed in one. They watched Jimmy and Lil Steve with dull, hazy eyes. Thin, papery skin held their skeletal bodies. They all looked two heartbeats from death's door. Some had mouths hanging wide, some of them drooled, but others had chapped lips with crevices so deep they were caked in dried blood, like a riverbed that hadn't seen water in years.

Jimmy looked in each room, inching his way down the hall. When he turned the right corner he found what he came for.

Trudy was leaning over this tiny, decrepit old woman. The old woman's once-braided plaits were now two fat dreadlocks. Loose, coarse hair sprung over the top. She was wearing an old, stained pair of men's pajamas. Another bony woman's face lay near her toes.

"Are you her kin?" the bony woman hoarsely said. Her voice sounded like someone shaking a big bag of rocks. "I knew someone would come. I been laying here praying."

Miss Dee tried her best to scoot up a bit but ended up slumped farther down. She seemed to be held by a string of IVs, like some old, worn-out, paper-thin puppet. A lunch tray with soup sat on a stand near her lap. And although a lone spoon slept on a napkin, her blotchy rheumatoid hands looked too gnarled to hold it.

"Oh, Miss Dee!" Trudy said, eyeing Miss Dee's wasted body. "Tony lied. He said you were dead!" When she leaned over to give Miss Dee's face a kiss, the bony woman's feet lying next to Miss Dee's head gently grazed Trudy's face. When Trudy felt those cold toes, she quickly pulled away. The toenails were ridged and completely curled in.

Miss Dee couldn't speak. A stroke had stolen her voice, but her twinkling eyes never looked more alive.

"I'm Agnes," the bony woman said. "She used to be down the hall but they put her with me month before last. Had a bad stroke and can't talk no more."

Miss Dee's face muscles rippled, trying to manage a smile. Her mouth was drawn and her skin was so deeply lined she looked like a plum left to rot in the sun. Her muscles were pulled so tight at the lip, it looked like a new baby's fist.

"My people don't never come visit me neither. But I knew someone would come. I told her I could feel it," Agnus said.

Miss Dee smiled again and grasped Trudy's hand. But as suddenly as the smile had appeared on her face, it immediately changed to pure fear. A tall man loomed behind Trudy's shoulders, but that's not what made Miss Dee yank the blanket over her face. Miss Dee hid when she saw the gun pointing at them from the door.

"Hey, girl," Lil Steve said low. Although it hurt when he

talked, he managed a smirk. "Bet yo' ass is surprised to see me." Jimmy stood hidden in the rest home's dark, gloomy hall. Lil Steve knew he was pointing a gun at his back, and a line of perspiration made its way along his jaw.

Trudy jerked her head up and lurched toward the corner.

"I must admit," Lil Steve stepped closer, "you had us all going. I didn't see none of this shit coming." Lil Steve chuckled. He did his best to appear friendly. But he kept smoothing the hairs on his mustache and goatee. Sweat rolled down to his ear.

Trudy inched farther back but there was no place to hide.

"You pretty slick, homegirl. Your game was real tight." Lil Steve clapped twice, miming applause. Now he was only a few inches from her face. "But quit trippin'. We don't need to play *Law & Order* no more." Lil Steve smiled inside Trudy's growing wide eyes. "Just give me the stuff back and I'll get it to Jimmy; then all this bullshit will be over." Lil Steve tried to act cool, but his worried eyes were pleading. He hoped Trudy listened. She better have that stash. He knew it would be over for him too if she didn't say where she hid the cocaine.

Lil Steve inched closer. Trudy felt his breath. "It's just you and me, baby. Ray Ray's in jail and Vernita is dead. You don't want to end up like them two."

Trudy looked at him in horror. This couldn't be true. "You're lyin'. I just saw Vernita, she's fine!"

"Well, I'm telling you, that nigga ain't playin' no more. Homeboy gunned her down. Executioner's style. Shot her point-blank in the dome," Lil Steve lied.

Trudy looked confused. This couldn't be true. "Well, then, how come he didn't kill you?" Trudy asked.

Even Jimmy had to smile when he heard Trudy say that. She was as sharp as a tree cutter's ax.

"I know you ain't willing to die for some ends!" Lil Steve grew impatient with her now. He shoved Vernita's purse into Trudy's hands. "Look at that and tell me if I'm lying or not. Come on, Trudy! Just give the shit back!"

Trudy examined the purse and looked back at Miss Dee, who

had pulled the blanket up to her eyes. This was definitely Vernita's purse. This was all of her stuff. Maybe Lil Steve was telling the truth. Trudy's whole body began filling with dread.

"Trudy, we don't have to go out like them," Lil Steve pleaded.

"Vernita?" Trudy asked. "Vernita's been killed!" Trudy felt so bad, she fell against Miss Dee's bed. But in the metal overhead light she saw something funny. A hand with a gun was right there in the hall. Lil Steve was setting her up.

"So what do we do now?" Trudy asked, stalling for time. Her eyes scanned the small room for some kind of weapon. But the only thing she saw was a paper towel holder on the wall and some antiseptic spray next to the food tray.

"Where's the coke?" Lil Steve demanded. He was really getting mad. He didn't like having that gun aimed at his spine. "Get the shit now and let's go!"

Trudy acted like she was about to go out the door. But instead she grabbed hold of Miss Dee's metal lunch tray and smacked it into Lil Steve's face.

Lil Steve yelled out in pain as the soup splashed in his eyes. The blow's impact killed his raw, throbbing jaw. Jimmy leaped, waving his gun, but Trudy held up the can. She sprayed the antiseptic right in his eyes.

With his eyes burning, Jimmy could barely see straight. He shot wildly around the room. Shots hit the ceiling and walls. There was a horrible, animal-sounding, blood-curdling yelp, like a mutt being struck by a car. But the yelp wasn't Trudy and it wasn't Miss Dee. Poor Agnes's head tilted down on her pillow. Blood oozed out of her nose. A bullet pierced through Agnes's neck. Miss Dee lay in fear. She couldn't do a thing. A lone tear rolled down the cracks of her face.

Trudy backed away toward the room's narrow corner. She was totally trapped. There was no place to hide. She felt like a roach underneath a huge shoe.

Jimmy grasped and held Trudy's quivering neck. "Where's the shit?" he screamed loudly. He was sputtering with rage. "I'll kill your whole fucking family if you don't tell me something quick!"

"I don't have it!" she screamed back. Trudy was scared out of her mind. She knew if she told him he'd kill her and be done. There was nothing else to do but try to stall.

"You a liar!" Jimmy spat. "Where's the shit at?"

Trudy tried to slither behind the IV and table but her foot got tangled inside the long see-through cord and the table crashed down to the floor. The IV ripped right out of Miss Dee's papery arm. A trail of dark blood flowed from her wrist.

During the blasting, Lil Steve dove to the floor. He inched toward the hallway, crawling on hands and knees. He figured it was best to get out if he could. He definitely didn't want to get shot.

When the table crashed down, Jimmy loosened his grip. Trudy grabbed the IV, dripping its clear liquid and rammed it inside his neck. Jimmy screamed in her face. He shot two more times, but they blasted the ceiling because he shot while snatching the needle from his skin, and the tall steel pole that was holding the IV came tumbling down on his back. At that point, Trudy scrambled and managed to get out of the room.

There were only two attendants working the late shift that night and one of them was out on his break. When the other attendant heard those gunshots coming from down the hall, she stuck her wet mop inside the bucket and left. The attendant snuck in a patient's room and ducked all the way down. She wasn't about to get herself shot on the job. Not on the bullshit minimum wage they paid her.

Trudy was almost at the front door. In a couple more steps she would be outside. It felt like it did when she'd shoplifted something, only a hundred and fifty times worse. Her heartbeat was pounding, her blood began to steam, and it was difficult to take a good breath. She put her hand on the handle, and the night air rushed in. She was almost there now. Her arm cleared the threshold. But just when her feet reached the darkness outside, just when she'd gotten her whole body out, just when her lungs finally took in some air, Jimmy hooked his thick arm around Trudy's waist and yanked her all the way back in. Trudy twisted and screamed but he had her this time. He slammed her so hard against the old stucco wall that the paint flecked down over the floor. The force was so strong she felt like she'd been whip-lashed. Jimmy brought her down, clutching both her wrists, nail-ing her against the hard floor like Jesus.

"Where's my shit?" Jimmy yelled. His sweat dripped on her forehead. But Trudy's lips didn't move, though they trembled a lot. Her tongue stayed lodged in the roof of her mouth.

"Oh, you ain't talkin'?" Jimmy sneered at her face. He snatched a shank out from the back of his pants. He cut Trudy's hoop ear-ring straight from the lobe. A piece of pink meat was still at-tached to the gold back.

The sight of her own blood immediately made her feel nau-seous. But Trudy's mind was set. She clenched her back teeth. She turned her whole brain into a strong steel vise. Vernita was dead. Ray Ray was gone; she'd be damned if she talked to him now. And even though her concrete eyes were desperate to cry, she willed the hot tears from escaping down her cheeks. Jimmy read the determined look in Trudy's hard eyes. He put the knife back and pulled out his Glock. Jimmy was a pro at breaking folks down. He lived for this kind of challenge. He slammed the cold gun upside Trudy's face. Explosions of pain flared all over her skull. He hit her again and blood drained from her lips, then he jammed the gun under her teeth.

"Gimme my shit or I'll mess you up for life. No man'll ever look at you twice!"

The pain was intense. Trudy struggled to think. But her mind said she'd die before giving him what he wanted. She was alive only because he needed her to talk. Her whole body became a tight steel pipe.

Jimmy's face scowled crazily. He breathed heavy and deep. Trudy felt his foul breath warming over her forehead. But then something crossed over his hard, ruthless mind. Something made his cruel lips almost curl to a smile. He dragged Trudy down, pulling her along the long hall. He yanked her back into Miss Dee's narrow room. The white sheet under Miss Dee had turned a deep crimson. Agnes's blood was all over the bed.

"I'ma give you something to make your quiet ass talk."

Jimmy aimed the gun over Miss Dee's shrunken frame.

"Wait!" Trudy screamed, but it was too late for that. Jimmy fired the gun straight into Miss Dee's spindly thigh. A raspy growl erupted from Miss Dee's parched throat and ricocheted down the hall.

"Oh God!" Trudy screamed. "I'll tell you, please stop!"

Jimmy held the gun over Miss Dee's concave chest. Miss Dee's face was knotted. It rippled in pain. Her pleading eyes focused on Trudy.

"The car!" Trudy screamed. "It's all in the car!"

"I been in the car and didn't see jack." Jimmy's finger tugged the trigger and almost fired again.

"It's there, Jimmy, I swear. Check the right side. I hid it inside the door panel."

Jimmy smiled when he heard Trudy say this last part. So that's where it was. This was one clever heifer. It was too bad she tripped out and stuck him like this. He and a cold bitch like her could have worked something out. Jimmy jammed his Glock up against Trudy's rib cage. He hustled her down the hall toward the door. A bucket and mop sat next to the wall.

Trudy kicked over the bucket. Water splashed across the floor. Jimmy's Stacy Adam boots slipped in the murky, soapy water and Trudy managed to pull away. Jimmy shot wildly at her big legs but missed. He put a hole in the wall and another in the counter. When a bullet hit the sharp spokes of a wheelchair in the hall, the wrinkled-up man in it smiled. He patted the lumpy pacemaker under his shirt. This was the best shit he'd seen in years.

Trudy was free. She leaped to the door. But suddenly her whole head and neck were snapped back. Jimmy had a fist full of her braids in his hand. Trudy heard the cold first click of the safety go off as Jimmy pulled back the trigger. Trudy couldn't even struggle. She was caught and held tight. With his fist at her head, Jimmy dragged her outside. Trudy saw the broken glass outside the VW's door. Jimmy reached in and yanked open the driver's door handle. He snatched the inside door paneling off. The money and cocaine were lodged down in the metal.

Jimmy let the tip of his finger trace the edge of her face. He actually felt bad. He hated to have to kill her. For a second his hard face revealed tenderness inside. He had liked Trudy. She was all right. But then Jimmy's face changed. The gentleness quickly turned sullen. He examined the coke and thumbed through the money. He stared back at Trudy with felonious eyes. The savage eyes of the betrayed. She didn't want him. All she wanted was his money. His index finger hooked the slim trigger of his gun. He pulled the gun's trigger back.

Trudy closed both her eyes and held in her breath. The blast was so intense the Bug's window blew out. Trudy stood frozen, unable to breathe. When she finally decided to open her eyes, Jimmy's large body was slumped on the ground.

Trudy panicked. It was getting harder to get air. She looked around but saw no one in sight. Her eyes drifted around the black desert night and the red sea of passing cars. Suddenly, Ray Ray's smiling face walked toward the car door.

Ray Ray rolled Jimmy over and took Jimmy's gun. He held two fingers at his neck to check for a pulse before sliding his own gun back in his holster. He found the bag holding Vernita's cut of the money. He found a metal container with two new cigars and put it inside his jacket. He grabbed Trudy's hand, lifting her up.

"Hey, girl. You okay?" He noticed the blood on her shoulder and her earlobe cut off. Ray Ray brought Trudy back into the rest home.

Ray Ray rummaged through a drawer and found alcohol and gauze. He swabbed Trudy's face and her badly cut ear. He covered the lobe with a bandage.

Trudy went down the hall to examine Miss Dee. The bullet was lodged in the sheet.

"Homegirl got lucky," Ray Ray said, lighting up. The bullet had gone straight through her flesh. Ray Ray bandaged her too and then picked up the phone. He lit a cigarette and dialed 911.

"Come on. We better leave before they all come."

"No! Ray Ray, wait." Trudy held Ray Ray's arm. "I have to see about Vernita."

"Don't need to. I've already been there." Ray Ray looked

down. He sucked in the smoke slow. "When she saw me she wouldn't talk. She just kept shaking her head. But Pearl showed up over there looking for you too. That's how I knew you were here."

"Tell me, Ray Ray!" Trudy said, worried. "Is Vernita okay?"

"Yeah, she'll make it, but she's hurt pretty bad. I stayed 'til the paramedics took her." Ray Ray looked over at Trudy's bandaged ear. "I hope all this bullshit was worth it."

Trudy looked at Ray Ray. His left eye was busted. He had bruise marks and welts all over his skin. A monstrous cut dissected his burn. Trudy held her head down. She'd never felt worse. She was responsible for everything that happened to her friends. All of them almost got killed. "If it wasn't for me, none of this would have happened."

Miss Dee looked at her bloody dead friend. Miss Dee stroked Agnes's head. Agnes had suffered. No one had been down to see her either. Loneliness had killed her a long time ago.

Trudy kept her head down. "I'm so sorry, Miss Dee. This was all my fault."

Miss Dee narrowed her eyes in worry.

Ray Ray smiled at Miss Dee while bandaging her leg. He whispered to Trudy, "We got to raise up, girl. Police'll be here in a minute."

Trudy cupped Miss Dee's face. "You gonna be all right?" She knew Ray Ray was right. They were fugitives now. She kissed Miss Dee's cheek. "See you, Miss Dee." She didn't have the heart to tell her she wouldn't be seeing her again.

Ray Ray and Trudy walked out the glass door. He lit a cigarette as they walked along the gravel road. The events of the last moments shook Trudy hard. A rush of tears streamed down her face.

"Dang," Trudy said, trying to stifle her crying, "you saved me, Ray Ray."

"Girl, you know I been had yo' back. I been telling you that shit forever." Ray Ray smiled and popped in a piece of Juicy

Fruit gum. "I knew that stone fool would be coming after you. Vernita told me y'all was coming up here, so I figured I'd better come too." He winked back at Trudy and she managed a weak smile.

"We better raise up," Ray Ray said calmly. "Am-ba-lance and po-po be all over this place." They walked toward the Volkswagen. The highway was blazing. It raced with the hot, fast-paced traffic to Vegas.

Ray Ray blew out his smoke toward the loud, violent highway. He felt free next to Trudy under the million-starred sky. He pulled her mouth over his lips. Trudy didn't resist.

Ray Ray wrapped one arm around both of her shoulders, the other arm circling Trudy's waist. He felt a warm, luscious heat erupt from his stomach. He'd been waiting for this moment for a very long time. He squeezed Trudy real tight.

Suddenly, the Volkswagen roared back to life. Ray Ray ran over and jerked open the door.

Lil Steve looked at Trudy and then over at Ray Ray. A perplexed look passed over his face. But Lil Steve quickly masked any emotion he had. A grin eased its way across his fat, swollen jaw. "Zap-nin', people?" he said, trying to sound casual. He rubbed the groomed hairs on his chin.

Ray Ray was stunned. What was Lil Steve doing here? "Man, where you been? I've been waiting on you all night." He was talking loud over the Volkswagen's rattling engine while Lil Steve sat squeezing the wheel.

"What, you fixin' to raise?" Ray Ray wanted to know. "Where's all the muthafuckin' bank money, G?" Did Lil Steve rob him? Was homeboy trying to leave? Ray Ray waited for Lil Steve to speak.

Lil Steve's jaw was so bashed in, it killed him to talk, but Lil Steve had to tell him something. He could see it in Ray Ray's eyes. Ray Ray was about two snaps from going off, so Lil Steve decided to try to catch him off guard.

"You stealing my woman? What's up with that, man?" Lil Steve came out the car door.

Ray Ray immediately felt awkward standing so close to Trudy. He dropped his arm from her waist and took a few steps away.

She was Lil Steve's ex. She was supposed to be off limits. He didn't know what else to say.

Trudy was just as nervous standing between them both. Because of her, both Ray Ray and Lil Steve were bleeding. All of them stood wondering who would speak first.

Lil Steve watched Trudy. He was glad he made her nervous. He walked up to Trudy and tried to slap her face but Ray Ray snatched back his hand.

"What's wrong with you, boy?" Lil Steve angrily said. "This bitch set us up! She played us both, Ray Ray! I know you didn't fall for her shit." Lil Steve tried to lunge at Trudy again but Ray Ray got between their bodies.

"Wait," Ray Ray said, holding Lil Steve back. "Be cool, man. There's no need to trip."

"Trip? Nigga, you the one trippin', cuz! I'm telling you, this bitch set us up!"

Ray Ray looked at Trudy but Trudy looked down.

"Tell him!" Lil Steve demanded. "Tell him how you got the money!"

Ray Ray eased his grip on Lil Steve's wrist.

"Man, she got the cash. She been playin' us all. She shot Charles and snatched up all the ends! He laying up in King Drew right now."

Ray Ray studied Lil Steve's face. Lil Steve was so adamant, so righteously pissed. He now knew Charles was shot, but Ray Ray didn't know by whom. Ray Ray looked back at Trudy again. Trudy wouldn't have crossed him. She wouldn't have set him up. She wouldn't do something that would send him back to prison. Trudy's dark eyes were glued to the ground. But maybe she would. He'd been gone for almost two years. Maybe she and Lil Steve used him all along. Maybe he was the one playing the fool. But then he remembered what Charles had said about the money.

"Naw, man, you wrong," Ray Ray said calmly. He spoke soft and slow, like he was sorting things together. "Charles got the money by selling Flo's car." Ray Ray waited for Trudy, expecting validation, but Trudy kept her eyes on the ground.

"Oh, wow. Come on, man, she's clowning you, dog. Charles didn't sell shit. Think about it, homie. Why the fuck would some drug dealer be tryin' to off us, huh? Where's our money from the bank? I bet we didn't get jack. I'm telling you this bitch set us up from day one."

Ray Ray looked confused. He didn't know what to say. It was true, his blue envelope only held newspaper shreds. He turned from Lil Steve and completely faced Trudy.

Trudy grabbed Ray Ray's arm. She tried to hold Ray Ray's hand.

"I told you don't do it, Ray Ray. I begged you, remember?" Trudy's pleading eyes tried to make Ray Ray understand.

Ray Ray pulled his arm away. He stared at her hard. She ground her right foot in the sand.

"See, man! I'm telling you she played you, my brotha. Didn't I say from day one she was foul."

"He's lying to you, Ray Ray. He's always lied to you about me."

Ray Ray backed away. He looked Trudy up and down. All he knew was that it was really getting hard not to smash one of these fools in the ground.

"She's been using you, Ray Ray. Selling you wolf tickets, homes. Your dick got your vision all twisted."

Ray Ray pushed past them both. He didn't want to listen to this madness. Though he couldn't hear them yet and they were miles away, Ray Ray could faintly see the flashing red and blue lights of the cops.

Trudy grabbed his hand and gently turned him around.

"Remember that party?" she asked. "The first time we ever spent together."

Ray Ray looked down. He bit his lower lip. It was the night he went to jail. Before he and Lil Steve did that robbery. "I try my best to erase it."

"Don't listen to her bullshit, man. All women lie. Lyin' and bitches is like dog shit and flies," Lil Steve said.

Trudy ignored Lil Steve and kept her focus on Ray Ray. "I felt something that night. I know you felt something too."

Ray Ray remembered that evening full well. Though he never spoke about it once, the memory loomed in his mind. In prison, he'd played it back hundreds of times. He used to lie on his cot and think about it for hours. With his eyes closed he could still see what Trudy had on. An ivory lace dress, with thin skinny straps, her hair piled high on her head. He remembered how good it felt to touch her. The rich brown warmth of her skin. But in a fraction of a second the whole thing was over. Next thing he knew he was stuck doing time and Trudy was with Lil Steve.

Lil Steve disgustedly spit on the ground. "Who gives a fuck 'bout some damn high school party! We talking about how we got pimped up here, G! We talking 'bout how this nasty trick dogged us!" Lil Steve turned to Trudy and got in her face. "Don't cloud it by bringing up that janky shit now!" Lil Steve didn't want Trudy to talk about the party.

"This 'ho got your nose blown open so wide you couldn't see this raggedy shit coming." Lil Steve stared at Ray Ray. He shook his head, disgusted. "She's working you, man, just like she worked Charles, and that nigga's laying in King Drew barely breathing." Lil Steve sneered in Trudy's fuming face.

But Trudy stepped up to Lil Steve this time. She whipped back her braids, putting one hand on her hip.

"You don't want me to tell him, huh? Look, you're scared as shit now. You're scared I'ma tell what really happened that night!" Trudy said.

But Lil Steve ignored her. He turned his back on her face. He laughed, leaning against Ray Ray's shoulder, rubbing his slender goatee. "Ain't this a bitch. She's trying to flip the script, man. She stuck Charles, dog. Shot him point-blank. Now she wants to tell some fairy tale shit about the past. I'm telling you, you're dealing with a garden tool, man. She ain't nothing but a cold-blooded 'ho!"

The cops were almost there, but suddenly they wildly veered off when they got a call that a drunk driver had hit the center divide.

"Go ahead, call me names," Trudy said boldly. "But I'm still gonna tell him what happened."

"Come on, man. Am I making this up? This bitch is just like her tired-ass mama," Lil Steve said.

Trudy ignored him. She wiped her braids back. "Yeah, I'm like Mama. We both got a few flaws but Mama could always recognize bullshit when she saw it. Your name-calling is not gonna stop me from talking. I'm telling this shit whether you like it or not." Trudy whirled around and faced Ray Ray full on.

"That night at the party, Lil Steve was watching us, I remember. I thought he looked worried. I was wondering why he kept staring. Next thing I know he starts blowing me kisses, licking his thin, nasty lips."

"That's a lie! I didn't even go to that party."

But Ray Ray remembered. Lil Steve definitely was there.

"First, I ignored him. Refused to look his way. But when you left to get a drink, Lil Steve came over. He told me you were high. He said he'd been listening. He said everything you told me that night was fiction and that you were nothing but a heroin addict who served time."

"That's a lie! I never said that!" Lil Steve wanted to slap Trudy's face.

Ray Ray looked at Lil Steve but decided to stay silent. He wanted to hear the rest of what Trudy had to say.

"He said y'all had business. Said you had to do some job and he'd be damned if he let some young trick like me mess it up. I thought he was crazy. I told him to leave. But Lil Steve just stood there and played with his mustache. I tried to push past him but he blocked my way. 'I'ma take you,' Lil Steve told me. 'Watch how I work it,' he said. 'Ray Ray won't never know what happened.'"

Ray Ray raised both his eyebrows but still he said nothing.

"Don't listen to this tramp. Can't you see she's crazy? Look at her, man. She ain't even fine. You seen my stable. None of my 'hos look like her." Lil Steve thought insulting her would make Trudy stop. But Trudy was already on a roll.

"What I remember," Ray Ray glanced at Trudy as he spoke, "is that I went to jail and then got sent to prison. When I came back you'd already been with my man."

Lil Steve smiled. "Yeah, I fucked her. So what? So had every other damn dick in town."

"He lied to you, Ray Ray! But you couldn't see. Lil Steve's been manipulating your ass from day one. And you walk around with your dumb little codes. Not talking to his girl. Shit, he didn't give a fuck! He didn't want me. He's always been selfish. He didn't want you near me because he wanted you to do that job. He wanted to use you so he could get some money, and you're the one who ended up doing time."

"Shut up!" Lil Steve screamed. "You fuckin' got damn slut!"

"Lil Steve was my first," Trudy said to Ray Ray. "I was a virgin and Lil Steve knew it."

Ray Ray could not believe what Trudy was saying. A virgin. That's not what he'd heard.

"She's a liar!" Lil Steve screamed. "That ain't how it went down!"

"He knew if you had someone decent in your life, you'd see him for the crackhead he is."

Lil Steve lunged at Trudy. "I ain't no crackhead, you bitch!"

But Ray Ray remembered. He had lots of time to think in prison. Lil Steve told him Trudy was no good. He'd told him everyone at that party had already had her. That she'd been with a whole bunch of men. But Ray Ray never heard that from anyone else. All Lil Steve kept saying was that he shouldn't trust no woman and that the only thing trustworthy was money.

"You listened to him and you ended up in jail!" Trudy said.

Ray Ray recalled the robbery. Lil Steve stayed in the car. He told Ray Ray he'd drive and would wait by the curb. But the liquor store had a security camera. They arrested Ray Ray and Lil Steve got away. And Ray Ray never ratted on his friend. He looked at Trudy again. Some of what she said made sense but he knew she had a part in this too.

"Well, you ended up with blood. You must have wanted him too." Ray Ray lit one of Jimmy's cigars and blew his smoke down the long dusty road.

"They put you away for close to two years, Ray Ray. Lil Steve kept coming. Kept sniffing at my door. He told me you didn't want me and that you were locked in there for life."

Ray Ray was pissed. "What difference does it make?" He tossed his lit butt down the long, littered highway.

"That's right, dog! None of that shit has to do with the bank. Yeah, I had her. So what? Shit, I had lots of women. It's not like the shit was a secret." Lil Steve spit down on the asphalt again. "The bottom line is this trick set us up. Keep yo' ass focused on that!"

"I set *you* up, punk! You dumb muthafucker! You made Ray Ray come, just like you did last time. You always make him do your dirty work for you, while you always hide in the car!"

Ray Ray asked Trudy point-blank, "So what is it, shorty? You did this bank shit with Charles?"

The way Ray Ray said "shorty" was like he separated himself from her now, like she didn't mean more than some chick on the street.

"Wait, Ray Ray, listen. Lil Steve got it twisted. Charles did help me out. But I didn't shoot him. Flo shot him because she thought me and Charles were messing around."

"Were you?" Ray Ray asked. He'd seen Trudy and Charles together a couple times. He didn't know which part was true.

"Hell, yeah, she was. I'm telling you she's scandalous! I saw 'em sneak away a whole gang of times. Creeping off after the show."

"Why are you lying on me, Lil Steve? What did I ever do to you?"

Lil Steve almost smiled. She really was cute. "Do to me? Ain't that a muthafuckin' blip. You used me and Ray Ray to take the fall for this job." He had Trudy against the ropes. There was nowhere for her to go, and he could see his boy Ray Ray was bending toward him.

"Something musta happened." Lil Steve sneered. "Nobody just comes after your ass with a gun. Yo' big ass musta done something."

Trudy saw the doubt entering inside Ray Ray's eyes. She ignored Lil Steve and tried to talk just to Ray Ray. She had to make him understand. "Look, Ray Ray, I did do the bank job with Charles. I tried to tell you that day but you just got out from prison. I didn't want to get you involved in a crime. I wanted to protect you. I wanted you to stay clean. But Lil Steve sucked you back in. I'm sorry. I didn't think it would turn out like this. All I wanted to do was pay his ass back and get the fuck out of L.A.!" Trudy tried to hold Ray Ray's hand but he moved.

Trudy stepped to Lil Steve. She got in his face. "Why don't you tell him about that videotape, huh? Same kind of videotape you made of me. Tell him how you finked on your friend."

Lil Steve swung at Trudy, but Ray Ray blocked his arm.

"He was so proud. He couldn't resist telling. Always talking about Teflon! How he's never been caught. He did get caught and would have definitely done time, but they let him go because he gave you up!"

"How the fuck would you know? You weren't even there." Lil Steve looked at Trudy with a confident air. He tried to leap toward her again but she moved farther away, backing up toward the highway. They were all standing right near the traffic.

" 'Cause you told! Vernita told me you bragged to her about it. Said it was business. That you had to give Ray Ray up. That you weren't going to jail no matter what," Trudy said.

See, that night, after the robbery, they picked Lil Steve up too. They kept him in a room asking him questions for hours. They played him the videotape again and again. The video showed a bandana-faced man holding a gun, running toward the liquor store door. It was Ray Ray but the cops didn't know it at the time. All they knew is they had Lil Steve. The cops worked a special deal for giving Ray Ray up. Ray Ray went upstate, got a year and a half at Norco. Lil Steve got a slap on the wrist.

Ray Ray was stunned. Was this really true? All this time he figured the storeowner was the one who popped him. He couldn't believe it was really Lil Steve. Maybe that's why they nabbed him so fast. Ray Ray looked at Lil Steve hard. He couldn't believe what he was hearing but deep down he knew it was true.

Lil Steve noticed the heat in Ray Ray's eyes, so he tried to quickly shift the blame to Trudy.

"She set us up, man," Lil Steve said fast. "Look all around you. Homeboy lying over there is shot. She dealt with that brotha. Charles is laying up bloody, that's another brotha she had, and we don't want to mention what happened to Vernita and that was her own got damn friend!" Lil Steve steeled himself when he said that last part. It was hard to lie about what had happened to Vernita. He felt guilty but he knew how to bury it well. "She fucked over us, man. That's a muthafuckin' fact. Ain't no two ways about that!"

"Ray Ray, I did pull this job," Trudy said, coming clean. "I didn't want you involved. I did try to stop you, but I didn't know nothing about taking that cocaine."

Hearing the word "coke" immediately triggered something inside Lil Steve. He looked at the cocaine bag in the paneling of the car. His mouth started to water. The cocaine called his name. He could see the loose duct tape flapping in the wind. He wiped his dry lips before speaking. "Don't trust a big butt and a smile," Lil Steve said. "They even make songs about raw chicks like her."

In the distance, there was the faint driving sound of sirens. The cops were trying to get the drunk driver to pull over.

Lil Steve inched close to Ray Ray. He stood right in front of his face.

"Man, this bitch gonna send yo' ass back to the pen. 5-0 is coming. We got to raise up. Let's off her ass and get in the car!"

Trudy looked horrified. What was Lil Steve saying? A second ago, Ray Ray had just saved her life. Now Lil Steve was trying to tell him to kill her.

"Come on, man. It's just you and me, homes. Get this shit over with once and for all and let's go sip some mai tais and see some titties on the Strip."

Ray Ray hesitated. He didn't want to shoot Trudy. He still couldn't believe his good friend had turned him in.

Lil Steve leaned closer to Ray Ray's suit jacket.

At that range Ray Ray noticed a powdery substance faintly sprinkled over his mustache. Lil Steve was definitely high.

Lil Steve felt the cocaine kicking in full steam. He'd snorted a whole lot while Ray Ray and Trudy were inside but now his body was aching for more. Lil Steve's arm started to mildly shake. Sweat leaked down his long, narrow back.

But before Ray Ray knew it, Lil Steve grabbed Ray Ray's gun from the underarm holster and pointed it at Trudy's head.

Ray Ray tried to reach for it but Lil Steve backed up.

"Get away from me, man. I'm not playing with you no more. I'm haveta put your work in myself."

"Dog, what are you doing?" Ray Ray said fast. "You ain't got to kill her. Let's just split the shit and go." Ray Ray tried to lunge toward Lil Steve's arm but Lil Steve jerked back. He raised the gun to Ray Ray's chest.

"Don't fuck with me, man. This ain't about you, dog." Lil Steve stared at the cocaine inside the car, then he stared back at Trudy. His tongue drew a line across his top lip. He wanted to kill Trudy, but he wanted that coke too.

He made Ray Ray take a step back. He got in and revved the VW engine. He pointed the gun back at Trudy. "I got business with this trick. Stay out of it, dog."

"Homegirl's always been my business," Ray Ray said loudly over the sound of the engine. He stood right in front of Trudy's body.

"She ain't worth it, man. Move over, G!" Lil Steve's hand shook while holding the gun. Sweat dripped down from his face.

"Naw, man. I can't let you go out like this, dog."

"She ain't shit. Don't let no tramp come between friends." Lil Steve pointed his gun at Ray Ray's scarred face. "Look what the last 'ho did to your mug. You better step off this bitch, homes."

But Ray Ray just stood there. He wouldn't move over. Car after car was whizzing by them now. The wind blew some sand into his eyes.

"She got you so whipped and your ass only smelled it. You tripping and you ain't even had you a taste." Lil Steve pulled back the safety on Ray Ray's large gun. "Sorry, dude, but I have to do this." His finger rolled over the trigger.

Suddenly, a red sports car came zigzagging up. The car came so close it whipped the gun from Lil Steve's hand. The gun danced across the thick double lines. Lil Steve was stunned. He turned his back to the highway. A semi was coming down the hill the opposite way. But the weaving red sports car made the truck driver brake hard. Lil Steve tried to get the VW Bug into gear but was shaking and couldn't find the right groove. The driver tried his best to keep the Mack truck in line. But the red car came so close, the truck driver had to swerve, forcing the semi to jackknife.

Ray Ray and Trudy raced out of the way. But Lil Steve was in the Bug. He struggled to get it going. The Mack driver honked the horn a long time. He lost control and hoped the Bug would move out of the way. But it was no use; he was coming too fast. He smacked the Volkswagen like it was a gnat. The hubcaps flew off. Smoke rose from the tires. The truck dragged the car over five hundred yards before the crumpled thing fell off the grill. The Bug was completely engulfed in dark smoke. The desert black night blazed with tall orangey flames. The red car kept going. It never eased its pace. Its taillights melted toward the gambling lights of the state line.

Ray Ray ran to the Volkswagen but couldn't get past the fire. He looked down the highway and saw a trail of approaching lights. The ambulance roared. The police sirens grew louder.

You could see Lil Steve struggling wildly with the driver's door. He was screaming and mouthing the word "help." Ray Ray ran into the fire. Ran straight through the flames but he couldn't open the Bug's smashed-in door. Lil Steve was frantic. He couldn't get out. His horrible screams didn't sound human. He was trying to open the door with one hand. The other clutched the cocaine and money.

Trudy yelled out, "Hurry up, Ray Ray! The police are almost here!"

The sirens grew louder. You could see the cars now. In a moment they would be at the scene.

Ray Ray struggled and pulled, but the front door was stuck. He ran from the flames. His clothing was scorched. He bent down and put both his hands on his knees. He struggled to catch his own breath. When he darted through the flames again he just came back choking.

"Ray Ray, come on!" Trudy said, worried about the fire. "Get away from there. It could explode!"

But he couldn't leave his friend burning up like that. He ran back but this time went to the passenger's side and pulled the door open wide.

Ray Ray noticed an oily trail leaking out from the tank. It was headed for the hungry red flames. Ray Ray was coughing hysterically now. The smoke fumes had ripped through his lungs. Lil Steve was passed out. The carbon monoxide got him. But Ray Ray was determined. He wanted to save his friend. So as the fire burned his skin, Ray Ray went all the way in and yanked Lil Steve away from the car.

He dragged Lil Steve away from the flames. Lil Steve's left leg was smoking and charred. One shoe was gone. His foot was burnt black. His pants leg had melted into his skin. Ray Ray started to drag Lil Steve farther out, but Lil Steve screamed out in pain.

"Leave him," Trudy said.

Ray Ray flashed her cold eyes.

"No, Ray Ray, look, you don't understand. If we take him with us he'll never survive the trip. We got two solid hours before we hit Vegas. If the ambulance takes him he still has a chance. But we gotta go now!"

Ray Ray and Trudy raced to Tony's black Caddy. Ray Ray revved the V8 and floored the gas pedal hard. In a second the cops had circled the scene. Trudy and Ray Ray were less than eighty feet away. But Ray Ray kept the lights off. Luckily the Caddy was black and there was a whole lot of smoke. It was easy to fade into the night.

Ray Ray looked in his rearviews at the wild flaming sky. The paramedics put Lil Steve on a stretcher.

Suddenly the Volkswagen blew up like a bomb. Shards of hot metal shot toward the sky. A fireball rose from the ground.

"Dayam," Ray Ray said looking at the flames. Trudy looked back and then fell against his shoulder. She felt like a wet sack of dirt.

Trudy's eyes followed the smoke to the sky.

"I'm sorry. I'm so sorry. This whole thing's my fault."

Ray Ray touched her cheek. He gently rubbed her back.

Trudy wept in her hands. She couldn't look again. Hot tears raced down from her eyes. That life was over. She couldn't go home again. But now she had no reason to keep going ahead.

Ray Ray wiped her face with the hem of his shirt.

His own eyes trailed down the dark two-way road. His brain went a million miles per hour.

They drove in cold silence for over two hours. Trudy couldn't look at Ray Ray. She just felt too bad, so she kept her head tilted toward her window instead. She only looked at Ray Ray in her peripheral vision. He was gripping the steering wheel tight.

Trudy couldn't take the silence and finally faced him full on. She wrung both her hands in her lap. "Ray Ray, I swear, I was telling the truth."

Ray Ray didn't speak. He kept looking straight ahead. Then he swerved the car over into the right lane and rolled into a rest area. He kept holding the wheel, staring straight at the trees. Finally Ray Ray turned to her and spoke.

"Listen. Prison gave me a whole lot of time to reflect. I knew Lil Steve worked something but I never was sure. That's what made doing my time seem so hard. Lil Steve was my boy. Me and him always been friends. We been hanging out in the streets since day one. When my brother died, Lil Steve was the only one I had left. I didn't want to fuck that shit up."

"I'm the one who fucked everything up," Trudy said. "I created all this mess and we still don't have jack." Trudy covered her face and just balled.

Ray Ray pulled a stuffed pillowcase out from the backseat. He placed the large sack in her lap. There was stack after stack of thick wads of hundreds, wad after wad of fifties and twenties, all held by fat rubber bands.

"Where'd you get all this? This is not from the bank." Trudy stared at the cash in complete disbelief.

Ray Ray didn't say this money came from Tony. He shifted the Caddy from Park and the tires ate the gravel. But he stopped before swinging the car back to the highway and pressing his foot on the gas.

"This is Ray Ray, remember. I still got skills, baby." Ray Ray smiled, letting his eyes leave the road for a moment. He rubbed his cross and tooled the car toward the bright Vegas lights, "but I'm ready to go legit, if you let me."

Ray Ray grabbed Trudy's body and squeezed her firm skin. He held her like he'd wanted to hold her for years. He kissed her long and hard, smothering her face and neck, tears brimming inside his eyes. His sincerity shocked her. She'd never felt so alive. She kissed Ray Ray like she had wanted to do that first night. Like there was nothing else she wanted more in life.

46

Flo and Charles

Now, most folks would have thought that after someone done shot ya, you'd never speak to their sorry ass ever in life. Not so with Charles and Flo. Soon as he got better he was back at the house. Screaming and fussing right where they left off. Cussing and saying stuff like "I never touched her." And Flo screaming back that she saw him. Round and around. Over and over. Oh, those fools fussed, cried and carried on so. Breaking things. Ripping stuff up like old sheets. Taking some of them fights to the street! But they stayed together. Never busted up. Bandages, bad feeling and all. Charles spent most of his time looking out of the window, wondering if one day she might show.

People talked about Trudy like she was some kind of legend. Gangbangers tagged the city with Ray Ray's face and name. Nobody they knew ever robbed them a bank. Or ever left a drug dealer to die in the desert. Beauty shops yakked, men in bars wondered. Folks who never spoke kindly to Trudy in life said that she was their very dear friend. Vernita was the only one who knew the whole truth. But she didn't see many of those folks anymore since she opened her new salon in Oakland.

Lil Steve lied to anyone who gave him a listen. He lost the use of his leg and was in a wheelchair now. Told everyone he saw that he'd thought of it all. That the bank plan was his invention. But most folks shook their heads and kept walking past. Only crackheads and drunks paid him any attention. If he was the big mastermind of it all, why did he live in that smelly flophouse up the block? Pearl would watch him outside from Dee's Parlor some-times, his one leg just as thin as a golf club. Sometimes he came in for a short stack or coffee and Pearl never charged him a dime. Dee's Parlor was a maple-smelling breakfast place now. Miss Dee lived there again and Pearl helped her run it, and at two ninety-nine for pancakes, grits and eggs, they were packed every day of the week. They even delivered food to shut-ins, like Ray Ray's mother, who now lived in a roomy apartment in View Park. Joan came once, turned her nose up at the place, then disappeared for a few weeks. She didn't answer her phone, didn't come out of the house and never told a soul that Mr. Hall left her. You just didn't see Joan around anymore. Pearl walked on over one day. Joan's Mercedes was there but when she called out her name, nobody came to the door, so she jimmied the lock and went in. She found Joan facedown with the oven turned on. Her bun was undone and her gray had grown out. She died with her face on the rack. She was clutching a tiny white sheet in her hand. It was a large Western Union check from Trudy.

See, a Western Union man showed up out of the blue once. He handed out checks to Pearl and Vernita. There was no return address or mention from whom.

Nobody, not one soul in the bucket of blood town ever heard from Trudy or Ray Ray again.

It's funny how you can want something so bad you can taste it. In your brain you can feel the thing touching your hand. Like if you don't get it now your whole arm might fall off. You can stretch but it always seems to keep out of reach. But wanting is like gnawing away at a flea or a howling dog scratching away at the screen. Sooner or later it just don't itch as much, or you just go someplace and lay down. And the next thing you know, a few months will go by and that feeling, that hot need, is a memory now and all of that wanting is gone.

Flo sat on the couch and quietly rolled up her hair, while their small baby napped on her thighs. Charles walked to the sink and drank his cold beer alone. It was March and already feeling like summer. Charles stared out the window a really long time. His eyes never left the hot scene beyond the screen. He scratched at his neck while swallowing slow. He licked his chapped lips and grinned toward the glass, as the big-legged girl across the street mowed her lawn.

Stay tuned for Pam Ward's next thrilling ride
BAD GIRLS BURN SLOW.
Available March 2008 wherever books are sold.

Until then, satisfy your craving with the following
excerpt from Pam Ward's exciting,
can't-put-down next book,

Enjoy!

Bernard glanced out his window and saw the girl in his yard. He hadn't seen her rip a sweater off another girl's back. He didn't hear the screams or see her pull the girl's hair. He didn't see her leave and go pick up a spade. He didn't see her dig the small hole in the ground or rip each silver button from off the front of the sweater and drop the thing down in the low bowl-sized hole, packing it back firm with her hands. No, all Bernard saw was the girl's dirty palms and her rinsing them off with the hose. He watched her walk toward the front and peek over the fence. She ripped a sharp leaf from one of the trees and tore the leaf into small bits.

The small girl and her mother had moved in last week. Though he'd met the girl's mother, he hadn't talked to the child. Her mother always yelled for the girl to come inside whenever Bernard was around.

The girl sat on the back step with her face in a book. She held it so close he could not see her face, like she was smelling each page.

She furiously sped through fat open textbooks, like she read to some internal clock.

Bernard hated being out when anyone was around. But this amazing-looking creature fascinated him. She invaded his space, though he rarely did see her. It was almost like they played this cat-and-mouse game. But her presence was hauntingly there. Like her schoolbooks left randomly under some shrubs, or her lunch bag being invaded by rows of black ants or a branch broken off one of his trees.

Though he hadn't seen her face, Bernard recognized her voice. With his ear to the floor he heard her talk to her mother. It was a sharp, controlled tone that was low and squeaked high. She was articulate and liked to use long, obscure words. She threw fits and would often stamp her feet against the floor. He heard the crashing of large items being thrown. One time he heard a long agonized sob gurgling out from the throat of her mother.

The duplex was stacked with his apartment on top. To get down he had to walk down a long flight of stairs. The girl's unit was at the bottom.

He went out and saw her sitting on the bottom two slats. She glanced at Bernard, watching him as he passed. She examined his clothes. His fingers looked soft, with nails clipped close and scrubbed so perfectly clean, they looked like a pink princess rose.

"Hello," Bernard said, passing the girl on the steps. He tried to make his tight voice not sound so annoyed. He was nervous. He took quick staccato breaths. His chest felt tight and his throat was now dry. But it irked him that she didn't acknowledge him at all. She never took her eyes from that thick beaten book. She held the pages so close to her miniature face that it looked like the book touched her lips.

"Maybe your mother should invest in some glasses." He said the remark sharply, thinking she'd speak to him then. But she didn't. She kept her face pushed in the spine. And then suddenly she sat back and snapped the book shut. She shot him a look filled with fury. There was so much raw heat in those gasoline eyes, he raced inside the garage and locked it.

Once inside, Bernard blotted his face with a cloth. Loosening the taut knot at the throat of his tie. Pushing the inhaler down past his two front incisors he blasted his mouth with the spray. Taking deep, measured breaths he began feeling calm. He cleaned off his frames and put the cloth in his pocket. He unlocked the door and swung the other side open.

Bernard got in and snapped his safety belt tight. He backed

the car out fast using only his mirrors. He was not going to get annoyed by some stupid young girl. He had to get back to work early.

Bernard pulled up at five forty-five. A protestor held up a large cardboard sign.

BAKE BREAD, NOT BODIES, the scrawling type read. His hair was the color of used-up gray coals. He looked over a hundred years old. People began protesting the parlor lately. The noise and the dust were bothering some who said the sound was like living by a freeway. There was no mistaking the sickening odor. The syrupy smell was like smoldering perfume and the bottom of a stuffed garbage can.

Bernard parked and the protestor ran to his car.

"The dental work of the dead puts mercury in the air. The EPA should shut this thing down."

Bernard ignored the protestor and walked to the mortuary's door.

"The homeowners have complained; we have signatures now. Our property values dropped when that smokestack went up."

Bernard walked down the hall toward the funeral parlor. Floral walls met up with solid gold trim and large planters filled with fake plants. He saw his boss talking with a closely huddled family. His boss's hand rubbed the shoulder of a slack-jawed old man with eyes so red they looked like they bled.

His boss was a broad, commanding man who stood six-feet-seven. His shock of gray hair only made him look grand. People liked him. He was good at talking to folks. His name was the main reason they came to this parlor. Reynolds. People remembered the place. Generations had been coming to see Reynolds for years. He was like a friend of the family, a long-distant cousin, a favorite uncle you rarely saw. He was there the time you buried your aunt. Or when the lady next door slipped and fell down the stairs. You came to viewings and wakes or celebrations of life where you sang to satin open caskets.

People said things like, "Reynolds sure made her look good." "Call Reynolds, honey, he'll handle everything for you." They liked the warm living-room elegance of his rooms, the chande-liers, the espresso machine in the corner, and the warm cookies on the buffet. He worked hard to make the living feel comfort-able with departure. And he was making a killing. They came to him in droves. Everyone went to Reynolds's Funeral Parlor off Third. He didn't have to advertise or market the place with brochures. He didn't have to make calls or knock on anyone's door. There was always a constant supply of bodies.

But when the crematory came, the parlor started to get a bad name. People complained about the foul odor. Or the ash that floated down on their cars. Ash that eased through your doors. Ash that came through the cracks, making dusting each day a mandatory chore. His boss was in the middle of a burned-body pickle. Though the cremation business was gaining each day, the locals began to abhor it.

"People are larger," his boss told him once. "Those big ones, hell, those suckers take a long time to burn. Stinkers," he called them, "they can burn for eight hours. Shoot, we used to do stiffs for under ninety-six minutes but those good old days are all over."

But Reynolds wouldn't stop burning. Crematories were big business.

"Hell, people can't afford to lay folks down anymore. Caskets and plots and the rental of limos can run you way up in the thou-sands."

Bernard liked his boss. He didn't require him to talk. He smiled when he passed and went back to the workroom. His boss seemed content with hearing his own voice. All Bernard did was sit back and listen.

"Now, your basic cremation run ya close to six hundred. You can take Grandma out in a little plastic box. Or you can put her in one of our decorative urns." Reynolds waved his gnarled hand to-ward a shelf of small vases. "We got blue ones and pink ones and some inlaid with gold."

Reynolds winked at the older red-eyed man. "If you're slick you can sprinkle her from a skyscraper downtown or the Nep-tune Society will take her for three eighty-five and scatter her ashes in the sea. I heard a feller take ashes to his lady's favorite store and scatter her all over the lot."

The red-eyed old man trembled and burst into tears. His whole back shook as he sobbed.

Bernard smiled at his boss. He opened a drawer. He pulled out what looked like a large pair of pliers and a small-tooth shiny saw.

Reynolds left the family to think things over. He came in the room and grinned at Bernard. "Poor fellow. He's too old to ever consider burning the body. There's some that can't stomach the notion."

Bernard took a small pipe to hold open the jaw.

"In Sweden those guys are trying new things."

"Like what?" Bernard asked. He loved hearing these stories.

Bernard's boss came close. He leaned in his face. "They're boiling them," he said, snapping his head back quickly.

Bernard listened intently with wide honey eyes.

"Them Swedes are cooking their bodies in lye. I ain't lying! I swear it's a natural-born fact! No dust, no bones and no odor either!"

Bernard stared at the face of the half-dressed young woman. She was turned to her side like she was watching a movie. Bernard picked her up and pulled down each sleeve. He carefully laid her down and buttoned her blouse and then rammed the large pliers through the roof of her mouth. Bernard was proud of his work. He wasn't hurried or untidy. His movements were careful yet firm.

His boss liked him too. He paid Bernard cheap. He did jobs the others did not like to do and worked hours that no one else wanted.

Reynolds scratched his head. He looked very concerned. "You see that family out there? Those were real nice folks. I had to talk to that father till I got blue in the face. He said he heard things. Things that weren't right." His boss crossed the room and looked down the girl's throat.

"Them damn crazy parlors give us good ones bad names. Like that Lake Ellsinore man. He started mutilating his bodies. Instead of burning them in retorts he sold them for parts. That man made money from toenail to beak, sold from both ends. He sold the organs, arteries and veins and then started harvesting bone. Dental surgeons are paying top dollar for the stuff. Look at all them implants we have now. You see them selling all over. There's a whole lot of folks walking around with crushed cadaver bone in their mouths. Plastic surgeons are turning into body snatchers too. They want muscle, fat or skin for reconstruction. They can put a car accident or burned person completely back together with parts supplied from a corpse."

"I'm telling you, Bernard, you picked the right business. Dealing in death has just shot open wide. Some say it's up in the billions."

His boss's eyes twinkled while talking about this subject. Especially when he mentioned the Lake Ellsinore man. The fact was, his boss admired the guy. He wished he had thought of it first. "Man had a steady flow of medical school money. He'd hand 'em a body and they gave him straight cash. No questions asked. Research, they call it. Research, my ass! Some of those bodies never even made it to class. You saw it! I know you saw it, Bernard! Story was all over the paper. Got the FDA champing at the bit about the mess. A slew of folks came down with hepatitis from one of them bodies. The FDA put the nails in the coffin on it quick. We have to fill out a bunch of papers on folks now to make sure we don't pass HIV."

His boss loved his job. His father had done it before him and his granddad had started the business. "We've been peddling death more than eighty-four years. You can't say I don't know this trade. Eternity's my middle name!" Reynolds stopped talking and watched Bernard use the saw. His whole hand almost fit in the dead woman's jaw.

"How's your mama? She's getting up in years, huh?" He smacked Bernard's shoulder and walked back outside. "Tell her Reynolds said hi! Don't forget, son. I hope to see her real soon."